College life 102;

Social Learning

J.B. Vample

Book Two

The College life series

COLLEGE LIFE 102-SOCIAL LEARNING

Printed in the United States of America

First Printing, 2016

ISBN-10: 099698173X (eBook edition)
ISBN-13: 978-0-9969817-3-6 (eBook edition)

ISBN-10: 0996981721 (Paperback edition)
ISBN-13: 978-0-9969817-2-9 (Paperback edition)

For information contact; email: JBVample@yahoo.com

Book cover design by: Najla Qamber Designs

Dedicated once again to my sister Jawhara; my number one fan and most loyal reader. Thanks for bugging me about writing the "documents". Also for entertaining the conversations where we talk about the characters like they are real people.

Thank you to all of my readers. Your questions, your comments, and your enthusiasm about my books make this journey so much more fun.

Chapter 1

"Welcome back, Chasity," a fellow Torrence Hall dorm mate called to the sullen Chasity Parker.

"Yeah, yeah," Chasity replied unenthusiastically, adjusting one of the carry-all bags on her shoulder. Pushing her long, black hair behind her ear, she let out a long sigh as she approached her room door. It had been a long morning. From being kept up late the previous evening by her aunt Trisha to get some last minute quality time in, to being stuck in bumper-to-bumper traffic on the way to Virginia with the rest of the returning Paradise Valley students and families, she was worn out.

Pushing her dorm room door open, Chasity was greeted by the sound of R&B music blaring from the small radio on her roommates' desk. Dropping her bags to the floor, she took stock of the open suitcases, their contents sprawled all over her roommate's bed.

"Sidra!" she called.

Snatching open the bathroom door, Sidra Howard smiled brightly. "Chasity!" she exclaimed, hurrying over to give her a hug.

"No, I don't do that," Chasity joked, holding her arm out.

Sidra playfully smacked Chasity's arm down. "Stop it," she scolded, giving her roommate a big hug.

With winter break now over, Sidra was excited to be back on the Paradise Valley campus for a new semester, and more importantly, in her spacious dorm room.

"All right, enough," Chasity jeered, jerking Sidra off of her. "Why are you so hype? I just saw you a few weeks ago on New Years."

Sidra put her hands on her hips. "I missed you and your evil self, okay. Geez." Bad mood aside, Sidra was glad that the Chasity before her was not the same coldly silent Chasity that she had met in the fall.

"Fine," Chasity sighed, feeling a little bad for her attitude.

Sidra watched her as she flopped down on the bed. "What's wrong? You look tired."

"Girl, because I *am*," Chasity complained, running her hand through her hair. "That freakin' drive down here from West Chester was ridiculous."

Sidra giggled as she grabbed some more clothing from her suitcase. "Tell me about it. My parents and I got stuck in some of it too," she sighed. "I guess everyone had the same idea of coming back on a Saturday instead of Sunday."

"Yeah well, people were pissing me off," Chasity sneered, unzipping her bag. "With their non-driving asses."

"Yeah, I'm sure," Sidra teased. She stopped suddenly as something caught her eye.

"What are you staring at?" Chasity asked, face frowned. Sidra knew that she hated being stared at.

"Did you cut your hair?"

Chasity rolled her eyes. "Just a few inches."

"It looks like *more* than a few inches," Sidra contradicted, walking over to touch Chasity's hair. The tall, light-brown skinned, slender Chasity was envied for her long, jet black locks, amongst other things. "It was almost to your behind before, and now it's just past your chest."

Chasity smacked Sidra's hand away from her. "It's not that serious. Besides, it was starting to get on my nerves."

"I like it," Sidra smiled, flinging her long ponytail over her shoulder. Brown-skinned, slim, Sidra could almost match Chasity in the hair length department. Most people were surprised that her ponytails weren't fake. "Malajia and Alex are back," she informed.

"So?" Chasity scoffed, hanging one of many expensive tops in her closet. She already had a wardrobe to die for, but that didn't stop her from dropping more of her aunts' money on new clothes.

"*So,* do you want to walk over there and see them?" Sidra returned.

"Nope."

Sidra shook her head. *Just plain stubborn,* she thought. "Chaz, have you talked to Alex since New Years?"

"No Sidra, I haven't." Chasity's tone was laced with frustration. She had no desire to talk to Alex; ever since their confrontation at Trisha's New Years Eve party where Alex criticized how Chasity was handling her relationship with her mother and the news of her adoption. She was sure that Alex wasn't too eager to speak to her either, since she threw up the fact that Alex spent so much time worrying about other people's issues and not the fact that she stayed in a dead-end relationship for three years.

"You two need to make up," Sidra persisted. "It's a new semester. There doesn't need to be any tension."

"There's no tension on my part, I'm fine," Chasity stated flatly.

Sidra sighed heavily. "You're lying...Let's just go," she commanded, pointing to the door.

Chasity narrowed her eyes at her roommate. She'd almost forgotten that Sidra wasn't afraid to challenge her. She had guts, not many people did.

"Fine," Chasity huffed, walking to the door.

Stacking her books neatly on her desk, Alexandra Chisolm wondered when her roommates would be returning.

She'd arrived by train the day before from Philadelphia; and although she enjoyed the peace and quiet, she was beginning to miss her friends.

Alex got her wish when the door opened and slammed against the wall. Startled, she spun around to see Malajia Simmons standing there, posing. Shaking her head, Alex ran over, arms outstretched. "Girl, you're a mess," she mused, hugging her.

"Yeah, so I've been told," Malajia laughed, dropping her bags to the floor.

"Where are your parents?" Alex asked, dragging one of Malajia's bags over to her closet for her.

"Those ignorant asses just left," Malajia jeered, moving some of her bobbed burgundy locks out of her face. "They literally dropped my ass off and drove away...So disrespectful."

Alex giggled. Malajia complained about being home with her family during the entire break. She guessed that they were sick of *her too*. "Well you're here now, so relax," she consoled.

Malajia looked at Alex as she went back to setting her things up on her desk. "To be honest, I didn't think you'd be too happy to see me," she admitted.

Alex looked up at her, frowning. "Why would you think that?"

"Come on, Alex. The last time we saw each other, we didn't really part on good terms," Malajia reminded her.

Alex folded her arms. "Oh, you mean since you and Chasity's little gang-up session on New Year's Eve?" she scoffed.

Malajia rolled her eyes. "First of all, Sidra voiced her opinion too, not just me and Chaz," she clarified. "Second, we weren't ganging up on you. We were just letting you know how you come off to us. We didn't mean to make you feel like we were attacking you."

Alex ran her hand through her thick, wavy, shoulder-length hair. For days after her confrontation with the girls at

Chasity's aunt Trisha's New Years Eve party, she felt personally assaulted and hurt. Being accused of being nosey and overbearing was a hard pill for her to swallow. But after having some time to think, she realized that they only did it because they cared about her.

"I know you didn't mean to hurt my feelings Mel," she replied. "And I know that I haven't spoken to you, but I was working these last few weeks. I've just been so worn out, I barely spoke to my own family."

Malajia waved a hand at her. "Okay...if you say so."

Alex watched Malajia with shock as she saw all of the skimpy clothes that her roommate was pulling out of her suitcase. "Mel, you don't plan on *wearing* those clothes, do you?"

Malajia looked up at her. The frustration clear on her brown face. "Well I *bought* them, so I guess that means that I'm going to *wear* them," she sneered. "You're starting again."

Alex rolled her eyes. "Me wondering why you packed all those skimpy clothes for the winter doesn't mean that I'm being nosey," Alex protested. "I'm just concerned."

"Well, concern yourself with something else," Malajia spat out. "You sound like my damn parents. Always complaining about how I dress." Malajia's skimpy wardrobe had become her trademark, much to the dismay of her parents and some of her friends. Her motto when it came to clothes was less is more.

"Good, *somebody* needs to," Alex grumbled. She admitted that Malajia had the height and slim frame to pull off every one of those items that she pulled out of her bag, but for her sake, Alex hoped that she planned on covering some of her assets up this semester. "You act like you have no sense."

Malajia was racking her brain for a snappy comeback when the room door opened.

"I knew that I heard Malajia's big mouth," Sidra joked, walking in.

Malajia jerked around. "Ponytail!" she exclaimed, running over to give Sidra a hug, only to be greeted by a scowl on Sidra's face and her hand out, halting her. "What?"

"You're being smart already," Sidra griped.

"You mad because I called you ponytail?" Malajia laughed "You should be used to it by now. It was either that or Prissy."

Sidra folded her arms. She was wondering when the jokes about her business attire or her ponytails and updo's would start. Malajia never disappointed in that aspect. Sidra unapologetically dressed like a professional at all times.

"Whatever, Malajia," Sidra sniped.

"Fine, I'm sorry," Malajia grinned, holding her arms out. "Come on, hug me Princess." Sidra let a smile creep up as she shook her head and hugged her outrageous childhood friend.

Chasity looked at Alex from where she stood several feet away, staring. She didn't know what to make of the silence. Was Alex still upset over the comment that she made about the situation with her ex-boyfriend? Was she afraid to approach Chasity because Alex thought she was still upset over her meddling ways? Her questions were answered when Alex smiled, walked over, and threw her arms around the reluctant Chasity.

"It's good to see you," Alex said. Chasity looked at Alex like she had ten heads as she released her from her embrace. "What?" Alex asked, noticing the stare. "I'm not mad."

"Really?" Chasity's voice dripped with sarcasm.

Alex chuckled. "Yes, really," she reassured. "I'm not angry at you anymore for what you said. I know it was just retaliation for how you felt I was coming off to you."

Chasity folded her arms. *Still not admitting your faults huh?* she thought.

"How I *felt* you were coming off, huh?" she hissed.

"Yes, how you felt," Alex persisted.

Noticing the tension building between them, Malajia intervened. "Satan, I missed you," she exclaimed, hopping over to her.

"Don't touch me, you jackass," Chasity snapped, nudging her away.

Malajia was shocked. "Damn! What did I do already? We just got here."

Chasity made a face at her. "Don't play stupid," she shot back. "How many times were you gonna play on my damn phone last night before you realized that I knew it was you?"

Malajia busted out laughing at the memory.

"Oh Lord, what happened?" Alex chuckled, grateful for the interruption. The last thing she wanted was another argument with Chasity.

Chasity removed her cell phone from her jeans pocket. "This idiot called my phone like ten times last night." She began to play the messages. The first few were of Malajia leaving messages pretending to be other people; then the next few messages were of Malajia screaming and making weird noises into the phone. "It's not funny," Chasity scoffed when the girls laughed.

"I was so bored last night," Malajia defended.

"Clearly," Chasity jeered, turning her phone off. Noticing Malajia staring at her, mouth wide open, she frowned. "What?"

"You did *not* cut your hair!" Malajia yelled.

Chasity rolled her eyes to the ceiling as she pushed some of her hair behind her ears. "Please stop talking."

Malajia made a face at her.

"Ladies, we just got back. Let's not start this bickering," Alex put in, voice laced with amusement.

"Where's Emily?" Sidra asked. She was sure that she would've arrived by now.

"Do we *look* like her driver?" Malajia sniped, ripping open a bag of chips.

Sidra cut her eye at her. *Smartass!*

The door opened, prompting Alex to get up. Excitement resonated on her face as she anticipated Emily walking through the door. The feeling quickly faded when she saw a woman walk through the door carrying a few bags.

The girls shot each other glances as the woman rudely walked over to one of the closets without saying a word. Malajia sucked her teeth and rolled her eyes as she sat on Emily's bed.

"Hello Ms. Harris," Alex greeted. She prided herself on respecting adults, even if they weren't respectful in return. Alex gave a slight frown as Emily's mother rolled her eyes and proceeded to unpack her daughter's items without so much as acknowledging her.

Sidra shook her head as Malajia leaned over to Chasity "No she didn't," Malajia whispered to her.

Chasity, who had been desperately trying to hold her tongue since the woman walked in, was glaring daggers at her.

Emily Harris walked into the room, holding a plastic container. Although she smiled at her friends, she didn't open her mouth to greet them. Her mother did not approve of them, and had been spewing off hatred of them during the whole car ride from New Jersey.

Emily, noticing the taut looks on the girl's faces as her mother began to place some of her items into a drawer, tapped her mother on the shoulder. "Um, Mommy that's okay, I can do that. You can go."

"Emily, I don't mind putting your things away," Ms. Harris insisted, folding one of Emily's many oversized sweaters.

"No, I can do it, really," she insisted. Ms. Harris stood there for a few seconds before smoothing her daughter's sandy brown hair away from her light brown face.

"Well, all right sweetie, I'll go," she relented, smiling. "Remember where your things go in the drawers okay, just like we do it at home."

Sidra rolled her eyes, tossing her hands in the air in frustration.

"I'll call you later," Ms. Harris continued. "I'll come down this weekend and we can go to lunch, okay?"

"Okay." Emily hugged her mother tightly.

Before Ms. Harris walked out, she turned to the other girls. "I might not have succeeded in getting my child's room switched this semester," she hissed. "But best believe *next semester* will be different."

"Why are you still here?" Chasity snapped; unable to hold her tongue any longer.

"*Thank* you," Malajia added under her breath.

"Who do you think you are? Talking to me like that, little girl," Ms. Harris fumed, adjusting her purse on her arm with a hard yank.

Chasity turned her lip up and went to put her middle finger up, when Sidra grabbed her hand.

"Goodbye, Ms. Harris," Sidra slid in, voice dripping with disdain.

Emily quickly shuffled her annoyed mother out of the room, breathing a sigh of relief once she closed the door behind her.

"Bitch," Chasity scoffed, flinging some hair over her shoulder.

Alex hugged Emily. "Chaz, that's still Emily's mom," she chided.

Malajia's jaw dropped. "Alex, are you serious?" she admonished. "Did you *not* see how she acted? She completely ignored you, and *you actually* spoke to her ignorant ass."

"Sorry about that girls," Emily apologized, voice low. "She doesn't mean it."

"*Yes* she does," Chasity declared bluntly

"Emily, stop apologizing for her," Sidra said.

Alex glowered at the other girls. "Ladies, let's not jump on her," she cut in, noting the somber look on Emily's face. "Anyway Em, how was your vacation?"

"It was—"

"Do you even have to ask?" Malajia asked, exasperated. "She was dealing with *that* the whole time."

"Malajia," Alex scolded. "Chill out."

Malajia waved her hand at Alex in a dismissive gesture and walked over to her closet to continue hanging her clothes.

"Well, it was fine, I didn't do much," Emily stated.

"Surprise, surprise," Chasity jeered, earning a glare from Alex.

"I really missed you all, though," Emily continued, trying to ignore Chasity's not so subtle disdain for her.

"We missed you too sweetie," Sidra smiled.

"Speak for yourself," Chasity hissed.

Alex's head snapped towards her. She'd almost forgotten how nasty Chasity could be…almost. "Chasity!"

"Yeah?" she responded nonchalantly.

"What? Did you hold everything in until you got here?" Alex groused. "Geez, give it a rest Satan."

"What? You thought that I changed over a four-week period?" Chasity shot back. "Yeah *that*'s cute."

Alex rolled her eyes, placing her hands on her hips. *I could slap her.*

"I have to go print my class schedule. Why don't you girls walk with me?" Sidra suggested, hoping to cut short the bickering.

"Yeah, let's go," Alex agreed, grabbing her coat. "We can grab ours too."

Chapter 2

"Oh, come on," Sidra complained, removing the royal blue gloves from her hands.

"Well I guess we better get used to standing for a while," Alex shrugged.

The line inside the Student Development Center began on the second floor and ended on the first.

Who knew so many students had the same idea to print out their class schedules at this time? Alex thought.

Letting out a loud sigh, Malajia took a step towards the line, when she heard a loud, familiar laugh. "Oh dear God, no," she groaned as the guy started making his way over to them.

"Ladies!" Mark Johnson exclaimed, accompanied by Josh Hampton trailing behind him.

"Ugh, go away," Malajia scoffed, shoving him.

"Malajia, don't freakin' touch me. I don't want your parasites," Mark shot back, dusting himself off.

Malajia made a face at him.

"Don't start you two," Alex interjected as she tried not to laugh. "How was your break?"

"Cool," Josh responded, adjusting the blue baseball cap on his head. "Didn't do much but work."

"Mine was all right, but y'all know that I had to get back here and see my ladies," Mark answered, adjusting the knit hat on his head.

Malajia stared at the stupid smile on Mark's face and nearly snapped. Even though he wasn't an unattractive man, with his dark brown skin, tall frame and athletic physique, Mark still annoyed every fiber of Malajia's being. "Nobody wants you! You're a freakin dog," she spat out.

"Sure they do, just ask your Mom," he shot back, ducking as she took a swing at him.

"Hey! Hey, quit it," Sidra hollered, stepping in between them. Playing the referee between Malajia and Mark was something that she was used to; it didn't mean that it wasn't irritating. Those two had been at each other's throats since they were children.

"Where's David?" Alex asked, changing the subject.

"His nerd ass been standing in that line for the past hour," Mark answered.

Josh shot Mark a glare. "Leave him alone, isn't he getting your schedule too?" he asked.

"So!" Mark shouted.

Chasity was about to say something, when she was interrupted by her phone ringing. "Hello?" she answered. "What do you want?...Huh...Why?...Where are you anyway?...All right fine...I said all right...Yeah."

"Who was that?" Sidra asked as Chasity hung up her phone.

"Jason," she informed her. "He wants one of y'all to hold a place in the schedule line for him. He said that he'll be here in twenty minutes."

"Man, ain't nobody doin' that bullshit," Mark scoffed, face turned up.

"Shut up," Alex charged. "Your freeloading behind is *always* asking for a favor."

He stared at her for a few seconds. "Aww, I missed you too, my nosey, chocolate, big-boned friend," he joked, going in for a hug.

"Get off me," she sneered, shoving him away. He got two things right, Alex's smooth dark skin rivaled his, and her frame was certainly thicker than that of her friends.

"Hey ladies," David Summers greeted as he hurried down the stairs. Alex smiled as she wrapped her arms around him.

"Did you get em'?" Mark asked.

Tall, toned, brown-skinned David handed Mark and Josh their schedules. "Yeah, here you go,"

"Good lookin'." Mark smiled at the girls. "Good luck standing in that line," he gloated, laughing.

"Can you guys wait with us?" Alex asked, smiling brightly.

"Hell no!" Mark yelled.

"Mark, do you have to be that loud?" Sidra questioned calmly.

"Sure *do*," Mark confirmed, fixing his collar.

Alex looped her arms through David and Josh's arms. "Please guys, it'll be fun," she persisted. "We can catch up."

"We would love to ladies, but, we have to go unpack," David objected, pushing his silver wire-framed glasses up on his nose.

Sidra and Chasity glanced at each other; then looked back at the one guy who could change their minds. "Josh," they crooned, voices low and sultry.

Josh looked at them. His brown face was flushed, eyes wide.

Mark noticed the girls' glances. "Hell no, don't give him that 'I wanna screw you look' to get your way," he jeered with animation. "No, it's not happening!"

"Please Josh?" they persisted, ignoring Mark's protest.

Josh gulped as he looked into Chasity's hazel eyes and Sidra's grey ones. "Um, guys maybe we could..."

"No!" Mark stomped his foot on the floor. "Come on man, I know this was Sidra's idea, she always does this."

"Always does *what*?" Sidra exclaimed, confused.

"Mark man, I'm sorry, but they got me too," David admitted, voice full of amusement. He didn't blame Josh for caving. The girls were beautiful.

Mark, ignoring Sidra question and not caring about the girls' good looks, held a scowl on his face.

"Oh, get over it," Alex said, pointing to the stairs. "Move your behind up those steps."

"Man, I need some ugly friends," Mark sulked.

Malajia shifted her weight from one foot to the other. "My damn feet hurt," she complained after just twenty long minutes of standing in line. "Why is this damn line taking so long to move?"

Alex glanced down at Malajia's red, knee-high stiletto boots. "That's what you get for wearing those hooker boots," she commented, adjusting the scarf around her neck.

"Well sorry that I don't wear ugly ass boots...you know, like the ones that *you* wear," Malajia shot back.

Alex looked down at her thick-heeled brown shoes and laughed. "At least my feet don't hurt," she retorted.

"Yeah, whatever," Malajia sneered.

Jason Adams approached his friends in line. "Hey, gorgeous," he whispered in the ear of the visibly annoyed Chasity.

Chasity went to turn around and was greeted by a hug from him. Not knowing how to feel about the tall, handsome, built Jason touching her, she shoved him off.

"Can you not touch me?" she hissed, straightening out her coat.

Jason shook his head; he missed her, bad attitude and all. "For now," he teased, a smile brightening up his light brown face.

"Jason! How is my favorite man?" Sidra greeted, giving him a hug. Then she caught the glances of the other guys.

"Why *he* gotta be your favorite man?" Mark asked, full of disdain.

She giggled. "I'm sorry, you know I love you guys too," she conceded.

As they inched their way to the print office, Alex held up her hand. "Now that we're all here, I can ask my big question," she began. "How was everybody's grades?"

"Well of course I received…"

"Straight A's," everyone spat in unison, cutting David's obvious words off.

"You know it," he boasted.

Mark stared at him with disgust. "You are a nerd!" he shouted.

"I wear the title proudly, thank you," David declared, unruffled.

"What about you, Mark?" Alex questioned. "I know that you had a lot riding on your grades."

Mark rubbed his hands together. "Let's just say that daddy will be receiving his car sometime this semester."

Malajia made a face at him. "Whose daddy are *you*?" she scoffed.

"*Yours,* smart ass," he shot back.

"I did pretty good," Jason chimed in. "I still have my scholarship, so all is well." Attending college on a football scholarship forced Jason to take his grades very seriously. He was never one to squander his opportunities.

"You?" Alex asked Chasity. "I know you struggled with math last semester."

"So did *you*," Chasity spat.

"She probably got all 'F's," Malajia cut in, fixing her red purse on her shoulder. "It doesn't matter; she gets spoiled by her aunt any freakin' way."

Chasity wanted to insult Malajia so badly; it showed in her face as her jaw tightened. "I got a 2.8," she answered after several seconds.

"That's it?" Malajia teased.

"It's higher than *yours*," Chasity shot back.

Sidra shook her head. "Malajia, don't tease my roommate about her grades when you know *you* didn't get one A last semester," she commented, successfully concealing a laugh.

Malajia's head snapped towards Sidra. "You know what? I hate your clothes!" she shouted. Sidra laughed at the out-of-nowhere insult.

"What the hell does that have to do with anything?" Chasity asked, obviously confused.

Malajia was equal parts angry and embarrassed. She knew that her insult made no sense.

"Wow," Josh laughed.

Alex went back to her original question. "Mel, how were your grades?"

"You know what, Alex? How were *your* grades?" Malajia snapped, annoyed with Alex for bringing up the topic in the first place.

"For your information, I ended up with a 3.5, so top *that* you slacker," Alex boasted, folding her arms.

Malajia sighed. "I got a 2.0," she mumbled.

"Damn, how did you get out of telling your parents *that* one?" Sidra asked.

Malajia waved her hand. "First of all, my mother is so damn busy with those brats that she doesn't even pay attention to what I do most of the time," she responded of her younger sisters. "And all I had to do was bend the truth and tell my dad that I got a 3.0, I mean what's he gonna do? Call the school?"

"Hey, don't underestimate your father now, Mel," Sidra warned. "Remember, he *has* caught you in many lies before."

"So what, I was new to lying back then," Malajia stated. "Anyway, there's nothing wrong with bending the truth a little."

"But you lie *all* the time," Mark butted in, tired of hearing Malajia talk.

"I *knew* I should've driven over here," Chasity complained, bundling her black coat up to her neck. Finally getting their printouts after another twenty minutes passed, the gang couldn't get out of the building fast enough.

"It's cold!" Mark shouted. The frigid winter air hit him like a ton of bricks.

Alex sighed loudly as she moved away from Mark. "Why is it that every time you start yelling, it just so happens that you're next to *me*?" she fumed

"Shut up!" he yelled, moving close to her ear.

Alex sucked her teeth as she fixed her leopard print earmuffs on her ears. *I wish someone would put a muzzle on him*, she thought.

Chasity opened up her schedule. "Nice," she mused. "I actually got a good one this semester."

"What is it?" Sidra asked.

"Monday, Wednesday and Friday I have class at eight, nine and ten in the morning. And on Tuesday and Thursday, I have an eight and a nine-thirty in the morning."

Malajia sucked her teeth. "That is *so* not fair," she complained. "*My* last damn class on Monday, Wednesday and Friday is at six in the evening. On top of that, I have stupid Mr. Bradley for Sociology," she seethed. Mark looked at her and frowned. "I mean, what the hell does Sociology have to do with fashion, huh? If I wanted to be a freakin' sociologist then I would have picked that as my major, *not* design and business."

Malajia's friends stared silently at her for several seconds. "You talk way too goddamn much," Chasity spat out.

"Thank you," Sidra agreed. *Leave it to Chasity to always say what others are thinking*, she thought.

"You know what? Now I have an attitude," Mark fussed out of nowhere.

Jason chuckled. "What's *your* problem?"

"I have that same damn class." Mark pointed to his schedule. "Meaning that I have to sit through fifty minutes of Mr. Bradley again, *and* I have to sit through it with *Malajia*."

"Nobody told your dumb ass to fail Sociology last semester," Malajia sneered. Mark gritted his teeth as he bundled his coat to his neck.

Chapter 3

"I really missed this place," Emily mused, stabbing her salad with her fork. The past few hours were spent unpacking. She was relieved when the group decided to take a break and head to the cafeteria for dinner.

Mark frowned in disgust. "You missed this crap?" he asked, pointing to a plate food that somebody left on another table.

"No not the food, but…"

"Mark you know damn well if nobody was here, you'd eat that," Jason joked, interrupting Emily's words.

Frustrated, Chasity tossed her fork onto her plate. "I'm not eating this bullshit," she sneered, folding her arms. "I'm gonna order out."

"You might as well add me to your order," Malajia declared. "You're not gonna eat fancy while the rest of us eat prison food."

"I'm not adding you to *shit*," Chasity ground out. "You're always trying to freeload."

"Shut up," Malajia snarled, taking a bite of her biscuit.

"Can you two just fight and get it over with?" Mark suggested, taking a bite out his turkey sandwich. Chasity and Malajia shot him venomous looks. "Come on, just rip each other's clothes off and go at it," he insisted.

"You're a dog," Alex exclaimed.

"I wasn't talking to you, *was* I?" Mark retorted. "What? You mad cause I didn't include yo*u* in my fantasy?" He punctuated his snide remark by throwing a french fry at Alex.

"Stop acting so childish," Alex scolded, tossing a tomato back at him. He quickly knocked it away, swatting it onto Jason's black, long-sleeved shirt.

"Come on man, that had ketchup on it," Jason exclaimed, picking up some of his fries and tossing them at Mark.

"Dawg, why you gotta throw that shit on *me*?" Mark complained, pointing to Alex. "*She* threw it."

"Go to hell, Mark," Alex snapped. "You play too damn much."

Mark glared at her. "Oh, go to hell, huh?" He tossed a piece of turkey at Alex, but it missed its target and landed on Chasity's expensive burgundy top.

She knocked the meat off, picked up a fork full of macaroni and cheese, and flung it at Mark. Laughter resonated through the booth as it splattered on his face.

Mark wiped his face clean with a napkin. "Oh, that's funny?" he yelled, picking up a slice of Emily's orange. He was about to hurl it at Chasity, but was stopped by a slice of onion hitting him on the side of the head. "Damn Jason, I thought we were cool!" he shouted, glaring at Jason.

"Mark, stop acting like an ass," Alex scolded.

"I act how I *want*," he shot back, tossing the orange at Sidra. "Here ya go, Sid."

"What are you doing?" Sidra gasped, knocking it away from her and hitting Josh in the face with it.

"Ow! The juice got in my eye!" he screamed, frantically rubbing his eyes.

Sidra covered her mouth with her hands and looked at him with shock. "Oh, I'm sorry honey."

Mark looked over at the big smile on Josh's face as Sidra began wiping his face with a napkin. Agitated, he pounded his fist on the table and shouted, "Man, what the hell are you smiling at?"

"Why are you so hype?" Josh shot back, tossing a roll at him.

Malajia suddenly perked with excitement as the mini food fight ensued between her friends. "Ooh I wanna play, I wanna play," she exclaimed, picking up a styrofoam cup and tossing it at Mark.

Her face took on a shocked expression as she watched the left-over fruit punch from the cup splash on Mark and Jason, who was sitting right next to him.

Malajia covered her mouth with her hands as the two guys glared at her. Suddenly, she got up from the booth and ran. Jason and Mark hurried out of the booth, chasing after her. Laughter erupted from the table as they heard Malajia scream.

"Now *this* is what I missed," Emily stated.

"I really need to stop buying stuff," Chasity complained tiredly, hanging the last of her many outfits in her closet. She'd been unpacking since they'd returned from the cafeteria hours ago.

Sidra giggled as she sat on her bed and grabbed the TV remote. "Girl please, my mama always says that a girl can never do enough shopping."

"Well next time, your mama can put my clothes away," Chasity jeered, stretching.

Ignoring Chasity's snide remark, Sidra flipped through the channels on Chasity's forty-two inch television. "God, why is there never anything on?" she grumbled.

Chasity shrugged, then heard a knock at the door.

"You expecting someone?" Sidra asked, sitting the remote on her nightstand.

"Hell no," Chasity replied. "You?"

"Not at *this* hour."

Chasity reluctantly opened the door, quickly moving out of the way as Malajia busted in, pulling Alex by her arm.

"What's going on?" Sidra asked as Chasity shut the door.

Malajia held her finger up as she tried to catch her breath.

Chasity looked over at Alex, who was clearly agitated. "What the hell is *your* problem?" she asked, voice laced with attitude.

Alex put her hand up. "Don't start with me, evil," she ground out, before walking over to the cream love seat and flopping down on it.

"Is somebody gonna tell us what happened?" Sidra persisted, voice raised.

"Jason and Mark are looking for me," Malajia informed her, finally catching her breath.

"They were chasing us for like ten minutes," Alex added.

"Why?" Chasity asked, standing with her arms folded.

"The whole thing is really immature," Alex scoffed, moving some hair from her face. "Malajia, I can't believe that I let you drag me out of my bed at eleven something for this mess."

"Why *are* you ladies out at this hour?" Sidra questioned. "And in pajamas?" She tried not to laugh at her friends' nighttime attire.

"Tacky pajamas at that," Chasity added. "This one looks like a street walker and the *other* one looks like she found hers in the dumpster," she continued, pointing to Malajia's slinky red night slip, paired with red tights and Alex's baggy gray sweatpants and green t-shirt. Their coats were open, so the attire wasn't hard to miss.

"Girl, I'm not in the mood!" Alex snapped, putting her hand up.

Chasity smirked, relishing Alex's annoyance.

Sidra giggled. "Tell us what happened."

"Go on, tell em' Malajia. Tell em'!" Alex yelled.

Malajia shot Alex a warning look before returning to Sidra. "Well, I was putting away the rest of my stuff, when I started craving a snack," she notified. "I wanted to go to a vending machine."

Sidra looked confused. "But you have a vending machine in your dorm," she pointed out.

"Go ahead. Tell them why we're out, when there is a perfectly good vending machine in our dorm," Alex fumed. Malajia looked at her. "Go on! Tell em'."

Malajia stared at her for a few seconds. "Why are you yelling at me?" she calmly asked.

Sidra chuckled. "Alex, you really need to calm down."

Alex leaned forward in her seat, shooting Sidra a shocked expression. "Sidra, this chick practically dragged my ass out of my bed to walk her to the SDC, to use their vending machine," she seethed. "At eleven at night, she wanted to go to the SDC. You wanna know *why* she wanted to go to the SDC vending machine and not the one in our own damn dorm? Huh?"

"Uh, I'm afraid to ask," Sidra joked.

"*I'll* tell you why!" Alex continued, exasperated. "Because our machine didn't have chocolate covered nuts—*nuts,* Sidra!"

Chasity laughed as Sidra shook her head and giggled.

"Is it *my* fault I like nuts?" Malajia jumped in, trying to defend herself.

Chasity put her hand up. "You wanna rethink that answer?" she chortled.

"Nope," Malajia returned. "I know how it sounded."

"And she didn't want just *any* kind of chocolate covered nuts," Alex added. "This fool, wanted the ones from that commercial where the stupid man dressed like a nut, was dancing."

Sidra put her hand over her face to keep from laughing out loud.

"He was killin' it on the commercial though," Malajia reasoned, much to Alex's annoyance.

"You know what, Malajia? You *look* like a damn nut," Alex yelled, tossing a pillow at Malajia.

"Anyway, Jason and Mark were in the SDC, and they started chasing us with a bottle of apple juice," Malajia continued.

"Wait, why would they be chasing you with a bottle of juice?" Chasity asked, curious.

"You remember when I accidentally splashed juice on them in the caf?" Malajia quizzed, Sidra nodded. "Well, they wanted to get me back by throwing the juice on me. But me and Alex dodged them by running in here."

"Where's Emily?" Sidra asked, standing from her bed.

"She's asleep," Alex answered. "Which is what *I'd* like to be doing right now."

"Oh shut up, I would do the same for you," Malajia snapped, tired of Alex's complaining.

"No, you wouldn't, because *I* would never drag *you* out of bed at night to walk out in the freezing cold to get some damn DANCING NUTS!" Alex shouted. Her rant was interrupted by a knock at the door.

"Are you kidding me?" Sidra complained, glancing at the clock on her nightstand, it was nearing midnight.

Chasity opened the door, only to be greeted by big smiles from Mark and Jason. "What?" she sneered.

"We know she's here, so you might as well let us in," Mark demanded as he and Jason pushed their way through the door.

Malajia screamed and hid behind Sidra as Mark opened the bottle of apple juice.

"Don't you bring that crap up in here," Sidra chided, putting her hand up.

"Sid, I love you like a sister. But you *will* get splashed with this juice if you don't move," Mark warned.

"You better not throw that damn juice in here. You wanna get slapped?" Chasity threatened, snatching Jason's bottle from him.

"Chasity, this has nothing to do with you," Jason declared. "We only want the thing behind Sidra."

Alex was fed up. "Are you serious?" she seethed. "Are you two really that immature? It's twenty degrees outside and you wanna throw cold juice on her? Then she still has to walk home in the cold. Are you really gonna be that petty?"

Jason and Mark glanced at each other before turning back to Alex "Yeah," they shrugged in unison.

Alex threw her hands up in frustration, flopping back against the chair.

"Come on Malajia, take it like a man," Mark urged, signaling for her to come forward.

"Why do you have to treat me like this?" Malajia whined over Sidra's shoulder. "If it was Chasity, Sidra, or even Alex, you would just deal with it and move on."

"Well, I wanna sleep with *her*," Jason joked, pointing to Chasity who in turn shot him a side glance. "So she can run me over with her car and I'll deal with it."

"I have other ways of getting Sidra back," Mark stated. Sidra raised an eyebrow as she placed both hands on her hips. "And Alex I can just fight like a man," he continued.

Alex threw a pillow at him. "And I would kick your ass," she spat out.

Mark flagged her with his hand as he turned his attention back to Malajia. "I just want to make *you* suffer."

Sidra was tired of this childish banter. "You two, get out," she demanded.

Mark was fuming as he stared at Malajia, who was still hiding behind Sidra. "Come here," he ordered through clenched teeth as he reached around Sidra to try to get to Malajia.

"Cut it out," Sidra exclaimed, shielding her from him.

Mark finally got hold of Malajia's arm, but didn't succeed in pulling her away, because she started screaming at the top of her lungs.

Alex jumped up from her seat. "Oh for the love of all things holy!" she shouted.

"That's it. Y'all are pissing me off, get out," Chasity demanded, pointing to the door.

"Okay, fine, we'll go," Jason relented, grabbing the doorknob. "But this isn't over Malajia."

"Just shut up and go," Chasity insisted.

"Come on Mark, let's let the ladies relax," Jason urged.

Mark glowered at Malajia, then he suddenly jumped at her, making her flinch.

"I hope you die in your sleep!" Malajia screamed at him.

Mark pointed at her. "Well I hope I do too, that way I can haunt *you!*" he hollered back. His comeback was met with confused looks.

"You're such an idiot," Alex concluded, too tired to yell anymore.

"Wow," Sidra chuckled.

As he and Mark walked out the door, Jason laughed. "What was that all about?"

"Man, I don't know, I couldn't think of anything else," Mark admitted, voice full of frustration as the door closed behind him.

Chapter 4

Malajia fixed a wayward curl on her head as she sauntered along the path towards her dorm. She smiled when she saw Chasity heading towards her on the same path. "Where are you going?" Malajia asked her, blocking her path.

"Bitch it's cold, move," Chasity snapped, trying to maneuver around Malajia. Every time she moved in another direction, Malajia jumped in her way. "Malajia!" she hollered, tired of the games.

Malajia laughed; she always got a kick out of pushing Chasity's buttons. "I just remembered, I need to go to the book store," she said. "Come on, walk with me."

Chasity pushed some of her hair out of her face. It was freezing cold, the heavy wind making the chill bone deep. "No, walk your damn self," she hissed.

Malajia stomped her foot on the ground. "Look, you're going," she commanded.

Chasity glared at Malajia, who in turn raised an eyebrow and folded her arms.

"Hey ladies," Jason greeted, heading their way.

Malajia turned around. As soon as she saw him, she shrieked and hid behind Chasity, who just shook her head and rolled her eyes.

"Relax Mel, I'm not gonna throw any juice on you," he assured, taking a sip from his water bottle.

"Oh please, like I'm supposed to believe you," Malajia sneered. "You're just as bad as Mark."

Jason's would-be retort was stopped as he saw Mark creeping up behind the girls, holding a jug of water. "Uh Chaz, can I talk to you for a minute?" he asked, reaching for Chasity's arm.

"About what?" Chasity asked with aggravation.

"Um…I overheard Jackie Stevens saying something bad about you on the way here, and I want to tell you about it," he lied.

Chasity's jaw tightened; it was easy for her to believe that, everyone was aware that Jackie Stevens was a loud mouth.

"Ooh, *I* wanna know," Malajia said, interest piqued.

"No, she'll tell you later," Jason protested, pulling Chasity aside.

Malajia stood there, hoping to overhear the gossip. But all thoughts stopped when she felt cold water hit her body. Mark proceeded to pour the entire jug of water on Malajia.

Chasity spun around as she heard Malajia scream.

Jason cracked up laughing as he and Chasity watched Malajia try to swing at Mark. "Stop it! It's cold!" she screamed.

"How's that? How do you like it?" Mark laughed. "Jase, get her!"

Jason proceeded to open his water bottle, but Chasity snatched it from him and shook her head 'no'. Malajia kept screaming as she took off running towards her dorm.

"She's colder than a muthafucka," Mark mused. "I let this jug thaw from the freezer."

Chasity narrowed her eyes as the guys high fived each other. "You two are fuckin' crazy," she concluded.

Mark shrugged. "What? It's only water," he joked. "It's not like she doesn't need a bath anyway."

"Oh calm down baby, it's just a little pay back," Jason chimed in.

Chasity rolled eyes before walking away. Jason and Mark continued laughing as they headed off in the other direction.

Malajia unlocked her room door and kicked it open, startling Alex, Sidra and Emily. "I'm going to kill Mark!" she shouted, slamming the door behind her.

"Girl what happened? Why are you soaking wet?" Alex exclaimed, focusing on Malajia's drenched coat. "It's freezing out there."

"Sweetie, don't you know that it has to be *hot* outside when you do your wet t-shirt competitions?" Sidra teased.

Malajia shot Sidra a lethal glance as she snatched her coat off. "Sidra, I will slice your fuckin' ponytail off if you don't quit playing with me!" she yelled.

Sidra made a face at her.

"What happened?" Alex enunciated slowly.

"Mark threw ice water all over me," she exclaimed. Before the other girls could respond, Chasity walked in the room and shut the door behind her. "Don't say anything to me, Judas," Malajia jeered, pointing at her.

"Oh don't blame *me* for that. You brought that on yourself," Chasity shot back, removing her scarf.

"You should've done something!"

"First of all, don't yell at me," Chasity warned. "Second, I didn't see him until *after* he started pouring it on you."

Sidra watched as Malajia snatched off her form fitting burgundy sweater. "Please tell me that they did not do that to get you back for throwing juice on them the other day," she broke in.

"Wow, I thought that they forgot about that," Emily said.

"You know what, that is so childish," Alex seethed, pacing back and forth. If there was one thing she hated, it was someone messing with her girls. "Don't worry honey, we're gonna get them back for that."

Chasity looked at her. "So who's acting childish *now?*" she mocked.

"Jason's dumb ass set me up," Malajia fumed, stomping her foot on the floor. "They fucked up my hair. Do you know how long it takes me to curl it like this?"

"Malajia just—"

"No Sidra, 'Malajia just' nothin'," she interrupted. "Now I have to go into that raggedy-ass bathroom that we share with half the damn floor to re-curl my hair."

Sidra glared at Malajia for a few seconds. She was willing to forgive the fact that the girl just cut her off because she was rightfully upset. "I was going to say—before you cut me off," she declared. "Just calm down. I will curl your hair for you."

Malajia glanced at Sidra, regretting her outburst. "Oh," she conceded. "Very well, I'll get the curling iron."

"So how are we gonna get those bastards back for what they did?" Malajia asked, slicing her french toast into pieces.

Sidra sat her cup of tea down on the table. "Malajia, come on, you threw juice on *them*; they threw cold water on *you*. It's even now."

With the first week of classes behind them, the girls decided to celebrate by having breakfast at the local diner, fifteen minutes off campus, as opposed to eating at the cafeteria.

Malajia narrowed her eyes at Sidra "You know what? Your stuck up ass is getting on my nerves," she snapped.

Sidra folded her arms and stared back at her; trying to suppress a laugh.

"God you even eat prissy food...What is that, crème brule?" Malajia mocked, pointing to the contents in Sidra's bowl.

"No, fool. It's a parfait," Sidra clarified.

"I don't care *what* it is." Malajia flicked her hand in Sidra's direction. "You just irk me."

Sidra, not feeling like going back and forth with Malajia, especially when the girl wasn't making any sense, just rolled her eyes and went back to eating her breakfast.

Alex laughed at their back and forth. *Malajia is always so hyper*, she thought.

"Anyway, what I did to those testosterone holders in the caf was an accident," Malajia pointed out, taking a bite of her food. "What they did to me was on purpose. I want payback, and I want it now."

"You know, usually I don't like to participate in juvenile behavior, but I'm actually with Mel on this one," Alex jumped in, gesturing to her friends with her fork.

"Do you really think that it's right to gang up on them like that? I mean, they didn't do anything to *me*," Emily added softly.

Chasity shot Emily a glare. "You know, I was actually enjoying your silence," she sneered.

Emily put her head down.

"Why do you keep picking on her?" Alex asked, frowning.

"Cause she's so damn annoying," Chasity snapped.

Alex waved her hand dismissively at Chasity. "Pay this witch no mind honey. You say what you want," she directed at Emily.

Emily hesitantly looked at Chasity. "Maybe you can learn to like me this semester," she hoped.

"Grow a backbone, and maybe I can try to tolerate you," Chasity spat.

Sidra shook her head, looking at her acerbic roommate. "Put a sock in it, ice queen," she ground out.

"Can we get back to *me* please?" Malajia cut in.

"Okay Mel, I'll help you," Alex chortled, taking a sip of juice.

"I am not entertaining this nonsense," Sidra scoffed.

"Oh you *will*," Malajia assured. "You may act all high and mighty, but deep down inside, you're a trouble maker."

Sidra's mouth fell open. "What are you talking about?"

"The same troublemaker that used to get me in trouble when we were kids," Malajia pointed out.

"But—"

"And the same troublemaker that manipulates Josh all the time to get him to do what you want, because you know he wants you," Malajia accused, pointing a manicured finger in her face.

"You lying little strumpet, I have *never* manipulated Josh to do anything for me," Sidra argued. "And he doesn't want me. We're just friends."

Malajia raised an eyebrow. "Yeah, okay," she jeered. "You helping or not?"

"Whatever, Malajia," Sidra relented, tossing her napkin on to the table.

"Yeah, that's what I thought," Malajia laughed.

Alex giggled as the waitress walked up and handed them the bill.

Chasity picked it up and looked at it. "Damn, what the hell did I eat that costs twenty dollars?"

"Oh please, just take the hundred dollar bill out of your wallet and pay the damn tab," Malajia sneered. Chasity glowered at her as she set the check down on the table. "And while you're at it, you might as well pay for mine too. God knows you can afford it."

"I'm not paying for shit for you. You annoying, whining idiot," Chasity hissed.

"Bitch! Why I gotta be all that?" Malajia exclaimed.

"All right ladies, enough," Alex broke in. "let's pay and get out of here."

As everyone gathered their money, Malajia hissed, "I'm sick of your damn mouth, Chasity."

"You must forgot whose car you rode in," Chasity shot back.

Malajia sucked her teeth.

"You two can*not* go an hour without insulting each other." Sidra recalled the many arguments that occurred between them just that morning.

Alex sighed as she pulled a ten dollar bill out of her purse. She'd forgotten that she spent most of her funds on books and essentials earlier that week, not leaving her enough to pay for her meal.

"Damn, I need a job," she mumbled.

Chasity glanced over at Alex as she continued to dig for change to cover the bill. Feeling sorry for her, Chasity took a twenty dollar bill from her wallet and slid it into Alex's hand without anyone noticing. Completely caught by surprise, Alex looked up at Chasity, who gestured for her to take it.

Alex gratefully took the money, mouthing the words 'thank you.' Chasity just nodded.

Feeling embarrassed, Alex was silent as the girls made their way to the parking lot. Chasity noticed the somber look on Alex's face, and handed her keys to Sidra.

"Go unlock my door," she commanded. Before Sidra could say anything, Malajia snatched the keys from her.

"Shot gun!" Malajia yelled, running for the car.

Sidra took off running after her, with Emily following close behind. "Why do you have to act so childish?" Sidra shouted.

"Chasity, I will pay you back," Alex assured her, once the others were out of earshot.

"Alex, why didn't you just say that you didn't have enough money?" Chasity asked.

"I didn't realize that I didn't have enough," Alex admitted. "Do you have any idea how embarrassing that was for me?"

"No," Chasity answered bluntly. "But I can imagine."

"I worked all through my winter break and it *still* wasn't enough," Alex grumbled, pushing some wavy tendrils back into its ponytail. "I swear, if it wasn't for my financial aid, I'd have to drop out of school."

Chasity frowned. She never had to worry about where money came from; it was always given to her freely. She couldn't imagine having to struggle financially.

"I have no choice but to get a part time job, I can't live like this," Alex declared. "Chaz, I'd appreciate it if you wouldn't say anything to anybody about this."

"Do I *look* like Malajia?" Chasity scoffed, causing Alex to chuckle. "Don't worry about it, all right."

Alex just smiled. Even though she suspected it, she was surprised to see that Chasity had a compassionate side. But she was sure that it wouldn't resurface for a long time to come, so she took care to appreciate it.

"Why don't we go to the mall?" Malajia suggested a few minutes after they pulled out of the parking lot.

"No," Chasity complained with frustration.

"Look here cranky, you're not the only one in this car," Malajia shot back "You don't decide what we do."

Completely fed up with Malajia's mouth, Chasity pulled over and turned the car off.

"What are you doing?" Sidra asked, voice full of amusement.

Chasity turned around and looked at Malajia. "Get out," she snapped.

"Bitch, you crazy. I'm not getting out in this cold," Malajia sneered, bundling her coat to her neck. "You're gonna have to physically put me out,"

Determined to do just that, Chasity unhooked her seatbelt. Sidra, trying to suppress a laugh, grabbed Chasity's hand from her belt.

"Okay Chaz, calm down," Alex said from the back seat, before nudging Malajia, who was sitting beside her. "And Malajia, stop being so damn annoying."

"Well seriously, *can* we go to the mall?" Sidra asked, once they pulled off yet again. "I have an idea about how we can get those boys back for what they did to Mel."

Alex was intrigued. "Okay, Miss Lady. I knew you had a nasty streak," she teased. "What do you have in mind?"

"Oh, nothing too serious, but it'll give them a taste of their own medicine."

Chapter 5

"This cold is just disrespectful," Mark complained, pulling the hood from his sweat jacket over his head.

"Nobody told you to come outside without a coat on," Josh chided. "It's like twenty degrees out here." A morning trip to the gym before classes was becoming a routine for the guys, but this particular blistering cold morning, they'd wished they had stayed in.

Jason wiped the sweat from his face with the sleeve of his jacket when he noticed the girls standing on the steps of Daniels Hall, arms placed behind their backs.

"Uh guys, what are the girls doing at your dorm?" Jason asked.

Mark rolled his eyes. This cold was too much for him to bear; he could care less what they wanted. "Who the hell knows," Mark ground out as they approached the steps. "What do y'all want?" he hissed at them.

"Well 'hello' to you *too,* ignorant ass," Malajia scoffed.

David chuckled and shook his head. "What brings you over here today?" he asked, adjusting the knit cap on his head. "Were we supposed to meet you for breakfast or something?"

"No," the girls replied in unison, shaking their heads.

The guys eyed them suspiciously. "Uh, o-kay," Josh replied. "It's too cold to be out here for no reason...I take it Emily had the right idea to stay in."

"Yeah well, she didn't want to join us for our little walk," Alex informed.

"All right, enough of this chit chattin' bullshit," Mark bit out, heading up the steps. "It's cold, and I need to shower."

"Ugh, you're not lying about that," Malajia scoffed, nose turned up. Mark sucked his teeth as the girls proceeded down the stairs.

"Bye you guys," they said in unison.

The guys followed their progress briefly before shaking their heads and proceeded to walk up the steps.

"Hey!" Alex shouted.

"What?" Jason replied. As soon as the guys turned around, they were met by a cold blast of water from the girl's water guns.

"What the hell man!" Mark shouted as a stream of water hit him in the face.

"Cut it out! Y'all play too much," Jason yelled, trying to shield his face.

"I didn't even do anything," Josh complained.

"Guilty by association," Alex laughed, continuing her stream.

Jason took off running in the direction of his dorm as Josh and David ran inside theirs.

Sidra, Alex, and Chasity dropped their soakers, and watched as Malajia ran up to Mark who had fallen on the steps and started spraying him at close range.

"How do you like it?" Malajia taunted. "It's cold isn't it? Huh? Isn't it?"

Mark put his hand up, trying to shield himself from the frigid spray. "All right Malajia, damn. You play too much." He jumped up from the stairs as the water hit him in the eye. "You know what!" he hollered, causing Malajia to quickly back up.

"Damn, you colder than a muthafucka," Malajia teased, pumping her water gun. "We let these thaw from the freezer."

"This shit ain't over, you freaks," Mark fumed, stomping inside.

"Well, we may have just started a war," Sidra predicted. The girls just shrugged before heading back towards their dorm.

Mark's anger only intensified when he busted into Josh and David's room. "It's on," he seethed.

"Still haven't learned to knock yet, huh?" Josh hissed, wiping his face with a towel.

David removed his glasses from his face. "Damn, that water pressure almost broke my glasses," he complained, examining them.

"Man, *fuck* your glasses!" Mark snapped, removing his wet sweatshirt.

David and Josh frowned at him. "Why are you so mad?" Josh calmly asked.

"I'm sick of those chicks!" Mark yelled, "They always tryna one up us and shit. They think they can get away with everything."

"Mark, it was just water," Josh chuckled. "Although, I do believe that they deserve a tad bit of payback."

"A *tad* bit—Man y'all fools are corny! Where's my partner in crime?" Mark snapped. He started tossing his friends clothes around in search of their room phone. Finally finding it, he dialed Jason's extension. "Jason," he hollered in the phone.

"What's up bro?" Jason laughed, grabbing a towel off of his bed.

"It's war, man," Mark declared.

"Oh, you better believe it," Jason confirmed.

"Come on guys, let's not take this too far," Josh stepped in.

"Man, shut your bitch ass up!" Mark shouted at him.

The light peeking through the blinds blinded Alex. "Ugh, eight already?" she groaned. She wished that she could close her eyes for a few more minutes, but decided against it, afraid that she would oversleep and miss her first class. She grabbed her bathroom essentials, walked out of the room, and into the shared bathroom. She turned on the sink and yawned.

Running her hands through her untamed hair, she let out a loud sigh. "You might need to start sleeping in a bonnet, Alex," she said to herself, staring at the mirror. She was in no mood to deal with her hair. She put on her clear shower cap before applying her daily facial mask. She chuckled as she looked at herself with that white mask on her face and the shower cap over her puffy hair. Grabbing her towel, she proceeded to walk to one of the shower stalls, only to be greeted by a bright flash.

"What the hell?" she exclaimed as the door closed. Rubbing her eyes, she walked into the shower.

Alex breathed a sigh of relief when her morning Algebra class was over. Looking at her watch, she hurried out of the math building and made a beeline for the path leading back to her dorm. *I guess I should get some studying in before this next class.*

She saw a few people stare at her, but she just brushed it off and kept walking. It's not as if she was unattractive; Alex was used to some stares now and then. It wasn't until a few people started pointing and laughing at her that she knew something was odd.

"What's so funny?" she asked a female upperclassman as she walked by, holding a piece of paper.

Alex looked around confused, until something caught her eye on the ground. Frowning, she bent down and picked up the piece of paper. Shock resonated on her face as she saw the blown up picture of herself from earlier that morning. The top of the page read *Meet Alexandra Chisolm*, in large bold letters.

"Oh my God!" she hollered.

It was then that she noticed copies of the picture littering the ground. Her eyes narrowed in anger as she spotted Mark and Josh walking across the path, laughing. "Mark!" she screamed, storming over to them.

The two guys continued laughing as Alex approached. "That's a good look for you Alex," Josh teased, holding the picture in front of her face.

Alex slapped his hand down. "Shut up!" she snapped.

"Damn, you're ugly in the morning," Mark teased. Alex gritted her teeth; she could have killed him right then and there. "What the hell is on your face?"

"You've gone too damn far you jackass!" Alex yelled, pointing at him. "This isn't funny."

"Why do you automatically assume that *I* did this?" Mark asked, fixing his book bag on his shoulder.

"Oh please Mark, either *you* or one of your smuts took this picture of me this morning," she argued.

Mark chuckled. "You can say what you want. But the bottom line is that *you* look like shit in this picture," he shot back, holding up his copy of the picture and pointing to it.

Unable to form any more words, Alex let out a loud groan before snatching the picture and storming off. As she hurried to the Science building to meet Sidra and Chasity, she saw Jackie, sitting on the steps with her friends.

"Nice look, Alex!" Jackie shouted, pointing to a picture on the ground.

Alex was in no mood to deal with Jackie; in her eyes, that girl was nothing but trouble. She just rolled her eyes and continued on inside.

Alex paced back and forth as she waited for her friends to come out. She was cursing to herself as Sidra walked out of the elevator.

"Hey, what's going on?" Sidra smiled, approaching. Not saying a word, Alex held the picture in front of Sidra's face. Sidra took the picture from her and stared at it. Alex folded her arms as Sidra put her hand over her face.

"It's not funny," Alex wailed as Sidra grabbed her stomach, doubling over with laughter.

"I'm sorry sweetie, I *am* but…you look like a hot mess," Sidra laughed.

Chasity walked out of the stairwell. "What's she laughing at?" she asked, pointing to Sidra. Too annoyed to say a word, Alex just looked at Chasity, who frowned in reply. "What? Why are you looking at me like that?" Chasity asked.

Sidra handed Chasity the picture, tears streaming down her face.

Chasity stared at it for a moment, before breaking into laughter. "Eww! What the hell is on your damn face?" she teased.

Alex tapped Chasity on the arm, snatching the picture from her. "It was a face mask," she snapped. "You know what? I don't appreciate you two laughing at me."

"Why does it look like you're posing for the picture?" Chasity questioned. Alex let out a loud sigh.

"That is the funniest thing that I have ever seen," Sidra concluded, wiping the tears from her eye.

"Whatever. Just come on," Alex seethed. "We need a plan to get them back."

"I won't be long in the store, I promise," Sidra assured, adjusting her purse on her shoulder as she and Chasity walked towards their dorm parking lot. "I know you're tired."

"Yeah, yeah," Chasity mumbled. For a half hour, Sidra begged and pleaded for Chasity to take her to Mega-Mart later that evening, before she relented.

Sidra chuckled at Chasity's surly response. "Oh, stop acting like you don't need stuff too," she joked.

Chasity was about to fire off a smart remark when she stopped in her tracks. "Oh...My...God." She drew her words out slowly.

Sidra shot her a concerned glance. "What's the matter with you?" she asked.

Without turning away from the sight, Chasity put her hands on Sidra's face and moved it in the direction of her expression of horror.

Sidra's eyes widened with shock. "Oooooohhh," she said, putting her hands over her mouth.

Chasity's black Lexus was covered with shaving cream and maxi pads.

Chasity stormed over to her car to examine the damage. "Are you fuckin' kidding me?!" she exploded.

"Can you believe that they took the time to stick all these damn pads all over the car?" Sidra admonished.

"I'm gonna beat the shit out of whoever did this," Chasity seethed, peeling the pads from the car. She sucked her teeth. "These damn things are leaving glue spots on my car!"

"This has the guys written all over it," Sidra assured. "Only *they* would think that this is funny." Sidra watched as her frustrated roommate went into the trunk of her car and took out a towel to wipe the shaving cream off.

Chasity's frustration grew into pure rage as she made a second discovery. "It's frozen!" she screamed.

Sidra tried unsuccessfully to contain her laugher. Chasity threw her towel on the ground and signaled for Sidra to get into the car.

Once they got in and Chasity started the car up Sidra asked, "How are you going to get it off?" Chasity stopped her words by quickly putting her hand up. She was so angry that she couldn't even say anything.

A loud bang on the door startled Jason out of his chill time. Frowning, he turned the TV down with his remote before walking over to his door. *Who is banging on my door all crazy?*

"Who is it?" he barked. Even though he heard no answer, curiosity begged him to open the door.

He laughed as he tried to close it on the person who was standing there.

Chasity and Sidra pushed their way through the door, sending him darting back. Sidra closed it behind them as Chasity walked up to him, forcing him to back away from her. The look on her face was one that, if he didn't know her, he would think that she was about to kill him.

"Hey baby, what—?"

"Don't 'hey baby' me, you jackass!" Chasity snapped, holding a white plastic bag in his face.

"What's the matter?" Jason asked, attempting to keep a straight face.

"Oh don't act like you don't know," Sidra sneered, walking over to him with her arms folded.

Jason held his hands up in the air. "Ladies, I swear I was in here the whole time," he declared.

"You're a damn liar!" Chasity yelled, throwing the bag full of pads at him. "You think it's funny sticking fuckin' maxi pads on my car?"

"Chasity, I swear, I don't know how the pads and shaving cream got on your car," Jason argued.

The girls glared daggers at him.

"What?" he asked

"Jason, I didn't hear either *one* of us mention anything about shaving cream," Sidra pointed out.

Shit, I'm busted. He stood there with a stupid look on his face, and put his hands on his head. "Damn," he said.

Sidra moved out of the way as Chasity proceeded to chase the laughing Jason around his room.

"Chaz, quit it," he urged. "It wasn't my idea."

"Oh please," Sidra scoffed.

"Don't you know that if you leave cream on a damn car in below zero weather that it freezes?" Chasity fumed.

"Oh shit, it froze?" Jason laughed. The fact that he kept laughing made Chasity even angrier.

"We were at the car wash for a half hour trying to get that mess off," Sidra interjected. "Hell, we didn't even get to the store."

"Well, you have to admit, it *was* kinda funny," Jason teased. Chasity glared at him for a few seconds; before reaching for the largest text book on his desk. Jason knew that in a matter of seconds, that heavy math book would fly right at him. He rushed over and grabbed her away from the desk.

"Look I *did* participate in that, but it wasn't my idea," he admitted, holding Chasity's arms behind her back.

"Oh whatever Jason," Sidra frowned. "It's just like a boy to stick pads on a surface for laughs."

"Come on Sid, do I *look* like I would come up with some corny shit like sticking pads to a car?" he asked.

"It doesn't matter. It's war anyway," Sidra concluded, walking towards the door. She turned back to him and said, "Stop trying to feel up my roommate so we can get out of here."

Jason looked at Chasity, whom he still held onto. "You do feel good though," he teased.

"Boy, get off me!" Chasity hollered, jerking away from him.

"Have a good night ladies," he called after the two angry girls as they walked out of the room. He flinched as the door slammed.

Chapter 6

Malajia and Mark approached Mr. Bradley's Sociology class at the same time. They stopped at the door, glaring at each other.

"Mark don't start your shit today," Malajia sneered. "I have to learn."

"What, you scared?" Mark taunted.

"Boy you can't scare nobody. Shut up," Malajia shot back.

Mr. Bradley made his way to his classroom. "You two better not start today, we have a lot to get through," he warned.

"Hey Mr. Bradley," Mark greeted with a big smile. He knew for a fact that he worked his teacher's nerves every class.

"Umm hmm, get in the room," Mr. Bradley commanded.

As his fellow classmates took their seats and began taking out their class materials, Mark reached his foot out and kicked Malajia in the leg.

"Cut it out, boy!" she hollered.

"Oops," Mark teased.

Mr. Bradley spun around to see Mark cracking up laughing. It was when he noticed the stern look on his professor's' face that Mark stopped. Mr. Bradley signaled for Mark to come up to his desk. Malajia stuck her tongue out at him as he got out of his seat and walked up to the front of the room.

When Mark got to the front of the class, Mr. Bradley leaned in close to him. "If you don't stop acting like a class clown, I'm going to kick your slacking behind out of my classroom," Mr. Bradley hissed. "Is that clear?"

Mark stared at him for a few seconds. "You seem stressed today," he assumed.

Mr. Bradley's eyes became wide with anger. Mark knew at that moment that this was not the time to try to be funny. "I'ma go head and sit down now," he said, pointing to his seat.

Walking back to his seat, Mark made a face at Malajia, who in turn rolled her eyes. He then pulled his pants up on his behind before flopping down into his seat, only to frown in confusion at the loud, strange sound that came from his seat.

"Eww Mark!" Malajia exclaimed, holding her nose. "You couldn't hold that until you left?"

Embarrassed, Mark turned and looked at his classmates, who were pointing and laughing at him. "I swear that wasn't me!" he exclaimed

"Mark, I warned you," Mr. Bradley sternly stated. "You need to leave my class right now."

"But I didn't do anything," Mark insisted, picking up a pink, rubber contraption from his seat. "It's a whoopee cushion," he informed. "Malajia put a freakin' whoopee cushion in my seat. Come on, how corny is that?"

"Oh please. Don't blame *me* because you can't hold your bodily functions," Malajia teased, moving her bangs out of her face. Mark glared at Malajia as he tossed the cushion at her, hitting her in the chest with it.

"Mr. Bradley! Mark's throwing stuff at me," Malajia wailed, pointing at Mark.

"Mark, leave," Mr. Bradley barked, pointing to the door.

Mark sucked his teeth as he quickly gathered his books from his desk. He turned to Malajia once he rose from his seat. "This ain't over," he warned.

Malajia flagged him with her hand. "Yeah, yeah. Just leave," she taunted. "The rest of us need to learn." She laughed proudly as Mark walked out of the classroom, shutting the door behind him.

The sound of the phone ringing stirred Josh and David awake. "Why is that ringer up so loud?" David asked tiredly, pulling the covers over his face.

Rubbing his eyes, Josh looked at the clock on his nightstand. "Three thirty in the morning? Come *on*," he complained before picking up the phone. "Hello?" he tiredly answered.

"Hello?" a deep voice responded.

Josh frowned. "Who is this?" he questioned.

"Who is this?" the voice repeated.

Josh let out a loud sigh. "Girls, stop playing," he hissed, before hanging up the phone.

"Who was that?" David grumbled, turning over in his bed.

"The girls trying to prank call us," Josh responded, lying back down.

"What kind of stupid shit was *that*?" Chasity scoffed as Malajia hung up the phone.

"Look, you know that I'm not good at prank calling people," Malajia argued. "Do you *not* recall the prank calls I made to *your* phone?"

Malajia and Alex, having lost track of time while studying in Torrence Hall, decided to stay over rather than walk back to their dorm. The girls had grown restless, and decided the best way to pass the time was to prank call the guys.

"Mel, all of your attempts at prank calling were just sad," Sidra chuckled.

Malajia narrowed her eyes at Sidra. "Then *you* try," she ordered, handing Sidra the phone.

"Oh honey, I'm no better," Sidra laughed, putting her hands up.

Chasity rolled her eyes and walked over to her desk. "I'm so over this," she complained. "I'm tired. So either y'all shut up, or get out."

"Oh no, one of these guys are getting pranked *tonight*," Malajia insisted, pointing to the phone. "I'm not losing sleep for nothing. So somebody else just give it a try." Malajia sucked her teeth and put the phone back to her ear when no one jumped at the opportunity. "Forget y'all, *I'll* go again."

"No. God make her stop," Chasity groaned as she put her arms on the desk and leaned her head on them.

"Shut up," Malajia retorted as she dialed a number.

Mark, having just fallen asleep not too long ago, was not happy to hear his phone ring. *First my damn mom talks my ear off for two damn hours, now this.*

Snatching his covers back in frustration, Mark picked up the phone. "Whhaattt?" he groaned.

"Hello?" a deep voice responded.

Mark frowned. "Who the hell is this?"

"Your mom!" the voice hollered.

Mark sucked his teeth as he hung up the cordless phone and tossed it across the room.

"Ouch!" his roommate shouted when the phone hit him on his leg.

"My bad, Rob," Mark apologized as he laid back down, pulling the covers up on his chest.

"Somebody take the goddamn phone from Malajia," Chasity demanded, pointing at Malajia from her bed, inciting laughter from Alex and Sidra.

"Look bitch, *you* try it!" Malajia snapped, holding the phone out for Chasity to take.

"I'm not getting involved in this mess," Chasity sneered, pulling her hair back into a ponytail.

"All you do is bitch about what *I'm* doing. Get over here and *help* me," Malajia challenged.

"I can help your stupid ass out my damn room," Chasity fussed, flipping Malajia off.

"All right you two, let's just focus," Alex cut in, voice full of amusement. "I have an idea," The other girls looked at her, waiting for her to talk.

Jason held his pillow over his ears, hoping that the loud ringing from his room phone would cease. When it didn't, he picked up the phone. "Hello?"

"Jason, its Chasity," the voice answered.

Jason instantly perked up. "Chasity?"

"Yeah, look I um…I really want to see you," Chasity replied, voice full with urgency. "I need to tell you something, but I have to tell you in person."

Jason sat up straight in his bed. "Chaz, are you okay?" he asked, concerned. "I mean, it's four in the morning and you want to talk to *me* of *all* people?"

"I know that it's weird but I just…I had—" Chasity paused and looked at the other girls, who were egging her on. Rolling her eyes, Chasity put her cell phone back to her ear. "I just really need to talk to you Jason," she replied.

"You want me to come over?" Jason asked, pushing the covers off.

"Yeah. Meet me in the parking lot outside my building in ten minutes," Chasity answered.

"Good work, girl," Alex beamed, patting Chasity on her back as she hung up the phone.

"This is really stupid, Alex," Chasity criticized, tossing her cell phone on her bed.

"It's gonna be worth it, I promise," Alex replied, gesturing to the cell phone that Sidra held. "All right Sid, your turn," she urged.

"Okay," Sidra sighed, and pushed a re-dial button on her phone.

"You're calling Josh and David's room, right?" Malajia asked.

Sidra nodded as she waited for one of the guys to answer. "Hey Josh," she said once he answered. "Listen I need a big favor from you—Yeah, but you don't even know what I—Okay, meet me in the parking lot outside my building in ten minutes." Sidra hung up and looked at her friends.

"Let me guess, he *jumped* at the chance to do something for you," Malajia assumed, folding her arms.

"Well, yeah," Sidra replied.

"Girl, you are so clueless," Alex teased; Sidra just rolled her eyes. "Ladies, it's show time," Alex mused, grabbing her coat.

Jason glanced at his watch, then shoved his hands into his coat pocket as he stood in the parking lot of Torrence Hall. The bitter cold wind whipped at him, and he wondered why he was out there in the first place. He was kicking himself because he was tired, but when it came to Chasity, he lost his right mind.

He looked at his watch again. *Where are you, Chasity? It's been fifteen minutes.*

Figuring that she wasn't going to show, Jason shook his head and took a step in the direction of his dorm. Seeing Mark, Josh and David walk up, he stopped in his tracks.

"What are you guys doing here?" he frowned, confused.

"Well, Sidra said that she needed me to do her a favor," Josh answered, rubbing his head.

"And your punk ass just jumped at the chance, *didn't you?*" Mark jeered.

Josh glared at him. "And why is *your* black ass out here?" he asked, voice filled with disdain,

"Man, that girl Serena called me and said she wanted some," Mark responded, adjusting the hood on his jacket.

"Some of *what?*" David questioned with disgust.

Mark glared at him. "Don't worry about it, dork," he shot back. "She wants this D, *that's* what she wants," he mumbled.

David rolled his eyes. *Lying ass.*

Jason looked at his friends. "Guys, I think we've been played," he concluded, looking at his watch one last time.

Mark stood there for a second, before stomping his foot on the ground. "Aww man, I'm *horny!*" he hollered, angry that he had been deceived.

"You could've kept that announcement to yourself," Josh jeered.

Fuming, Mark was about to fire off a retort when he felt something hit him on the side of his head. The other guys looked at the blue paint dripping down Mark's face as he stood there seething,

Jason started to laugh. "What the hell?" he said, just as something smacked him in his chest. All traces of laughter now gone, he slowly looked down at the red paint dripping down his black jacket. The guys turned to find Malajia, Sidra, Chasity, and Alex standing several feet away, holding water balloons full of paint.

"Are you *that* damn bored?" Jason yelled.

"Red's a good color for you, Jason," Chasity teased.

"Are you really gonna do—?" Josh's words were stopped by a balloon hitting him on his arm.

David was cracking up laughing, but soon stopped once a balloon full of yellow paint hit him in the neck, splashing paint on his neck and face. "Sidra, I thought we were cool," he exclaimed.

"Well that was before you started acting like *them*," Sidra shot back, an innocent smile on her face as she gestured towards Mark and Jason.

"Y'all are a bunch of—" Mark started as he pointed at the girls, but was stopped by a balloon hitting him in the stomach.

"You—"

He was hit by another.

"Stop it!"

"Who the hell are you yelling at?" Malajia fired back, before throwing another balloon, hitting Jason in the leg.

The guys took off running as a hoard of balloons went flying at them. David nearly tripped as a balloon hit him on the back of the head. "Ow!" he wailed.

Chapter 7

Today's Biology class is gonna be awesome, Emily thought, excited. Taking her seat and placing her book bag down on the floor next to her, she anticipated the professor's arrival. She smiled up at Mark as he walked into class and headed over to her.

"What are you so happy about?" Mark sneered, taking a seat at a table behind her.

Emily spun around to face him. "Didn't you hear during the last class?" she beamed. "We get to dissect fetal pigs today. Isn't that exciting?"

"Um, no," Mark answered slowly, eyeing her skeptically. "It's *class*. Nothing that has to do with class is exciting," he jeered.

Emily faced forward as she clasped her hands together. "Well, *I'm* excited," she maintained. "I never did that before. I think it'll be fun."

Mark removed his hat and ran his hand over the black waves on his head. *I need a damn haircut*, he thought as he watched the professor walk into the classroom, holding a tray full of small fetal pigs. Eyeing Emily's open book bag at her feet, Mark smiled slyly as a plan formed in his head. He rubbed his hands together in anticipation.

Professor Jennings sat a tray consisting of one fetal pig, latex gloves, and dissecting instruments in front of each student. "Class, I have to run to my office just down the hall. I will be back in just a second," he announced. "Please review your notes from last class, and we'll get started when I get back."

Mark followed the professor's progress out of the classroom with his eyes before turning his attention back to the front desk.

Emily turned and looked at Mark. "Hey, if Professor Jennings comes back before I do, can you tell him that I went to get a drink of water?" she whispered.

"Sure thing, little one," Mark smiled. *Perfect timing.* Waiting until Emily left the room, Mark seized his opportunity and put his plan into action.

Professor Jennings returned to the room right before Emily walked back in. "I see you're excited for today's activity," he smiled.

"I sure am," Emily replied, pushing some of her hair behind her ear. "I never got to do this in high school."

Emily smiled to herself as she returned to her seat. She opened her notebook then reached into her book bag for a pen. A frown formed on Emily's face as she felt something weird in her bag. *What in the world is this?*

Emily held the frown as she pulled the unknown object out of her bag. She screamed in shock, tossing the oily fetal pig onto the table. Emily looked around mortified as her classmates began laughing at her. She fought to keep her tears in as she frantically searched around for something to wipe her hands on.

"She had a pig in her bag," Mark laughed.

Emily spun around and faced him. "I didn't even do anything to you," she fumed, figuring that he was responsible.

"Guilty by association," Mark countered.

Emily turned back around to find the professor staring at her with anger.

"Miss Harris," Professor Jennings scolded. "Those are not toys for you to play around with."

"But—"

"I expect more from you," he chided, interrupting Emily's excuses.

Emily lowered her head. "I'm sorry," she mumbled, trying to hold back tears.

"One more interruption, and I will ask you to leave," Professor Jennings warned, going back to writing notes on the black board.

As the class started preparing for the dissection, Mark snickered loudly. "Pig in the bag," he teased.

Emily solemnly leaned her head on her hand as she picked up her gloves.

"Pig in the bag," Mark repeated, earning snickers from his classmates.

"Mark, one more word out of you, and you'll have to leave," Professor Jennings warned, pointing at him.

"I'm starving. Please be on time Alex," Sidra said to herself as she made a quick departure from the English building. After spending nearly an hour in her Creative Writing class writing poetry about food, Sidra couldn't think of anything else and was eager to meet up with Alex outside of the cafeteria for a quick lunch.

Sidra stopped her walk short when she saw Mark and David approaching her. "Don't you two dare start with me," she hissed, pointing her gloved finger at them.

"Even if we *felt* like starting with you, we would have every right considering what you girls did to us last night," Mark griped, adjusting his book bag.

"Oh, you deserved it," Sidra shot back with a wave of her delicate hand.

"Whatever Sid," David scoffed, rolling his eyes. "Have a nice day."

Sidra watched them skeptically as they continued their progress down the path; *don't trust them. They're up to something,* the voice boomed in her head.

"Hey lady," Alex greeted, walking up to Sidra. "You ready to hit the caf? I figured we could just head over together."

Sidra spun around to face Alex. "I sure am," she smiled. "I've been writing about food, and now I want some."

Alex chuckled. "Creative Writing assignment, huh?" she assumed.

"Yeah, exactly."

"I think I'm going to take that class next semester," Alex informed her, moving some of her hair out of her face.

Suddenly, Sidra felt something hit her in the back. "Ouch!" she exclaimed. "What the hell?" Startled and angry, she spun around to see who or *what* had hit her. Just as she turned, something hit her in the chest. She let out a scream.

Alex frowned in disgust as she looked down at what had hit Sidra. "What the hell is that?" she asked, pointing to it.

Sidra's eyes widened as she looked at what Alex was pointing to. "Is that an animal?!" she shrieked.

"Oh my God, it's a damn fetal pig!" Alex admonished, backing away from it. Having dissected one in high school, she was able to identify it. Before Alex could say or do anything else, a pig hit her on the side of her head. Disgusted and horrified, Alex began to frantically wipe the liquid from her face and hair.

"That is so gross," Sidra whined, eyeing the wet spot on her dark blue, double breasted coat.

"Pigs in ya hair!" Mark shouted from across the path, giving a laughing David a high-five.

"You two are *beyond* childish!" Sidra screamed, storming over to the guys with Alex following close behind. "Do you realize how completely gross this is?" Sidra hollered, coming face to face with them.

"Pigs on ya coat," Mark teased, pointing to the stain on Sidra's coat.

Fuming, Sidra hit him on the arm with her purse. "You're paying for my dry cleaning," she demanded.

"Yeah, I'll do *that* when you pay to get the paint removed from *my* coat," Mark shot back, folding his arms.

"David, I would expect this from *Mark*, but not you," Alex hissed. "I mean, who does this? Who throws freakin' fetal pigs at people?" she chided.

"Who throws balloons filled with nasty paint at people at four in the morning?" David countered, pushing his glasses up on his nose.

"You can get in trouble for stealing those, you idiot," Alex seethed. "What's wrong with you?"

Mark flagged her with his hand. "Ain't nobody worrying about those greasy ass, dead pigs," Mark scoffed. "They were left over from our class anyway." Eyeing the wetness on Alex's hair, he laughed. "Pigs in ya hair," he teased, reaching out to touch her hair.

Alex quickly smacked his hand away. "Don't touch me," she snapped.

Sidra hit both Mark and David with her pocketbook again before stomping off.

"You salty you got hit in the face with a pig," Mark taunted at Alex as she stormed off.

"This isn't over," Alex threw over her shoulder.

"Bring it on, pig hair!" Mark shouted after them.

Confidence and relief showed on Malajia's face as she sauntered her way through the campus after her Calculus class. She received gazes of admiration from her fellow male students, something that she always welcomed. Besides her pretty face, she knew that her outfit: a stylish red leather coat, tight dark blue jeans that hugged her slim figure just right and high-heeled knee boots, was a contributing factor. Her wine-colored bob, which she spent two hours curling just right, and her silver jewelry, capped the look off perfectly.

"Hey baby, looking good," an upperclassmen who she'd become friends complimented in passing.

"Every day Praz, every day," Malajia responded with confidence, waving her delicate hand at him.

The tall, dark-skinned junior stared at her, a smile plastered to his face. "Ain't that the truth," he mused

Malajia halted her stride and spun around to face him. "When are you having a house party?"

"On Valentine's Day, at my house off campus. You gotta come," Praz said, adjusting his book bag on his shoulder. "And bring those sexy friends of yours."

"We'll be there, baby," she promised. He gave her the thumbs up sign before walking away, leaving her standing there, staring at his back.

"You sexy, chocolate man you," she cooed to herself. Fixing her satchel on her shoulder, she continued on her path back to her dorm.

The feeling of a cold substance hitting Malajia on the side of her neck stopped her dead in her tracks. She slowly wiped the thick substance from her neck and looked at her hand. Horrified, her eyes widened. It was chocolate pudding. She let out an ear piercing scream.

"Puddin' on ya face!" Mark hollered from across the walkway.

Malajia spun around. Seeing Mark and Jason doubling over with laugher, she snapped. "Are y'all serious?!" She began, charging in their direction, but was struck in her chest with a pudding filled paper towel, splashing the substance on her coat. "Jason, this is a new coat, you bastard!"

"Sorry, I was aiming for your face," Jason laughed once he and Mark jogged over to her.

"Why the fuck did you have to do this bullshit in broad daylight?" Malajia fumed. "Are you that damn bored?"

Mark reached out to touch Malajia's soiled hair. "You got puddin' on ya hair," he teased.

Malajia smacked his hand out of the way "Don't touch me," she snapped, delivering a punch to his chest. "You're such an asshole."

"Ow!" Mark complained, grabbing his chest. Surprisingly, the punch hurt.

Malajia, feeling a knot form in her throat, made a quick departure. "It's on," she threw over her shoulder. She screamed as she felt another pudding bomb hit the back of her jeans, sending her running.

"Hey everybody! Malajia got shit on her jeans," Mark shouted.

"Damn, that was wrong," Jason admitted, trying to control his laughter.

Malajia reached her room in record time. Busting through the unlocked door, she found Alex, Emily, and Sidra sitting around talking. The girls stared at her in confusion as Malajia threw her bag across the room in a fit of anger. "Don't say a fuckin' word," she hissed before anyone said anything.

Alex looked Malajia up and down, taking in the brown substance all over her clothes, hair, part of her face and neck. "I'm not even gonna ask," she said, trying unsuccessfully to conceal a laugh.

Malajia snatched her boots off and threw one across the room, hitting the closet door. "I fuckin' hate Mark and Jason," she hollered, flinging off her coat.

"Mel, don't drop that on the floor," Alex said. "You'll stain the carpet."

"Bitch, don't nobody care about this ugly ass carpet!" Malajia snapped, throwing the garment to the floor.

Alex looked at Malajia as if she had lost her mind. "Was calling me a bitch really necessary?" she bit out.

"Yes," Malajia shot back, putting her hands on her hips. "I got attacked in front of the whole campus, and you worried about some beige ass carpet that needs to be cleaned *anyway.*"

"Hey, don't get mad at *us*," Sidra interjected. "You're not the only one who had something done by the guys," she informed. "Alex and I had freakin' dead pigs thrown at us."

"And Mark put a pig in Emily's bag," Alex added in. "The professor practically yelled at her."

Emily nodded in agreement.

Malajia stared at the girls with a blank expression for several seconds. "Are you…" she paused in an effort to remain calm, "comparing finding a damn biology pig in your book bag to getting chocolate pudding thrown on you in broad daylight?"

Emily put her hand over her mouth in an effort to keep from busting out laughing at Malajia's question.

"Malajia—"

Malajia's hand jerked up. "No!" she yelled, interrupting Alex. "I got pudding thrown at my *face,* and you're comparing *that* to finding a small ass, dead pig that y'all were gonna cut up *anyway* in your book bag?"

"Hey! I got hit in the *head* with one of those nasty ass pigs, so shut up," Alex shot back, pointing to herself.

Malajia looked over at Emily who was cracking up laughing. "You think that's funny?" she hissed.

"I'm sorry, but yes," Emily laughed. She couldn't help it. Even though she had been embarrassed earlier that morning, it in *no* way compared to what had just happened to Malajia.

Furious, Malajia walked over to Emily. Emily let out a scream as Malajia tried to sit her pudding stained behind on her lap.

"No! Malajia no," she screamed, trying to block Malajia's pants from coming in contact with her.

Alex, fed up with Malajia's antics, grabbed her arm and gave her a little shove in the direction of the door. "Mel, leave Emily alone and go take damn a shower," she urged. "And you better wash your clothes now, before they stain."

"*You* wash em', you fat ass mop," Malajia spat, before grabbing her essentials and leaving the room. The offhand remark made Sidra burst out laughing at the annoyed look on Alex's face.

Reaching the bottom of the dorm steps, Chasity searched through her small black purse for her car keys. Finished with classes for the day, Chasity was going to take a much needed trip to the mall for some retail therapy.

As she closed the front door behind her, she accidentally dropped her keys. "Shit," she hissed to herself, bending down to retrieve them.

The sound of something hitting the door behind her startled her. Chasity quickly stood up, looked at the thick white substance on the door, and spun around to see who threw it. Her eyes widened when she saw Josh standing on the sidewalk, holding two small freezer bags filled with the same substance.

"Are you freakin' serious Josh?!" Chasity snapped.

"Oh *very*," Josh ground out. "Nothing like whipped cream bombs to get back at someone."

"Wow," Chasity said, amazed. "You must *really* have a lot of time on your hands."

Josh narrowed his eyes at her. *Smart ass*, he thought. Taking a few steps towards her, he repeatedly tossed the bag in the air. "Hey, did I ever get you back for almost running me over last semester?" he asked.

Chasity's face took on a worried look as she backed up against the closed door. She held her hand out. "Josh, you better not—"

"Better not *what*?" Josh taunted, interrupting her warning. Not wanting to end up covered in whipped cream, Chasity's eyes darted around in search of a quick exit. "Hmm? Were you going to say something?" Josh goaded, raising his eyebrow.

"Look, you really don't need to do this," Chasity pleaded, her voice not hiding her nervousness. "You don't have to be like the others, you're the nice one."

Josh stared at her for a few seconds. He had to admit to himself, if he wasn't so in love with Sidra, he would actually be competing with Jason for Chasity's affection. He then quickly dismissed the thought, knowing that his docile personality couldn't handle someone as fiery as her.

"You know you're right, I *am* nice," he agreed. "But not *that* nice,"

Chasity watched as Josh lifted the bag, preparing to hit her with it. Unable to make a getaway quick enough, she held her hands up to shield her face. Chasity was relieved when the door opened behind her just as Josh hurled the bag. She managed to duck inside the dorm at the exact same time that one of her dorm mates walked out.

Josh's eyes widened as the bag hit the girl in the chest, splashing whipped cream on her coat.

"Ooooohhh," Josh responded, putting his hand over his mouth. "I'm sooo sorry," he apologized as the horrified girl began breathing heavily.

"Not as sorry as you're gonna be when this mace gets in your eye," the girl hissed, reaching into her purse.

"Oh crap," Josh blurted out, and took off running.

"I can't believe that Professor Jackson yelled at me for speaking my mind," Alex vented, setting her dark brown book bag on a counter top.

"Alex, nobody told you to insult the man," Chasity replied, handing Alex the brush that she was holding for her. On their way to the cafeteria for lunch, Alex, Chasity, Sidra, and Malajia made a pit stop at the student lounge so that Alex could use the bathroom.

Alex frowned at Chasity as she snatched the brush from her. "Whatever, Chasity," she hissed.

"Snatch from me again," Chasity warned. "I'll punch you in your damn face."

"First of all, you don't scare me," Alex returned, vigorously brushing her hair into a ponytail. "Second, I didn't insult him. *You* should know what an actual insult sounds like. You're the queen of them."

Chasity slowly folded her arms. "Turning this around on *me* isn't gonna erase the fact that you got your ass embarrassed today in front of the entire Women's Studies class," Chasity shot back, much to Alex's chagrin.

Alex let out a frustrated sigh. "It was uncalled for."

"Alexandra, you called the man a jerk," Sidra cut in, voice full of laughter.

"I don't know *why* you thought he wouldn't say anything back to you," Malajia chimed in, examining her face in a small pocket mirror.

Alex pointed at Sidra. "No, I said that he was *acting* like a jerk, there's a difference," she retorted. Sidra rolled her eyes to the ceiling. Alex then pointed to Malajia. "And *you* stay out of this," she hissed. "You were so busy passing notes to that guy from the basketball team that I'm surprised you heard *anything*."

"Girl, he was fine, wasn't he?" Malajia mused, Sidra just shook her head.

"Hell, I don't know why a damn man is teaching that class in the first place. It's called *Women's Studies*," Alex bit out, tossing the brush in her bag. "But the bottom line is that there is a difference," she concluded.

"So, if I say that you were *acting like* a bitch, that would be different than me saying that you actually *are* a bitch?" Chasity asked, casually examining her nails

Alex narrowed her eyes at her. "Always the smart ass," she sneered, earning a smirk from Chasity.

In the middle of glancing around the open room, Sidra noticed that Mark and Jason were resting on one of the cushy, blue couches.

"Hey," she whispered, grabbing the girls' attention.

"What?" Malajia said, curious.

Sidra pointed at the sleeping guys. "Look."

Malajia sucked her teeth as she eyed them. "Nasty bastards," she scoffed. "They sleeping on those dirty ass couches."

"The couches are *not* dirty," Sidra contradicted. "I have an idea, come on," she added, signaling for them to follow her.

The girls stood in front of the two sleeping men, studying them. "They're knocked out," Alex chortled, giving Mark's arm a soft poke.

Sidra, seizing the opportunity, went into her handbag and pulled out a tube of a light, shimmer lipstick. The others watched as she proceeded to carefully apply it to Jason's face.

Chasity, following suit, pulled a black eyeliner from her purse. Alex looked over at Malajia as she dumped a large amount of makeup contents out of her red bag.

"Are you serious?" Alex questioned. "All that damn makeup?"

Malajia looked at her. "What? You act like you've never seen me use this stuff," she replied.

"Yeah, I know, but it's still a lot," Alex chuckled. "You don't need all that."

"Less talking, more vandalizing faces," Malajia shot back, exasperated. The girls spent the next few moments quickly applying their products to the guy's faces. Once finished, they stepped back to examine their work.

"They look like clowns," Alex admitted, amused.

"Good, then our job is done," Malajia boasted. "They shouldn't be sleeping in a public place that hard."

"Let's get out of here before they wake up," Sidra urged, making her way to the exit. Alex, having a bright idea, took a piece of paper out of her book bag, folded it into a hat, wrote something on it, and carefully stuck it on top of Mark's head. Snickering, the girls made a quick departure out of the lounge.

Ten minutes passed before Jason and Mark began to stir. Mark stretched, glancing at his watch. He instantly popped up. "Shit, I'm late!" he exclaimed.

"Aww man, me—" Jason couldn't finish his sentence, too busy staring at Mark's face as the guy frantically looked around for his coat and books. Jason busted out laughing.

"What's so damn funny?" Mark frowned. His anger turned to amusement as he noticed Jason's face.

"What are *you* laughing at?" Jason laughed.

"Your face," Mark answered,

"*Mine*? You should take a look at *yours*," Jason shot back.

Both guys stopped laughing and thought for a second. Then they both jumped up and made a mad dash for the men's room.

"What the fuck?" Jason exclaimed, laying eyes on his makeup-covered face in the large mirror.

As Jason ran water and began frantically rubbing his face, Mark focused on his head. "Why do *I* have a damn 'dunce' cap on my head?" he questioned.

"Who gives a shit?" Jason seethed. "The more important question is, what's *in* this stuff?" He wiped a wet paper towel across his face and stared at it. "It's not coming off!"

"It's those damn girls and their waterproof shit," Mark assumed, pouring hand soap in his hands and rubbing it on his face. "Ow, this soap burns!" he howled.

Mark and Jason slowly turned to face a few students who had walked into the bathroom. Their peers began laughing at the sight, and Jason and Mark stood there seething.

Chapter 8

"I'm so glad this dumb ass week is over," Malajia grimaced, sprinkling salt on her french fries.

"Tell me about it," Alex agreed, shaking a sugar packet. "This prank mess has been so damn draining."

The prank war between the girls and guys had gotten old. Tensions rose each day as they tried to one up each other. By the time Friday arrived, neither team was on speaking terms.

Sidra rolled her eyes as she noticed the guys approaching their booth. "Are you kidding me?" she mumbled.

"Y'all might as well move over," Mark demanded, signaling for the girls to make room.

"Boy, y'all better get away from here. There are *other* places to sit," Alex sneered, pointing to a table across the cafeteria.

"Look, we have every right to sit here, this is *our* booth too," Jason pointed out.

"You're name ain't on it," Malajia snapped.

"Neither is *yours*," Jason shot back, narrowing his eyes at her.

Malajia sucked her teeth and flagged him with her hand. "Whatever," she huffed.

"It doesn't matter, because you're *not* sitting here," Sidra snarled, folding her arms.

The guys looked at each other before nudging the girls over, forcing their way into the booth.

"God, why can't y'all just go away?" Malajia snapped, slamming her hand on the table.

"Shut your whining ass up!" Mark barked. "You haven't gotten tired of your damn voice yet?"

"Bitch," Malajia bit back.

"Freak," Mark countered.

Malajia sucked her teeth. "Bastard."

Mark flipped her off. "Stupid."

"Punk."

"Your Mama," Mark hissed. Frustrated, Malajia let out a loud sigh and folded her arms.

Fifteen minutes were spent in silence as the group ate dinner, with occasional nasty glances at one another in between sips of their drinks and bites of their food.

Fed up with seeing the guys' faces and the awkward quiet, Malajia pounded her fist on the table. "This is all y'all fault!" she wailed, pointing at them.

The guys looked at Malajia as if she had lost her mind. "*Our* fault?" Jason asked in disbelief, pointing to himself.

"Malajia, please. *You're* the one who threw juice on us first," Mark pointed out, picking up his cup of juice.

"I *told* you that it was an accident," Malajia argued. "You should've let it go."

Mark removed the cup from his lips and frowned. "Oh *really?*"

"Did she stutter?" Alex snapped.

Mark focused his angry gaze on Alex as he raised his cup, then tossed its remaining contents at Alex. The red juice splashed on Alex *and* Chasity, who was sitting right next to her.

"Are you crazy?" Chasity screeched, tossing a balled up napkin at Mark.

"It was an accident, you should let it go," Mark shrugged.

Alex glared at Mark, while the guys snickered. "You gonna finish that?" she asked, sticking her finger in the middle of his burger.

Mark's laughter halted abruptly. "No, but are *you* gonna finish *these*?" he asked, picking up a handful of her curly fries and squeezing them. He smiled at her as he dropped the squashed fries back onto her plate.

"You are such an ass!" Alex seethed.

"Oh what? You think you can stick your long ass finger in my food and I'm not gonna do nothin' about it?" Mark bit out. "Please, baby, you got me twisted."

"I swear, I hope you choke on your fuckin' food and die," Malajia hissed.

"You just mad cause you got puddin' thrown in your face," Mark threw back. Jason erupted with laughter. Shock and embarrassment flooded Malajia's face as Mark laughed too. "Puddin' in ya face," he mocked.

"Shut up," Malajia fumed.

"You looked like a shit-covered blow up doll," Mark howled, unable to contain his laughter.

"David, I don't know what *you're* laughing at," Sidra jumped in. "*You* got busted in the back of the head with paint."

"*You* got hit in the back with a dead pig," David shot back

Fuming, Sidra folded her arms and sat back in her seat. *Asshole*, she thought.

"Oh yeah, oh yeah, didn't you get hit in the face with a pig, Alex?" Josh laughed.

"Pigs in ya face," Mark taunted.

Alex's mouth had grown so tight from anger that it looked like her jaw was about to snap. "You know what—" she began.

"Aye Chaz, exactly how long *did* it take you to wash that frozen shaving cream off your car?" Mark teased.

Chasity glared at him. Suddenly she took her hands and pushed all the leftover food from her plate in the guys' direction. They complained as food landed on their clothes.

"You startin'?" Jason sneered, plucking a cherry tomato in her direction. It missed its target and hit Malajia in the mouth.

Malajia screamed as she frantically wiped the tomato juice from her face. She then picked up the rest of her sandwich, and hurled it at Jason with force, but he knocked it away, and it hit David in his face.

The girls busted out laughing as one of the lenses from his glasses popped out and fell into his soup.

"His glasses broke!" Malajia screeched, pointing to the now soiled lens.

"Lens in ya soup," Chasity teased, making Malajia laugh louder.

"Naw man, y'all ain't gonna be playin' my boy like that," Mark fumed, grabbing a handful of spaghetti off of Josh's plate.

"You ignorant—" Alex words were cut off as the spaghetti smacked her in the face. Chasity pointed to the horrified Alex and laughed as the noodles slid down to her neck.

Jason looked at Malajia, who had her mouth wide open from laughing, and threw a small piece of bread in it.

Malajia immediately spit the bread on the table. "You dumb jock," she snapped, throwing a dinner roll at him and hitting him in the chest.

"Emily, don't act like you ain't in this," Mark said, tossing ketchup-covered veggies from his burger at her. Emily gasped as the veggies splattered on her pink sweater.

Sidra tossed a few croutons from her salad at Mark. "Don't drag her into this."

Emily picked up one of her soft baked cookies and threw it at Josh. Josh, quick to react, smacked the cookie away from him, causing it to hit a guy sitting at the next table. The food throwing ceased as they anticipated how the guy would react.

Emily's eyes widened. "Ooooohhhhh."

Embarrassed and angry, the guy picked up his slice of apple pie and hurled it at them. Emily and the others watched as the pie soared through the air, then splattered on their table, sending slices of apple and pieces of crust flying at them.

"That was uncalled for!" Malajia hollered, plucking a slice of apple from her red shirt.

Jason gritted his teeth as he watched the guy laugh. "Oh, that's funny huh?" he asked, before picking up the rest of his chicken sandwich and throwing it at the guy. But it missed the guy and hit a girl at another table, smacking her in the head.

"Nice aim, star player," Chasity mocked.

"Shut it," Jason bit out, shooting Chasity a side glance. He then looked at the girl and sincerely said, "I'm sorry."

"Sorry my ass," the girl fumed, picking up a handful of fries and throwing them. The fries missed Jason completely and hit a group of people sitting nearby.

"What the hell is up with you people?" Alex chortled, "Can't any of you aim?"

"I have a bad feeling about this," Emily whispered as half the cafeteria, including her friends, rose from their seats.

Emily's apprehension became a reality when she heard a deep male voice, shout, "Food fight!"

"Now that's what *I'm* talkin' 'bout!" Mark shouted over the commotion.

"What is this, middle school?!" Sidra shrieked, trying to shield her head from the food that began flying around the cafeteria. There were salad fixings, dessert slices, and sandwiches flying everywhere.

Mark watched a girl slip and fall on a piece of fruit. He was pointing and laughing, until he got hit on the back of the head with a tuna fish sandwich.

Alex picked up a cup of red gelatin and held on to it as she stood up on a chair. "Guys, y'all need to stop this," she cautioned as she watched her friends and classmates throw food at each other. "We could get in trouble."

"Then what's with the cup of gelatin, Alex?" Sidra pointed out.

"Girl, if one of these sandwiches hits me, somebody is getting a face full of this wiggly mess," Alex promised, inciting a giggle from Sidra.

Emily had thrown a few pieces of sliced fruit at someone before ducking and hiding underneath one of the tables. David slid under the table with her.

"You okay under here?" he asked.

"Yeah," she replied. David's face took on a shocked expression once he felt something squishy hit the back of his head. He turned around to see if there was anything for him to throw back, and that's when Emily spotted the slice of pizza stuck to his head. She put her hand over her mouth to avoid laughing in his face.

"It's on now," David promised her, before getting back on his feet. He grabbed a half-eaten burger from the floor and tossed it across the room.

Malajia screamed as spaghetti splattered all of over her. "Somebody hype as shit throwing these bland ass noodles!" she barked. Spotting a jelly donut laying on a nearby table, she quickly scooped it up and threw it. Seeing the jelly-filled pastry splatter onto a girls face made her forget about her sauce-covered clothes.

Sidra, who was hiding under a table, watched as a skinny guy ran around the cafeteria, holding a large, clear plastic bowl full of chocolate pudding. He was flinging it at people while he screamed like a fool. She shook her head in disgrace. She had no intention of participating in this nonsense. But her mind changed once a slice of coconut pie landed in front of her, splattering on her clothes.

"Eww, goddamn it!" she yelped, making a mad dash from under the table. Searching for the nearest item, she grabbed a plastic ketchup bottle and began squirting random people. "I'm not gonna be the *only* one washing clothes tonight," she assured as people scattered.

Jason, having been watching the pudding slinging guy run around, picked up a bowl of vanilla pudding and dumped it on his head as he approached. Jason's laughter was short lived as pineapple slices hit the back of his head. He turned around and saw Chasity standing there with a stunned look. She hadn't meant to hit *him* with them.

"Oops," Chasity shrugged. Before she could react, a guy ran up and threw a hand full of pasta salad at her chest. She gave him a shove, then grabbed a handful of strawberry jelly from a plastic bowl and shoved it in his face, causing him to slip and fall.

Jason ran over. "Ammo! I need ammo!" he urged. Chasity shook her head at the sight of potato salad in his hair. Jason picked up a bowl full of rolls and tossed it, sending rolls soaring in the air.

"Hotdogs! Get your dry ass hotdogs!" Mark shouted, throwing hotdogs and buns at people.

Josh was about to throw a piece of lasagna when he noticed the lunch staff enter the room, accompanied by campus security. Quickly, he grabbed Sidra, who was standing next to him squeezing mustard out of a bottle, and pulled her towards the back door.

David saw them and followed suit, pulling Emily out from under the table.

"Look, if we get caught in here, we're in serious trouble, especially since we technically *started* this," Josh pointed out.

"Let's get the others," David said, signaling for Sidra and Emily to wait by the door. He and Josh took off running in search of their friends as the guards began to round people up.

While Josh grabbed Alex and Malajia, he hollered to Jason, "Jase! Get Chaz, we need to go!"

Jason nodded, grabbed Chasity's arm and pulled her towards the door. "Mark! Time to bounce," he yelled.

Mark put down the cake and ran to the door.

"Let's go, let's go," Alex panicked, holding the back door open.

As the gang slipped out the back door and ran, Emily panted, "After all of this, we still look out for one another."

"Less talking, more running," Mark urged as they continued to make their getaway.

Chapter 9

"Girl, you've got to get a date and go out tomorrow," Malajia cooed, fluffing her curls with her fingers. "You don't wanna be sitting around looking all lonely and salty."

Chasity rolled her eyes. "I'm *aware* that tomorrow is Valentine's Day," she sneered, "and I don't give a damn."

Both girls stood in the hallway of the Science building after their morning class had ended. Friday had arrived, and the students of Paradise Valley were not only excited about being class free for the next two days, but that Valentine's Day was just hours away.

Malajia sucked her teeth. "God, why do you have to be so damn miserable?"

Chasity's retort was interrupted when two guys walked up, immediately grabbing Malajia's attention. She had a thing for tall, dark, muscle-bound men.

"What's up, Mel?" one guy said.

"Hey Ron, what's good baby?" Malajia smiled, pushing some hair out of her face.

"Nothing much," Ron returned, adjusting his book bag on his shoulder. "You got a date for tomorrow?"

"No, not yet. Why? You want to be mine?" Malajia's grinning and hair twirling annoyed Chasity and it showed in her face.

"Please," Chasity mumbled, earning a side glance from Malajia.

While Ron was busy grinning at Malajia, the second guy was busy staring at Chasity. His tongue was practically hanging out of his mouth. "How about y'all double date with me and Ron," he proposed.

Chasity shot the guy a frown, His staring was creeping her out. *No damn chance in hell*, she thought as she began to look at her phone. If she didn't think that Malajia would start yelling after her, Chasity would have simply walked away.

"Look, you know *me*, *I'll* go," Malajia assured, before gesturing to Chasity, "but this chick over here ain't goin' for it. Trust me."

Ron simply shrugged as his friend rubbed his lips with his hand. "Hey, Chasity," the guy called.

Chasity let out a loud sigh, her head jerking up from her phone. "What?"

"You don't wanna go out with me?" he asked, taking a step towards her.

"Get out my face," she spat.

The look on his dark face went from lustful to angry. "What's *your* deal?" he hissed. "I mean, I heard you were a virgin and all that, maybe I could help you out with that problem."

"Boy!" Malajia jumped in. "Don't come at her like that. What's wrong with you?"

"*Never*, would I let you touch me, you fuckin' bastard," Chasity barked.

Jason was just stepping out of his Physics class when he frowned, recognizing Chasity and Malajia's hostile voices. Protection mode kicked in as he made his way over.

"Please, Miss Evil is just scared," the guy taunted, looking Chasity up and down.

"Don't nobody want your overly strong ass," Chasity hissed, earning laughter from Malajia. "You sure you can find your dick under all that?"

"Looking like a stack of black ass dumplings with a small ass head," Malajia joined in.

The guy sucked his teeth, "You know what, you better watch your damn mouth before your stuck up ass gets hurt," he warned.

Chasity was confused. "I'm sorry, are you threatening me?" she sneered.

"Yo Ron, get your friend before he gets slapped," Malajia urged. She smiled slyly once she saw Jason walk up behind them, fists balled up with a mask of anger on his face. "Never mind," she said.

"Yo, do we have a problem here?" Jason fumed.

The guy spun around, coming face to face with Jason. "Naw, no problem. Just handling this chick here," he boasted, unaware of the hole he was digging himself into.

Jason moved closer to the guy, eyes burrowing through him like a laser. "If you *ever* disrespect her again," he began, drawing his words out slowly in a low, menacing tone. "I will personally tear you apart."

"You better run, boy," Malajia warned, amused at the scared look on the guys face.

"Dude, stop being a dickhead and come on," Ron ground out, giving his friend a nudge towards the exit. Before he made his exit, Ron turned to Malajia. "You still wanna go out tomorrow?"

"Yeah, call me," Malajia nodded.

Jason shook his head as both guys made a hasty departure, before turning his attention to Chasity "Are you okay?"

"Aren't I always?" Chasity replied. Even though she didn't say it, she appreciated how Jason stood up for her.

Malajia glanced at her watch and sighed. "Booo, I gotta go study for this raggedy Econ test," she grumbled. "I'm so not ready, I need more tiiiiiime."

"Should've studied last night," Chasity chided evenly.

"You should mind your business," Malajia shot back, sauntering off.

Chasity glared at Malajia's departing back for several seconds, inciting a chuckle from Jason. "You know tomorrow is Valentine's Day right?" he reminded.

She rolled her eyes. "Yes, I know that, as everyone keeps reminding me. I don't give a shit."

"Well, it would be the perfect opportunity for me to take you out," he smiled.

"No." Chasity's response was instantaneous.

"Damn, can you at least *think* about it?" he chortled.

"I did," Chasity jeered.

Jason was so busy rubbing his hand over his head, trying to cope with Chasity's stubbornness, that he didn't see Jackie Stevens approach, "Fine, at least—"

"Hey, Jason baby," Jackie crooned, sidling up to him, twirling a few of her blond and brown micro braids with her finger.

Jason turned around and looked at her at the same time that Chasity shot her a glare. *Go away, Jackie,* he silently wished. He knew what Jackie wanted, what she's *always* wanted, ever since he stepped foot on campus last semester— him. The feeling wasn't mutual. Jason's interest remained with Chasity alone, and the entire campus knew it, Jackie included.

Jackie was tall and slender, with a brown complexion. The long blond and brown braids that she wore didn't complement her face. She wasn't considered pretty. The only reason guys went out with her was because she was an easy lay.

Even though Jason was annoyed with the interruption, he still didn't want to be rude. "Nice to see you Jackie, but don't you see that I'm in the middle of talking to someone?"

Jackie sucked her teeth and looked Chasity up and down. "Please, I don't know why you talkin' to this chick anyway," she hissed.

Oh, this bitch is testing me, Chasity fumed. Jackie had been a constant thorn in her side ever since their first confrontation in the beginning of the previous semester.

Since then, she had been hearing how Jackie was running her mouth about her all over campus.

"You better move your ugly ass away from me," Chasity warned.

Jackie sucked her teeth as she stared at Chasity. Jackie hated her, not only was she prettier and had a better body than she did, but Chasity had the attention of the one guy she wanted.

"Don't make me punch you," Jackie threatened. "I still owe you an ass whoopin' from last semester."

Chasity did not take threats lightly; she dropped her book bag to the floor. "Bitch! I will break your fuckin' neck," she snapped.

"You ain't gonna do shit!" Jackie hollered. She was forced to take a step backwards when Chasity lunged at her.

Reacting quickly, Jason grabbed Chasity and held her back. "Chasity, she's not worth it," he pointed out, holding on to her.

Fired up and ready to attack, Chasity tried to maneuver around Jason to get to her target, but to no avail.

Jackie was feeding off the presence of the students gathering around watching, hoping for a fight to break out. "Ain't nobody scared of you, bitch," she laughed. "Wait till' I get my girls—we're gonna stomp your ass."

Chasity managed to break away from Jason for only a split second, but was stopped again a second too soon. Jason wrapped his arms around her waist and held on.

"Jackie, get the hell out of here!" Jason shouted, keeping his grip tight on Chasity.

"You just wait," Jackie threw over her shoulder as she hurried off.

As several professors and other students began to walk out of nearby classrooms, Jason shuffled the fuming Chasity off to a corner and backed her against the wall.

"Look, she's *not* worth it," he urged. "She's nothing but a troublemaker. You need to calm down."

"Don't tell me to calm down!" Chasity snapped, slapping his hand away. "You think I'm supposed to stand there and let her threaten me? Are you out of your fuckin' mind?"

Jason ran a hand over the back of his neck. "I get why you're mad, trust me, I'm pissed off too," he assured her. "But you can't let her miserable ass drag you into a fight. You could get kicked out of school."

"Were you *not* just about to fight that bastard who was messing with me?" Chasity threw back.

"Oh absolutely," Jason admitted confidently. "And I'd do it again if I had to." When she shot him a confused look, Jason let out a sigh. "Look, I just don't want you to get hurt," he admitted, "I know you can handle yourself, but Jackie is sneaky and I don't want her to pull something on you, or get you jumped."

Chasity was furious at Jason, but instead of continuing to lash out at him, she just rolled her eyes and sighed. "Fine, I'll let it go this time," she promised through clenched teeth. "But Jason, if that bitch gets in my face again, I swear, I'm knocking her teeth right out of her face."

Jason shook his head. He knew that Chasity had every intention of carrying out that promise, but he was glad that at least for now she'd let it go.

"I'll take that," he said. He went to retrieve her book bag from the floor. "Let's get out of here," he said, gesturing towards the exit.

"What?!" Alex exclaimed.

"Yeah, I heard that Chaz was about to fight her right in the Science building," Malajia informed. "One of my acquaintances that was there, told me what happened when I was on my way back to the dorm."

After her six o'clock class, Malajia headed back to the room to kill time with Alex and Emily. She couldn't wait to fill the girls in on what she had heard.

Alex shot her a side glance. "Did you just say acquaintance?"

Malajia nodded. "Sure did, the chick ain't my damn friend," she dismissed.

Amused, Alex just shook her head. "Anyway, I had a feeling that Jackie was gonna start her mess this semester," she huffed, folding her arms.

"I don't understand why she has to be so rude," Emily softly put in. She didn't have any run-ins with Jackie herself, but Emily had witnessed her nasty behavior around campus.

"Who cares? The bitch is ugly anyway," Malajia spat with a wave of her hand. "So let's just go to the girls' room and see what they're doing,"

"Yes, cause I want to hear what happened first hand from Chaz," Alex proclaimed, walking out the door.

Sidra was enjoying the soft music coming from her radio when she heard her door knob turn.

"It's locked Malajia, I *lock* my door," she barked, walking over to the door. "Ugh!" she scoffed, seeing Malajia standing on the other side of the door with a grin plastered to her face. Alex and Emily were behind her.

"Oh shut up, you know you love seeing us," Malajia beamed, pushing her way into the room.

"When do I *not* see you?" Sidra chuckled.

"Where's your roommate?" Alex asked, removing her long, brown coat.

"Not sure," Sidra answered, reaching for a pack of candy on her nightstand. "She wasn't here when I got back, and I've been here for a while."

"Ooh, give me one," Malajia demanded, walking over to Sidra with her hand out.

Sidra narrowed her eyes at Malajia. "Try asking," she stated.

"Just give me a damn piece," Malajia snapped, exasperated, then shielded herself as the pack came flying at her.

Chasity walked through the door. As soon as she saw the girls, she turned right back around. She wasn't in the mood for any company.

"Chasity!" Alex barked.

Chasity turned back around. "What?" she hissed, not bothering to hide her frustration.

Alex placed her hands on her hips. "Why were you about to fight Jackie today?"

Sidra's face took on a shocked expression. "You were about to do *what*?" she wailed.

"The people on this campus talk too fuckin' much," Chasity hissed.

"You already knew that," Malajia put in. "Why do you think Ron's ugly ass friend assumes you're a virgin?"

"You mean *you* didn't tell him?" Chasity sniped, shooting Malajia a glare.

Malajia made a face at her. "No, I *didn't*, smart ass," she sneered. "I didn't know you really *were* one to be honest."

"Shit," Chasity mumbled, realizing that she inadvertently shared a secret about herself.

"I'm not surprised though," Malajia added, taking a bite of her candy. "You were named after a certain belt, anyway."

Chasity sucked her teeth. "Funny."

"Anyway, all these people do is run off at the mouth and spread gossip," Malajia continued.

Sidra shot Malajia a glance. "Don't act like you don't partake in it too."

"Oh, I never said I *didn't*," Malajia admitted. "I'm all for finding out information."

Alex wasn't going to let this side conversation distract her from the answers that she sought. "Chasity, what the hell—"

"Alex! I didn't start it okay," Chasity snapped, cutting Alex off.

"I didn't say that you *did*," Alex replied, voice now calm. "But you don't need to get in to any fights. Don't let Jackie drag you down with her."

"Whatever," Chasity huffed, tossing her book bag on the floor "Why are you here anyway?"

"We're bored, want to do something," Malajia answered, flopping down on the love seat. "So, what is everyone doing for Valentine's Day?"

Chasity rolled her eyes, "What's with you and this stupid holiday?" she bit out.

Malajia looked at her as if she was crazy. "Well, excuse *me* if I want to do something fun for the damn holiday," she threw back. "Just because *you're* miserable, doesn't mean that the *rest* of us has to be."

"I'm *not* miserable," Chasity spat.

"Could've fooled *me*," Malajia jeered, examining her long red nails.

"Okay, okay you two, stop it," Alex slid in. "Come on, let's go grab dinner from the cafeteria," she suggested.

Malajia turned her lip up. "I don't wanna go to that dirty ass caf."

"Well you know what, some of us don't have a *choice*. Now let's go," Alex barked, pointing to the door with authority.

Sidra, Malajia, and Chasity glowered at Alex. The nerve of her trying to control where they eat. Emily slowly grabbed her jacket and headed for the door.

"Bitch, sit your spineless ass down," Chasity snapped.

Startled, Emily quietly returned to her seat. Sidra couldn't help but snicker at Chasity's outburst towards Emily, she actually agreed with her.

"Man, fuck outta here, I'm going off campus to eat," Malajia insisted, ignoring Alex's protest. "*You* eat them old ass chicken wings if you want to."

"Yeah, I'm not for cafeteria food either," Sidra added, grabbing her purse from her closet door knob. "Chaz, are you coming?"

"Nope," Chasity said, sitting on her bed.

Sidra sucked her teeth. "Fine, Chaz." Sidra noticed that her roommate seemed to be in a foul mood, and that had started even before her confrontation with Jackie.

Alex let out a loud sigh as Sidra and Malajia walked towards the door. She really didn't want cafeteria food either, but she couldn't afford to go out to eat. She had spent the last few dollars that she had washing clothes the day before.

"Emily, will you go to the cafeteria with me?" Alex asked.

"Sure," Emily beamed.

Malajia and Sidra turned around; Malajia stomped her foot on the floor. "No! Bring your fat ass with *us*," she hollered at Alex.

Alex frowned. "You think that calling me fat is gonna make me come with you?"

Sidra glanced at the dumb look on Malajia's face, shaking her head.

Chasity, watching the byplay between Alex and the other girls, stood up from her bed, walked over to her desk, and pulled something out of her top drawer.

"Alex, come here for a second," she called.

"I'm sick of you calling me fat, Malajia," Alex snarled at Malajia, as she walked over to Chasity.

"Whatever, all I'm saying is—"

"Malajia, *please* stop talking," Sidra ground out, pinching the bridge of her nose with two fingers.

"Bitch—" Malajia's insult was halted once Sidra mugged her on the side of the head.

"Call me another bitch, hear?" Sidra warned. "You know I don't like that word."

"Damn, I was just playin' Sid. You didn't have to do that," Malajia complained, rubbing her head.

"Take this and get out," Chasity said to Alex, voice almost a whisper as she handed her a folded twenty dollar bill.

Alex was shocked. This was the second time that Chasity had offered her money. "Chasity, I can't accept this," she whispered, placing her hand over her cheek.

"Yes you *can*," Chasity insisted, shoving the money into her hand.

Grateful, Alex discreetly pocketed the money, then threw her arms around Chasity. "Thank you sis," she whispered.

Chasity rolled her eyes as she nudged Alex off of her. "No need to touch me," she jeered. Alex giggled. Even when she was trying to be nice, Chasity still had to let her snarky behavior come through.

"Will you bring your *rotund* ass on?" Malajia exclaimed, tired of standing around.

Spirits now lifted, Alex chuckled at Malajia. "You make me sick."

"If you and Em are going to the cafeteria, Mel and I can walk you on our way off campus," Sidra suggested.

"On second thought, I guess I can scrape up a couple bucks to eat off campus," Alex said, grabbing her coat off of the chair.

Malajia looked over at Chasity who was busy looking at her phone. "Well, since Chasity probably isn't going anywhere else today, her car is just gonna sit in the parking lot," Malajia hinted. "Maybe, she'll let us borrow it."

"Maybe you can take the bus," Chasity bit out.

Malajia stomped her foot on the floor. "Why you gotta be so damn mean?" she sneered, storming out of the room with the other girls following behind her.

Chapter 10

Bright light blared from Chasity's laptop. Eyes tired from looking at the screen's contents, she rubbed them. It was nearing midnight, and she'd been working on a webpage for her aunt Trisha for hours. She'd taken a quick break an hour before, just to change into her pajamas, only to come back to it.

At midnight exactly, her cell phone rang. Without looking at the caller ID, Chasity grabbed her phone and put it to her ear. "Yeah?" she answered, voice flat.

"Happy birthday to you, happy birthday to you," a soft female voice sang.

Recognizing the singer, Chasity chuckled.

"Oh really? Is my singing *that* bad?" Trisha asked with laughter in her voice. She'd always called Chasity exactly at midnight to wish her a happy birthday, and this year was no different.

"Yeah," Chasity bluntly stated.

"Happy birthday honey," Trisha replied, voice filled with amusement. "And happy Valentine's Day."

"Thanks," Chasity's tone was even.

"So? How does it feel to be nineteen?" Trisha prodded.

Chasity typed on her keyboard. "Same as it did when I turned eighteen."

"What are you doing? Were you sleeping?"

"No, I'm working on your webpage."

Trisha sucked her teeth. "While I appreciate you doing that for me, I don't want you to sit in your room on your birthday with your face stuck in your laptop all day," she sternly put out. "You can worry about finishing my webpage tomorrow."

"Trust me when I say, it needs to be finished *now*," Chasity replied. "The guy you hired to do this did a crappy job. Your page looked like trash."

Trisha's soft laugh erupted over the line. "Yeah well, that's what happens when my computer whiz of a niece goes off to college and stops doing them for me," she joked. Chasity created and had been updating Trisha's business web pages since she was a sophomore in high school. Trisha, not wanting to burden Chasity with that task once she left for college, hired someone else to work on them. A decision that she had since regretted.

"Anyway, I'm serious. I want you to have fun," Trisha insisted. "I'm sure your friends have something planned for you to do."

Chasity shook her head. "Trisha, I highly doubt that they even know it's my birthday," she ground out. She figured with everybody caught up in all of the Valentine's Day hoopla, nobody would even care.

"Sweetheart, I'm sure that's not true," Trisha replied, tone comforting.

"It is," Chasity assured her. "I never told them when it was."

"Well, first off, I don't know why your mean behind *didn't*," Trisha chortled. "Second, your friends are resourceful. I'm sure they found out one way or another."

Chasity was silent for a moment. For days, her mind had been racked with thoughts that she desperately wanted to get away from. But now that her birthday was upon her, she couldn't escape them.

"Well, it's probably not my birthday today anyway, so who cares what anybody does for me," she spat.

"What are you talking about?"

"I'm talking about the fact that I'm adopted. Which means that my actual birthday might be on some other day," Chasity blurted out. "How can I celebrate something that might not even be true?"

Trisha sighed. She had been dreading this conversation for weeks. Even though Chasity hadn't said much about her adoption, she knew that the questions would come eventually, and she wasn't sure how to answer them.

I fuckin' hate Brenda for telling her, she fumed of her older sister and Chasity's adopted mother.

"Listen honey, trust me when I say that you don't have to worry about not knowing if today is your birthday, because it is," she promised.

"You don't know that for sure," Chasity insisted.

"Yes I do," Trisha answered, bite in her voice.

Chasity rolled her eyes. "*How*?" she shot back, bite now in *her* voice too.

"Chaz, I just *do* okay?" Trisha's voice was full of compassion for her niece. "I want you to stop this. Stop questioning everything about yourself. Yes, you may have been adopted, but that doesn't change who you are, or our relationship."

Chasity cursed as she continued to stare at her screen. She wasn't in the mood for Trisha's lecture. She had a right to feel how she wanted, and hated when Trisha tried to force her to believe otherwise. "Can this phone call be over now?" she spat out.

"If that's what you want."

"It is."

"Very well," Trisha relented. There was no need in upsetting her any further. "I love you, and I'll talk to you later."

"Um hmm," Chasity responded flatly.

Trisha sighed loudly; it bothered her when she said 'I love you' that Chasity hardly ever said it back. Normally, she let it slide, but not tonight. "Chasity Taj-Marie Parker!"

Chasity flinched at the base in Trisha's voice. Trisha only ever called her by her full name when she was upset with her, which was hardly ever.

"Yeah?" she answered.

"I said I love you."

Chasity rolled her eyes. "I love you too," she responded, voice low and teeth clenched. Even more irritated, she abruptly ended the phone call and tossed the phone on the floor.

Fatigue now setting in, Chasity closed her laptop and put it back on her desk. She pulled the covers up, ready to drift off to sleep, when she heard keys jiggling in the door.

She rolled her eyes; she was really enjoying the quiet. "Ugh, fuck my life," she sighed to herself.

Seeing a flicker of light out the corner of her eye, Chasity turned over only to see the girls walk in singing 'happy birthday' to her, while Alex held a cake with a lit number nineteen candle on top.

Chasity covered her face in embarrassment as she sat up in bed. "Oh my God."

"What? You thought we wouldn't find out?" Sidra assumed, a smile on her face

"I was *hoping* you wouldn't," Chasity joked.

"Yes, we're aware. Which is why we found out from Ms. Trisha the night of your New Year's Eve party," Alex bragged, passing the cake to Sidra. "You *would* be the only one who wouldn't give out that information freely, with your evil self," Alex teased, giving Chasity a hug, before sitting on the bed.

"So I guess all that Valentine's Day talk was just to piss me off, huh?"

"Oh absolutely," Malajia boasted. "Seeing the look on your face every time we asked you what you were gonna do for Valentine's Day was priceless."

Chasity made a face at Malajia as Alex nudged her over. "Move over."

"Come on, the bed isn't big enough for your wide ass," Chasity complained, moving over.

"Shut it up," Alex shot back, making herself comfortable. "And there's nothing wrong with a large behind. No man has ever complained," she laughed.

"Probably because you were sittin' on their damn faces," Malajia mumbled.

"Oh, absolutely," Alex joked.

Malajia shot Alex a confused look, before processing what she meant. "Eww!" she complained as Alex burst out laughing. "Now that image is gonna be in my head."

"That's what you get for always running your mouth," Alex fired back.

Emily looked around. "What are you guys talking about?"

"Nothing, Emily," Chasity bit out. It irritated her how clueless Emily was. Sure, Chasity may have been a virgin, but at least she knew about sex, in all of its forms.

As Malajia inched her way onto the bed, Sidra set the cake down in front of Chasity. It was round, covered in white icing and lined with big fluffy pink flowers. Written in the same shade of pink were the words *Happy Birthday Chasity* and underneath her name, in parentheses, said *Satan*.

She chuckled at the writing, then scoffed "Ugh, its pink."

"Yes, we know that you hate the color, and that's why we picked it," Sidra teased.

Malajia rubbed her hands together as she eyed the cake. "Hurry up and cut that thing," she urged. She was starving; she barely touched her dinner because she didn't like what she had ordered, "Oh!" she exclaimed. "Almost forgot, we have a party to go to later tonight."

Alex frowned. "A party, *where?*"

"Off campus, at a friend's house," Malajia explained. "Shut up, Chasity," she spat, once Chasity opened her mouth to protest. "It's your birthday, bitch. You're gonna get drunk, and have fun."

"Fine," Chasity ground out.

"Well what time is—"

"Alex, don't ask me no more goddamn questions," Malajia snapped, slamming her hand on the bed. "Now cut the damn cake, I'm hungry." When nobody moved, Malajia leaned over the cake. "Y'all think I'm playin'," she grumbled before blowing out the candle.

"Your hype ass just spit all over the cake," Sidra wailed, tossing a pillow at Malajia.

"Good, now I don't have to share," Malajia taunted, reaching for the cake.

Chasity grabbed a handful of it and smashed it on Malajia's face, inciting a scream from Malajia and laughter from the other girls.

Chapter 11

Chasity searched through the mounds of clothes in her closet. "Why do I buy so much shit?" she grumbled to herself. Trying to find her scarf was becoming tiresome as she pushed through hangers full of clothes and piles of accessories.

She slammed the closet door shut and threw her hands up. "Fuck it." She'd gone this long without wearing one, what would it hurt to continue not wearing it. As she began placing her diamond drop earrings in her ears, she heard a light tap on the door.

Jason was standing on the other side when she opened it. She shot him a skeptical look. "Yeah?"

"First, hello to you too," he replied. "Second, I was dropping by to wish you a happy Valentine's Day."

Chasity rolled her eyes. "Jason, please."

Jason stood there for a second. "Well, if not a happy *Valentine's* Day, then how about a happy *birth*day," he amended, pulling a basket filled with red and pink roses, candy, a card, and a white teddy bear from behind his back.

Chasity couldn't help but smile. Unable to speak, she moved aside to let him in.

"Uh huh, you thought I wouldn't find out," Jason chortled. He handed her the basket, "here, I picked this up for you. There were balloons on it, but they weren't tied tight enough so they flew away."

Chasity giggled. "That's okay," she assured him. "I guess I should say thank you."

"That would be the non-evil thing to say," Jason teased.

"Well, thank you," she replied, setting the basket down on her desk. She faced him and folded her arms. "So," she began, leaning up against the desk. "Which one of them told you?"

"Malajia," he confirmed.

Chasity shook her head. "Not surprised."

Jason sat on the arm of the love seat. "So, what do you have planned for today?"

"Malajia is dragging me to some house party tonight."

"I think I know which one you're talking about," he said. "I'm going to that too...Not unless you let me take you out tonight. For your birthday at least."

"Give it a rest, Jason," she bit out.

Jason chuckled. "Fine, I'll leave it alone for now," he promised. "Just make sure you have fun tonight. You deserve it."

Chasity just shook her head, and then her eyes focused on his as he stared at her. She hated when her eyes caught his stare; it was always so intense that it made her uncomfortable.

She frowned. "Why do you keep looking at me like that?"

"Do you really have to ask?" Jason huffed with a seriousness that she wasn't expecting. "I think you're beautiful."

Fighting the urge to blush in front of him, she went into defense mode. "Could you not do that? It...makes me uncomfortable."

"Why?" he asked, standing up, "Do I scare you?"

"Hell no," she exclaimed.

Jason slowly walked up to Chasity and stood as close as he could without actually touching her. "Then what is it?"

Chasity tried to back up, but she couldn't move anywhere; she was backed up against her desk. Jason being that close to her was getting her hot and bothered, but that wasn't something that she wanted him to be aware of.

"You already know that I don't like being stared at." When he kept staring into her eyes, she narrowed them. "What?!" she snapped.

He smiled. "I think that I'm beginning to wear you down."

She turned her lip up. "Get over yourself." She put her hand on his chest and tried to push him away, but Jason just grabbed her hand and held it.

"So, you're telling me that I'm lying?" he asked.

She was trying not to focus on the way that his rock hard chest felt against her hand, or the way that his muscular body looked in his dark blue jeans and black long-sleeved shirt.

"What? Yes, you're lying," she stammered. "I don't want you."

Jason squinted at her. *You're lying*, he thought.

"Well that's a shame," he said as his eyes roamed over her. He liked the way that her dark blue skinny jeans and her black fitted turtleneck looked on her slender, toned frame. "Because I'm sure you're already aware that *I* want *you*."

Chasity was speechless. She already knew that he wanted her, and she did a pretty good job of resisting his advances. But Jason being this close to her was making her wish that he would just take her right then and there. Chasity didn't know exactly when it had happened, but the next thing that she knew, Jason was leaning in to kiss her and she wasn't making any move to pull away. His lips barely touched hers when the doorknob began to turn.

Jason, irritated at the interruption, let out a sigh as Chasity quickly pushed him aside.

"Chaz, we're about to take a trip to the mall, you want to come?" Sidra asked, barging through the door.

"Yeah, let's go," Chasity nodded, relieved for the interruption. She snagged her coat from her chair, grabbed Sidra's arm, and proceeded to pull her towards the door.

Sidra frowned as she studied Chasity's face. "Why are you so red in the face?"

"I'm hot, let's go," Chasity spat. That was true, in more ways than one.

Sidra giggled as she waved to Jason.

"Hey Sid," he replied. "See you later Chasity."

"Uh huh," Chasity threw over her shoulder as she walked out the door.

Jason shook his head as he walked out of the now empty room. He was disappointed that he didn't get to kiss her. *There will be another opportunity*, he reminded himself.

Malajia stormed into Torrence Hall around ten that same evening. She was meeting the girls there so they could all ride to her friends' off-campus party together. She barged through the door, startling them.

Alex spun around. "What's wrong with *you?*" she asked, noting the irritated look on Malajia's face.

Malajia kicked her high-heel boots off. "I am *never* going out with Ron again," she fumed.

"Why not?" Sidra giggled, handing Malajia a blue gym bag.

"These the clothes I asked you to get?" Malajia asked her. Sidra nodded. "Oh, well anyway, this damn asshat took me to a club…a *club!*"

"Well what's wrong with that?" Emily asked, opening a box of microwave popcorn.

Malajia shot her a glare. "A club is not where you take a woman on a damn date, *Emily*," she spat out.

Alex chuckled at Malajia's reaction. "Okay, don't take your frustration out on Em," she urged, brushing her hair. "Tell us the rest."

Malajia snatched her long-sleeved dress off and tossed it on the floor. "So, he takes me to this club that, by the way, looked like a damn crack house from the outside," she vented. *"Then*, we couldn't even get *in* the damn thing because this bitch didn't realize that it was a twenty-one and *over* club…We're nineteen."

"Oh wow," Sidra chortled.

"Yeah, *wow*," Malajia fussed. "It's cold as shit outside, and he had us standing out there looking all stupid. Then he gonna look at me talking about 'oops, my bad. You wanna go get a burger?'…I told his stupid ass to bring me back. Never again."

"Well, sorry you had such a bad time," Alex sympathized.

Malajia sucked her teeth as she looked through the bag that Sidra had given to her. "Sid, where's my belt?"

"You didn't say grab a belt. You said get your white bra with all the designs on it, your white netted tank top and your jean shorts," Sidra replied, counting each item on her fingers. "And let me say that I was *completely* grossed out going through your underwear drawer…I have never seen so many damn thongs in my life, don't ever put me through that again."

"I don't do panty lines, darlin'," Malajia retorted.

Sidra waved her hand at her. "Whatever, like I said, you didn't ask me to get a belt."

Alex looked at Malajia with shock. "Shorts? Girl, its freezing outside."

"*So*," Malajia ground out, face scrunched up. "We're going there in a car, and coming *back* in a car. Plus, it's a *house* party, and you know it's gonna be hot as shit with all those black people in there."

Alex shook her head as she gave herself a once over in the mirror. The jeans that she had on hugged her curves just right, and the form fitting white short-sleeved shirt accentuated her top half.

Chasity grabbed a belt from her closet and put it on as she stood next to Alex in front of the mirror. She nudged her over as she too gave her outfit a once over. The light denim jeans and sleeveless white tank hugged her body in all the right places. She was just putting the finishing touches on her hair; she had pulled her long-layered hair back into a ponytail. Her bangs were perfectly styled, with the majority of them laying over one of her eyes.

Alex laughed a little. "Try using your words Chaz," she jeered. "Saying 'excuse me,' can't be that hard."

"Just move," Chasity snapped, inciting a poke in the arm from Alex.

"Anyway Malajia, why do we all have to wear jeans and white tops anyway?" Alex asked, fluffing her hair, which she had pulled into a wild ponytail.

"Girl, cause Praz is a weirdo," Malajia joked. "He likes to keep stuff uniform I guess." Gathering her undergarments and a towel from the gym bag, she made a beeline for the bathroom, intending on hitting the shower.

Ten minutes later, showered and feeling much better, Malajia stepped out the bathroom and grabbed her outfit from Sidra's bed. She paused as she shot Sidra a confused look.

"Uh Princess, why aren't you dressed?" she asked, noticing that Sidra had not changed into her required denim and white attire. Sidra rubbed the back of her neck, letting out a sigh.

"She's not going," Chasity answered, as she grabbed a pair of gray and white sneakers from her closet.

"What do you mean you're not going?!" Malajia hollered, putting her hand on her hip.

"First off, stop yelling," Sidra sneered. "Second, put your damn clothes on. I'm tired of looking at your ass cheeks bounce around in that thong."

"You mad cause I'm sexy," Malajia taunted, much to Sidra's disgust.

"And *third*...Emily doesn't want to go, so I'm going to stay in with her and watch a movie."

Malajia stared at Sidra with a blank expression, then turned to Emily, who in turn caught her angry gaze and looked down at the DVD box that was in her hands.

"*Movie?* You're gonna sit in this room on a Saturday night to watch a corny ass *movie?*" Malajia was in disbelief. "Are you crazy? Do you know how hot this party is gonna be?"

"There will be other parties," Sidra frowned.

"And Emily will miss *those* too," Chasity chimed in. "So be prepared to sit your bored ass in the room with her quite often."

Sidra rolled her eyes as Emily fiddled with the strings on her pink hoodie

"I just don't feel well," Emily informed, voice low and soft.

"Don't nobody *care*," Chasity hissed, inciting laughter from Malajia. Embarrassed, Emily looked down at the floor.

"Look you two—"

"Stay out of it Alex," Malajia and Chasity spat in unison.

"No, I will *not* stay out of it," Alex persisted, hands on her hips. "Y'all need to stop picking on her. That's mean."

Malajia sucked her teeth. "Ain't nobody picking on her."

"You *are,* and it's not right," Alex insisted.

"She don't like it? She needs to say something," Chasity bit out, placing a pair of diamond studs in her ears.

"Boom!" Malajia exclaimed, pointing to Alex.

Annoyed, Alex shot Malajia a piercing stare. "Will you put your damn clothes on?!" she barked.

Chasity pulled her black Lexus into the first available spot that she could find in front of Praz's house. "I can't believe it's almost eleven thirty," Malajia complained, jerking out of her seat belt. "All the drinks are probably gone."

"You were the one who took forever getting ready," Alex pointed out, tossing her gray sweat jacket in the back seat. "You kept saying 'it's only a ten minute ride, why do we have to rush?'"

"*I* know what I said," Malajia snapped, opening the car door. The loud reggae music could be heard from outside of the one-story house. They could only imagine how loud it would be once they got inside.

Malajia folded her hands to her chest as she darted for the door. "It's cold. It's cold, it's cold!" she shrieked.

"Um hmm, I told you not to wear those damn shorts," Alex teased as she and Chasity approached the door.

Malajia gave a hard knock on the door and smiled once it opened. As she and the other girls walked in, they were hit by a wave of heat from all of the bodies crammed inside. The smell of cigarette and cigar smoke filled the air, and the volume of the music made hearing virtually impossible. The small house was packed; the living room was lit by the moonlight pouring through the open shades and some strobe lights in each corner of the room.

"God, I can't breathe," Chasity complained of the heat and smoke.

"Well, there goes my hair," Alex chuckled. She knew that by the end of the night, her natural curls would tighten even more.

"Hooooo partay, partay!" Malajia screeched. She then grabbed Chasity's arm. "Come on, birthday girl!" she yelled over the noise.

Of course Malajia's big mouth would carry over this noise, Alex mused to herself. She watched with amusement as Malajia pulled the reluctant Chasity to the middle of the dance floor. As her friends began to dance, Alex, once approached by a handsome partygoer, began to join them.

Malajia caught sight of Alex and hollered, "Work him, girl!"

Praz, taking a sip of his drink, danced his way up to Malajia as she and Chasity continued to dance to the reggae music blaring from the speaker. She pointed to the plastic red cup in his hand. "What's that?"

"A drink I made," he announced.

Malajia, not wanting to go into the tiny kitchen to make her own, grabbed the cup from him and took a sip. She made a face as she swallowed the strong alcoholic beverage.

"Ooh, that's good," she beamed, handing the cup back to him. "Make me one," she demanded.

Praz chuckled, "you got it."

"Oh, make *her* one too," Malajia said, pointing to Chasity, who wasn't paying her any attention. "It's her birthday." She continued her wild dancing as Praz walked off.

Alex approached soon after. "Girl, did I just see you take a sip from that guys cup?"

Malajia rolled her eyes. "Yes, you did, stalker," she confirmed. "I know him, he's my friend, so chill. And don't start your under-age drinking bullshit. I'm having several, so get over it."

Alex just shook her head as she danced in place. She may not be able to stop Malajia from drinking, but she would still keep an eye on both her and Chasity.

Praz walked out of the kitchen holding two drinks in his hands a moment later, and handed them to Malajia,

"Here drink this," Malajia urged to Chasity, handing her one of the cups.

Chasity was so hot from dancing that she needed a drink bad. She took the cup, and, without thinking, took a big gulp.

Malajia started laughing as Chasity began coughing hysterically as the strong red liquid poured down her throat.

"What the fuck!" she exclaimed, holding her hand to her chest.

"Good, isn't it?" Malajia asked, taking a sip of hers.

Alex pinched the bridge of her nose with two fingers as she heard a familiar voice holler over the music.

"Somebody make me a drink!" Mark hollered, walking into the party, followed by his roommate and Jason.

Jason noticed the girls across the room and nudged Mark to get his attention. When Mark didn't respond, Jason glanced over and saw him dancing wildly with his eyes closed. Amazed at how stupid he looked, Jason watched him for several seconds. It wasn't until Mark grabbed one of his legs with his hand and began doing a silly dance while the other hand was on his head, did Jason backhand him with force.

"What dawg?!" Mark shouted, rubbing his arm.

"You looked stupid," Jason bit out, before pointing to the dancing girls. Mark, glad to see them, danced in their direction with Jason in tow.

"Whachu got?" Mark asked Malajia, as he grabbed for her cup.

Without saying a word, Malajia handed it to him as she started dancing with him. Mark took a quick sip. "That's what *I'm* talking about!"

Arm propped up on a pillow, Sidra let out a sigh as she stared blankly at the TV screen. She couldn't figure out if it was the bad movie, or the fact that she was missing out on a party with the other girls that had her in a sour mood.

It was when she glanced over at Emily who was sitting next to her, shoveling popcorn into her mouth, that Sidra realized it was the latter. She found herself glaring at the side of Emily's head for several seething moments.

Why did I have to be the nice one and stay? She could've watched this sorry ass movie by her damn self! She screamed to herself. *Freakin' child.*

"Do you want some popcorn, Sidra?" Emily smiled, unaware of what Sidra was feeling.

Sidra feigned a smile. "No, thank you."

Emily shrugged as she continued in the bag. "I appreciate you staying in with me," she said.

Sidra once again sighed, trying to keep her irritation in check. She might have been mad, but she didn't want Emily to know that. After all, she didn't ask Sidra to stay. "You're welcome, Emily." After looking at the screen for several more minutes, Sidra rubbed her face in frustration. "Can we watch something else?" she asked, with a bit of bite in her voice.

Emily looked at her, "Um, sure. What did you have in mind?"

"Not *this*," Sidra responded evenly. Still clueless about Sidra's mood, Emily hopped off the bed in search of a different movie.

Alex glanced at her watch; it was nearly two in the morning. Using her shirt to wipe the sweat from her face, Alex made her way into the small kitchen in search of a bottle of water.

As she grabbed a bottle from the cooler, she glanced over and saw Chasity leaned over the counter, her head resting on her arms. Concerned, she walked over and tapped her on the shoulder. "Chaz, you okay?"

Chasity slowly lifted her head and looked at her. Her hazel eyes were unfocused.

"Are you okay?" Alex repeated.

"I don't know," Chasity slurred.

Alex's face frowned as she made a realization. "Are you drunk?" she asked.

"Maybe." Chasity responded, honestly.

Frustrated, Alex looked down at the keys chained to Chasity's jeans. "Give me the damn keys," she insisted, holding her hand out. When Chasity struggled to remove the keys from her belt loop, Alex sucked her teeth and snatched them off.

"I can't believe you," she hissed. "Where's Malajia?"

Chasity just shrugged before putting her head back on the counter.

As soon as Alex turned around to walk back to the dance floor to find Malajia, she saw her dance into the kitchen. Alex stared at Malajia with annoyance as she slowly danced up to Alex. It was clear from the way that Malajia was dancing and the clown-like smile on her face that she was drunk too.

Alex grabbed Malajia's arm. "We're leaving," she snapped. Grabbing Chasity's arm, she pulled both girls out of the kitchen.

"Y'all leaving?" Mark yelled as he danced with a girl.

"They're drunk, I'm taking them home," Alex announced, heading for the door. The cold air hit Alex like a ton of bricks once she stepped outside. She hit the automatic unlock button on Chasity's keys and began shuffling the wobbly girls to the car.

"I wasn't ready to leave yet," Malajia slurred.

"You don't have a damn choice," Alex ground out. Both Chasity and Malajia were stumbling down the path, laughing and making pointless drunk comments. "You two are sickening," Alex hissed. "You just *had* to go overboard with the damn alcohol." She sucked her teeth as Chasity busted out laughing for no reason. "And *you*, Chasity, I'm disappointed in you. I expected this from Malajia's careless behind, but I thought you knew better."

"Shut up." Although Chasity's speech was slurred, it didn't mask the annoyance in her voice. When Chasity reached for the driver side door, Alex shoved her away.

"Get your ass in the back," Alex urged, opening the door.

Chasity stumbled over her own foot and fell to the ground. "Ow!" she yelped. "You pushed me."

"I did not," Alex argued.

"Alex, why you push her?" Malajia whined, trying to sit on the trunk of the car. "Why is my ass cold?"

Alex grabbed Malajia off the car and pushed her towards the back door. "Get in the damn car, Malajia."

Malajia snatched away from her. "No, I have to help my friend up," she slurred. Alex watched as Malajia wobbled over to Chasity who was still sitting on the ground, and grabbed her hand.

"Why are you touching me?" Chasity barked, before giving Malajia a yank, pulling her to the ground. Instead of screaming, Malajia rolled on the ground laughing.

Alex let out a loud sigh. She pulled Chasity from the ground and maneuvered her into the back seat. Next she did the same for Malajia, who was cackling the entire time. Finally able to get in and start the car, she was ready to go home.

"Jason!" Malajia screamed, startling Alex.

"Girl!" Alex seethed, banging on the steering wheel. She'd had enough.

Jason, who had just stepped outside for a breather, walked over to the car. "You ladies okay?" he asked, resting his hands on the hood of the car.

"I'm taking drunk one and two home," Alex answered.

"Drunk huh?" Jason chuckled, glancing at both girls laid out in the back seat. "Do you need help with them?" he asked, focusing on Chasity, whose eyes were closed.

"No, I can handle them, sweetie," Alex assured him, rubbing the back of her neck.

"All right then," Jason said. "Tell Chaz I'll call her later on, will you?"

"I will," Alex promised.

"Hell, damn the call. Just fuck her," Malajia put in. "You know she wants it."

Alex sucked her teeth as Jason put his hand over his face and laughed silently. "You know what Jason, let me get them outta here," she insisted. "Malajia is on ten right now."

"Be careful." Jason watched as Alex sped off, holding his gaze on the car until it turned the corner.

Alex was five minutes from campus when she heard Chasity say, "Alex, pull over."

"We're almost there," she replied, looking in the rear view mirror.

Chasity held her stomach and leaned against the door. "Alex, pull over," she repeated, this time a little louder.

"Chasity, we're almost there," Alex declared. "I don't feel like stopping."

Malajia looked over at Chasity, who had just put her hand over her mouth. "She's gonna throw up, pull over!" Malajia shrieked.

Alex quickly pulled over to the side. Chasity immediately opened the back door, leaned over, and threw up on the curb.

"Eww," Malajia complained, before hitting her head on the door as she leaned over. "Ow. Who put that there?" she whined

Alex shook her head as she watched Chasity pull her head back inside and shut the door. "I am gonna cuss y'all out *so* bad tomorrow," she promised.

Chapter 12

Malajia held her head in her hands as she sat up on her bed. "I...feel...like...shit," she groaned.

"Here you go, Malajia," Emily said, handing the girl two aspirin and a bottle of water.

Malajia slowly popped the pills in her mouth and took a sip of water. The last thing that she remembered was dancing at the party the night before. Everything after that was a blur, but the hangover was quite vivid.

Alex barged through the door, purposely slamming it. Malajia winced at the loud noise "Good morning sunshine!" Alex yelled.

"Will you shut your loud, wide ass up?" Malajia moaned, voice full of disdain.

"Oh don't get mad at *me* because you're hung-over," Alex teased, setting her books on her bed. "Nobody told you to go overboard with the drinks."

"I didn't even drink that many cups," Malajia argued, rubbing her temples with her fingers.

"Apparently whatever was in those drinks was so strong, you didn't *have* to," Alex returned, folding her arms.

"Alex, don't be so hard on her," Emily softly put in, sitting on her bed, "she's been throwing up all morning."

Malajia grabbed her stomach and laid back down. "What time is it?"

Alex looked at the alarm clock on her desk. "After eleven," she informed.

Malajia let out a loud sigh. "Shit, I missed class," she realized.

"It's Sunday," Alex informed, laughter in her voice.

Malajia sighed again. "I didn't ask you what day it was." she snapped, slamming her hand on the bed.

Annoyed, Alex stared at Malajia for several seconds before walking over to the top bunk and clapping her hands several times in Malajia's face. She then darted from the bed as Malajia jumped up.

"Seriously?!" she exclaimed, before grabbing her head. "Owwww," she whined.

Curled into the fetal position, Chasity laid in the bed, unable to move. *God, please just kill me now*, she thought.

She woke up a few hours earlier feeling like she'd been hit by a truck. As if the nausea wasn't bad enough, the throbbing pain in her head and stiff neck were making it impossible for her to function. She painstakingly showered and dressed for the day with every intention of heading to the library, but once she threw up whatever contents were left in her stomach from the night before, she realized her bed was where she was going to reside for the day.

Sidra was sitting at her desk studying when she turned around and looked at Chasity. "Chaz, do you want to try to eat something?" she asked.

"I can't," Chasity whined.

"Well you have to put *something* in your stomach," Sidra urged, rising from her seat.

"Why? It doesn't stay down," Chasity sneered, rolling over on her back.

"Well, you can't take any aspirin unless you eat. So you're just going to lay there and suffer?"

"Sure, why not?" Chasity mumbled. Feeling another wave of nausea, Chasity hopped up from the bed and made a dash for the bathroom.

Sidra shook her head. *Stubborn.* Hearing the room phone ring, she quickly grabbed the receiver. "Hello?"

"Hey Sidra, its Jason."

Sidra smiled. "Hey Jase, I heard you guys were at the party last night; did you have fun?"

"Yeah, it was cool. Your boy was acting a damn fool though," Jason chuckled.

Sidra laughed. "Oh lord, what did Mark do?"

"Sid, he got so drunk. He started throwing paper cups at people," he chortled. "Then he started taking the pillows from the couch and tried to build a fort in the corner of the room."

Sidra grabbed the bridge of her nose with her fingertips. "Why am I not surprised?"

"Wait, then he started *yelling* at people and threatening them if they went near his fort."

Sidra giggled. "I wish that I was there to see that."

"Hey, why *didn't* you come out anyway?" he asked.

Sidra rolled her eyes to the ceiling and let out a sigh. "I was here watching movies with *Emily*." She hadn't meant to sound so bitter when saying the girl's name, but she was unsuccessful.

"Is Chasity awake?" He asked, smoothly changing the subject. "I called her cell a few times and she didn't answer."

"Yeah, she's up," Sidra rubbed the back of her neck, "but she's pretty hung-over."

"I figured that. She and Malajia were pretty tore up last night."

"Yeah, Alex, Em, and I had a hell of a time getting her and Mel in the rooms," Sidra revealed. "I don't know how we did it."

"You ladies should've called me," Jason said. "Anyway, can you tell her that I called to check on her?"

"Will do," she replied, then hung up the phone.

Sidra walked out of her Science class Monday morning.

"I wish spring would hurry the hell up and get here," she complained to herself as she bundled the collar of her blue coat. The frigid February weather was getting to be too much for her.

On her way towards the building exit, she spotted Malajia coming out of the bathroom with sunglasses on her face. "Girl, what's up with the sunglasses?" she chuckled.

Malajia slowly took her glasses off and rubbed the bridge of her nose. "It's bright as shit out there," she replied, voice scratchy.

"Still feeling sick, huh?"

Malajia nodded. "My damn head is killing me." She rubbed her forehead. "My throat is sore too. Damn those tasty, strong drinks."

"Yeah, I don't think the drinks made your throat sore," Sidra said, adjusting her pocketbook on her shoulder. "You can thank stepping outside in those booty shorts after sweating at that party, for that. You better hope you don't catch the flu."

Malajia glared at Sidra. "Didn't nobody ask you to bring up my shorts," she hissed. "And why you gotta say 'booty'? Just say '*ass*'."

Sidra sucked her teeth at Malajia's nasty tone. "Because I don't need to curse every five minutes to get my point across," she shot back.

"You just sound corny saying it," Malajia snapped, flicking her hand in Sidra's direction.

Sidra shook her head. She wasn't about to go back and forth with Malajia over something so trivial. Especially when it was clear that the girl was still suffering. "Feel better, cranky," Sidra threw over her shoulder as she walked away, leaving Malajia to roll her eyes before heading off to class in the opposite direction.

"I'm just running into all of my hung-over friends today, huh?" Sidra joked, seeing Mark lying on a bench outside.

Mark looked up at her with tired eyes. "Sid, I think I'm still drunk," he groaned, grabbing is stomach.

"You know that bench is cold," she said, folding her arms.

"It sure is," Mark admitted, too tired and sick to move. "Yo, they told me that I was trying to eat styrofoam cups at the party."

Sidra pinched the bridge of her nose. "You don't need to drink, you're silly enough already," she concluded.

"They told me that I said that styrofoam was good for their insides," Mark added.

Sidra busted out laughing.

"It's not funny."

The seriousness in Mark's voice made Sidra laugh even more.

Chasity opened her eyes a little. The bright sun beaming through the blinds practically blinded her tired eyes. She wasn't sure why she was still feeling sick. *This can't still be a fuckin' hangover*, she thought. *I may not have had one before, but this can't be it. Come on.*

The stiffness, first only in her neck, had migrated to the rest of her body. Her head pounded, her throat was sore and nose was stuffy. On top of that, the nausea that she still felt made it impossible for her to keep anything down, food or medicine. Chasity closed her eyes as she heard the door open.

Sidra walked in, setting her books on the loveseat. Chasity was lying on her bed, dressed for the day, but dead to the world. She glanced at her watch. "It's after ten. You're late for your Calculus 2 class."

Chasity opened her eyes slightly, then closed them back.

When she didn't see her move, Sidra walked over to Chasity's bed. "You okay?" she asked, concerned.

Chasity shook her head 'no' as she grabbed her stomach and turned on her side, away from Sidra.

"Do you need anything?" Sidra pressed.

"Just leave me alone," Chasity hissed, voice low and deep.

Sidra sighed, patted her on her back, and headed for the bathroom. Chasity laid there and closed her eyes, trying to will her pain away.

Propping a pillow under her back, Emily sat in bed watching TV, eating a bowl of cold cereal. She enjoyed the downtime before her next class of the day.

She leaned over and grabbed the phone from her desk when it rang. "Good afternoon," she answered sweetly.

"Hello baby girl,"

Emily smiled at the sound of her mother's voice. "Hi Mommy."

"So, I was thinking…how about I drive down to your school this weekend?"

Emily's eyes widened. She loved her mother dearly, and she missed her, but the last thing that she wanted was to be subjected to a visit which consisted of criticizing who she spent her time with. "Oh really?" was all that Emily could say.

"Yeah, I'm going to rent a motel room and—"

"Wait, Mommy, you're *staying*?" Emily asked, shocked.

"Well, yes." Ms. Harris's tone was sharp. "Do you have a problem with that?"

Emily sat her bowl down on the desk beside her. "Um…" She tried to think of an excuse, any excuse to change her mother's mind. She had none. "Never mind, I'll see you this weekend," she answered finally. The tone in her voice didn't match the panic that she felt. She let out a long sigh once her mother ended the call. Placing the phone back in the cradle, Emily looked over at the door as Alex and Malajia walked in.

"Hey Em, did I get any phone calls?" Malajia asked, tossing her book bag on the floor.

"Um, your mother called earlier," Emily informed.

Malajia rolled her eyes. "Any calls that *mattered*?"

Alex laughed at Malajia's disgusted tone. "Girl, cut it out," she teased, nudging her slightly.

"Whatever," Malajia sneered, slowly removing her boots. "God, can this hangover or cold or *whatever* it is be gone already?" she complained, lying down on the floor next to her boots.

Alex shook her head. "Next time, maybe you'll listen to me." Malajia just sucked her teeth. "Chaz *too*. Sidra said that she's not better yet either."

Emily fiddled with her hands as she tried to think of the best way to tell the girls her news. She already knew they weren't going to be happy. "Um, girls, I have something to tell you."

"Is Alex moving out?" Malajia jeered, throwing her arm over her face. Alex made a face at her as she sat on her bed.

Emily smiled nervously, "Well…" She paused for a second. "My mother is coming down this weekend."

Malajia let out a loud groan as she sat up right. "Why?!" she exclaimed.

Emily pushed some of her hair behind her ears "She's my *mother,* Malajia."

"*So*?" Malajia scoffed.

"Well, she misses me, and I miss her too," Emily admitted. "I'll try my best to keep her away from you all as much as possible."

"Where is she going to stay?" Alex asked.

"She's not staying *here*," Malajia answered before Emily had a chance to.

"No, she's staying at a motel," Emily informed.

"You already know, she won't be at nobody's motel," Malajia spat. "Every chance she gets, she'll be here sitting in our damn faces."

"I'll try to be nice as much as possible for *your* sake, Emily," Alex promised.

"I appreciate it," Emily smiled, before looking over at Malajia who was fingering the curls on her head. Alex looked over at her as well.

Malajia caught their stares. "I'm not gonna *try* to do nothin'," she hissed, pointing to herself. "I'm not gonna *be* here."

Alex placed her hands on her hips. "And where do you think your gonna stay?"

"In Sidra and Chasity's room," Malajia answered confidently. "Good luck with that, Alex."

Alex rolled her eyes as Emily let out a giggle. "Yeah, Chaz and Sid aren't going for that. You'll be in this room right alongside me," Alex assured.

Every hour that passed, Chasity felt worse and worse. It was now the evening. She hadn't left the room and barely even left her bed all day. It was official, she was sick. She laid awake for hours, hoping to fall asleep, but her stuffy nose made it hard to breathe and the cough that she had developed wasn't helping.

Chasity groaned at the sound of a tap on the door. She felt like crying as she slowly stood up from her bed. Her body was so stiff and her head throbbed as she walked. Opening the door, she found Jason standing there.

Concern was all over his face once he laid eyes on Chasity. Her already light brown face was pale; she looked drained. "You okay?"

"No," she sneered, voice barely audible.

Jason stepped in and guided Chasity back to her bed to lay down. Noticing that her arm was warm, he felt her forehead with the back of his hand. "Damn, you're burning up," he observed. "Is there anything I can do?" Jason made no attempt to mask his concern for her.

Chasity simply shook her head 'no' as she turned on her side. "Can you just leave?"

Jason removed his coat and put it on the back of the chair. "No I can't," he refused, voice stern. Jason didn't care how much she didn't like it, he was going to stay with her until either she fell asleep or Sidra returned to keep an eye on her. "I'm going to make you some tea."

As Jason began gathering the items needed for the tea, Chasity just laid there and rolled her eyes. She was annoyed that he didn't honor her wish and leave. But she had no strength or voice to argue with him.

"I feel sorry for you, Alex, and Mel," Sidra chuckled. She, Malajia, Alex, and Emily were approaching Torrence Hall. After hearing about Emily's mother's impending visit at dinner, she was so glad that she wouldn't have to be subjected to the pettiness of that woman.

"A tee hee *hell*," Malajia scoffed, pushing some hair from her face. "I'm staying in *y'all* room while she's here."

Sidra shot Malajia a glance as she stuck her key in the dorm front door. "Oh no you're *not*!" she exclaimed

Alex and Emily bundled their coats up to their necks; the freezing night air was unbearable. "Uh, lady, can you curse her out inside? It's freezing," Alex suggested, gesturing for Sidra to open the door.

"Oh, sorry," she shrugged, pushing the door open.

"Thank God," Alex rejoiced as a blast of heat greeted her from the corridor.

As they made their way up the steps, Malajia continued her complaining. "Sidra, I'm telling you, if I have to stay in that room with Emily's mom all weekend, I'm gonna kill her," she grumbled. Malajia faced Emily. "I'm gonna kill your mom, Emily."

Emily shook her head and rolled her eyes to the ceiling.

Sidra turned and faced Malajia once they approached her room door. "Malajia, we have no room for you," she spat out. "Besides, you can't just *tell* me you're going to stay here, you have to ask Chasity too, and Lord knows she won't go for it."

Malajia made a face at her. "Please, I'm not scared of that chick," she ground out. "I'm gonna stay here no matter *what* she says. Hell, I'll even sleep on the floor."

"Why? So we can hear you complain all night about how hard the floor is?" Sidra shot back.

Malajia sucked her teeth. "Y'all got me chopped," she mumbled, twisting the door knob and pushing the door open. "Chasity, guess who's staying with you this weekend!" she hollered.

Jason, who was sitting on the bed next to Chasity, quickly turned around and put his finger to his mouth, signaling for Malajia to be quiet. Chasity had just fallen to sleep after trying for the past hour.

"How long has she been asleep?" Sidra whispered, removing her coat.

"Not long," Jason responded, pulling the covers up on her.

Sidra walked over to Chasity's bed and glanced over her. Chasity's breaths seemed short and labored. "She looks like she's gotten worse from earlier," she observed.

"Is she gonna be okay?" Emily asked, concerned as she removed the pink and purple stripped gloves from her hands.

"I'm sure she will be, Emily," Jason replied. "She just needs rest...and quiet, *Malajia.*" Jason focused his attention on Malajia, who looked back, shocked.

"You *would* look at me when you said that, wouldn't you?" Malajia sneered.

Jason shook his head as he stood up from the bed. "Don't act so surprised." He grabbed his coat and headed for the door. "I mean it, don't bother her," he warned.

Malajia made a face behind Jason's back as he walked out of the door.

Sidra looked at Malajia with amusement. "I guess he told *you.*"

"Oh yeah? That's why I'm sleeping in *your* bed this weekend," Malajia countered, tossing one of her red gloves at Sidra.

Chapter 13

Sidra awoke the next morning to the sound of whimpering. She sat up and looked over at Chasity, who was laying on the edge of the bed sobbing. Her body was in so much pain, she could barely breathe. The constant coughing was hurting her chest, and she was too damn hot. It had taken her almost an hour to get herself together. She was going to attempt to make it to class, but the more she moved, the more she felt like passing out.

Sidra jumped out of the bed and hurried over to her. "Chasity, you need to see a doctor," she urged her roommate, kneeling down in front of her.

"I don't wanna go," Chasity cried as she tried to move some of her long hair out of her face.

Sidra saw her struggling and moved it for her. "Where's your phone? I'm calling your aunt," she demanded, standing up.

"Sidra, no, I'm fine," Chasity whined, trying to roll over and grab her cell phone before Sidra could.

"Girl you're over here dying!" Sidra exclaimed, moving the phone out of Chasity's reach. "I'm not going to stand here and let that happen, I'm calling her." Sidra searched through Chasity's contact list. Once she found Trisha's name she pushed the talk button. "Hi Ms. Trisha this is Sidra,

Chasity's friend," she announced once Trisha answered. "I'm fine, thank you. Listen, Chasity is really sick and I think she needs to see a doctor...Yeah, she's laying here crying. She can barely move."

"I'm fine," Chasity snarled. Her voice was barely there.

"No, you're *not*," Sidra argued, putting the phone back to her ear. "Yes...Okay, hold on." Sidra handing the phone to Chasity. "Your aunt wants you."

Chasity slowly grabbed the phone. "Huh?" she answered. She had planned on down-playing her illness, but as soon as she heard her aunt's voice, she broke down. "I'm sick," Chasity whined, letting the tears flow. "Okay...bye."

Sidra stared at Chasity with sympathetic look. She'd never seen her roommate look so fragile and vulnerable. *Poor thing. The toughest ones usually suffer the worst,* she thought.

"What did she say?" Sidra asked as Chasity ended the call and let the phone fall to the carpeted floor.

"She's coming to get me," Chasity answered, closing her eyes. Sidra just sat next to her and rubbed her shoulder.

Malajia, Alex, and Emily walked into the room later that day. Alex walked over to Chasity's bed and looked at her. "You feeling any better, sweetie?" she asked.

Chasity just glared up at her, not saying a word. *Do I look better?* she thought.

Malajia frowned when she noticed that Sidra was putting several items into a large overnight bag. "Where the hell are *you* going?" she asked.

"Nowhere," Sidra confirmed, zipping the black bag. "This is Chasity's stuff."

"Oh...Where then where the hell is *she* going?" Malajia asked, confused.

"Her aunt is coming to pick her up," Sidra answered. "Chaz is really sick."

"Aww Chaz, I'm sorry," Alex sympathized, rubbing her arm.

"Don't touch me," Chasity mumbled, struggling to sit up. Ignoring Chasity's request, Alex grabbed her arm to help her up.

"Wait, how is Ms. Trisha coming here to get her? Doesn't she live in Florida still?" Malajia asked.

"She moved to West Chester last month," Sidra informed. "And why does it matter?"

"Maybe I just don't want the bitch to leave," Malajia argued, earning confused looks from the girls.

"Wait, what does that have to do with you asking about Ms. Trisha and Florida?" Alex chuckled.

Malajia sucked her teeth and flagged Alex with her hand. She didn't care what the other girls thought; she was going to miss Chasity, no matter how mean she was.

Chasity let out a groan at the arguing. That was the last thing that she wanted to hear. If she had the strength, she would have cussed them all out.

A knock at the door broke the bickering. Alex opened the door and smiled. "Hi Ms. Trisha," she greeted, giving the tall, slender woman a hug.

Trisha took her leather gloves off after exchanging pleasantries with the girls, then she looked at her niece. "Aww baby girl, look at you," she sympathized. She walked over and gently grabbed her arm. "Come on sweetie, let's go home."

"Why are you taking her home?" Emily asked.

Chasity rolled her eyes. "Somebody shut her up," she complained, much to Malajia's amusement.

Trisha cut her eye at Chasity. "Be nice," she demanded before looking at Emily. "Her doctor is back home. Besides, I think she needs a few days to rest, away from everybody," she answered, pulling Chasity up from the bed. "Don't worry, she'll be back terrorizing you ladies in no time."

As Trisha and the girls made their way out the door, Malajia grabbed a piece of paper from Sidra's notebook and started writing some things down.

Trisha opened the passenger door of her silver Mercedes Benz and helped Chasity inside. As she proceeded to place Chasity's bag in the trunk, the four girls stood by the car.

"I hope that you feel better soon roomie," Sidra said, folding her arms across her chest.

"Yeah get better okay. I can't go *too* long without hearing you say something ignorant," Alex teased.

Malajia stuck her hand through the window and handed Chasity the note that she had written. "Hey girl, I need you to sign this."

Chasity took the paper and looked at her skeptically. "What the fuck is this?" she asked.

"Oh just a little agreement," Malajia smiled. Chasity raised an arched eyebrow at her.

"Oh don't get me *wrong*, I hope you get better and everything," Malajia clarified. "But just in case you should like; you know, *die*, this is just a little something saying that if that happens, I get to keep everything that you left in your room." Chasity frowned at her. "You know, the clothes, the TV, stereo, jewelry; *everything*," Malajia added.

Chasity sat the paper on her lap, and, with her finger, signaled the smiling Malajia to come closer. Malajia stuck her head through the window. Chasity narrowed her eyes at her as she put her finger on a button. Before Malajia could figure out what was happening; the window had rolled up until it couldn't go anymore, Malajia started screaming as her head became stuck in the window.

"Ms. Trisha! Ms. Trisha!" Malajia screamed. Chasity started laughing.

Trisha, who had just sat down in the driver seat, looked over. She leaned over and grabbed Chasity's hand from the button. "Chasity!" Trisha hollered. "Girl, chill out."

Chasity started coughing as Trisha rolled the window down far enough for Malajia to pull her head out.

Malajia quickly backed away from the car, holding her neck. "Witch! I hope you choke on your own mucus," she yelled, embarrassed.

"Eww," Sidra complained, backhanding Malajia on the arm.

"Okay, we have to get going," Trisha announced, putting the car in gear. "I'll have her call you when she feels better."

The girls waved as they watched the silver vehicle drive off. It was silence for a few moments. "I'm going to miss her evil self," Sidra pouted. She couldn't believe she was saying those words, considering how much they disliked each other when they first met. What a difference a semester had made.

"Cheer up, Sid," Malajia urged, folding her arms. "There's a bright side."

"What's that?" Sidra asked, unenthused.

"You get to have *me* for a roommate for the next few days!" Malajia exclaimed, holding her arms up in the air.

Sidra's eyes widened in horror. "Oh fuck no," she scoffed.

Alex laughed. "Ooh, Mel, she just used the 'F' word," she pointed out. "She's pissed."

"She'll get over it," Malajia promised with a wave of her hand. "I'm gonna get my stuff and I'll be over later."

Sidra stomped her foot on the cold ground. She already knew that she had no choice. Malajia would stalk her until she got her wish. "Wait a minute, hold on," Sidra barked, putting her hand up and grabbing the girls' attention. "What do you mean *later*?" she asked. "As in later *tonight*?"

Malajia nodded enthusiastically.

"Malajia, you said that Emily's mom is coming on the weekend," Sidra pointed out.

"So?"

"So today is *Tuesday*!" Sidra exclaimed, exasperated. "If you think you're going to be in my face all week, you've got another thing coming, Simmons."

"You saying my last name in that hype tone don't mean shit," Malajia countered. "I'm getting my shit and I'm staying in your room," she promised, pointing her finger in Sidra's face. "And I'm sleeping right in Chasity's—ouch!" she yelped as Sidra grabbed her finger and twisted it. "I should slice your damn ponytail off!"

"Do it and I'll dye your hair back to its natural color," Sidra shot back. "*And* I'll throw away that old ass perm you got in your closet so you can't do a touch up on those roots."

"First of all, bitch, my perm ain't old," Malajia countered. "Second, if you take my perm, I'm stealing your gel, so you can't slick those edges for those wack-ass ponytails you always wearing."

"Fine, take it. My edges slick just fine without gel," Sidra assured, pointing to her perfectly slicked hair. "I have baby hair."

Malajia made a face. "Baby hair?" she scoffed. "Heifer please, that ain't no damn baby hair. That's some *senior citizen* hair around those edges."

Sidra's mouth fell open as she resisted the urge to burst out laughing at Malajia's offhand insult. "I hate you so much for that comment," she spat.

Alex shook her head and turned to Emily as Sidra and Malajia continued their pointless, childish bickering. "Well, Em, at least it'll be quiet for a few days with Mel gone," she joked.

"Yeah," Emily giggled.

"I heard that, nappy roots," Malajia directed at Alex, who shot her a glare as she folded her arms.

Alex shot Sidra a side glance as she busted out laughing.

Chapter 14

Alex tapped her pencil against her textbook in a rapid motion. She'd been in the library for over an hour with Josh, and hadn't gotten anything accomplished. Alex had a lot of things on her mind, and American Literature wasn't one of them. Letting out a loud sigh, she ran her hands through her hair and sat back in her seat.

Josh looked up from his notebook. "Everything good with you, Alex?"

"Sure, why do you ask?"

Josh closed his notebook. "Well, aside from the fact that you've been tapping your pencil for like ten minutes straight and sighing every five minutes, you just *look* like something's up."

Alex once again sighed. *He's on to me.* She chalked her bad mood up to the letter that she received from the financial aid office earlier that morning. She knew that the amount that she was receiving from financial aid would cover only the bare necessities, but to find out that the amount was being reduced really threw her for a loop. She was barely making it as it was; now she would have no money left over for anything.

"I'm okay, just have some stuff on my mind," she answered finally. "Nothing for you to worry about."

Josh shrugged, "Well, if you want to talk, just let me know."

Alex nodded as Josh went back to writing in his notebook. She pushed herself back from the library table. On her way to the bathroom, something caught her eye—a flyer stuck to the bulletin wall. Removing the pink piece of paper, her eyes lit up as she read it.

"Waitresses needed at the Paradise Valley Pizza Shack. That's just what I need." Alex hurried back over to her table and tapped Josh on the shoulder. "Josh, can you come with me somewhere?"

He looked up. "Sure, where do you need to go?"

Alex quickly gathered her coat and books from the table. "I need to go get a job," she said.

"Okay then, let's go," Josh replied, standing up from his seat. "I'm tired of looking at this book any way."

The walk off campus to the Pizza Shack took nearly twenty minutes, but the route was scenic. Passing several tree-lined streets full of small shops, the Pizza Shack was the smallest one on the block.

Alex and Josh walked into the cozy little pizza parlor and looked around. "I haven't been in here since last semester around finals," Alex remembered, eyes roaming.

A short, heavy-set man walked from behind the counter. "Can I help you?"

"Um yes, I saw a flyer that you were hiring and I came here to inquire about it," Alex answered, shaking the man's outstretched hand.

"Okay great," he smiled. "Just have a seat anywhere and I'll bring you an application."

Josh looked at Alex and gestured for her to walk ahead of him. The two of them sat down as the man walked behind the counter.

He brought out an application and handed it to Alex, along with a pen. "When you've finished, just give me a holler and I'll come and get it. My name is Leroy."

Alex smiled as he walked off. "Josh, I appreciate you coming with me," she said as she began to write.

"No problem. I understand what it's like to need extra money," Josh sympathized. Alex looked at him in disbelief. "Oh what? You think I don't need extra?" he chuckled, noticing the way she looked at him.

"Well, to be honest, I thought that *I* was the only struggling friend," Alex huffed.

Josh shook his head. "Not at all," he assured her. "I just don't make it known, but I'm struggling too."

"You're on financial aid?"

Josh nodded.

Alex was intrigued; she had no idea that she wasn't the only one feeling the pinch. He did a good job of hiding it. "You always seem to have extra money when we go out."

"Yeah well, I worked my ass off every chance I got while I was home," he revealed. "So I was able to save a little extra. But now the well is running dry."

"Yeah, I worked all winter break. It still wasn't enough," she sulked.

"It never is."

"Tell me about it," Alex said. "I'm the oldest child, so I've always worked to help my family out. I never minded, but now, I'm just tired of struggling."

Josh understood how Alex felt; he was faced with a similar problem.

"Are you the oldest?" Alex was enjoying her one-on-one conversation with Josh. She was learning so much about who he really was.

Josh shook his head with a sigh. "I have an older sister."

Alex smiled. "Oh yeah? What's she like?"

Josh frowned. "I'd prefer not to talk about her," he replied, tone not hiding his agitation.

The sudden change in demeanor wasn't lost on Alex. *I wonder what she did to make him so angry at the mention of her.* She kept her curiosity to herself and honored his wish of dropping the subject.

"Do you have an extra application?" Josh asked. Alex nodded, handing him one, along with her pen.

They called for Leroy once they were finished. He looked them over with enthusiasm as both teens stood, watching in anticipation.

"Alex, it's your lucky day. I can use you as a waitress. Can you come in Saturday at ten in the morning?"

"Absolutely," Alex beamed, clasping her hands together.

Leroy looked at Josh. "Can you come in Saturday too? I also need a pizza cook, and it says here you were a junior cook at a diner back in Delaware."

Josh smiled. "I sure can."

After exchanging handshakes with Leroy, Alex and Josh hurried out of the parlor. Alex jumped up and down while she clapped her hands. She wrapped her arms around Josh and hugged him tight. "This is such a relief," she gushed. "Oh, do me a favor, and please, don't tell the others about this."

"Believe me, I'm not in a rush to say anything," he assured, putting his arm around Alex's shoulder. "Once Mark finds out that I'm working where food is, he'll always be in here looking for a free meal."

Alex giggled as they walked off.

Malajia sat her fork onto her empty plate and looked at Sidra, who was poking at her pasta. "Are you ready to go back to the room, *roomie*?" she smiled.

Sidra stopped poking at her food and glared at Malajia. "You left your damn clothes all over the bathroom sink this morning," she sneered.

"So? I was rushing," Malajia returned defensively. "And it wasn't *clothes*. It was one shirt. Stop exaggerating."

"You *know* how I feel about mess," Sidra hissed.

Alex laughed as she speared her steak with her fork. "Having a tough time being in the room together, huh?"

"I hate her being there," Sidra amended, pointing to Malajia who was doing a silly dance in her seat. "She watches music videos all night long, then she spends like three hours looking in the mirror trying to copy the dances. I don't want to watch her shake her ass all night."

"You're lying out your ass, Sidra," Malajia bit out. "I don't even spend three hours doing that."

"It's only been two days. What are you gonna do for the next three?" Alex asked.

"She's about to get sent back to *her* damn room," Sidra grumbled, pushing her half eaten plate of food away from her.

Malajia sat back in her seat and calmly examined the polish on her nails. "Sidra, you, Alex *and* Emily can kiss the blackest part of my ass if y'all think I'm stepping anywhere *near* my room before Monday."

Emily nearly spat out her drink as Alex shot Malajia a glare. "Was saying all of that really necessary?" Alex hissed.

"Yep, every last part," Malajia nonchalantly returned.

Sidra rolled her eyes at Malajia before turning her attention to Alex. "Anyway, Alex, do you want to go to the movies with me Saturday?" she asked. "I could use the break from *this*," she pointed to Malajia, who just sucked her teeth.

Alex looked up from her food. She knew that her first day of work was on Saturday. "Um, I can't. I have a prior engagement," she answered.

Malajia looked at her skeptically. "No you don't. You *have* no life," she ground out.

"Shut up, Malajia," Alex huffed, reaching for her cup of juice. "You always have something smart to say."

"Well it's *true*," Malajia joked. "Sid, I'm tired, give me the room key so I can go," she demanded, holding her hand out.

Sidra looked at Malajia as if she had lost her mind.

"Mommy!" Emily exclaimed, throwing her arms around the smiling woman.

"I missed you," Ms. Harris gushed, squeezing her daughter tight.

"I missed you too," Emily smiled, pulling her mother into her room and shutting the door. Emily was nervous about her mother's visit, she didn't know what to expect. But when she finally arrived that Saturday morning, all anxiety vanished. She really was happy to see her.

Ms. Harris sat down on her daughters neatly made bed, and looked around. She took one look at the posters of half-naked men that Malajia had hanging on her side of the room and shook her head.

"Naked men on the wall? Hmm, that doesn't surprise me."

Emily rolled her eyes behind her mother's back. "Mom, they're just *pictures*," she pointed out.

Her mother turned to her. "That's not the point. Those girls should be respectful enough not to have things like this hanging around someone as innocent as *you* are," she fumed.

Emily let out a sigh. *And it starts.* "Mommy, can you not talk about my friends?" she pleaded.

Ms. Harris folded her arms across her chest. "Where are those heathens anyway?" she grumbled, ignoring her daughter's wishes.

Emily pushed her hair behind her ears. "Mommy *please*?"

Ms. Harris huffed. "Fine, I won't say anything about them right now," she complied, touching her daughters' cheek.

Emily smiled gratefully. "Thank you."

"Well, come on, let's take a walk around campus," her mother suggested, returning Emily's smile with one of her own.

Emily had taken her mother around the entire campus, not leaving a stone or building unturned. Working up an appetite, they decided to take a drive off campus to go to lunch.

"Emily, where do you think that we should eat?" Ms. Harris asked, stopping at a red light.

"I know this cute little place called the Pizza Shack, the food is really good," Emily suggested.

Her mother smiled. "Okay, I haven't had pizza in a while."

Emily and her mother walked into the crowded parlor once they found a parking spot. The wait for seats was long. Emily didn't mind waiting, but her mother wasn't that patient. "Why don't we go somewhere else, honey?"

"No, this is a good place," Emily insisted.

Ms. Harris sighed as her daughter tugged on her arm. "Fine, we'll wait," she relented.

Emily checked her watch, then looked up and saw a familiar face. She frowned in confusion as Alex walked out of the back, holding a tray full of drinks in her hands. She was wearing the parlor uniform: a white button-down shirt, black pants, and a black apron. Alex rushed over to one of the many tables and sat the drinks down.

Emily held her confused look. *Alex works here? Since when?* She wondered why Alex didn't tell them that she had a job. Emily didn't want Alex to see them. She turned to her mother. "Mommy you're right, it *is* a little crowded in here. Let's go someplace else." Then she grabbed her mother's hand and led her out of the parlor.

"Aye, Jase man, pay attention," Mark barked, slamming his hand on the card table.

"Why are you yelling at me?" Jason asked, visibly annoyed.

"Cause, you not payin' attention to the cards," Mark hissed, shuffling the deck in his hand. Jason had been sitting in the lounge of his dorm playing cards with Mark, Josh, and David for the past hour. Although his body was present, his mind was far from the game. He was plagued with thoughts of Chasity. He hadn't spoken to her since he left her room days ago. When Sidra told him that Chasity had gone home, he couldn't focus. He was worried and he missed her, but had refrained from calling her because he figured that she was getting some much needed rest.

"Mark, you yelling isn't gonna help you win this spades game," Josh teased, tossing a card on the table.

Mark shot Josh a side glance. "You hype cause you and dork David won a hand."

David sucked his teeth at the name calling.

Jason, fed up with Mark's talking and with the game in general, tossed his cards down on the table. "Man, I'm sick of this damn game." He stood up in a huff and walked off.

"Come on man, get back here!" Mark shouted. He pounded his fist on the table when Jason ignored him. He then caught the glares from Josh and David. "What the hell are *y'all* staring at?"

Without saying a word, both guys sat their cards down and walked off, leaving Mark feeling and looking stupid.

Jason reached in his pocket for his cell phone as he shut his room door. *I can't take it anymore, I have to check on her.*

Sitting down on his bed, he dialed Chasity's number and put the phone to his ear. He breathed a sigh of relief when she answered. "Hey Chaz, how are you feeling?" He made no attempt to hide his concern.

"Um, I'm feeling better," Chasity answered, voice now back to normal.

"That's good to hear. When are you coming back?"

"Probably in another day or so."

Jason nodded, even though she couldn't see him. "Well...I just wanted to check on you. I...was worried." There was a pause on the line. "Hello?"

"I'm here," Chasity assured him. "I appreciate it."

Jason smiled as they said their goodbyes. Once the call disconnected, he tossed the phone on his pillow and grabbed the nearest text book from his desk. Now that he'd spoken to Chasity, he could focus on studying for his American History test that was coming up on Monday.

Emily flipped through the channels on the TV in her room. Her mother had gone back to the motel and she was waiting for Alex to return. She really wanted to get to the bottom of what she had witnessed earlier.

As if on cue, Alex walked through the door with her coat and book bag. "Hey Em."

Emily watched as Alex dropped her belongings to the floor. "Tired?" she asked, picking up on her friends tone.

"Girl, yes." Alex flopped down on her bed. "It's been a long day."

Emily looked down at her hands as she figured out the best way to bring the topic up. "So um..."

Alex let her ponytail down and ran her hands through her hair, fluffing it out. "Is something wrong, Em?" she asked, noticing her hesitation.

Emily took a deep breath. "I saw you at the Pizza Shack earlier today," she blurted out.

Alex sighed. *Shit.* "Oh yeah?"

"Yeah...You work there?"

Alex slowly removed her boots. "Yes, I work there," she confirmed. "Just started today."

"Why didn't you say anything?" Emily asked, confused.

"Because Em, I just want to keep my money troubles to myself," Alex said. "I would appreciate it if you wouldn't tell the girls."

Emily simply nodded. Alex had nothing to worry about on that front. Emily wasn't one to run off at the mouth about anything, let alone a secret.

"I appreciate it," Alex smiled, laying her head on her plush pillow. Although she wasn't happy about Emily finding out about her job, Alex was grateful that it was Emily who saw her, not Malajia. If it was the latter, her troubles would have been out before she stepped foot back on campus.

Sidra rubbed her temples with her fingers as she tried to concentrate. She'd been suffering through Malajia's constant presence for days. Now Sunday arrived, and she prayed that Chasity would return soon and rid her of Malajia. Sidra, tired of her temporary roommate dancing around her room, slammed her hand on her desk.

"Malajia, will you cut the shit?!"

Malajia stopped dancing and spun around to face Sidra "What do you mean, roomie?" she smiled.

Sidra put her hands up. "Okay *first* of all, stop calling me that," she snapped. "You are *not* my roommate. You are Alex and *Emily's* roommate. Now get out!"

Malajia flagged her with her hand. "Nope. Until Satan comes back, I'm *your* roommate," she taunted, fluffing her hair with her hand.

Sidra groaned loudly as she turned back to her books. *I hope Chasity kills you*, she fumed internally.

Malajia flopped down on Chasity's bed. "You know what Sidra, you should really get used to me being here."

"And why is *that*?" Sidra asked dryly.

"Because, Chaz may still be in bad shape," Malajia said. "So she may be gone for a while."

"I talked to her earlier, she's better."

Malajia shrugged. "*I* talked to her too, it don't mean shit," she declared. "She may decide to stay for another week. Which means, *I* get to stay *here* for another week."

"I don't think God would be that cruel to me."

Malajia made a face.

Malajia's eyes snapped open the next morning at the feeling of someone squeezing her nose. "The hell?!" she exclaimed, slapping the person's hand away. Malajia wiped her eyes, looked up, and was surprised to see Chasity standing there with her arms folded, an angry gaze on her face.

"Chaz. Hey girl, you look all better and stuff. You so pretty," Malajia stammered.

"Uh huh," Chasity replied, still holding her gaze.

Sidra hopped on the bed next to Malajia and started laughing in her face. "I *told* you she'd be back," she boasted. "Now she's gonna kill you and you'll be out of my life forever."

"Get away from me!" Malajia barked, shoving Sidra away from her.

"Malajia, I suggest that you say your goodbyes now, cause I'm gonna kill you," Chasity calmly threatened, examining her painted nails.

Malajia snatched the covers off, hopped out of bed and stood in Chasity's face. "You know what—"

Chasity put her hand up to silence Malajia. "Before you continue your nonsense, *please* take into consideration that you just woke up and your breath ain't all that fresh," she pointed out.

Malajia closed her mouth, rolled her eyes, and headed for the bathroom.

"Get your crap and get out," Sidra teased, dancing in a circle.

Once the bathroom door closed, Chasity said, "I guess I'll have to burn my sheets."

Sidra giggled. "I tried to stop her," she assured. "One minute I turned away, and when I turned back, she was all up in your bed talking about, 'rich sheets, rich sheets'."

Chasity shook her head as she walked over to her closet to pull out a new set of bedding. "I'm not surprised."

"So, do you feel like your old self again?" Sidra asked, sitting down on her bed.

"Yeah, I guess."

"Did you ever find out what was making you sick?"

"A really bad flu," Chasity revealed, stripping the sheets from her bed.

"Is there any other kind?" Sidra chortled.

Chasity flipped Sidra off for her smart comment. Sidra in turn just giggled. "It's good to have you back…Seriously. Malajia has been a pain in my ass this past week."

"Why the hell was her dumb ass staying here, anyway?"

Sidra ran her hand over her ponytail. "Emily's mother came for the weekend and she didn't want to be anywhere near her," she replied. "Can't say that I blame her."

Chasity didn't get to respond because Malajia walked out of the bathroom. "Chaz, as much as I love seeing your face, you sure you're not still sick?" Malajia pressed. "You don't need to go back home for a few more days?"

"No, stupid. Get the fuck out," Chasity hissed, pointing to the door.

Malajia turned her lip up. "Damn, you would think suffering would make you nicer."

"You thought wrong," Chasity bit out.

"Malajia, you're stalling," Sidra pointed out.

Malajia spun around, pointing at Sidra. "Mind your business, Ponytail," she snapped, Sidra smirked.

Chasity looked at Malajia as if she was crazy as the girl grabbed hold of her arm.

"Chaz please, just go back home for a few more days," Malajia begged.

"Malajia, you're touching me," Chasity pointed out with a deceptive calm.

"*Please*, you can*not* send me back to my room, not today please," Malajia whined, tugging on Chasity's arm. "You don't know what it's like living there. Alex is always in my business and she makes me call my mother every week…my *mother,* Chasity. Seriously, she will sit there and annoy me until I do it. And Emily, she is so annoying! All she does is smile, what the hell is she smiling at all the damn time?"

Sidra put her hand over her face to suppress a giggle. Malajia had always been dramatic.

"Malajia, you have five seconds to let go of me before I slap you," Chasity warned

"Look, you don't even have to go home. I can sleep on the loveseat," Malajia proposed. "Shit, I'll even take the floor."

Chasity was silent for a second. "Malajia."

Malajia looked up at her with hope in her eyes.

"Five seconds are up," Chasity confirmed before knocking Malajia's hand off of her and delivering a stinging slap to her arm.

Malajia let out a shriek as she grabbed her arm and backed away. "That was uncalled for!"

"Oh my God, Malajia, just get out," Sidra groaned, rubbing her face with her hand. The sooner that peace and quiet was restored to her room, the better.

Chapter 15

"Where's Alex?" Malajia asked, highlighting lines in her notebook. "She usually studies with us."

"I think she had study group," Sidra informed. The girls had been studying at the library, later that evening, for hours, in a private room.

Emily looked up from her book, but didn't say a word. Alex told her earlier that she had to work.

Chasity rubbed her eyes as they began to get blurry. She had a weeks' worth of assignments to catch up on for five classes. While she was grateful that her professors took pity on her due to her illness and allowed her to make up the work, she almost wished that they hadn't.

"I can't take this shit anymore," Chasity complained, rubbing the back of her neck. "I'm tired."

"You and me *both*," Sidra agreed. "And I'm hungry."

"Let's get out of this dry ass library and get something to eat," Malajia suggested, leaning back in her seat. "Let's go to the Pizza Shack."

Emily looked up from her book again.

"I don't want no damn pizza," Chasity scoffed.

Malajia slapped her hand on the table. "I don't care *what* your uppity ass says, you're *going*," Malajia snapped.

Chasity gritted her teeth as Sidra sucked hers. "Always so damn loud," Sidra commented.

"Um, why don't we go somewhere else to eat?" Emily cut in. "Maybe to the burger place up the street."

"Who said that we *wanted* burgers?" Malajia sneered.

Emily resisted the urge to roll her eyes at Malajia's nasty tone. She was more concerned with trying to keep the girls away from Alex's place of work. "Well if not *that* place, what about someplace else?"

The girls regarded her suspiciously. "Why do I get the feeling you're trying to keep us away from there?" Chasity charged, folding her arms.

"I'm not, I just—"

"You're lying," Chasity hissed, interrupting Emily's stammering.

"Maybe she just doesn't want pizza, ladies," Sidra jumped in. "No need to get nasty with her." Even though she was getting irritated with Emily's personality herself, Sidra still couldn't stand by and watch her get jumped on by Chasity and Malajia.

"I was just..." Emily was trying to think of a reason to keep the girls from going to the Pizza Shack. She knew that Alex didn't want the girls knowing her personal business. But not being able to lie without getting caught, she just sat there.

"You know what, let's go to the Shack," Malajia demanded, grabbing her coat. "Emily's tryna keep shit from us, and I wanna know what it is."

Emily sighed as the girls gathered their belongings. *I shouldn't have said anything. If I would have kept my big mouth shut, they would have changed their minds eventually.*

"It's all dry in here," Malajia complained, looking around the half empty pizza parlor once she and the other girls walked in. "There's nobody for me to talk about."

Sidra rolled her eyes. "Well, we *could* have gone somewhere else, but you and Chasity wanted to play 'secret agent'," she ground out.

Malajia waved at Sidra dismissively, "Whatever, I know Em is hiding something," she replied.

"I am *not*," Emily insisted, voice low.

Chasity put her hand to her ear. "I didn't hear you," she hissed. "You might want to speak louder when you're trying to be convincing."

Emily looked down at her shoes as Malajia snickered.

"Chasity, chill out," Sidra chided, noticing a sign next to her. "I guess we can seat ourselves."

"Seriously?" Malajia scoffed. "We were standing here all this time looking stupid, waiting for someone to seat us."

"It doesn't matter, let's just go," Sidra urged, pointing to a booth off in the corner of the parlor.

Once situated in the booth, the girls began removing their coats. Sidra frowned in concern when she noticed that Emily kept looking around, almost as if she was searching for something, or some*one*.

"Sweetie, are you okay?"

Emily looked at her. "Yes, I'm fine. Just seeing where our waiter is."

Alex walked out of the back, placing her order pad and pen into the pocket of her apron. She paused when she saw her friends sitting at the booth, talking amongst themselves.

"Oh God," she groaned to herself. If she could have darted out of the door without being noticed, she would have. But there was no other waitress available. Alex sighed and headed over.

The girls were laughing at something, when they heard a voice say, "Good evening, are you ready to order?"

Looking up, they saw Alex standing there, decked out in the parlor uniform. "Well, well, look who it is," Chasity smirked.

Emily put her hands up. "I tried to keep them away," she assured.

Alex smiled at her as she mouthed the words, 'It's okay.'

"What the hell are *you* doing here, dressed like that?" Malajia loudly asked.

"I work here," Alex answered.

"You work here? Why?" Malajia asked.

"I need the money."

"You need the money?" Malajia repeated.

Chasity shot Malajia a glare. "Why do you have to repeat shit? Shut up!" she snapped, slamming her hand on the table.

"Thank you," Sidra cut in. She'd had enough of Malajia's big mouth.

Alex chuckled. "Chasity, I'm glad that you're feeling better. I missed you."

"Shit, she need to go back home," Malajia mumbled, rolling her eyes.

"How long have you been working here, Alex?" Sidra asked, changing the subject.

Alex ran her hand over her high ponytail. "A few days."

Sidra nodded slowly. "Do you like it?"

"Sidra, don't nobody like working at no dead ass pizza place," Malajia sneered before Alex had a chance to respond.

"Why did we bring her?" Chasity spat out, exasperated. If Malajia said one more ignorant thing, Chasity would slap her.

Alex shook her head at Malajia. "It's not bad," she answered. "Like I said, I need the money."

"Please. Alex, you're in college. You shouldn't be working," Malajia put in. "Just sponge off of your parents like the *rest* of us do."

"I don't sponge, it's given to me willingly," Chasity shot back. Malajia made a face at her; Chasity in turn, flipped Malajia off.

"Well Malajia, some of us *can't* sponge from our parents because our parents have nothing to *sponge*," Alex replied, not hiding her irritation. *Will she shut up already?*

Malajia looked at her as if she was crazy. "Why are you so mad?"

"Because you always say things without thinking," Alex fumed.

"We'll just order," Sidra quickly slid in before Malajia had a chance to say anything else.

Without saying a word, Alex pulled a pad and pen out of her apron pocket.

"It's about time," Malajia sneered once Alex brought their food to the table later on.

"It's only been fifteen minutes," Sidra pointed out, sticking a straw into her cup of iced tea.

"It shouldn't have been *that* long. It's not like there's anybody else in here," Malajia complained, folding her arms.

Alex stared daggers at Malajia as she sat the large veggie pizza on the table. "Don't start your shit tonight, Mel," she warned.

Chasity made a face of disgust as she looked at the pizza. Seeing all of the cheese and grease on the pie made her nauseous. Maybe her stomach wasn't all the way back to normal after the flu after all. Eyeing the small salad in front of Malajia, Chasity realized that's what she should have ordered.

Alex noticed the sick look on Chasity's face "Are you okay, Mama?"

Chasity put her hand over her mouth. "Um hmm," she nodded.

"You're not going to be sick, are you?" Sidra asked, frowning.

"Eww, you better not throw up on this table!" Malajia exclaimed, picking up her fork.

Chasity looked at her, then started dry heaving in her direction.

"Oh my God! No, don't do that," Malajia shrieked, dropping her fork on the plate. She started pushing Emily out of the booth so she could get out. "Move Emily, mooooove."

Once Malajia was out of the booth, Chasity reached over and grabbed her salad. "False alarm," she taunted.

"Are you serious?" Malajia glared at her. "You could've just ordered your own, you asshole."

Chasity shrugged at her as she smiled.

"You two are crazy," Alex chortled. "Mel sit down," she commanded, putting her hand on Malajia's shoulder.

Alex brought out the check once the girls finished eating. As Chasity picked it up and looked at it, Malajia looked at Alex. "Don't think you're getting a tip," Malajia said.

Alex put her hand on her hip. "And why *not*?"

"Cause this pizza was wack and I just didn't like your attitude," Malajia joked.

"Pay the complaining diva no mind, Alex," Sidra said, wiping her hands with a napkin. "You're a good waitress."

"Sidra, don't lie to her. You know she sucks," Malajia jeered.

Alex glared at her. "You got one more time, hear?"

Malajia ignored Alex as she focused on Chasity, who was pulling her wallet from her pocketbook. "You might as well pay for mine too," she demanded.

Chasity looked at her. "Malajia, no matter how many times you say that, it's *never* going to work." Her voice was deceptively calm as she put a ten dollar bill on the table.

"Why *not*?" Malajia hissed. "At least *I* ask. Alex doesn't say *anything,* and you pay for *her* shit."

Alex looked at her with astonishment.

"What are you talking about?" Chasity asked, confused.

"When we went to breakfast at the diner a while ago, you slipped Alex money to pay for her food," Malajia reminded, playing with her straw.

Chasity looked away from Malajia; she did in fact remember the incident.

Alex stood there, embarrassment resonating on her face. "You *saw* that?"

"Sure did," Malajia confirmed, "and I saw Chaz give you money the day before her birthday."

Sidra looked at Malajia with confusion. "How the hell do you *see* all that?"

"Don't worry about what I see or how I see it," Malajia shot back.

"You're too damn nosey, that's the problem," Sidra ground out.

"Whatever," Malajia threw back. "Anyway, I don't think it's fair that Chasity paid for *Alex's* food and gives *her* money, but she won't do it for the rest of us."

Chasity closed her eyes, rested her elbow on the table and grabbed the bridge of her nose with her fingertips. She felt terrible for Alex; she couldn't imagine the humiliation she was feeling at that moment.

"Malajia, shut up," Chasity softly warned as Malajia rambled on.

"No, *you* shut up," Malajia countered, pointing at Chasity. "You just mad cause I'm making a good point, and—"

"Malajia, shut up," Chasity repeated, voice rising. When Malajia wouldn't comply, Chasity picked up a balled up tissue and threw it at her.

Malajia shrieked as the tissue hit her in the face. "Use your damn words, Chasity!" she exclaimed, moving her hair out of her face. "You don't have to throw shit, you child."

Alex felt like crying. *I'm so humiliated.* "I'll see y'all later," she mumbled, making a hasty departure from the table.

"Why is she leaving?" Malajia asked, completely unaware of what Alex was feeling.

Chasity held a fiery gaze on Malajia, as Sidra threw her crumbled up straw paper at her. "Isn't it obvious?" Sidra asked.

"*No!*"

"She didn't want us to *know* that Chasity gave her money. She's working because she doesn't *have* money. She can't go to her parents like *we* can," Sidra pointed out. "She didn't tell us about the job because she didn't want us feeling sorry for her."

Malajia looked around with a shocked expression. "Well if I would have *known* all of that, do you think that I would've said all that stuff?" she replied, defensively. "Do you think I'm *that* insensitive?"

"Oh absolutely," Sidra seethed. "You say ignorant shit all the time."

Malajia's mouth dropped open as she pointed to Chasity. "*I* do? When the queen of ignorant is sitting right here."

"Don't deflect," Chasity sniped. "I told you to shut your dumb ass up, but you *had* to keep talking."

"She *always* does that," Sidra put in, voice filled with disdain over Malajia's antics. Emily, who had been a quiet spectator during the entire conversation, just sipped what was left of her soda.

Malajia sucked her teeth as she sat back in her seat. "Whatever," she mumbled.

Alex dropped the towel that she used to clean all seven tables of the parlor onto the counter top. It had been a long day for her, now almost ten, and she was finally off. Alex was happy to be finished, but was dreading heading back to campus. The last thing that she wanted to do was face the sympathetic looks of her friends.

Alex slipped on her coat, stuffed her tips into her bag, and said goodbye to her manager before walking out of the door, wrapping her orange scarf around her neck. She didn't even make it to the curb before she heard a car horn. Startled, she looked across the street and saw Chasity's car. Hesitantly, she walked over.

"Are you going to get in?" Sidra chuckled from the passenger's seat as Alex just stood there.

"I appreciate you offering me a ride, but I'd rather walk," Alex replied, adjusting her bag on her shoulder.

"Alex, get your black ass in this car," Chasity demanded.

Alex complied, climbing into the back seat. "Thank you," she said, removing her scarf. The car was so warm. "How did you know what time I got off?"

"We didn't exactly," Sidra answered. "We just figured that when the place closed, you'd leave. We've been out here for about fifteen minutes."

"Makes sense," Alex shrugged. "Malajia and Emily didn't want to ride?"

"I told them no," Chasity answered evenly, maneuvering her car through the quiet street.

Alex fished in her bag and pulled out several crumbled up bills. She straightened them out as best she could, leaned up in her seat, and stuck her arm next to Chasity. "Here's half the money I owe you," she offered.

Keeping her eyes focused on the road, Chasity smacked her hand away. "Keep it."

"No, I want to pay you back," Alex insisted.

"Alex, it's just twenty dollars, it's not that serious," Chasity countered.

"To *you* it's just twenty dollars," Alex argued. "To *me,* it's a debt that I owe, and I want to repay it." Chasity rolled her eyes.

"Alex, if she said keep it, then *keep* it," Sidra cut in softly.

Alex pulled her hand back in a huff. "Sid, you don't understand. I never wanted anyone to give me anything," she sulked. "This is really humiliating for me."

"What's humiliating exactly?" Sidra asked, confused. "The fact that your friend wanted to help you out when she saw you struggling? Or the fact that you have a job and we know about it?"

"Both," Alex spat. "You have no idea what it's like to be around people who don't have to worry about money. I try to keep up with you guys all the time, and I'm just tired."

"What do you mean 'keep up' with us? As in going out and stuff?" Sidra asked.

"Exactly," Alex confirmed, tone dripping with disdain.

"Alex, at any time you feel like you aren't able to go out or do certain things, then you need to tell us that. We're not mind readers," Sidra replied. "And contrary to what you think, *all* of us aren't well off. Josh is on financial aid, and if it wasn't for David's four year scholarship, *he* would be too," she informed. "Emily's family struggles too, and Malajia *thinks* she has it easy, but I'm almost certain that her parents are two seconds from cutting off her extras."

"How do you know all of that?"

"Because they talk to me," Sidra said. "They're not ashamed of their situations, and *you* shouldn't be either. Keeping stuff bottled up isn't good, Alex. You should know that from last semester."

Alex sighed. Sidra had a point. Last semester, Alex kept her issues with her then boyfriend Paul to herself and ended up exploding on Malajia. She vowed not to do it again. *Might as well get it all out*, she thought. "You know what the worse part of all of this is?"

"What's that?" Sidra asked.

"For the first time in my life, I resent my parents," Alex shamefully admitted. "Don't get me wrong, I love them. But...I hate the fact that we struggle so much. I can't run to them when I need a new book or a new coat or even a few extra dollars. I've been working since I was fourteen, and I'm over it."

"Alex, I'm sure your parents feel bad when they can't give you what you want," Sidra sympathized. "But I'm sure they do all that they can."

"I know but—"

"You think that having money makes life so much better?" Chasity asked, not masking her agitation.

"It's not *everything,* but—"

"Well then shut up," Chasity snapped. She tried to be silent for the ride back to campus, having deep conversations wasn't one of her strong points. But hearing Alex complain about not having money, when she had parents who loved her, irritated her.

"Chaz," Sidra frowned.

"No, I have to say this," Chasity insisted, putting her hand up. "Alex, you sound crazy. You may not have money, but you have two parents who love you," she pointed out. "I may be able to buy anything I want, but my family is fucked up. My mother hates me for whatever reason. My father is so damn detached, he doesn't even have a relationship with me. And less you forget, I'm adopted. I don't know where I come from and why I was given up. So you need to be grateful for what you have, and stop stressing over stupid shit."

Well damn girl, just smack me in my face with the truth. Alex smiled and nodded. She was so caught up in her lack of finances that she forgot that her family was perfect the way that they were. "You're right," she admitted. "Thank you for that."

"Um hmm," Chasity bristled.

Alex giggled at Chasity's unenthused response. "And thank you both for being there for me. I love you girls."

"We love you too," Sidra said at the same time that Chasity said, "Shut up."

Feeling much lighter, Alex rested her head back against the seat and laughed.

Chapter 16

Chasity had barely a few minutes between her eight o'clock and nine o'clock classes as she walked along the crowded path towards the Science building. Being back to school for a full week, she finally felt one hundred percent better. Finally caught up on all of her assignments from when she was out sick, Chasity's mood was brighter than usual.

She glanced down at her silver and diamond watch, then looked up and frowned as she saw Jackie heading in her direction. *There goes my damn mood.*

She hadn't seen Jackie since they almost came to blows before her birthday. Not being one to run scared, she kept her stride as Jackie kept hers.

The girls stopped short of bumping into each other and just stood there. Chasity waited in anticipation. She wondered if Jackie had the guts to try something with her again.

Jackie simply made a face at her. "Bitch move!" she yelled.

Chasity stared at her, blinking slowly. In her mind, Jackie needed a major lesson in fashion. She seemed like she was trying too hard to be 'trendy.' The fads were fast fading, and so was the color on her clothes. Her braids were in dire need of a touchup, and it was clear that cheap braiding hair was used to put them in.

"Is that all you're gonna do? *Yell* at me?" Chasity taunted, Jackie rolled her eyes. "What, no threats? What happened to 'you owe me an ass whoopin'?"

"You don't want none. I'll beat your ass."

"And yet, you *still* stand there…doing nothing," Chasity smirked, folding her arms. She knew it. This jealous girl, like many others, was all bark and no bite. "So I guess your ugly ass isn't as big and bad as everyone thinks, huh?"

"Whatever, bitch," Jackie shot back, flinging her braids over her shoulder. *"You* ain't."

"Oh no, I'm *just* like everybody says, and you know that," Chasity threw back confidently.

Jackie looked at this girl in front of her, this girl who had everything that *she* wanted. Money, nice clothes, good looks, men's attention—more importantly, *Jason's* attention. Jackie hated her. Every time she laid eyes on Chasity, she watched to scratch up her pretty face.

"Whatever Chasity, I don't have time for your bullshit right now," Jackie ground out as she tried to walk off.

Chasity blocked her path, glaring at her. Jackie swallowed hard, hoping that Chasity wouldn't swing. She may have hated her and let it be known, but what she didn't want known was the fact that Chasity made her nervous.

Chasity could tell, and she relished seeing Jackie squirm. Normally she would ignore anyone who annoyed her, but for the sake of proving a point, she couldn't do that with Jackie.

"You lucky I gotta go to class, but I *will* see you later," Jackie promised, scurrying off.

"Yeah okay," Chasity laughed, walking in the other direction.

Mark wiped the sweat from his face and neck with his towel as he stepped into his room. He'd worked up a major appetite playing basketball at the gym, but before heading to the cafeteria, he needed a shower. His roommate handed him the room phone.

"Who's this?" Mark frowned.

"Your mother," his roommate replied.

Mark put his hand over the receiver, stomping his foot on the floor. "I don't feel like talking to her," he fumed.

His roommate shrugged and walked out of the room.

Mark huffed and put the receiver to his ear. "Hi Mom," he said, feigning excitement.

"Uh huh, you don't feel like talking to me?" Mrs. Johnson hissed.

Mark's eyes widened. *Shit, she heard me.* "Um, what I meant to say was—"

"Oh, shut up," she snapped, interrupting his lying. "Listen, I need for you to come home next weekend."

"Why?!" Mark barked, slapping his forehead with his hand.

There was silence on the phone for several seconds. "Boy, are you snapping at me?" Mrs. Johnson snapped back. "Have you lost your damn mind?"

"No Mom, I'm not snappin'," Mark temporized. "But, don't nobody wanna come home for the weekend. It's corny there. Why come home just to look at you and Dad do nothing all day, when I can stay *here*, drink, and party."

"You better not be drinking."

"I didn't even *say* that I was drinking, you trippin," Mark lied, nervously.

"Mark, I don't have time for your nonsense," she ground out. "Just do what I said and bring your behind home this weekend. Play with me if you want to."

Mark rubbed his eyes in frustration. "Huh? Mom, I can't hear you," he lied into the phone before abruptly ending the call. "I'm gonna get cussed out so bad for that," he admitted to himself, staring at the phone, bewildered.

Chasity headed to the bathroom in the Science building once her Intermediate Programming class let out. She began checking her appearance in the large mirror, when she saw Malajia walk out of one of the stalls.

"Ugh," Chasity jeered.

"Good morning to you too, evil ass," Malajia returned, washing her hands at the sink. "You done with class for the day?" she asked.

"Yep," Chasity answered nonchalantly.

"I hate that your damn day ends so early," Malajia huffed. "I'm ditching my eleven o'clock today. I hate History."

Chasity shook her head as she ran her hands through her hair.

"I'm going to the computer lab upstairs," Malajia informed, drying her hands. "I swear, I can't wait to get a new damn laptop. I'm tired of sitting in these damn crowded—"

"I promise, I don't care," Chasity spat, walking out of the bathroom, leaving Malajia standing there looking stupid.

"Ignorant bitch," Malajia grumbled to herself.

Chasity was making her way towards the exit when she saw Jackie again. Chasity didn't say a word; she just smirked as she continued to pass her.

Jackie, feeling like Chasity was trying to punk her in front of people, stopped walking and glared at Chasity's departing back, "Yo Chasity!" she hollered.

Chasity turned around and shot her a challenging look.

"See me outside," Jackie demanded.

Chasity knew exactly what those words meant. "Let's go," she shot back, snatching her coat of and heading for the doors. Hearing Jackie's challenge and seeing Chasity's reaction, nearby students in the hall ran outside as Jackie followed Chasity out.

"It's about to be a fight!" a fellow student exclaimed.

Jackie threw her coat on the ground and snatched her large, gaudy gold earrings off from her ears. "I'm sick of your mouth, and I'm gonna shut it now," she warned.

Chasity stood there, her angry gaze piercing right through Jackie. There was no need for her to exchange any more words.

Jackie ran up to Chasity and swung at her, Chasity knocked her hand out of the way with so much force that it caused Jackie to stumble. Angry and embarrassed that she had missed, Jackie charged at Chasity and grabbed on to her. Chasity pushed her off, delivering a punch to her stomach, followed by a one-two punch to her face. Jackie doubled over and fell. Chasity jumped on top of her and started raining punches down on her. As each blow was being delivered, the crowd went crazy.

"I hate these dumb ass computers in here," Malajia complained, clicking the mouse with her finger. "I can't even download any damn music."

Malajia's solo complaint session was interrupted by a fellow classmate running into the computer lab. Malajia looked at her and chuckled at the wide eyed look on her face. "Girl, what were you running from?" she teased.

"I was looking for *you*. Somebody said they saw you come in here," she informed, out of breath.

Malajia sucked her teeth. "What? Is Professor Hamilton looking for me?" she assumed. "I'm not going to stupid History today. He can forget that, with his boring self."

"No, Malajia, your girl is outside fighting."

Malajia frowned, as she jumped up from her seat. "What?! Which one?"

"Does it *matter*?"

"No." Malajia took off running out of the lab. Running down the steps and outside, Malajia pushed her way through the rowdy crowd and laid eyes on the scene in front of her. She was shocked to see Jackie lying on the ground, screaming at the top of her lungs and trying to use her hands to shield her face from Chasity's blows.

Malajia, not thinking straight and happy to see Jackie get what she deserved, started jumping up and down. "Beat her ass, Chaz!" she exclaimed.

The student who had informed Malajia about the fight glanced back inside the building, and saw a few of the professors hurrying out the door.

"Yo, Malajia! We better break this up before your girl gets in trouble."

Malajia caught sight of the professors. "Shit," she admonished, before running over to the tussling girls. She grabbed Chasity and tried to pull her off, but Chasity just snatched away from her and continued punching Jackie.

"Girl, come on, before you get in trouble!" Malajia urged, grabbing Chasity's arm again and giving her a hard yank.

As the crowd began to quickly disperse at the sight of the authoritative figures approaching, Malajia pulled Chasity to her feet and guided her away in a hurry. Another student helped the bruised and bloodied Jackie to her feet.

"You're dead, bitch!" Jackie screamed in Chasity's direction before scurrying off.

Once Chasity and Malajia reached Chasity's room, Malajia barged through the door. "Introducing the fighting champion of Paradise Valley University, Chasity muthafuckin' Parker!" she proudly announced, much to Alex and Sidra's confusion.

"Malajia, what are you talking about?" Sidra frowned. She looked over at Chasity. The girl was seething: her long hair was disheveled and her gray shirt was ripped at the collar. "What happened?!" Sidra exclaimed as Chasity tossed her coat on the floor.

"Jackie got the bullshit beat outta her," Malajia boasted, removing her coat.

"Wait, what?" Alex asked, confused.

"By *who*?" Sidra followed up.

Malajia sucked her teeth. "Who do you think?" she jeered. "Did I *not* just come in here and introduce her?"

Alex was both shocked and disappointed. She managed to show both feelings on her face at the same time. "Chasity, you fought?"

"Don't ask me stupid questions, Alex," Chasity snarled. Those were the first words that she had spoken since Jackie called her out.

"It was great, you should've seen it," Malajia laughed, grabbing a pillow off of Sidra's bed. "I ran outside and I saw *my* girl on top of Jackie like this," Malajia threw the pillow to the floor, kneeled on top of it and started punching it. "She was like pow, pow, pow, all in her face right, and Jackie was laying there like this," she picked the pillow up, laid flat on her back and kicked her legs wildly in the air, "Ahhhh, get her off me, get her off me, no, nooooooo!"

Sidra put her hand over her face in an effort to keep from laughing at Malajia's silly antics. Chasity just rolled her eyes as she removed her ripped shirt and threw it in the trash.

"Bitch face was tore all the way up," Malajia laughed, standing up from the floor.

Alex wasn't amused. "This isn't funny, Malajia," she barked, folding her arms. "This is serious. Fighting isn't the answer to everything."

Malajia sucked her teeth. "Alex, shut up already," she snapped. "You know Jackie is an asshole. She's been talking shit about Chasity and every-damn-body else since we got here."

"So?" Alex countered. "You can't go around fighting everybody who says something about you."

"First of all, I don't do that," Chasity fumed, pulling a white t-shirt over her head. "Second, the bitch threatened me on *more* than one occasion. If you thought that I was gonna ignore that shit, then you're just as dumb as *she* is."

"She's got a point Alex." Sidra slid in. Sidra didn't agree in pointless fighting, but like her roommate, she didn't take threats lightly. If she was in Chasity's shoes, she knew that she would have done the same thing. She may be dainty, but she was no punk.

Alex let out a loud sigh as she ran her hands through her hair. "Look, I know you think I don't get it, but I do," she assured. "I'm just looking out for you. I don't want you to get kicked out of school, or worse, get hurt."

"*Obviously* Jackie can't fight worth shit," Malajia put in.

"Maybe *not*, but I don't put it past her to try to get her little ghetto friends that she always hangs with to try to retaliate," Alex pointed out. "Jackie doesn't seem like the type to lose gracefully."

"Fuck her. I'm not scared." Chasity assured. "This isn't the first fight I've been in...or second...or tenth."

"Clearly," Alex replied.

"If she and her friends try any-damn-thing, I'm smacking a bitch," Malajia warned. "Nobody's gonna retaliate on *my* girl."

"You got that right," Sidra added, examining her nails.

Alex tossed her hands up in the air in surrender. "Fine! Just, be careful."

Chapter 17

"Yo, I heard Jackie got the bullshit beat outta her yesterday," Mark joked, shifting his books from one arm to the other.

"She sure did," Malajia confirmed. "Chasity wore that ass out."

Alex shook her head. "You need to stop going around bragging about that, Malajia," she warned. Just leaving the bookstore, Alex, Mark and Malajia were standing in front of it, killing time before their respective classes.

Malajia stomped her foot on the ground. "Why, Alex?" she ground out. "You scared? You think she's gonna come over and breathe her ugly on you?"

Alex shot Malajia a side glance. "First off—no, I'm not scared of Jackie, or anyone *else* for that matter," she clarified. "Second, even though I'm sure she deserved what she got, I don't believe in fighting. I think it's unnecessary."

"You've never been in a fight have you?" Mark joked.

"I didn't say that," Alex replied. "I've had to fight before. But I learned that there are better ways to resolve conflict."

"Alex got her ass beat," Malajia concluded, pointed to her. Mark laughed.

Alex sucked her teeth, but didn't get a chance to respond. They saw Jackie approaching the store. As Jackie got closer, Alex could see just how much damage had been done to her. If the noticeable black eye and swollen jaw weren't bad enough, the bruise on her cheek certainly was. Alex wondered how she could breathe with her nose as swollen as it was.

Alex had heard that Jackie refused to go to campus infirmary out of embarrassment. *That girl is a fool, she better get that face checked out.*

Jackie rolled her eyes at the smirk on Malajia's face as she walked pass. "Something funny, whore?" Jackie hissed in passing.

"Yo, what the hell Jackie?" Mark commented. Even though Malajia annoyed him, he wasn't a fan of people insulting her.

"Calling her a whore was uncalled for," Alex jumped in.

Jackie ignored Mark and Alex as she focused her attention on the still smirking Malajia. "You heard what I said. Something funny?"

"Oh *very*," Malajia ground out, unnerved. "Your fucked up ass *face* is funny. Who beat your ass? Oh, I know, that girl you're jealous of. How does that feel, huh?"

"Oh, you think that shit with Chasity is over?" Jackie spat.

"Judging by the way you look right now, I'd say it is," Malajia countered. "Guard your face next time," she sneered, before sauntering away with a proud Mark walking along side of her.

Alex frowned at Jackie. "I hope you learned your lesson," she said. "You need to find something else better to do with your time than messing with people." Jackie gritted her teeth as Alex turned on her heel and walked off.

Furious, Jackie walked inside the bookstore. She felt the urge to knock every text book from the shelves, but seeing two of her friends standing in one of the aisles, she changed her mind.

"From now on, we need to travel together at all times," Jackie spat, walking over to them.

"Damn girl," one friend said, reaching out to touch Jackie's face. "You look worse than you did yesterday."

Annoyed, Jackie smacked her hand away. "Don't worry about that," she spat.

"Yo, you need to make that bitch pay for what she did to you."

"Oh don't worry, I will," Jackie assured. "I got a plan in mind."

"What's that?" the other girl asked. "Whatever it is, we're down. Shawna's still in class, but I'm sure she'll be down too."

Jackie managed a satisfied smile.

Sidra shoved a stack of notebooks and papers into her book bag as Chasity paced back and forth, talking on the phone. Sidra kept quiet, but her ears were perked. Although she only heard one side of the phone conversation, she assumed that Chasity was getting an earful from her aunt Trisha, judging by the looks on her face.

"Everything okay?" Sidra asked, once Chasity disconnected the call.

"I just got chewed the fuck out," Chasity spat, tossing her cell phone on her bed. "Trisha found out about the fight."

Sidra frowned in confusion. She knew that Chasity wouldn't tell her aunt that, knowing that she would get yelled at. "Who told her?"

Chasity shot Sidra a knowing look, but didn't get a chance to respond because Malajia, Alex and Emily walked in. Before anybody could say anything, Chasity pointed to Malajia. "Bitch you got a big ass mouth!" she snapped.

Malajia was taken back. "Huh?! What the hell did I do *now,* Parker?"

"What did I tell you about touching my fuckin' phone?" Chasity barked.

"Wha—"

"Wait, what happened?" Alex asked, putting her hand up. It wasn't rare for Chasity to snap on Malajia without an explanation, but Alex was curious as to what the reason was for this tongue lashing.

"I was on the phone with Trisha for a half hour; she was on my case about that damn fight."

"But what does that have to do with Malajia?" Alex was totally confused.

Chasity glared at Malajia as she spoke to Alex. "Trisha told me that she answered her phone call the other day and told her about what happened."

Malajia looked away; she knew exactly what Chasity was talking about. She put her hands up cautiously. "Okay, just hear me out," she bargained.

"No, come here," Chasity demanded, signaling for Malajia with her finger. She could've choked her right then and there.

"Yeah, that's not happening," Malajia assured. "Do I *look* like an idiot?"

"Yeah, a little in the face," Chasity sneered, inciting a snicker from Sidra.

Malajia narrowed her eyes at Chasity. "Anyway, I only answered your phone because I thought it was mine."

Every girl in the room looked confused by Malajia's explanation. "But your cell phone looks nothing *like* Chasity's," Sidra pointed out.

"Didn't nobody ask you that, Sidra!" Malajia yelled, clapping her hands with each word.

Sidra stared at Malajia in stunned silence for several seconds. She was amazed at how simple Malajia could be. "Let me get to the library, before I smack her," she said to the other girls, slinging her book bag on her shoulder. "I have an English paper to research. I'll be back in time to go to the movie."

Malajia turned to Chasity as Sidra walked out of the room. "Chaz, look—"

"Are you seriously talking to me right now?" Chasity spat, folding her arms.

"My bad sis, it just came up in my conversation with Ms. Trisha," Malajia defended. "You have an awesome aunt, by the way," she smiled. Chasity wasn't amused. "If it makes a difference, she wasn't shocked."

"*No?*" Chasity bit out. "Well, I never would've guessed by the way she was cussing me out."

"Serves your violent behind right," Alex chimed in, sitting down on the couch.

"Fuck off," Chasity shot back.

Alex sucked her teeth. "Oh yeah, real mature Chasity," she ground out.

Sidra yawned as she rubbed the back of her neck, staring down at the books spread out on the small wooden table. She glanced at the silver watch on her slender wrist.

Shit, I've been here for three hours. She was going to make them late for the movie if she didn't hurry. Quickly, Sidra gathered up her belongings, and looked through her purse for her cell phone to call and let them know that she was on her way. She closed her eyes and sighed loudly as she came to a realization.

"Left the damn thing in my other purse," she groaned to herself.

Slinging her bag over her shoulder, she made a dash for the door. The area around the library was practically desolate, which was normally the case around nine in the evening when it wasn't midterms or finals. Sidra quickened her pace down the library steps. She was almost to the bottom when someone bumped into her.

"Damn it," Sidra barked, rubbing her shoulder.

"Watch where you going," a familiar voice snapped.

Sidra frowned. The light from the street lamp illuminated the culprits face. "Jackie," Sidra hissed. "You bumped into *me*. What are *you* mad for?"

Jackie, recognizing who she'd bumped into, managed a smirk through her swollen face. As Jackie's three burly friends walked up behind her, Jackie rubbed her hands together. "Well, well, look who it is."

Sidra rolled her eyes. "Stop acting like you know me," she sneered, glancing at her watch. "I don't have time for your nonsense."

As Sidra went to walk away, Jackie blocked her path. "Not so fast," she taunted, stepping close to Sidra's face.

Sidra glared at her. "What's your problem, Jackie?" she asked, not hiding her annoyance. The sneaky look on Jackie's face sent chills down Sidra's spine, *Something's not right,* she realized. She looked around her and noticed that Jackie's friends were surrounding her.

"And to think I was almost *disappointed* that I didn't see Chasity out here by herself," Jackie said, cracking her knuckles. "But I guess her *roommate* will do just fine."

Realizing what was about to happen, Sidra looked around nervously, dropping her bag to the ground.

"Where is that girl? I'm starving!" Malajia complained, flopping on Sidra's bed like a fish out of water.

"Will you be patient? I'm sure Sid will be here soon," Alex placated. "You know how much research goes into a paper. Especially for Professor Harris's class."

Malajia rolled her eyes as she sat up on the bed. She didn't care what Alex was talking about. It'd been over three hours since Sidra left for the library. She was hungry and bored.

"God Alex, you're so damn useless," Malajia sneered.

"Excuse me?" Alex exclaimed.

"Why didn't you bring any of that dirty ass pizza from your job?"

"I didn't work today, first of all," Alex returned. "And you're calling it dirty, but your hungry butt wants some, don't you?"

Malajia sucked her teeth. "Who the hell is at the damn door?" she sniped when someone knocked.

"Nobody for *you*, that's for damn sure," Chasity jeered, rising from her chair.

Alex chuckled at the irritated look on Malajia's face

Chasity opened the door and grabbed the small, flat pizza box from the young delivery driver and handed him her money.

"What's that?" Alex asked, craning her neck to see what the box said.

"My dinner," Chasity responded evenly, sitting back in her seat and placing the box on her lap.

"Did you get *us* anything?" Emily smiled, hopeful.

Chasity made a face. "Why would I do that?" she bit out.

Malajia was in disbelief. "So your selfish ass sat there and ordered food for yourself when you *know* the rest of us are hungry?" she chided. "That's that only child shit."

"She *is* an only child," Alex put in.

"Alex! Shut the fu—" exasperated and starving, Malajia vigorously rubbed her face with both hands. "Chasity, give me a piece of whatever you got," she demanded.

"You must be crazy," Chasity shot back, opening her box. The aroma of her stromboli wafted through the room and into the hungry girls' noses.

"Yesssss, that smells so goooood," Malajia crooned, sidling up next to her.

Before Chasity could say anything, Alex and Emily gathered around her. "If y'all don't get the hell away from me."

"Chaz, I will let you slap me in my face with a pillow if you just give me a piece," Malajia propositioned. "Just that piece in the corner with the cheese spilling out."

Chasity glanced at her. "Instead of the pillow, can I use my fist?"

Malajia frowned. "What? Hell no!" she exclaimed.

"Then no deal, fuck off."

Malajia gritted her teeth as Alex snickered at Chasity's retort. Eyeing the folded pie in the box, Malajia figured she would just have to take drastic measures and deal with the consequence later. Before Chasity could react, Malajia reached in the box, broke off a piece of the stromboli and darted away.

Chasity tossed the box on the floor. "I'm gonna kill you, Malajia," she fumed, chasing after her.

"It's hot, it's hot!" Malajia howled as she felt the melted cheese slide down her hand. Before Chasity could get her hands on her, Malajia escaped into the bathroom, slamming the door.

"Malajia, I can't believe you put your hands on that girl's food," Alex scolded as Chasity pulled on the door knob.

"Chaz I'm sorry, I'm just so hungry," Malajia reasoned through the door.

"Open the goddamn door, Malajia," Chasity urged, banging.

"You must be crazy."

Chasity's anger intensified once she heard her own words thrown back at her. She stepped away from the door. "I'll take that bitch off the hinges," she warned.

Alex's response to Chasity's threat was interrupted when the room door opened, grabbing the girls attention. Sidra slowly limped in, dragging her book bag in her hand. Her coat was hanging off of her, the buttons of her white blouse had been ripped off, exposing much of her bra. Her long brown hair looked to have been forcibly pulled from its ponytail as it swung wildly past her shoulders.

"What happened?!" Alex exclaimed.

Sidra painstakingly removed her coat and dropped it to the floor. "I was jumped," she replied.

"You were *what*?" Chasity fumed.

"I was jumped!" Sidra barked, moving hair from her face.

Stunned, Emily gently grabbed Sidra's arm and led her to the loveseat.

"*Who* jumped you?" Alex fumed.

"Fuckin' Jackie and her fat ass friends," Sidra revealed as tears started to flow from her eyes.

Chasity was so angry, she couldn't form any words. While she tried to compose herself long enough to form a sentence, Emily pointed to Sidra's shoe.

"Your heel is broken," Emily pointed out.

"Why the fuck would she care about that right now?" Chasity snapped.

"I *know* that, I broke it while I was fighting," Sidra spat, wiping her eyes with her shirt sleeve.

Alex gestured for the trembling Emily to move away from Sidra. She knew that Emily meant well, but with everyone so riled up, she would do better staying out of the way.

"I can't believe they pulled this shit," Alex seethed, grabbing tissue from a small box on Chasity's dresser.

Hearing the commotion, Malajia walked out the bathroom. "What the hell is all this noise about out here?" she asked. Noticing the rage on her friends' faces and Sidra's disheveled appearance, she frowned. "Sidra what happened to *you*?"

"Jackie and her hood rat gang jumped her," Alex answered, rubbing Sidra's shoulder.

Malajia's eyes and mouth widened. Seeing her friend sitting on the couch, trembling with her face in her hand, made Malajia snap.

"Hell no!" Malajia began pacing back and forth as she breathed heavily. "They jumped *my* friend? Hell fuckin' no!"

"I don't understand why they would do that to you Sidra," Emily softly put in.

Sidra raised her head and took a deep breath, trying to keep calm. "Jackie basically said that since she couldn't get to you, Chasity, that she was gonna get *me* because I'm your roommate."

Chasity clenched her fists and began pacing back and forth along with Malajia. She darted for the door, but was blocked by Alex.

"No, where are you going?" Alex barked, grabbing Chasity's shoulders

Furious, Chasity knocked Alex's hands off of her. "Get the fuck out of my way, Alexandra," she barked.

"Why? So you can go out looking for Jackie and those goons, alone?" Alex argued. "What do you think they'll do to you when they see you, their *intended* target?"

"Oh, she won't be alone," Malajia assured, walking over. "Cause I'm going with her. Come on Chaz, let's go fuck some shit up."

Alex let out a sigh. She understood that the girls were angry; *she* was too. She didn't want to admit it, but she wouldn't mind going to search for those girls alongside them. But for their sake, she had to be the voice of reason.

"Look, we can handle this in a different way," Alex suggested.

"You're a freakin' idiot," Chasity seethed.

"What other way *is* there?" Malajia followed up, equally annoyed. "Those bitches jumped your damn friend, and you think there is some *other* way to handle it besides beating the shit outta them?"

Alex rubbed the back of her neck. *Good point*, she thought.

"Well, maybe we can go to the Dean, or the President of the school even," Emily quietly put in.

"You know what—What the f—Emily just shut up!" Chasity yelled, causing Emily to flinch.

"Chasity! Stop taking your anger out on her," Alex scolded. "Focus."

"I *am* focused," Chasity assured. "Focused on putting my fist through somebody's face."

"You got *that* right," Malajia put in.

"I can't believe this just happened," Sidra sobbed.

Alex gave Sidra a once over, aside from her ripped shirt and messed up hair, she barely had a scratch on her. *She must have put up a good fight.*

"I'm not going to the damn Dean. I want payback, and I want that shit now," Sidra fumed, slamming her hand on the arm of the chair.

"But if we go to the Dean, at least they could be kicked out of school," Alex pointed out.

"I don't give a flying fuck about them getting kicked out!" Sidra snapped. "That won't make me feel any better. I…want…payback."

Alex was shocked. She knew that Sidra was angry, but this was a side to her that she'd never seen. "Well…whatever you want to do sweetie," she relented, knowing that nothing that she could say would change the girl's mind.

"About time," Malajia sneered. "Let's go find them."

Alex had a thought as she put her hand up. "No, not tonight," she urged.

Chasity threw her head back and groaned as she stomped her foot on the floor. "Am I gonna have to knock you out to get out this door?" she challenged.

"No, that won't be necessary," Alex hissed, making a face. "Do you ladies realize that they will be expecting for us to retaliate tonight?"

"Don't nobody care—"

"Just listen to me," Alex ordered, interrupting Malajia's rambling.

"Hurry up and fuckin' talk," Malajia spat, waving her hand at her.

Alex looked at Emily, "Em, don't you have class with Jackie tomorrow?"

"What the *fuck* does that have to do with anything? I'm sick of this talking bullshit!" Chasity shouted.

"You know what, you need to calm your ass down okay!" Alex yelled back, pointing at Chasity.

Malajia gently grabbed Chasity's arm. "All right, just let her talk," Malajia suggested, trying to keep calm. "This better not be nothin' dumb."

"My five o'clock is with her," Emily answered in between biting her already short fingernails.

"What does she usually do after class?"

"She waits for her friends to come in and they sit and talk for a while."

"Can you do us a big favor?" Alex asked. Emily stared at her in anticipation. "Can you tail them for us?"

Emily looked at Alex with shock and fear. "Um…tail them? As in follow them?" she stammered.

Chasity sucked her teeth. "Forget her scared ass. She's *not* gonna do that," she pointed out.

"Right," Malajia chimed in. "Why can't *we* just tail them?"

"If they notice any one of *us*, then they're gonna know that something is up. They won't suspect Emily," Alex pointed out. She looked over at Emily, who was clutching a pillow to her chest. "Sweetie, we're not asking you to fight, we just need your help...but if you don't want to do it, then we won't pressure you."

Emily thought for a moment. Although she was terrified, Emily hated what was done to Sidra and she wanted to help any way that she could. "Okay, I'll do it," she replied softly.

Alex sighed. She hated to drag Emily in, but she would make sure that she was protected the best that she could. "If you change your mind, don't hesitate to say something," Alex urged.

Malajia sucked her teeth. "She gonna follow the wrong people and shit."

Alex shot Malajia a side glance.

"And she's tailing them *where* exactly?" Chasity sneered, folding her arms. She just wanted to fight, and Alex was trying to form some pointless plan.

"Somewhere that prevents us from being kicked out of school…how's *that*?" Alex bit out.

"Man, screw this damn school," Malajia spat, sitting on the floor.

Chapter 18

Emily kept her face buried in her notebook as she secretly waited for Jackie's friends to arrive after her class. Like clockwork, the girls walked in, just as loud as ever. Even from the back of the classroom, Emily noticed that Jackie's friends had scratches and bruises, especially one in particular.

Once the group exited the classroom, Emily rose from her seat, grabbed her book bag, and followed them. She lingered several feet behind, blending in with the other students as she followed Jackie and her friends through campus. Her eyes widened when she noticed that they were heading away from the school.

Pulling out the cell phone that Sidra had loaned to her, she started texting Alex what was going on. Alex told her to fall back after she learned that they were heading off campus, but Emily kept going. Luckily, the girls stopped in a mini-store right outside of campus, only two minutes away. Emily texted Alex the location and waited outside for her friends to come.

The girls arrived to the store in record time. Emily pointed out their location, and they waited until they saw Jackie's group go into the bathroom before heading inside.

"Did you see the look on that stuck up bitch's face when she realized that she was about to get jumped?" Jackie laughed as she primped in the large bathroom mirror.

"Stuck up or not, she can fight," one girl said, checking out her bruises and scratches in the mirror.

Jackie sucked her teeth. "Suck it up, you seen *me* after *my* fight," she mocked. Looking over, she noticed the bathroom door was open. "Let me close this shit before somebody barges in here."

Jackie was about to shut the door when Chasity appeared from out of nowhere and blocked the door with her arms. Jackie was startled, seeing the rage in Chasity's face.

"And here I thought you were *tired* of getting your face beat in," Chasity taunted, taking her hand and pushing Jackie back into the bathroom by her face.

Jackie's friends turned when they saw her stumble back into the room with Chasity following her.

"What the—"

The question was interrupted as Alex, Sidra, and Malajia hurried in behind her.

"Shit," one of them stammered.

"What? You thought you was just gonna jump my girl and we weren't gonna *do* anything?" Malajia taunted as Emily snuck into the bathroom, shutting the door behind her.

"We wanted *that* one," another friend argued, pointing to Chasity. "The other girl was in the wrong place at the wrong time, so she had to take it for her little friend."

Enraged, Sidra tried to charge at the girl, but Alex held her back. "You talking a bunch of shit with your face all fucked up! I pulled *all* your damn face out of my nails last night, you fat freak!" Sidra screamed.

"Sidra jacked y'all up," Alex boasted. "By her-damn-self. You trifflin', punk ass bastards."

"So, what y'all tryna do?" the third friend challenged, throwing her hands up.

"Enough of this talking bullshit," Chasity spat, charging at Jackie, pushing her into one of the stalls. As Jackie stumbled back and fell, Chasity jumped on her and started striking her, at the same time as the other girls rushed the rest of Jackie's friends.

Emily watched in horror as her friends fought Jackie's friends. Sidra had one girl on the ground in a strangle hold, while Alex had another one in a headlock. Another girl rushed Malajia, pushing her against the wall. Furious, Malajia pulled a loosened plastic soap dispenser from the wall and threw it at her, striking the girl in the chest with it and sending her falling to the ground. Malajia ran over and started kicking the already injured girl in her ribs.

Jackie was screaming and struggling to break free of Chasity's grip. Chasity had her by the back of the hair, smashing her face into the hard floor as she continuously punched her back and sides.

The girl that Sidra was fighting pushed Sidra off of her and threw her up against the wall. As she charged, she was greeted by Sidra's fist to her face. Sidra then grabbed her hair while she continued to punch her. The girl screamed at the top of her lungs.

Emily moved away from the door as it swung open. In charged a whole group of police officers. Emily stood in a corner as the officers rushed over, pulling the girls apart.

Sidra screamed obscenities as one officer hauled her away from her opponent. One officer grabbed Chasity around her waist, while another had to unwrap Jackie's braids from around Chasity's hand. As Malajia was being dragged out of the bathroom she pointed at Jackie and laughed at all of the braids that Chasity had in her clenched fist.

"You salty, you bald headed bitch!" Malajia taunted.

As Alex was being pulled out of the room, along with the other girls, she looked over and saw one of the officers try to grab Emily. "No! She didn't do anything," Alex exclaimed.

The officer looked at the trembling Emily. "Get out of here," he ordered. Patrons were gathering around to watch the officers drag the arguing girls through the store and out of the door,

"What's going on?" one patron asked as he heard Malajia shout, "You fat ass owl! I hope you die in your sleep."

"Damn girls from that college were fighting in the bathroom," the cashier said.

The officers' handcuffed the girls; they put Jackie and her friends in one patty wagon and put the other girls in the other. As the doors were being closed Jackie yelled, "This ain't over!"

"Oh my God! You just got the shit kicked out of you and you're *still* talking!" Sidra snapped back.

It was silent as the wagon pulled off. Chasity looked over at Malajia, who was seated next to her, and asked, "Did you call one of them a fat ass owl?"

"Oh, so what. I couldn't think of anything else to say," Malajia sneered, fidgeting in her seat.

"A fuckin' owl though?" Chasity scoffed.

Malajia stared at her for a second, and with a straight face said, "*What*? Owls are fat, aren't they?"

Chasity was so disgusted by Malajia's stupidity that she couldn't even laugh. She just glared at her.

"She said Owl. Out of *all* animals," Alex commented.

The local police station of Paradise Valley housed two small cells. When the girls arrived, they were placed in one of them.

As the officer locked the gate, Malajia stood there with her hands on the bars. "Are you seriously locking us in here?" she exclaimed.

"Settle down," the officer ordered.

Malajia let out a loud sigh and walked over to a bench, squeezing onto it with her friends. "My parents are gonna kill me," she complained, leaning her head on Alex's shoulder.

"*Yours?*" Sidra scoffed, pushing some of her disheveled hair over her shoulder. "My parents would have a fit if they found out that their Princess ended up in a nasty jail cell."

The girls watched as the guard led Jackie and her friends down the hall. "You better *not* put them in here," Malajia warned.

"Wouldn't dream of it," the officer sneered, leading them to the nearby cell.

"I meant what I said. This ain't over," Jackie threatened.

"Yeah, you talk big shit now that we have these bars between us," Chasity mocked. She rubbed her wrist, the same wrist that she sprained last semester, lifting weights. She knew by the twinge of pain that she had aggravated it. "This is freakin' gross, it smells like somebody just pissed on the floor," Chasity scoffed.

Alex looked at her, "You act like you never been in jail before," she said.

"That's cause I *haven't*," Chasity spat.

The girls looked at her in astonishment "You've really never been in jail before?" Malajia asked.

Chasity matched their looks with one of her own. "What is *that* supposed to mean?"

"We're sorry, but as many fights as I'm sure you've been in, I'm surprised that you *haven't* been," Alex temporized.

Chasity clenched her teeth "Yeah, well, I *haven't*."

"Well damn, shocked the hell outta *me*," Malajia joked.

"God, I gotta get out of here," Sidra whined.

Malajia glanced over at Chasity. "Chaz, can't you just bail us out?"

"No, I can't," Chasity spat.

"Come *on*, you know you have the money," Malajia barked.

Chasity took a deep breath in an effort to remain calm. "I *can't* because there is no bail," she hissed.

Sidra frowned in confusion. "What are you talking about?"

"There is no bail," she repeated. "They're gonna make our parents come get us."

"She's right," Alex added. "Because we're college students and the school owns the store that we fought in, they're not charging us. But we're gonna sit until a parent comes to pick us up."

"Why the fuck are we in here then?" Malajia sneered. "If we're not being charged with anything…which by the way, I'm not complaining about," she clarified. "I'm too cute to have a criminal record."

"Because we still fought in public and caused a disturbance," Alex said. "They also want us to cool off, I guess."

"How the hell do you know all this?" Malajia asked.

"While you were running off at the mouth about how justified you were to call that damn girl an owl, and while Sidra was staring off into space like a crazy person, the nice officer explained things to me and Chasity," Alex revealed.

"So which one of us are gonna call a parent?" Sidra asked.

"Shit, not *me*," Malajia assured, folding her arms.

Emily sat on her bed with her head in her hands, rocking back and forth, tears staining her cheeks. She had run all the way back to campus from the store. Scared, worried, and not knowing what to do next, she just sat there in a full blown panic.

"I never should've gone along with this," she sobbed to herself. "They wouldn't have fought if I didn't."

I need to tell the guys what happened. Wiping her face with her sweater, she grabbed the phone from her desk and dialed David's room number. After asking him to gather the guys and meet her in the Wilson Hall parking lot, she ran her hands through her hair.

"What am I gonna do?" she sniffled. "Think Emily, think." A light bulb went off in her head. Hopping up from the bed, she grabbed Alex's phone book from her dresser.

Not more than ten minutes later, Emily was down in the parking lot meeting with the guys. "What's wrong?" Jason asked, noticing the troubled look on Emily's face.

"The girls are in jail," she blurted out

Mark's mouth fell open. "*Whose* girls? *Our* girls?!"

"What? Why? What happened?" Jason fumed.

Emily could see that they were just as upset and worried as *she* was. "They got into a huge fight with Jackie and her friends off campus; they were all arrested."

"What!" Josh hollered, putting his hands on his head. "Oh my God, Sidra must be freaking out right now."

Jason glared at him. "Sidra is *not* the only girl in jail," he spat.

"Yeah, well neither is *Chasity*," Mark chimed in.

"Mark, you do *not* want to start with me right now," Jason warned, facing him.

"Guys, please stop arguing," Emily urged.

"We're sorry," Josh said. "Do you know where the jail is?"

"Yes, here are the directions." She handed Josh a piece of paper. "I got them from one of the officers before they took them away."

"Cool." Mark snatched the paper from Josh's hand. "Guys, let's be out," he ordered, before they took off running for the bus stop.

David turned around and looked at Emily, who was just standing there. "Aren't you coming?"

"No, I have to wait for someone," she answered.

David shot her a confused look, before taking off after the guys.

"I have to get out of here. My clothes stink, and I have to pee," Sidra fumed, stomping her foot on the cement floor. It'd been an hour since the girls were placed into that cell and they didn't see their release any time soon. No one wanted to be the one to call their parents to tell them what happened.

"It's cold in here," Malajia complained, flopping around in her seat. "I want my bed. Alex, call your parents."

"You call *your* parents," Alex shot back, rubbing her head.

"Bullshit," Malajia refused.

"Ladies, you have visitors," an officer announced, just as the guys darted around the corner. Excited, the girls jumped up and ran to the bars.

"Are you all okay?" David asked.

"David, we're in jail, what do you *think*?" Malajia sneered.

"What are they saying? Do you have to spend a night here?" Jason asked.

"Spend a night?!" Sidra exclaimed, grabbing her stomach. "Oh God, I'm gonna throw up."

"The sooner they call their parents, the sooner they can leave," the officer declared, folding his arms.

"You want me to call them?" Josh asked a panicked Sidra.

"No, are you crazy?" Sidra barked. "Vanessa and Joseph would kill me."

"Just calm down Sid, it'll be okay," Josh assured her, holding her hands through the bars.

"I gotta get the fuck outta here," Chasity vented to Jason as he held her hand. "It smells like hard piss in here."

Malajia looked at her. "I'm sorry, I tried to hold it."

Chasity's head snapped towards her; she was in no mood for Malajia's attempt at jokes. "Malajia, get away from me with that shit, I swear I'm not for it right now," she snapped.

"I was just kidding."

"Where's Emily?" Alex asked, craning her neck to see if she was lurking around a corner.

"Man, she gave some damn excuse, talking about she was waiting for someone," Mark scoffed.

"Waiting for *who*? *Nobody* comes to see *her*," Malajia seethed.

"Don't start Mel, *she* didn't put us in here," Alex pointed out.

"So what, we're all friends, she should *be* here," Malajia countered.

Mark reached his hand through the bar and gently palmed Malajia in the forehead. "Hey big head, how you doin'?" he asked.

Malajia glared at him. "Why can't you be nice like the rest of them?" she hissed. "Why you always gotta be the ignorant jackass?"

Before Mark could respond, the lurking officer walked around the corner. "Okay fellas, visiting time is over," he declared.

"What?! No, you guys can't leave us in here like this," Malajia whined.

"Mel, it's not up to *them* to get us out of this mess," Alex informed, watching the officer show the guys the way out.

Jason looked at Chasity sympathetically. "Don't worry, it'll be okay," he said. He, like the other guys, hated to leave the girls there, but they had no choice.

As the officer tried to move the guys away from the bars, Malajia reached out and grabbed onto Mark's shirt. "No please, get me out of here," she pleaded. "I swear I will kiss your ass for an entire week. Please don't leave me in here. I'm going crazy, and it smells like ass."

"All right Mel, calm down," Mark said. He heard a tearing sound and realized that she had ripped his shirt. "Damn Mel!" he shouted, jerking her hands off of the fabric. He pointed to the officer. "Yo my man, make sure you keep her ass in here."

"No! Mark I swear that's not funny," Malajia spat.

As the guard led the guys down the hall, Josh turned to him. "How about we make a deal? I'll bring you free pizza every day for a month if you let them out," he proposed.

Mark smacked the back of his head. "Come on man, with that sorry ass bribe," he bristled.

"I don't see *you* doing anything," Josh snapped, rubbing the back of his head.

As Alex and Sidra went to sit back down, Malajia looked at Chasity, "Call Ms. Trisha," she urged.

"I'm *not* doing that," Chasity hissed.

"Why the hell *not*?" Malajia frowned. "She's not like the rest of our parents, she's cool. She'll understand."

"You know how you don't wanna call your parents and tell them that you're in jail? I don't want to call my aunt and say that," Chasity explained. "The last thing I need is for *her* to be disappointed in me."

Malajia sighed; she understood where Chasity was coming from. Nobody wanted to disappoint their parental figures, no matter how laid back they were.

Emily jogged down the hall and stopped in front of the jail cell. "Girls," she announced, grabbing hold of the bars.

"Emily," Alex exclaimed, jumping up along with the other girls.

As the girls congregated around the bars, the officer approached with keys in hand. "You're free to go."

Malajia sucked her teeth. "After damn near six hours, you finally decide to let us go," she sneered. The office smirked.

"Oh yeah, that's smart. Go ahead and get flip at the lip with the officer, Malajia," Alex chided.

"No, one of your parents is here," the officer revealed, much to the girls shock.

"What? *Whose* parents?" Sidra stammered.

Before he could answer, Trisha walked around the corner and up to the gate.

Chasity's eyes widened once she saw the angry gaze fixed on Trisha's face. "Shit," she whispered. Trisha's piercing gaze never left Chasity as the girls walked out of the jail cell.

"All right ladies, let's go." The officer shuffled the girls down the hall to small office. As Trisha signed some papers, the girls stood there, silent. Sidra, Alex, and Malajia were relived to be free, and even more relieved that it wasn't their parents that were standing in that room with them. But they felt for Chasity, and could only imagine what she was feeling at that moment.

After signing the last paper, the officer began to make copies. "Do you have *any* idea how pissed off I am with you all right now?" Trisha seethed, slamming her pen on the desk. When no one answered, she folded her arms. "Nothing to say? Nobody?" She directed her gaze to her niece. "Chasity, you got all that damn mouth. Nothing to say?"

Not sure what to say, Chasity simply shook her head.

"What kind of shit are you girls on?" Trisha fumed. "Fighting? Landing in jail? Do you care about your future at all? You put yourselves and Emily in a fucked up position."

Emily looked down at the floor.

"Good thing she thought to go through Alex's phone book and call me. I had to drive four hours to get here!" Her gaze roamed over Malajia, Sidra and Alex. "I should call all three of your parents right now."

"Please don't," Malajia mumbled, resulting in a nudge from both Alex and Sidra.

Trisha shook her head as she looked at Chasity. "And *you!*" she yelled "You already got into *one* fight, now you go and get in another. What the hell is wrong with you girl? You think this is the life that I want for you? What do you have to say for yourself?"

Chasity pinched the bridge of her nose with her fingers. Aunt or not, justified or not, Chasity couldn't stand there and be yelled at in front of everyone and not say anything. "I really don't know what you want me to stand here and say, Aunt Trisha," she spat.

"I know you're not trying to get smart with me, Chasity Taj-Marie!" Trisha yelled, pointing at her. "Don't make me slap you."

Chasity frowned. She hadn't meant to, but that was an instant reaction when someone threatened to do something to her.

"Ms. Trisha, please don't be mad at her." Alex cut in, stepping forward, "We all take full responsibility for what happened."

"Are we finished here, officer?" Trisha asked as he approached her with a stack of papers. She gestured for the girls to walk once the officer confirmed that everything was in order.

The ride back to campus in Trisha's car was awkward for everyone, to say the least. Between the silence and the tension, they couldn't wait to get out of that car. Chasity stared out of the passenger side window as the girls in the backseat continued to exchange glances.

Trisha let out a loud sigh as she pulled into the parking lot of Torrance Hall. "I just have *one* more question for you girls," she declared, earning nervous looks throughout the car. "Did y'all at *least* beat their asses?"

Chasity shot Trisha a confused look "What?"

"Well, *did* you?"

Chasity, not sure if she should still be nervous or not, just nodded.

Trisha nodded in satisfaction. "Well, good."

"You're not mad?" Malajia asked.

"About you getting locked up and me having to drive all the way from Pennsylvania to get you out? I'm *annoyed*," Trisha clarified. "About you defending yourself? No...Emily told me the whole story. Those girls are disgusting."

"So...you're *not* gonna disown Chasity and adopt *me*?" Malajia joked. Chasity rolled her eyes.

"No, I'm not," Trisha chuckled. "I know my niece, she's not as violent as she seems. I know she only fought because she was being provoked. I understand that, I used to go through the same thing at her age…I just want you girls to be careful."

"Trust us, we're done with that situation," Alex assured her, putting her hand up.

"As long as they don't try nothing else," Malajia added.

"I doubt that they will. They got embarrassed on more than one occasion," Alex said.

Trisha looked back at Sidra. "Sidra, I heard how you barely had a mark on you after being jumped."

Sidra ran her hand through her hair. "Yeah well, when they started swinging on me, I grabbed one of them and backed myself against a wall," she said. "Every time they hit or pulled on me, I hit and clawed *her*. She blocked a lot of those hits."

"Smart girl," Trisha approved.

Chapter 19

Sidra dropped her book bag into the trunk of Chasity's car. "I need for spring break to hurry up and get here," she complained. "I'm over these stupid research papers."

Malajia chuckled as she opened the back door. "I'd take that over History *any* day," she jeered. "If I have to read about anything else from the sixteenth century, I'm gonna slap something."

"Get in the car now, or I'm pulling off without you," Chasity warned, starting the car up.

"All right, cranky," Sidra giggled, settling into the passenger seat. "I know Alex is waiting for us anyway."

Just as Malajia stepped her foot in the car, she noticed Mark making his way through the parking lot. "What the hell is *your* black ass doing over here?" Malajia sneered at him.

"Damn Malajia!" Sidra exclaimed. Malajia could be so belligerent at times; it really rubbed Sidra the wrong way.

"Damn Malajia, *what*?" Malajia scoffed. "He know he black."

Mark made a face at Malajia as he approached the car. "Always gotta be the asshole," he spat.

"Whatever," Malajia returned. "Where are you going?" she asked, noticing the overnight bag in Mark's hand.

Mark threw his head back and groaned loudly. "I'm going home for the weekend. I'm meeting my ride over here."

Sidra stuck her head out of the window. "What did you do, Mark?"

Mark sucked his teeth. "Why you gotta assume that I did something?"

"Because it's *you*," Malajia cut in, before dissolving in a fit of laughter. "You salty, you gotta go home on a Friday. You on punishment and shit."

Too angry to think of a quick retort, Mark stood there gritting his teeth.

Irritated with being held up, Chasity honked her horn, startling them both. "Get in the damn car, Malajia!" she ordered. Not saying another word, Malajia sat in the car as Mark stormed off in search of his ride.

"It's about time," Alex joked, putting her hands on her hips. It'd been nearly an hour since she called the girls to have them meet her at the Pizza Shack.

"It's Sidra's fault," Malajia said, approaching the empty booth that Alex had reserved for them.

Sidra's mouth fell open. "I had to finish my paper," she argued. "What was *your* excuse for making us wait after I got back from the library?"

Malajia sucked her teeth as she removed her coat. "I was doing my hair," she mumbled.

"What was that?" Sidra pressed, putting her hand to her ear.

"I was doing my damn hair, okay?" Malajia barked. "You already know I need to get my curls just right."

"Okay, none of that is important," Alex cut in, sitting down. "You're here now."

"Why *are* we here?" Chasity asked tiredly. The last thing she felt like doing was sitting in a pizza parlor. She would much rather be in bed after the week that she had. Having major assignments due and quizzes in all five of her classes that week had taken its toll.

"Well, I wanted to talk to you about Emily's upcoming birthday," Alex revealed, removing a large gold hoop from her ear. "It's in a few weeks."

Chasity narrowed her eyes at Alex. "And you couldn't talk to us about this back on campus?"

Malajia snickered at Chasity's snarky question.

"No, I *couldn't*," Alex hissed. "You know Emily usually tags along when I come to your dorm, or she's in our room. I don't want her to know that we're planning anything."

"Planning what, exactly?" Chasity spat. "A fun-filled night of sitting in the damn room? Cause you know that's what's gonna happen. The girl never does any-damn-thing."

Alex glowered at Chasity. She could have shaken her. "You're banned from saying anything for the next five minutes, evil ass."

"Yeah, *that's* gonna happen," Chasity shot back sarcastically.

Alex sighed loudly. "What is your problem with Emily now?"

"What do you mean *now*? She's *always* gotten on my damn nerves."

"Seriously? Even after the girl came through for us?" Alex reminded. "You forget, she was the one who played a major part in our retaliation plan."

Chasity and Malajia looked at Alex with confusion. "She didn't even *fight*," Chasity pointed out.

"Right," Malajia agreed. "I mean she could have thrown a punch, a tissue or *something*."

Alex glared at them. "*First* off, you already knew that she wasn't going to fight anybody. She barely wanted to tail them. Second, it was four on four so there was no need for her to get in it."

"Shit, when that fat owl pushed me into that damn wall, that was the time for her to get in it," Malajia commented, folding her arms.

"Think about it, miserable and stupid," Alex bit out. "If Emily had fought with the rest of us, she would've gotten locked up. *Then* how would we have gotten out? *She* was the one who called Ms. Trisha, after all."

Chasity rolled her eyes as Malajia pointed at Alex. "Call me stupid one more time, hear?" Malajia warned.

Ignoring Malajia, Alex focused on Sidra, who was busy examining the silver polish on her nails. She noticed that Sidra hadn't jumped to Emily's defense once.

"So Sidra, are you on *their* side?"

Sidra looked at Alex. "Meaning?"

"Well, these two have basically destroyed Emily's character, and you haven't said anything."

Sidra sighed. "Regarding Emily not fighting? No, I don't agree with them. She didn't need to do that, and she came through when we needed her," she said. "*However,* I *am* starting to get annoyed with her childish behavior."

Alex tossed her hands in the air. "Really, Sidra?"

"Look, I'm not saying that I don't *like* the girl, because I do," Sidra amended. "I love Emily to death, but she has got to get out of that childish, my-mama-won't-let-me-do-anything mentality...I mean the girl is about to turn eighteen, she needs to change that."

After a few seconds Malajia slammed her hand on the table, "Boom!"

Sidra laughed as Chasity shook her head.

"And you did that for *what*?" Alex hissed.

"She told *you*," Malajia shot back.

Alex waved a hand at her dismissively. "Whatever, you three are no help at all."

"We *will* be," Sidra promised. "We'll think of something nice for her...something that she will comfortable with doing."

"So no reggae parties with drinks, huh?" Malajia joked.

"No, nobody needs a repeat of the last one," Alex laughed. "Isn't that right, vomit Parker and stumbling Simmons?"

"You're corny Alex," Chasity spat.

"Yes! Always," Malajia added, then erupted with laughter at the annoyed look on Alex's face.

"Why are we out here?" Jason asked, looking at his watch. He'd been standing in the parking lot of Daniel's Hall for nearly ten minutes with Josh and David, Sunday evening.

"Don't know, Mark called me about a half hour ago and told me to get everybody and meet him out here," Josh replied, scratching his head. He smiled when he saw the girls approaching.

"What's this about?" Sidra yawned. "It's almost nine."

"Mark wanted us to meet him down here," David informed, pushing his silver glasses up on his nose.

"Knowing Mark, it's something stupid," Malajia grouched. She craned her neck when she heard a car horn.

A dark blue Nissan Altima pulled in front of them. "Who is that? And why are they so close?" Alex frowned.

Chasity shot her a side glance. "Yeah, cause we can see who that is in the dark?" she jeered.

"That was a rhetorical question," Alex returned, putting her hand up.

The driver's side door opened, peaking the curiosity of the group and ceasing the impending bickering between Alex and Chasity.

"Seriously?" Sidra jeered, seeing Mark step outside wearing a pair of sunglasses.

Alex sucked her teeth as she watched him lean against the door and fold his arms across his chest. "It's not even any *sun* out here!" she exclaimed.

"Mark, whose car did you steal?" Malajia teased, folding her arms.

Mark snatched the sunglasses from his face "This is *mine*, you fool," he shot back.

A big smile crept across Malajia's face. "Yours? As in *you* can drive us places now too?" she asked, reaching out to touch the car.

"Get your nasty fingers off it," Mark barked, smacking her hand away.

Malajia reached out and touched Mark's arm. "Ooh, this car is making you look kinda cute," she mocked.

"Oh, *now* you think so huh? *Now* you want me. Get off me." Mark jerked his arm out of Malajia's grasp.

Malajia busted out laughing as Mark gave her a little push. "Boy please, *nothing* on this earth will make me want you."

"How did you pull this off?" Josh asked, changing the subject.

"Remember last semester around finals when Mom said that if I brought my grades up, I can get a car?"

"Not really?" Josh joked, he snickered at the silly look on Mark's face. "I'm kidding man. I'm surprised you pulled it off, when you failed Sociology."

Mark frowned. "Why you always gotta be up in my business?"

Josh rolled his eyes. "Whatever dawg, I'm going to bed," he declared, walking off along with the rest of group.

"So, nobody wants to go for a spin?" Mark yelled after them.

"No boy, it's late," Sidra threw over her shoulder. "Take your butt to bed."

The past few weeks were a blur to the students at Paradise Valley University. Besides the slow weather changeover from winter to spring, midterms had the stress level of the students at an all-time high.

"What is it about tests that make me crazy?" Sidra whined, flopping down on her bed.

Malajia shot her a glance. "Whatchu mean *tests*? Girl, when the cafeteria runs out of *coffee,* your butt gets crazy," she said.

Sidra sat up on her bed. "You're exaggerating, as usual," she bit back.

"Okay, let's not start with the arguing," Alex slid in, removing her jacket and tossing it on the chair. "Midterms are over, let's try to relax."

"Shit, I'm ready for spring break," Malajia put in. "Where are we going and how long is it gonna take us to get there? I'm hype."

"I have no idea," Sidra shrugged. "But I know where *Chaz* is going."

Chasity rolled her eyes at Sidra as all eyes fixed on her.

"Where are *you* going? And without *us*?" Malajia sneered.

"Miami," Chasity answered evenly.

"What?!" Malajia exclaimed, jumping up. "No invite though? Damn bitch, you're just selfish."

Chasity glared at her. "If I didn't invite you before, you think calling me a selfish bitch is gonna make me do it now?" Chasity shook her head at the silly look on Malajia's face. "You really *are* as stupid as you look."

Sidra opened a bottle of water from her mini fridge. "You know what the worse part is?" she asked the girls. "Chasity owns the condo that she's staying in down there."

"Really, Sidra?" Chasity exclaimed. She revealed to Sidra a while ago of her plans to go to Miami for break, and that she would be staying in the condo that Trisha bought for her when she graduated high school. "And here I thought *Malajia* was the one with the big ass mouth."

"Hey! I resent that," Malajia scoffed, putting her hands on her hips.

Sidra giggled, "I'm sorry Chaz, blame it on my lack of coffee this morning," she defended.

"You might as well just let us come to Miami with you," Malajia pressed. "You know you'll be bored without us."

"Bullshit," Chasity spat. "I need a damn break from y'all."

Malajia sucked her teeth. *Selfish, spoiled heifer.* A sly look appeared on Malajia's face as she had a thought. Reaching into her purse, she pulled out her cell phone and dialed a number.

"I can't believe you actually own a condo…in *Miami* of all places," Alex said. "Not to get all in your business, but why would Ms. Trisha buy you your own condo?"

"Not to get in my business, huh?" Chasity ground out.

"Okay, maybe I want to get *all up* in your business," Alex chuckled.

Chasity rolled her eyes. "I was originally supposed to go to a college in Florida, so she bought me a place in her building," she revealed. "I decided not to go there, but she still kept it for me."

"I'm jealous," Alex admitted.

"I've told you before, you don't want my life," Chasity assured, evenly.

Malajia walked up to Chasity and handed her the cell phone. Chasity eyed Malajia skeptically. "What are you doing?"

"It's for you," Malajia smiled

"Why would anybody who wants to talk to *me* be on *your* raggedy phone?"

"Cause I called Ms. Trisha; she's the one on the phone."

Chasity's mouth dropped open as she snatched the phone from Malajia and put it to her ear. "Yeah?"

"Let them come down to Miami with you," Trisha urged.

Chasity looked at Malajia, who was doing a silly dance. "You fuckin' snitch," she barked.

"Watch your mouth, baby," Trisha warned. She knew that Chasity used quite a bit of profanity, that didn't mean that she liked it. "And, stop being mean. There is more than enough room in that condo for them, and they'll have a great time."

Chasity was too irritated to say anything but "fine," through clenched teeth.

"Just let me know what day you girls will arrive, and I'll make sure you have everything you need. Everything is on me," Trisha promised. "I'll talk to you later, love you."

"Mmm hmm." Chasity abruptly ended her call. Before Malajia could react, Chasity tossed the phone at her. Malajia let out a shriek and ducked. The phone hit the door behind her.

"Damn it Chasity!" Malajia hollered, grabbing her phone from the floor. "Look what you did, you cracked the screen! You owe me another goddamn phone."

"Sue me, bitch," Chasity hissed.

Malajia's eyes widened. "Fuck you," she threw back.

"Well…at least we get to go to Miami now," Sidra said after a few moments of strained silence.

"Good point Sidra, good point," Alex agreed, smiling. She could care less about Chasity's attitude, or Malajia's broken phone. Alex was just happy to have the opportunity to go on an all-expense-paid trip to Miami.

Chapter 20

Emily quickened her pace along the path back to her dorm. She'd spent the majority of her time after her last class of the day sitting in the library, trying to concentrate on studying. But she couldn't. It was a Friday, and more importantly, it was her eighteenth birthday.

The look on her face was somber. Not only had her mother informed her earlier that morning that she was coming down to bring her home for the weekend, none of her friends wished her a happy birthday.

Why am I not important to them? Do they not care? were the questions that played in her head all day.

Emily was so lost in her thoughts that she almost didn't see Chasity and Malajia in front of her. She stopped just short of colliding with them.

"Hi girls," she stammered, removing her gray sweat jacket. The breezy weather was perfect for late March, but her quick pace made her hot.

"Whatcha doin?" Malajia asked, smiling brightly.

"Um, going to the room, I have to pack," Emily revealed. "My mom is coming to get me later tonight to take me home."

Chasity rolled her eyes. *Not surprised.* "Look, we need you to come with us right now," she demanded. "We want to show you something."

Emily felt nervous. The big, sneaky smile on Malajia's face and the urgency in Chasity's voice didn't sit well her. "Um, where's Alex and Sidra?"

Malajia and Chasity exchanged a quick glance, before turning back to Emily. Malajia frowned. "They're not here, obviously."

Emily looked at the ground. "Oh," was all that she could say. "I was just wondering."

"Why does it matter where they are?" Malajia asked. "What, you don't wanna hang with *us*?"

Emily stared at them. *The question is, do you guys really wanna hang out with me?*

"You're not *afraid* of us, are you?" Chasity smirked.

Yes. "Well…Um…" Emily hesitated.

Chasity frowned, "You're not *serious* are you?" she hissed.

"Um, can you blame me?" Emily asked softly.

Chasity sighed loudly. "You know what, I don't have time for this Emily," she barked. "Let's go and let's go now."

Emily swallowed hard as she watched Chasity and Malajia turn and walk off. Emily clutched her books to her chest and slowly trailed behind.

The ride in the back of Chasity's car was nerve-wracking for Emily. She didn't know exactly how long the ride was, but she was almost certain it had been over fifteen minutes. The fact that she was blindfolded only made matters worse.

"Um, where are we?" Emily asked, once she heard the car turn off.

"The cemetery," Chasity joked, earning a snicker from Malajia.

"Huh?" Emily exclaimed.

"Don't move, we'll be right back," Malajia said, laughter filling her voice.

"Wh—Where are you going?"

"To dig a ditch," Chasity replied, with a seriousness that caused Emily to gasp. Malajia busted out laughing as she stepped out the car and shut the door.

Chasity and Malajia headed inside the Paradise Valley Arcade Palace. Although frequented by children, this, besides the mall, was a major hangout for the local college and high school students. One section held wall-to-wall arcade games, and another section was strictly for eating. Finding Alex and Sidra in the food section, decorating a table, the girls walked over.

"Did you get her?" Alex asked, tying several pink and white balloons to a chair.

"Yeah, she's in the car," Malajia laughed.

"What's so funny?" Sidra asked, straightening out the plastic pink table cloth.

"This chick had the nerve to ask us where you two were when we went to get her," Chasity scoffed. "Like she was scared to come with us alone."

Alex placed a large birthday card and a small, wrapped gift in front of the decorated chair. "Do you blame her?" she asked. "You can be very intimidating, Chasity."

"What about *me*?" Malajia asked as Chasity sucked her teeth at Alex's comment.

"*You're* just simple," Alex joked. Malajia wasn't amused and it showed on her face.

"We're finished; can you two go get her?" Sidra asked, removing a plastic cover from a small round birthday cake

"I should've put her ass in the trunk," Chasity jeered, turning to walk out.

"Be nice Lucifer, it's her birthday," Alex called after her.

Chasity and Malajia walked back inside with a nervous, blindfolded Emily not even five minutes later. Alex signaled for Malajia to remove Emily's blindfold.

Emily put her hands over her face in shock as she eyed the scene in front of her: the balloons, the decorated table, the birthday cake. *They remembered!*

She gave each of her friends a hug. "Oh my gosh! Thanks you guys!"

Emily's eyes began to glisten with tears. Chasity shot her a confused look. "You're not gonna cry, are you?"

"No," Emily lied, smiling.

"Aww, come here and sit down," Alex chortled, putting her arm around Emily. "You know we couldn't forget to do something for you on your birthday."

"I kinda did," Emily admitted, pushing herself up to the table. "This means a lot to me that you girls did this."

"Well, we love you Emily," Sidra smiled.

"Thank God, I'm starving," Malajia said as the waiters came to the table to begin setting up a small taco bar.

Alex shot Malajia a stern look as she watched her grab her plate and pile ground beef, taco shells, veggies, sour cream, salsa and refried beans on it. "Malajia, can you let the birthday girl go first?"

Malajia paused, mid scoop. "Emily know it's her birthday. Not getting her food first isn't gonna change that," she sneered, setting the full plate in front of her. "Always up in my business."

Emily giggled as she began to fix her plate.

"Girl, you eat like food is going out of style," Sidra directed to Malajia. "I'm surprised you're as skinny as you are."

"Fast metabolism," Malajia shrugged, preparing her tacos. She looked around the table. "No drinks?"

"As in liquor? No you fool," Alex bristled. "We're under twenty-one remember?"

Unable to think of anything else to say to that, Malajia waved her hand at Alex dismissively. "So Emily, you going to Miami with us for spring break?" she asked after several seconds of silence.

Emily looked up from her freshly made tacos. "Um...probably not." She let out a sigh as she went back to eating. Emily recalled that the girls told her of their planned trip to Miami for spring break a few days ago. She also recalled the feeling of sadness that she felt—going would be out of the question.

Malajia slammed her hand on the table. "Seriously Emily? What else can you *possibly* be doing that would be better than that?"

Nothing, Emily thought. "Well…I have to go home," she answered. "My mom—"

"Can kiss my ass, because you're *going*," Malajia snapped, cutting Emily off.

"Malajia, back off of her," Alex cut in, pointing her fork in Malajia's direction.

Malajia put her hand up, signaling Alex to be quiet while she stared at Emily. "So, you're gonna miss out on spring break...In Miami?" Malajia was so irritated with Emily; she wished that the girl would take a stand for once.

"Malajia, she'll never let me go," Emily pointed out.

"Well, you better get to lying then," Malajia shot back.

Sidra hated that Malajia was coming down so hard on Emily, but she did have a point. "Emily listen, you're eighteen now, legally you're an *adult*," Sidra cut in. "And you're in college. This is supposed to be the best time of your life and you're letting your mother take that from you."

"Why are you two even wasting your time on this shit?" Chasity hissed. "You already know the girl is too damn scared to ask, let alone lie."

Emily put her head down. "I really don't know what you girls want me to do." she stammered.

"I *want* you to stop whining," Chasity bit out.

"Grow a pair and tell your lonely ass mom that you're going," Malajia added.

"Chasity, Malajia, that's enough," Alex barked. She'd had enough with the girls jumping down Emily's throat. "If Emily isn't comfortable with asking her mother, then we just have to accept that she won't be going."

"I don't really give a shit if she goes or not," Chasity sneered, earning a glare from Alex.

"Fine," Malajia huffed, picking up another taco. "Nobody bring her back any souvenirs." Sidra put her hand over her face to suppress a snicker at Malajia's silly comment. "Let her stay home and sniff her dirty ass stuffed animals."

"Malajia, you're about to get slapped," Alex warned.

After spending approximately a half hour of talking and eating, the girls decided to take full advantage of their outing and play some games.

Malajia grabbed her stomach as she waited her turn on the car racing game. "My stomach is acting like a complete asshole right now," she groaned.

Chasity chuckled, standing next to her. "That's what your greedy ass gets for eating all those nasty refried beans."

"Nobody asked you," Malajia spat. "And they're not nasty…I just ate too much."

"Whatever you say, bubbles," Chasity teased, earning a sidelong glare from Malajia.

Malajia stomped her foot on the floor. The two college-aged guys playing in front of them had already gone for three rounds, and didn't look like they planned on getting up any time soon.

"Dude, you continued the game like five times, give somebody *else* a turn," Malajia seethed.

"So?" one guy countered, eyes not leaving the game. "We have plenty of tokens. We're not moving."

"So you're just gonna sit your dumb ass on this game all night?" Chasity spat, folding her arms.

"Yep," the other guy laughed, as their game ended. "We're gonna continue as long as we can."

Malajia and Chasity watched as the time began to countdown on the screen in front of them. Exchanging glances, Chasity slowly walked up beside one guy who had his cup of tokens sitting on the floor next to him.

As he was about to reach for some tokens, she raised her high-heeled boot-covered foot and gave the large cup a kick, spilling its contents to the floor.

"Both guys looked up at her, shock written on their faces. "What the hell?" one exclaimed.

"Oops," Chasity smiled, voice filled with feigned innocence.

"Oops for *me* too," Malajia added, walking over and with her foot, kicking the tokens across the floor.

"That was uncalled for!" the other guy yelled, as he scrambled for tokens. He put his hands on his head in astonishment as a zero appeared on the screen, ending their long streak. "I can't believe you just did that."

Chasity and Malajia just stood there smiling in satisfaction. "Oh, you know what Malajia, this isn't even the game that I wanted to play," Chasity mocked.

"Oh well," Malajia shrugged. Both girls turned on their heels and walked away, leaving the guys fuming.

Sidra vigorously pushed several buttons on a joystick. "Come on, why won't this damn man kick?" she fumed, watching her player lose for the third time on a fighting game.

"You lose again!" a middle schooler boasted, jumping up and down.

Sidra shot the girl a seething look.

Seeing that Sidra was at her boiling point, Alex giggled and put her hand on her shoulder. "Relax Sid, it's only a game."

"Let's go again," Sidra challenged, ignoring Alex. She put tokens into both her and the little girls' game. "It's on."

"Okay, but don't get mad when I beat you again."

Sidra clenched her jaw. *Smart ass.*

Emily and Alex watched with amusement as Sidra tried her hardest to beat the girl, but she once again proved to be a better opponent. Sidra slammed her hand on the screen. "Seriously?" she exclaimed.

"Ha ha, you lose again," the girl taunted before skipping off.

Sidra followed the girls' progress for several seconds, before spinning around to face her friends. "Did you see that cheating mess?"

"Sid, it's a game and she's a child," Alex chortled. "Don't get so wound up."

"You didn't lose four games in a row to a damn twelve year old, or *however* old that little ball of sunshine was," Sidra spat.

"No, you got me there," Alex giggled, earning a glower from Sidra.

"Very damn funny," she seethed, flinging her ponytail over her shoulder and sauntering away.

Alex shook her head. "Come on Emily, let's get the others and get out of here before Sidra cusses somebody's child out," she urged.

Alex and Emily rounded up the girls and were on their way to the exit when something caught Emily's eye. "Ooh, the ball bin," she beamed. Grabbing Alex arm, she took off for the large bin filled with colorful plastic balls. "Let's go get in."

Malajia sucked her teeth as Alex and Emily jumped into the bin. "Don't nobody wanna jump in no damn balls," Malajia scoffed, putting her hands on her hips.

Sidra rolled her eyes. "Your English is terrible," she complained. "You were taught better than that."

Irritated with Sidra's critique, Malajia spun around and stood in Sidra's face. "You know what, you prissy ass—" Malajia's rant was halted as Sidra gave her a push, sending her falling backwards into the bin. As she fell, Malajia reached out and grabbed Chasity's arm pulling her in with her.

Sidra laughed as both girls came to the surface.

"What the hell did you do that for?" Chasity fumed, tossing one of the balls at Malajia.

Malajia ducked out of the way, sending the ball flying passed her. "Were I go, *you* go," she taunted.

Alex dove in and once back to the surface, looked at Sidra who was standing arms folded, watching. "Sidra, get in. It's fun," she pressed.

Sidra shook her head as she turned her lip up. "I wish I *would* jump in that nasty bin."

Alex reached out and grabbed hold of Sidra's ankle. "Girl, get your snobby butt in here," she said, teeth clenched as she pulled a screaming Sidra into the bin.

"You salty," Malajia laughed, pointing to the visibly irritated Sidra.

While the girls were playing, a few children walked over to the bin and picked up balls to throw.

Chasity looked up as one of the boys raised his hand to throw one at her. "You better not," she warned. "I'll punch that fuckin' smile off your face."

Alex was astonished. "Chasity! He's a *child*," she exclaimed, as the boys took off running.

"So?" Chasity returned.

Alex sighed. "First Sidra is about to cuss a child out over a game, and now *you* threaten one. It's safe to say it's time to go."

Chapter 21

Emily sat on her bed in her bedroom in New Jersey, staring out of the small window. The cloudy weather on that Saturday afternoon matched Emily's somber mood. While her mother talked during the ride from campus the previous evening, Emily's thoughts were focused on spring break, merely weeks away. She wanted to go have fun with her friends, and hated that fact that she couldn't.

Emily let out a long sigh, clutching her pillow to her chest. She heard a light tap on the door and turned around just in time to see her mother walk in.

She rolled her eyes when her mother wasn't looking. *What is the purpose of knocking if you're just going to walk in anyway?* She thought to herself.

Ms. Harris walked over and gave her daughter a big hug. "How did you sleep sweetie?"

"I slept okay," Emily shrugged.

"I have a great day planned for us," Ms. Harris promised, sitting on the bed next to Emily.

Emily feigned a smile. She'd much rather be back on campus with her friends. She doubted that anything that her mother planned would be half as fun.

"Oh," her mother started, having a thought. "I know that spring break is coming up, so why don't the two of us go away together?"

Emily's eyes widened, the smile still plastered to her face. *Oh no, no, no!*

"We can go to South Carolina to see Grandma."

Emily put her hand over her face. As much as she adored her grandmother and would love to visit her, she didn't want to spend her spring break down there. Not when she should be having fun in Miami. *I can't do this. I can't waste my spring break…It's now or never Emily.*

Emily took a big deep breath before grabbing her mother's hand. "Mommy Um…I can't come home for spring break." She winced once she saw the look of shock and anger on her mother's face.

"And why *not?*"

"Well…" *Think Emily, think!* "Truth is…I didn't do so well on my Science midterm so the professor said that if I stay for the week and help her with an experiment, she will give me some extra credit towards my grade."

Please buy it, Mommy. Emily sat there in anticipation as she waited for her mother to respond.

Ms. Harris sighed. "Well, I must say that I'm disappointed that you won't be coming home for your break…*and* at the fact that you didn't do well on your midterm." She frowned at her worried daughter.

Emily lowered her head. "I know, I'm sorry," she mumbled.

Ms. Harris's face relaxed into a smile. "But at least you're trying to do better. School is more important, so you do what you need to do."

She bought it. Emily smiled as her mother patted her hand. She held the look of relief as her mother rose from the bed.

"I'm going to make some lunch, would you like some?"

"Sure," Emily beamed, mood lifted. As she watched her mother walk out of the room, Emily did a little dance in her seat. "Yes," she celebrated to herself.

"Dude, you've washed that car five times this week," David chortled, watching Mark meticulously wipe smudges from his car. "And it's about to rain, you're just wasting your time."

Mark cut his eye at David. "Why are you always up in my business, dawg?" he roared. "You're just jealous because you don't have a car."

David shook his head. "I'd rather have a new laptop than a car," he shot back.

"Well you don't have that *either*, dork," Mark spat.

David opened his mouth to make a comeback, but Josh walked up, freezing his thoughts.

"Hey guys," Josh greeted, slinging his book bag over his shoulder.

"It's Saturday, what's up with the book bag?" Mark laughed.

"I'm going to work, my stuff is in here," Josh informed. "As a matter of fact, I'm running late, can you give me a lift?"

Mark looked at Josh as if he lost his mind. "I hope you got gas money."

Josh's eyes widened. "Gas money? Really Mark? For a ride that's not even fifteen minutes long?"

"You damn skippy," Mark confirmed.

Josh looked at his watch; he had no time and wasn't in the mood for Mark's nonsense. "Look here brotha, you're *going* to give me a ride," Josh demanded.

Mark sucked his teeth. "Man—"

"All the money you owe me, I should make you give me rides every damn day."

"He has a point," David agreed, folding his arms.

"Man, your damn head has a point, *David*!" Mark barked. Ignoring the confused look from David at his comeback, Mark rubbed the back of his neck. "Just get in the damn car."

Satisfied, Josh removed the bag from his shoulder and got in the front seat.

"You didn't have to bring up old shit either," Mark grumbled, settling in the driver seat.

"Yeah, yeah. Can we just go?" Josh replied, fastening his seat belt.

Mark looked over at David as he jiggled the door handle to the back seat. "I hope you don't think you're getting in this car," he bit out.

"Mark, stop playing, it's starting to rain," David replied, banging on the window.

"Oh well, your glasses need a bath anyway," Mark laughed, starting the car.

"Dude, I don't have time for this. Let David in the car and come on!" Josh snapped. He already didn't feel like going to work anyway, Mark's childish antics were making things worse.

Mark sucked his teeth as he pushed the button to unlock the door. "Hey man, watch the leather," he shouted as David hopped in to the car.

"Just shut up and pull off!" David barked, slamming the door.

"*You* shut up," Mark mumbled, pulling off.

Josh hopped out of the car as soon as Mark pulled into a parking spot in front of the Pizza Shack. "Good looking bro," Josh said, hurrying inside. He was shocked to see Mark follow him in. "What are you doing?"

"Damn, can I get a pizza? Is that okay with you?" Mark scoffed.

"Oh," Josh shrugged. "Knock yourself out."

As Josh headed behind the counter, Mark tapped him on the shoulder. "Yo, you gonna put that pizza on your tab or what?"

Josh narrowed his eyes at Mark. He knew it. He knew Mark had an ulterior motive for coming inside of the parlor. "If you don't get your freeloading ass out of here, I'm gonna smack you with this pizza dough," Josh slowly warned, pointing to a freshly-made ball on the counter behind him.

"Your tone is uncalled for," Mark jeered.

Josh shook his head just as Alex walked up, notepad in hand. "Mark, nobody is giving you any free pizza today," she commented. "Pay like everybody else."

"What good is it having friends who work at a pizza place if I can't get free food?" Mark said, leaning over the counter.

"I don't have time for this," Josh seethed, walking away.

"Pay, or get out of here, fool," Alex ordered. "And stop acting like you don't have any money. Your parents just bought you a car, so I know they give you spending money on the regular."

Mark waved his hand dismissively at her as David stormed inside.

"Mark, will you come on? You have me sitting in that car looking stupid," David fumed.

Mark checked his reply as he saw the manager head to the counter. He pointed to David. "Aye, my man, he's tryna get free pizza."

David stood there confused as Mark hurried out of the door. "Huh?" David exclaimed.

Alex concealed a laugh as she began putting her orders into the computer.

Alex looked up from her notebook. Stretching, a frown of concern crossed her face. "Mel, did you hear that?"

Malajia, with her notebook over her face, sat up on her bed. "Hear what?"

Alex paused for a second as she listened. Not hearing anything, she shook her head. "Never mind."

Malajia stood up from her bed and headed over to grab a brownie from the top of her microwave. "What did you hear, crazy?" she joked.

Alex leaned back in her seat and ran her hands through her hair, scratching her scalp. "I don't know exactly," she admitted. "It sounded like somebody was yelling or something."

"Well its midnight, so I sure hope it wasn't," Malajia observed, glancing at the clock on her nightstand. "It was probably one of those weird ass animals that keep showing up on campus."

Alex laughed as she pushed herself back up to her desk.

"I swear, the other night I saw something that looked like an alligator with a cat head," Malajia added.

"You're silly," Alex commiserated, picking up her pencil. She spun around when the door opened. "You're back, finally," she smiled to Emily, who walked in, carrying her overnight bag. "I'm surprised your mom dropped you off this late."

"Shit, *I'm* not surprised," Malajia sneered, cutting off Emily's reply. "She probably wanted to sit on Emily as long as she could."

Emily shook her head at Malajia's snide remark before turning to Alex. "Well, she took a nap earlier and overslept." Emily sat on her bed and folded her arms as Alex and Malajia went back to their books. "So, I have some news," she announced.

"What's that Emily?" Alex asked, eyes not leaving her book.

"If it has anything to do with your mom, you can keep it to yourself," Malajia joked, closing her textbook. She giggled as Alex threw a balled up piece of paper at her.

"Well, that's a shame, because if I keep it to myself, then you won't know that I'm coming to Miami with you guys."

Malajia and Alex looked at her with shock. "Really?" Alex exclaimed.

Malajia scratched her head. "How the hell did you pull *that* off?"

"I actually told a...um...tiny lie," Emily admitted, much to Alex's dismay.

"You *lied*?"

"Come on Alex, you know that if I told her the truth she would never let me go," Emily defended. "You know how she feels about you all, not to mention she wouldn't want me traveling across the country without her."

"I understand that and all Em, but lying isn't the answer," Alex chided. "We wanted you to stand up to her, not lie."

"Alex, leave the girl alone," Malajia cut in as Emily sighed. She was impressed with her roommate. She finally did something that took guts. "You heard what she said; the truth wasn't an option for her. Stop acting like you never lied to your parents before."

Alex folded her arms. "I never said that I *didn't*," she clarified. "But it was never anything this big."

Malajia waved her hand at Alex. She could care less about her nagging. She was more concerned with something else. "So Em...what lie did you tell her?"

"I told her that due to a bad midterm grade in Science, the teacher said that if I helped her with an experiment for the week than she will give me extra credit."

"Oh *really?*" Malajia, nodded in amazement, as she grabbed a piece of paper and a pen from her bed.

Alex glanced over at Malajia, who began jotting something down. "Girl, what are you doing?"

"Nothing, nothing," Malajia said, writing. "Emily you told her that the teacher said *what?*"

Alex walked over and snatched the paper from her. "Cut that out."

"Oh come on, If 'mama-smother-em' fell for that, *my parents* are definitely gonna fall for it," Malajia argued, trying to get her paper back.

"Girl, please! Like your parents are gonna believe that a teacher is really gonna raise *your* sorry grade," Alex shot back, ripping the paper to shreds.

Malajia rolled her eyes as she picked up the phone. Tapping her nails on the nightstand, she waiting for the person on the other end to answer. "Chasity," she beamed. "Listen girl, I've got some news...Emily is going to Miami with us. Let me tell you, she lied to—"

Alex frowned, noticing the shocked look on Malajia's face. "What did Chaz say?"

"Her ignorant ass just hung up on me," Malajia exclaimed, slamming the phone down. Alex and Emily dissolved in a fit of laughter.

Malajia scribbled in her notebook as Mr. Bradley lectured. Sociology was the farthest thing from Malajia's mind. With twenty minutes left to her class, this was the last thing between her and spring break.

Mark, who was sitting in the seat next to her, leaned close. "Are you taking notes?" he whispered.

"Nope," she returned, eyes not leaving the doodles on her notebook.

Mark looked at the chalk board, before leaning back over to her. "Yo, what is he talking about anyway?"

"Who knows," Malajia's tone was low and flat.

Mark suddenly raised his hand as Mr. Bradley was in mid-sentence. "What is it Mr. Johnson?" he asked, voice not hiding his frustration.

Mark slowly put his hand back down. "Um...What are you talking about?"

Mr. Bradley glared at Mark as a few students snickered. He pointed to the door. "Get out."

Mark's eyes widened as Malajia put her hand over her mouth, trying to silence her laughter.

"Mr. Bradley, why are you putting me out?" Mark asked, holding his hands up. "I only asked a question."

"Mr. Johnson, this is the third time that you have interrupted my class today to ask me that question. It's clear that you're not paying attention, and I will not continue to let you disrupt the lesson for the rest of your classmates."

Mark grabbed his notebook and shoved it in his book bag. "This is some bull, man," he mumbled, rising from his seat.

Malajia felt tears pouring out of her eyes at the result of her trying to hold in her laugh. As Mark hurried out of the room, Malajia, not being able to hold her laughter in any longer; stood up and ran out after him.

"You're gonna fail if you keep getting kicked out," Malajia laughed, shutting the door behind her.

"Man *fuck* that class, I wanted to leave early anyway," Mark jeered. "So what are you and the rest of the banshees doing for spring break?"

"Going home," Malajia answered, moving some hair from her face away.

Mark stared at Malajia skeptically. *You answered that too damn fast.*

"What?" Malajia snapped, noticing his staring.

"You're going home, huh?" he asked, slowly folding his arms.

She frowned at him, placing her hands on her hips. "Yes," she answered, tone sharp.

"So you ain't doin' nothin' the entire break, huh?" he challenged. "*You*, Malajia I-can't-stand-my-family Simmons; is gonna go home and sit there for the *entire* week without anything to do, huh?...I smell bullshit."

Malajia's mouth fell open. "Are you calling me a liar?" she exclaimed.

"You damn right." Mark pointed his finger in her face. "You bitched nonstop about Thanksgiving, and that was just four days."

"So?"

"You and the other witches are doing something fun, and you don't want me and the other fellas to know about it. You holdin' out."

Malajia rolled her eyes. "I don't have time for your mess, I have to finish learning." As she went to open the door, she was greeted by her book bag and jacket.

"You might as well stay out here, since you like it so much," Mr. Bradley hissed, before closing the door in her face.

Malajia stood there, astonished for several seconds, before sauntering off. Mark followed her progress, laughing after her.

Sidra grabbed a steaming bag of freshly popped popcorn from the microwave. "I can't believe we're leaving for Florida tomorrow," she mused, sitting on Alex's bed.

Friday evening was upon the students, thus beginning their spring break week. The girls planned on getting an early start the next morning. Bags already packed, Sidra, along with Chasity, headed to the other girls' room to kill time.

"I still say we should've flown," Malajia said, folding one of many skimpy clothing items and shoving it into her small suitcase.

"Flown *where*? To the poor house? Cause that's where I would end up if I would've paid for a plane ticket," Alex sneered, pulling a dark green duffle bag from the bottom of her closet.

"And so *now* we have to suffer through a twelve hour drive from Virginia to Florida," Chasity bit out, grabbing a handful of popcorn out of Sidra's bag.

"Relax, we already agreed to take turns driving down there," Sidra slid in. "Three hours each."

"I wish I could help drive," Emily put in, opening her suitcase. "No license."

"Shit, y'all can take the car. I still have time to buy a plane ticket," Chasity jeered.

"Oh bitch, get over it," Malajia hissed, zipping her suitcase. "We're all riding down together."

Chasity's eyes became slits. "Please don't make me slap you tonight," she warned.

"Do what you want, but come tomorrow, I'll be in Miami in *your* condo," Malajia taunted, sticking her tongue out at the visibly fuming Chasity.

Emily grabbed a few pairs of pajamas out of her drawer. "Hey, what do you think the guys will do for the break?" she asked.

"I don't know and don't care," Malajia scoffed.

Emily pushed some hair behind her ear. "Do you think we should invite them?"

"No," Chasity and Malajia spat in unison.

"Don't nobody wanna see Mark's raggedy ass all week," Malajia added. "I see *enough* of his beggin' behind."

Sidra shook her head. "Uncalled for insults aside," she ground out, pointing her finger at Malajia. "This is a *girls* trip, sweetie."

Emily slowly closed her drawer. "But...I think it'll be nice if they came along too," she insisted.

"And why is that Emilyyyyy?" Malajia groaned, flopping around on Alex's bed.

"Girl, get off my damn bed doing all of that," Alex snapped, tossing a pillow at Malajia. "Was that really necessary?"

Malajia sat up straight. "It *wasn't,* but she pissed me off," she clarified, turning her attention to Emily. "Look, they're not coming. So stop asking about it...Well maybe *Jason* can—"

"Jason's not coming *either*," Chasity spat out, earning a giggle from Malajia.

Emily just shrugged. "I was just asking," she mumbled.

"Alex, no!" Malajia exclaimed as Alex proceeded to place a shirt in her bag. "You better not put that in there."

Alex looked up with confusion. "What is your loud butt talking about, Malajia?"

"Take that ugly ass shirt outta your bag," Malajia scoffed, pointing to the brown and yellow stripped shirt in Alex's hand. "I swear Alex, don't put that mess in there; nobody wants to walk down the street with you while you're wearing that."

Alex shot Malajia a glare as she pointed at her. "Malajia, in the words of Chasity, please don't make me slap you tonight," she hissed.

Chapter 22

"How are we going to fit all of these bags in this trunk?" Sidra yawned, standing over the open trunk of Chasity's car around seven the next morning. There were several suitcases sitting on the ground waiting to be loaded.

"*I* know, somebody's shit is going back in the room," Chasity answered. "You know it's mostly Malajia's anyway."

Malajia looked at the one small carryon bag that Chasity stuffed in the corner of the trunk "I'm surprised *you* only have one bag Miss I-own-half-the-damn-mall," she sneered.

"Yeah well, I have a closet full of clothes in that condo already," Chasity taunted. "So I'll let y'all fight over which one of your raggedy bags stays."

Malajia glared at Chasity's retreating back. "Spoiled bitch," she mumbled as Chasity disappeared in the dorm.

Sidra and Malajia exchanged glances before grabbing their bags and struggling to get them in the trunk.

"Oh I'm gettin' all *my* bags in here," Malajia assured, bumping Sidra with her hip.

"Mel stop playing!" Sidra shouted.

Jason and Mark, gym bags in their hands, walked the path towards the gym. With the weather now much nicer, the two guys decided to do their workouts earlier. They knew they would have free reign over the weights and machines. "You going home or staying on campus for break?" Mark asked.

Jason shrugged. "Not sure yet," he admitted. "I don't have anything to do at home, so I may just chill here."

"Yeah, Mom wants me to come home, but I told her I didn't wanna be all bored with her and Dad," Mark said, he laughed slightly. "Naw, I'm lying, my parents told me to stay where I'm at. I guess that one weekend I went home was enough for them."

Jason was about to take a sip from his water bottle, when he noticed Alex and Emily heading outside of their dorm, each holding a bag.

"What are you two doing out here this early?" Alex smiled, seeing the guys approach.

Jason raised an eyebrow. "We should be asking *you* the same question."

"Going somewhere?" Mark asked, folding his arms.

"Yeah, I'm going home to Philly," Alex answered. "I'm riding with Chasity."

"Yeah and my mom is waiting for me," Emily carefully added. "In the parking lot…at Torrence Hall."

Mark looked both girls up and down as he sucked his teeth. "That's a real coincidence," he nodded. "You're leaving now, Chaz is leaving now, Sidra's gone, Malajia's gone and Emily's leaving….at the same time…Since when does *everyone* leave at the same time?"

"He has a point," Jason chuckled.

"We all leave around the same time every damn break," Alex spat, shifting her bag from one hand to the other.

"Whatchu mean *every*? We've only had two of em' so far," Mark shot back. "Well…Besides this one."

Alex rolled her eyes. "Mark, you're holding us up," she ground out.

"I think you girls are up to something," Mark maintained, "Mel was acting all weird the other day and now y'all are up all early and to do what?...To go *home*? Come on now."

"Look, some of us miss our home and want to get there early. So leave us alone," Alex fumed, maneuvering around him and walking away.

Emily's departure was halted by Jason and Mark, who stepped in front of her "Not so fast little one," Mark said.

"What's up you guys?" she asked innocently.

Mark waved his hand at her. "Don't give us that cute little innocent act," he bit out. "Now, you and the girls are going somewhere, and we want to know where."

Emily looked back and forth between Mark and Jason, and swallowed hard.

"Come on, I need everything that I have," Malajia whined, trying to shove another one of her overnight bags into the trunk of Chasity's Lexus.

"Mel you have four bags...*four*!" Alex hollered, holding four fingers up in Malajia's face.

"*I* know what the number four looks like," Malajia shot back.

"Whatever," Alex countered. "The point is that *I* only have one bag. Chasity has one bag, Emily has one bag, and there is one bag of snacks and Sidra—"

"Has two bags, but one of mine is sitting on the floor of the front seat with me," Sidra slid in, from the passenger seat.

Malajia stomped her foot on the ground. "Alex, it's not my fault that you have your shit balled up in that raggedy duffle bag of yours," she spat.

Chasity, fed up with the bickering, stepped out of the driver seat, stormed around to the rear of the car, grabbed the largest bag and pushed it into Malajia's hands. "This isn't going," she sneered.

"Chasity I *need* this," Malajia whined.

"Mel! It's nothing but shit for your hair in here and you know that," Chasity snapped.

Malajia took the bag and rolled her eyes. "So what, I need my hooded dryer."

"Get rid of it, or you stay," Chasity warned, heading back to the front of the car.

Malajia stomped over to Sidra's side. "Can I use your key to get in your room?"

Sidra laughed as she handed her keys to Malajia, who just stormed off.

Emily headed up to the car and placed her bag into the trunk just as Alex slid into the back seat. "I'm so excited for this trip," she beamed, sliding next to Alex.

Malajia walked up to the car and got in after a few moments. "Are you happy now?" she directed towards Chasity.

"I'd be happier if you died," Chasity shot back, adjusting her rear view mirror. Malajia sucked her teeth.

Josh rubbed his eyes and sat up in bed. "Who is knocking this early?" he asked, yawning.

David covered his head with his pillow as the knocking got louder. He wished that his roommate would just answer the door.

Josh stumbled out of bed and headed to the door. As soon as he opened it, he groaned. Mark pushed his way into the room, followed by Jason.

"What are you guys doing here so damn early?" Josh yawned as Mark jumped on David's bed.

Mark slapped David on the back of his head. "David! Get up man, we're going on a road trip."

"Get off," David groaned, nudging him away.

"Man, I said get up!" Mark yelled, snatching the pillow from under his head.

"Come on man! Josh, get him off me," David fumed as Mark began hitting him with the pillow.

Josh, still tired and irritated with the noise, rubbed his face frantically. "Mark will you chill out?!" his loud voice boomed off the walls.

Mark slapped David in the face, then jumped off of the bed and darted towards the door. "My bad Dave, my bad." Mark put his hands up as David approached.

"You play too damn much," David wailed, reaching for Mark's collar.

"Okay, guys just chill," Jason put in, stepping in between the two guys.

"What is this all about anyway?" David asked, straightening out his t-shirt.

"We're going on a road trip," Jason revealed.

"Where?" Josh asked, confused.

"To Miami," Mark answered. "The girls lied to us. Emily told us that they're on their way to Chasity's condo in Miami, and they didn't even invite us."

Josh was still confused and it showed on his face. "So why are *we* going?"

"To crash their trip, of course," Jason boasted, folding his arms.

"If they don't want us there then *why* are we going?" David asked.

Mark was fed up with all of the pointless questions. "Man!—you know—fuck y'all corny, bitch ass fools," he snapped.

"Why are you so damn mad?" Josh shot back.

"Cause, we wanna go have fun and y'all over here acting like some nuts," Mark seethed. "What, are you scared of the girls? You think they're gonna throw their tampons at you?"

Jason chuckled. "Come on Mark, forget them."

"Man they—"

"No listen," Jason urged, grabbing Mark's attention "*We'll* just go and see the girls in their bathing suits...that includes *Sidra*." Jason gestured his head towards Josh who stood there wide eyed.

Mark, having caught on to what Jason was trying to do, smiled as he rubbed his hands together. "Oh yeah, let's just go without them."

As Mark and Jason headed for the door, Josh glanced at David, who in turn just shrugged.

"Um, let me grab a quick shower and pack. I'll be right down," Josh relented.

As David made a mad dash for the closet in search of his suitcase, Mark and Jason gave each other high fives before walking out the door.

Chasity let out a loud sigh as she kept her eyes on the road in front of her. She'd driven three hours before passing the wheel to Sidra, who had taken them off of the highway.

"Sidra, why the hell did you take us on these damn back roads?" Chasity fumed.

"I don't like the highway," Sidra shrugged, checking her phone.

"What do you mean?" Malajia sneered from the backseat. "You live in Delaware, the damn highway state. How don't you like driving it?"

Sidra gritted her teeth. "I don't like the highway," she repeated.

"That's why you got kicked off the wheel after a damn hour," Malajia teased.

"Leave me alone, Malajia," Sidra fumed.

"Shut up, shut up," Chasity barked as Sidra and Malajia began to bicker. "I need to get out of this damn car for a minute. I'm pulling over," she announced, pulling her car off to the side of the road. One plus to being on the back roads, there was hardly any traffic.

Alex stepped out of the car and stretched. "I'm starving," she said, walking over to the trunk. "Anybody want anything from the snack bag?" she asked the other girls as they stepped out of the car.

"Why didn't you put the snack bag in the car with *us*, Alex?" Sidra giggled.

"I figured that we would be cramped enough in that back seat without added stuff in there," Alex shrugged.

"Okay, crazy," Chasity jeered.

Alex searched in the open trunk. "Where's the snack bag?" she asked.

The girls walked over. "I thought you put it in there," Sidra assumed, helping Alex search. "The juice is in that bag too."

"I *did*," Alex assured. "It was a red duffle bag. I packed it myself and put it in the trunk before I got in the car."

Chasity sucked her teeth. "Oh but *look*," she groused, grabbing a bag and pulling it out of the trunk. "Malajia's hair bag is back in here."

Malajia's eyes widened as all sets of eyes fixed on her. "What are you looking at *me* for?" she exclaimed.

Chasity threw the bag on the ground. "You took out the damn snack bag while we were in the car and put *your* stupid ass bag back in," she fumed, pointing at her.

"Oh so what," Malajia boasted. "I'd be damned if I go to Miami without my hair stuff. You won't catch me down there looking like a fool."

"Malajia are you *that* self-centered?" Alex asked, folding her arms.

"Yes! And you already know that," Malajia returned. "Don't ask stupid questions, Alex."

Chasity feigned calmness as she pulled her hair back into a ponytail.

Sidra watched as Chasity bent down to tie her sneakers. When Chasity began to stretch her legs Sidra shot her a confused look. "Girl, what are you doing?"

Without answering, Chasity took off running towards Malajia, who shrieked as she fled.

Sidra put her hand over her face. "Oh Geez," she mumbled. "Chaz, the girl has on sandals, for goodness sakes," she called after them.

Alex slammed the trunk. "Malajia has issues," she concluded.

"Don't I know it," Sidra agreed, heading over to the driver's side.

Malajia, tired of running down the dirt road, turned around and put her hands up to stop Chasity from colliding with her. "Okay, quit it," she panted.

Chasity smacked her hands down. "You never cease to prove how fuckin' stupid you are," she seethed.

"Oh please. The only one who cares about the damn food is Alex's big ass," Malajia returned, putting her hands on her knees.

Chasity didn't get a chance to respond because the car pulled up beside them.

Sidra stuck her head out the window. "All right ladies, enough playing. Let's go,"

Chasity and Malajia glared at each other as they walked over to the car. "I shoulda tripped your ass," Chasity bit out, snatching open the passenger door.

"Yeah, yeah," Malajia mocked, sliding next to Emily in the back seat. "Sidra get us off this deserted ass road!"

Hours later, tired and on edge from being held up in the car with the girls for a long period of time, Chasity breathed a sigh of relief when she finally pulled into the garage of her Miami condominium.

"I can't believe we've been riding for over twelve hours," Sidra yawned as she and the girls approached the front door. "Next trip that's over four hours long, we fly."

"Sidra, us being in that car longer than we should've been was *your* fault," Chasity declared.

Sidra rolled her eyes. "I know, I know."

Opening the front door, Chasity walked into the air-conditioned condo and dropped her keys on a nearby wooden stand.

The four girls walked in and looked around in awe at the huge, beautifully decorated interior of the condo. "Look at this place," Alex gushed, slowly walking across the hardwood floor entryway, which led into the fully-furnished living room. She looked up at the high ceilings and large windows. "How many rooms are in here?"

"It's three bedrooms and two bathrooms," Chasity answered evenly, checking out a note on the glass coffee table.

"Ooh!" Malajia exclaimed, making a dash for the kitchen. "Yo, check out all this food," she beamed, searching through the dark wood cabinets which were filled to capacity. Opening the stainless steel refrigerator, Malajia reached for a bottle of soda. "I hate you…I really hate your life Chasity."

Chasity shook her head. "Stop acting like you never seen a damn condo before."

"Not like *this*," Malajia clarified, flopping down on the cushy cream couch in the living room. "This place could be in a magazine…I swear, if you were a dude, I'd kiss you for letting us come."

Chasity made a face. "Eww," she scoffed, smacking Malajia on the top of the head with her paper.

"I guess we should pick out which rooms we're going to share," Sidra suggested, dragging her bags into the living room.

Malajia jumped up from the couch. "I call the biggest room," she announced, taking off running down the hall.

"Fuck outta here," Chasity called after her. "The first room is mine, so stay your hype ass out of it."

Malajia sucked her teeth as she stuck her head through the largest room in the condo. The queen sized four-poster bed, loveseat, beautiful dresser and nightstand set, fifty-five inch flat screen TV and, walk-in closet made her fall in love. "Can I at least be your roommate?"

"No!" Chasity exclaimed.

"I call the second room," Sidra giggled, darting past Malajia.

"Shit!" Malajia stomped her foot on the floor. "Well Alex and Emily, I call the third room. So either, one of y'all share with Sidra or hit that floor in the living room."

Alex laughed. "I don't care where I sleep, I'm just happy to be here," she declared, plopping down on the loveseat. "I'll take the couch."

"It's a pullout bed," Chasity informed.

Alex put her hands up. "Even better," she smiled. "Em, we can share if you want. This couch is pretty big."

"Sounds good to me," Emily agreed.

Chapter 23

The early morning sun beamed through the sky as Mark pulled his car into a parking lot near the Miami condominium

Josh, Jason, and David emerged from the car stiff and tired.

Mark on the other hand seemed to have a burst of energy, which intensified once he stepped foot out of the car and laid eyes on the palm tree lined street, and more importantly, the bikini-clad girls sauntering past him.

"Hooooo! Party time," Mark beamed, dancing in a circle.

"Shut your dumb ass up," Jason snapped, slamming his hand on the hood of the car.

Mark stopped dancing and looked at him wide-eyed. "Hey, don't hit my shit," he bit back. "And what's your damn problem?"

"Mark, I will tear the roof off this damn car for all the shit that you put us through," Jason fumed, pointing at him. "We could've been here last night."

"Oh what? You mad we got lost?" Mark sneered, removing his bag from the trunk of his car. "You were the one with the GPS. That was *your* fault."

"I told you what the GPS was saying. Hell, you *heard* it!" Jason fumed. "You just went your own damn way."

"Yeah Mark, Jase is right," David put in. "We almost ended up in Pennsylvania because of you. The complete opposite direction."

"Well look damn it, we're here ain't we?" Mark concluded, removing his sunglasses.

Josh chuckled at the angry look on Jason's face. "Never again will I take a road trip with you guys," he declared.

The guys stepped out of the elevator and walked along the massive hallway before ending up in front of Chasity's door.

"They're gonna so be pissed," Mark laughed, ringing the doorbell. The four guys had big smiles on their faces as the door opened.

"What the hell?!" Alex exclaimed, all traces of smile gone from her face.

"What happened?" Sidra asked, hurrying to the door along with the other girls.

"Greetings ladies," Josh smiled, walking in and setting his bags on the floor.

"What the fuck are you doing here?" Chasity fumed.

"Good morning to you too, beautiful," Jason teased.

"You guys weren't invited," Malajia slid in.

"*Clearly*," Jason responded, voice dripping with sarcasm.

"How y'all just gonna come to Miami and not tell us?" Mark charged, dropping his small suitcase. "I feel some kind of way about that. That was some triflin' selfish shit."

"Don't nobody give a damn about how you feel," Malajia returned, hands on her hips.

"Hold on, how did you get pass security?" Chasity asked.

"Oh, Ms. Trisha cleared us," Jason revealed, much to Chasity's astonishment. "When we found out about this place, I called your aunt and she gave us the address and said that she would clear us with the front desk."

"Ain't this about a bitch," Chasity hissed, folding her arms. Once again, meddling Trisha goes and does something behind Chasity's back, knowing that it would upset her.

"Time out," Malajia barked, grabbing everyone's attention. "Jason, you called Ms. Trisha *after* you found out about where we were going right?"

Jason nodded.

"So, who told you in the *first* place?" Chasity added.

Mark folded his arms. "I will not reveal my sources," he promised.

Chasity, Alex, Malajia and Sidra exchanged glances, then on instinct, slowly turned to face Emily, who was in the middle of taking a bite of bagel.

Emily gave a nervous laugh. "Anybody want a piece of bagel?"

"You know nobody wants that bagel with your teeth marks all on it," Malajia snapped.

"Emily, you told?" Sidra exclaimed. "Why would you do that?"

Emily's eyes shifted as the girls eyes cut through her like a laser. "Um...I...Uh," she stammered. "They threatened me!" she blurted out, pointing to Mark and Jason.

"We did *not*," Mark assured.

"Emily, all we said was that we would take you for ice cream if you told us," Jason revealed, folding his arms across his chest. "Don't lie."

Unable to say anything else to defend herself, Emily just looked at the floor as she took a bite of her bagel.

"Ice cream? You ratted us out for *ice cream*?" Malajia charged.

"We should've let her snitch ass go home and sniff up under her mom all week," Chasity barked.

Alex let out a loud sigh. "Well, you drove all the way here, you might as well get comfortable," she relented. "You guys want some breakfast?"

"Hold on!" Chasity exclaimed. "This is *my* house, y'all gotta go," she spat out, pointing to the door.

"Chasity, it's done, just let it go," Alex said on her way to the kitchen.

Mark walked up to Chasity and placed his hand on her shoulder. "It's done. Just let it go," he teased.

Fuming, Chasity grabbed Mark's arm and twisted it behind is back. "I've told you before not to touch me."

"Ow! Ow, ow," he howled. "Damn your strong ass!"

"Mark, leave her alone and come eat," Alex yelled from the kitchen.

Chasity let go of Mark's arm and stormed off.

"You punk," Malajia laughed, pointing to him.

Mark glared at Malajia before letting out a scream, running past her, and giving the back of her head a light tap.

"You play too damn much," Malajia yelled, chasing after him.

The sun-filled sky turned cloudy and opened up, dampening the city and the group's mood.

"This rain is in the waaaaaay," Malajia groaned, rolling around on the carpeted floor of the living room where she and the rest of the gang were spread out.

"Tell me about it," Mark grouched. "I was planning on getting in that ocean today."

"You can still go," Chasity assured, voice even. "Maybe the extra water will sweep your stupid ass out and drown you."

Mark shot Chasity a glare. "Do you wake up evil?"

"Sometimes," Chasity said, propping a throw pillow under her head.

"You guys wanna watch a movie?" Emily asked, changing the subject.

"We're in Miami, Emily," Malajia sneered. "You think we wanna waste time watching some sorry ass movie?"

"I was just trying to help," Emily shrugged.

"How about we play spades?" Mark suggested.

"No!" was yelled in unison from the group.

"All right fine," Mark ground out. "I'll save my victory for another damn day."

The silence around the room was torturous. Chasity slammed her hand on the couch, "Okay, I'm raiding the fridge," she announced, jumping up from the couch.

"Dibs on the ice cream," Sidra said as she and the others headed for the kitchen.

While everyone raided the cabinets and refrigerator, Mark made his way over to a small cabinet in the corner.

"Hey Chaz, what's in here?" Mark asked, hand on the silver handle.

"Boy *I* don't know, just look," Chasity hissed.

Mark shrugged, then opened the door. "Yeeeeesssss," he rejoiced, pulling out a large bottle of vodka.

Malajia hurried over to him "Whatchu got?" she asked, peering over his shoulder.

"I found the liquor," he answered, showing her the bottle.

"You found the liquor?" Malajia repeated.

"I found the liquor," Mark confirmed, before both of them broke out into a dance.

Alex walked over, watched them dance like idiots for several seconds, and snatched the bottle from Mark's grasp. "I don't think so."

"Hey, give that back!" Malajia wailed, reaching for the bottle.

Alex held it out of the way. "Haven't you learned your lesson from your *last* encounter with alcohol?" she chided. "Do you want to end up hung-over again?"

Malajia rolled her eyes as Alex continued to scold her. In the middle of Alex's rant, Jason snuck up behind her, snatched the bottle, and ran into the living room.

"Hey!" Alex exclaimed.

"Run man," Mark laughed.

Alex ran into the living room just in time to see Jason, along with Chasity, Mark, and Malajia play keep away with the bottle.

"You four are so juvenile," Alex seethed. "You know that your parents would have a fit if they knew y'all were out here drinking."

"Well our old ass parents aren't here now, *are* they?" Malajia taunted, opening the bottle.

"Chug, chug, chug," Mark egged on, as Malajia took a sip from the bottle.

"Oh my God," Malajia coughed, patting her chest. "Why is it that damn strong?"

"What? You thought it would taste like fruit punch?" Alex spat, folding her arms. "It *is* straight alcohol."

Malajia flipped Alex off as she passed the bottle to Jason, who then took a sip.

"Come on Jase, you spittin' in it," Mark complained. Jason shot Mark a glare as he passed Chasity the bottle.

"You guys, this isn't right. You're all underage," Emily pointed out, sitting on the couch. She had no plans on joining her friends for that activity.

"Thank you Emily," Alex said. "At least *you* have sense."

"But she's corny!" Malajia exclaimed.

Alex looked at Sidra. "Sid, come on back me up, here."

Sidra scratched her head as she looked at her four friends taking turns drinking from the bottle. "Honestly Alex...I kind of want a drink too," she admitted.

"Sidra!" Alex exclaimed.

"I just want to know what it tastes like," Sidra explained, as Chasity handed her the bottle.

"It taste like that bullshit," Chasity jeered, patting her chest.

Proud that Sidra was joining them, Mark stood in her face as she began to take a sip. "Take that, take that, take that," he egged on.

Sidra glared at him. "You're all up in my face!"

"My bad," Mark apologized, taking a step back. "Take that, take that, take that," he repeated.

She took a quick sip from the bottle, then began coughing. "Eww," she complained, voice scratchy. "Can we at least mix this with something?"

"I'll get the orange juice," Mark announced, running for the kitchen.

Alex threw her hands up in the air as she flopped down on the couch.

"You're not going to try to stop them anymore?" Emily asked.

"Nope," Alex relented. "They're gonna do what they want to do. I might as well let them go at it and worry about damage control later."

Alex let them go at it for a few hours; they finished the entire bottle as well as a bottle of rum that they found later. Both empty bottles were now lying in the corner of the living room. Resting her head on her hand, Alex shook her head as she watched her now intoxicated friends maneuver around her. Mark turned the stereo up as he and Malajia danced wildly around the room.

Josh tripped over a pillow on his way to the bathroom and fell, making Sidra double over with laughter. Alex sighed loudly as she watched Sidra roll around on the floor.

"We need more liquor," Josh slurred, still laid out on the floor.

"Your drunk behind don't need another damn drink," Alex hissed. "You can't even walk straight."

"I'll be right back," Chasity slurred, slowly standing from the floor.

Alex watched as she walked down the hall, leaning to the side in the process "Where are you going?" she asked.

Chasity ignored her as she continued towards her room. Alex was about to go after her when Malajia's hollering caused her to turn around.

"Turn up my song!" Malajia bellowed.

"You don't know nothin' 'bout this!" Mark yelled, doing a silly dance in Malajia's face.

Malajia fell to the floor in a fit of laughter. "He's killin' it!" she screamed.

"Oh Lord Jesus, Malajia please," Alex barked. "Is the screaming necessary?"

Chasity held on to the wall as she stumbled into her bedroom. "Why did I come in here?" she asked herself. Her mind was cloudy. She ran her hands through her hair, and figuring that she must have come in the room in search of something, started looking around the room.

While searching for her unknown item, Chasity bumped into the dresser. "Shit," she hissed, grabbing her knee in pain.

Jason, in the process of heading for the bathroom, walked into the room. "I heard something," he announced, resting against the open door.

"I hit my damn knee," she groaned, rubbing it.

Jason pushed himself from the door and stumbled into the room. "You okay?" he asked. When Chasity nodded, he pointing to the hallway. "Come on, let's go back out there."

"I can't feel my legs," Chasity slowly informed. Jason chuckled as he reached for her arm.

"I'll help you," he assured her. Chasity tried to walk, but ended up stumbling into Jason. He caught hold of her, but was too drunk to stop her from falling. Jason lost his balance and both of them fell to the floor.

"Josh, why are you chewing on the pillow?" Emily asked, trying to pry the white throw pillow from Josh's strong hand.

"It's not a big marshmallow?" Josh slurred.

"Never again will I babysit a bunch of grown babies," Alex fumed, assisting Emily in pulling the pillow from Josh's grip.

Sidra stared at her reflection in the floor length mirror. Seeing her disheveled hair, she ran her hands through it. "I *so* don't look pretty right now," she whined.

"Sidra, you look fine," Alex sighed, pulling Sidra's hair back into its loosened ponytail.

"You're beautiful, Sidra," Josh put in from the floor.

"You hype, she don't want you dawg," Mark teased.

Hearing a noise from the hall, Alex looked at Emily. "Keep an eye on them, I'm going to see where Chasity is; I heard a noise."

"Okay," Emily agreed, tossing the empty liquor bottles in the trash. Alex hurried down the hall as Emily looked at Josh, who had confiscated the white pillow yet again. "Josh no! You can't eat the pillow."

Alex checked in the bathroom for Chasity before sticking her head in her room. She frowned in confusion when she saw Jason pull Chasity up from the floor. "What are you two doing?"

"I fell," Chasity bit out, straightening out her shirt.

"That's what your drunk butt gets," Alex returned. "You two bring your selves out of this room, where I can keep an eye on you."

"What's that supposed to mean?" Jason frowned.

Alex gave him a knowing look. "It means that I'm not leaving you two alone in this room." She folded her arms. "Liquor and raging hormones lead to big mistakes being made."

"You really think I would take advantage of Chasity like that?" Jason asked, offended.

"No, not you," Alex clarified, eyeing Chasity who was busy scratching her head with her eyes closed. "This one over here looks like she's a horny drunk," Alex jeered, pointing to her.

"Bite me," Chasity hissed, passing Alex out of the room.

"No, thank you," Alex jeered, signaling for Jason to walk out.

Alex walked in the living room, and frowned at the argument taking place between Mark and Malajia.

"What are you two arguing about?" Alex asked. "I was gone for less than five minutes."

"Mark and Malajia were having a dance battle and Malajia accidentally poked Mark in the eye and when he started yelling, he accidentally spit on Malajia," Emily informed.

Alex shook her head before pointing to Jason and Chasity. "Well, I found these two back in Chasity's room."

Malajia put her hands over her mouth as she jumped up and down, screaming. "You two did it?"

"No," Chasity scoffed.

Jason looked at her. "Damn, why did you have to say it like that?" he chortled.

Malajia stopped jumping and regarded Alex angrily. "You always ruining shit. You cock blocker," she barked.

"Malajia, shut up already," Alex ground out.

Mark glanced over at Chasity. "Hey Chaz." She looked up at him. "You wanna take *me* to your bedroom?" he joked.

Chasity narrowed her eyes at Mark. "Not even if you were the last living thing on the face of this earth," she sneered, earning a loud, exaggerated laugh from Malajia.

Jason wobbled over to Mark. "Say some shit like that to her again, hear?" he warned, pointing in his face.

Mark, having stumbled back into the wall, pushed himself up. "Man, I say what I want," he boasted. "You're *not* her man."

David, who'd been busy playing a video game on the fifty-seven inch television, rose from his seat and darted over just as Jason grabbed for Mark's collar "Guys, chill out," he said, stepping in between them. Shaking his head, he nudged Jason in one direction and Mark in the other.

"Anybody wanna go in the room with *me*?" Malajia asked, trying to steady herself. "Just know that I'll have no idea what I'm doing," she joked.

"Seriously, Malajia?" Alex exclaimed. She was appalled at the proposition that came out of Malajia's mouth. "Don't be that sloppy, whorish drunk. It's not cute."

Malajia leaned against the wall. "All right, fine," she relented, before falling to the floor. "I'm okay," she assured everyone.

Alex relished the quiet. David continued with his video game. Emily was curled up on the loveseat, nodding off. The others were sprawled out around the room, still buzzed…but quiet.

Malajia inched her way over to Chasity, who was sitting on the floor with her back against the wall staring blankly out ahead of her.

"Hey, hey Chasity…guess what?" Malajia whispered, tapping her shoulder

"What…what…what!" Chasity fumed, knocking Malajia's hand off of her.

"Guess what?" Malajia smiled. "Out of all these heifers in this room, you're actually my favorite one."

Chasity shot Malajia a confused look. "Get away from me, Malajia," she bit out, grabbing her head. Everything in the room was spinning.

"No, seriously," Malajia slurred. "I hate you the most, but I love you the most…Does that make sense?"

"Nothing you say makes any damn sense," Chasity hissed. "Get away from me."

Malajia sucked her teeth. "Fine," she huffed, rolling away.

Josh looked around the room. "Hey everybody," he said, trying to push himself up from the floor. "I love you guys."

"Josh, please don't start that sentimental shit," Mark scoffed, rubbing his face.

"No seriously, y'all are the brothers and sisters that I always wanted," Josh revealed.

"Man, you already got a sister," Mark pointed out.

"To hell with her!" Josh barked, pointing at Mark, who put his hands up in surrender. Alex grabbed Josh's arm and guided him back to the floor.

"Sleep it off, sweetie," she said, handing him a pillow.

"My fault bro," Mark said. "Damn."

A smile broke across Josh's face. "It's cool bro," he assured him, holding his arms out for a hug.

"Get outta here with that Josh," Mark ground out. "Nobody's hugging you right now. Chill."

"Please, please go to sleep you guys," Alex begged.

"We got any more liquor?" Malajia asked.

"No, nobody gets another damn drink. Go to sleep!" Alex snapped stomping her foot on the floor.

"Boooo," Malajia jeered, earning snickers from around the room.

Alex gritted her teeth as she sat down on the couch. "Y'all are gettin' on my nerves," she seethed. Mark began singing at the top of his lungs, and Alex put her head in her hands. *Never again*, she thought, popping her head up as Mark hit a bad high note. "Mark! Shut the hell up."

Chapter 24

Ms. Harris placed a teapot full of water on the stove and cut the burner on. After cleaning her home from top to bottom, she was ready for a much needed break. *A cup of tea and my TV shows will do me some good.*

Realizing that she forgot to put the folded laundry away, she grabbed the large green basket and headed upstairs. Stepping foot into her daughters' room, she looked at Emily's side and sadness fell over her. She missed her baby girl.

The first few days of Emily not being home, Ms. Harris resisted the urge to drive down to the school and see her. *No, she's taking the initiative to bring her grade up, let her be,* screamed in her head every day. She even overlooked the fact that Emily had not called her or answered her room phone for four days straight. But as she began putting her oldest daughter Jazmine's clothes in her drawer, her eyes made their way to a picture of Emily on top of the dresser.

"I have to call her," she concluded, heading downstairs.

Grabbing the cordless phone from its cradle on the wall, she dialed the number to Emily's room back on campus and waited patiently while it rang. She frowned when the answering machine picked up.

"How are you out of the room every single time?" she said aloud, waiting for the beep. "Emily honey, it's Mommy again. I know that you're working hard, but give me a call okay, I miss you. Bye."

Hanging up the phone, Ms. Harris began to feel really uneasy. Even if Emily was busy, it was unlike her to not return one single phone call. For four days? She dialed another number.

"Good afternoon, Wilson Hall," a pleasant female voice answered.

"Hello, my name is Kelly Harris. When Emily Harris gets back to the dorm from class, can you tell her to call her mother please?"

"Emily?" the girl asked.

Ms. Harris frowned. "Yes Emily Harris, slim girl, light skinned, sandy brown hair—"

The girl laughed. "No, I *know* who she is; she hangs out with her roommates, Malajia, Alex, and those other two girls, all the time."

Ms. Harris resisted the urge to make a nasty comment. "Uh huh," was all that she could manage. "Can you please give her my message?"

"Sure, I'll give her your message, but she won't be back until Sunday."

A frown appeared on Ms. Harris's distinguished face. "Why wouldn't she be back until Sunday?" she asked.

"Well, she's in Florida for the week."

"What?!"

There was silence on the other line for a few seconds. "I'm sorry Ms. Harris. I'm friends with Malajia, and she told me where they were going. I just assumed that you knew," she stammered finally.

Ms. Harris was so angry, she slammed the phone down without saying a word. She could have torn the whole house apart.

"How *dare* she lie to me!" she fumed.

"I'm glad that damn rain stopped," Malajia mused, rubbing sunscreen on her already glistening brown skin. "Having us stuck inside all day every day."

"Yeah, as much as I love you guys, I needed to get out of the condo," Alex agreed.

Weather now cooperating, after being cooped up in the condo for days due to the rain, the gang were finally able to take an excursion to the beach.

"Damn *love*, I was two seconds from taking every last one of y'all outta here," Chasity sneered, pushing her designer sunglasses from her face to the top of her head.

Sidra rested her head against the back of her lounge chair. "Those guys didn't hesitate to run for that water," she chortled, watching the guys swim in the blue ocean. "Thank God for this umbrella, the sun is beaming today."

"I guess it's making up for all that rain," Alex giggled, reaching for a bottle of water from the cooler.

"Anybody mind if I take my top off to get an even tan?" Malajia asked, reaching around her back to grab for her bikini straps.

"Yes, we mind!" Alex and Sidra exclaimed, putting their hands up.

"You pull those tits out and I'll kick sand in your damn face," Chasity warned.

Malajia sucked her teeth. "Y'all are some hatin' ass chicks," she scoffed, putting her sunglasses on.

"Far from a hater, Malajia," Alex assured. "We just don't want to see your breasts, okay."

David ran over. "Hey ladies, you should come get in the water, it feels great," he said, grabbing water from the cooler.

"Naw, water and my hair don't mix," Malajia replied, moving curls from her face. "I need a damn touch up, so this stuff will turn ugly real quick."

David shrugged before heading back to the water.

"Yeah, we know," Chasity laughed. "We all saw your roots snatch back after Mark locked you out on the balcony in the rain yesterday."

Malajia shot Chasity a glare. "I know *you're* not talking," she bit out. "I've seen *your* hair after you wash it. Looking like damn lion's mane."

"A *long* mane, get it right sweetheart," Chasity bit back. "And I have an excuse, I don't get perms."

"You're a whole liar," Malajia accused. "There is no way in hell your hair gets that damn straight and behaves that well without a perm."

"It's called training. And my hair has been trained since I was a child," Chasity clarified. "So no, I don't get perms...You salty."

"I am, just a little," Malajia admitted, laughing.

"Yeah well, that was the *one* thing that Brenda did right for me," Chasity joked.

"Clearly," Malajia chuckled. "Maybe you can train Alex's mop," she teased.

"Uh no, Alex is perfectly happy with her natural mop, thank you very much," Alex put in, flinging her hair over the back of the chair.

Emily stood from her lounge chair. "I'm gonna go get in the water," she announced, jogging away.

Once Emily was out of ear shot, Malajia leaned over to the other girls "Now *why* does she have that outfit on, at the beach?"

Alex glanced at Emily, who was dipping her feet in the water. The gray sweat shorts and pale pink tank top that Emily had on wasn't necessarily standard beach wear, but she didn't look bad in it.

"Mel, stop being so two-faced," Alex scolded. "Emily obviously feels comfortable in what she has on, let her be."

Malajia glared at Alex. "*Two-faced*? I'm *not* two faced," she scoffed. "Everything I said to you just now, I said to *her* this morning." Malajia pushed her sunglasses up on her head. "I mean, the girl cut an old ass pair of sweatpants to make those shorts. I even offered her one of my bathing suits and she insisted on wearing that baggy mess. That's not cute."

"Girl, you already knew she wasn't going to wear those strings that you tried to give her," Sidra bit out.

"Well, she should've bought her own," Malajia shot back.

"She doesn't own a bathing suit," Alex argued. "Shit *I* shouldn't own one with my big thighs," she chuckled.

Glancing down at her brown and gold two piece bathing suit, paired with a sheer brown sarong, Alex smiled. *Thick thighs or not, I sure look good.*

Sidra fanned herself with her hand. "Alex, pay Malajia no mind. The girl's always talking about somebody's clothes," she said. "You remember she talked about both mine and Chasity's bathing suit earlier."

Malajia rolled her eyes. "I was just suggesting that you wear a two piece, Sidra. You have the body for it," she clarified.

"My one piece is just fine. I don't need to flaunt it just because I have it," Sidra replied, voice haughty. She knew that she had the slim body to wear what Malajia suggested, but the royal blue strapless one piece bathing suit was comfortable.

"Yeah, and I already told you that if you suggest a thong to me one more time that I was gonna choke you with yours," Chasity spat, before taking a sip of water.

"But you act like your two piece is more concealing than mine," Malajia shot back.

Alex gave Chasity's black two piece and Malajia's red two piece suit a once over. "Yeah Mel, Chasity's covers her better. Yours looks like fabric and strings," Alex concluded. "One hard sneeze and everything you got is gonna pop out."

Sidra suddenly sat up right in her seat. "Girls, check out that wave." She pointed to the ocean, her eyes widened once she saw it approach her friends in the water. "Oh my God!" she exclaimed.

"Ooh, take a picture," Malajia laughed as she and the girls stood from their seats to get a better look.

"Do they even know it's behind them?" Alex scratched her head.

Chasity grabbed her phone and began recording. She laughed once she heard Mark's loud voice shout "Oh shit!"

"*Now* they do," Chasity laughed.

They watched the guys make a run for the beach. Some guys made it to the beach, but others weren't so lucky. Laughter resonated through the girls as they watched the wave push Mark and Josh down on the water.

"Of course, Mark would be one to get caught," Malajia laughed. "With his dumb looking self."

Malajia was so busy laughing that she never saw the guys approach. Mark glared at her for several seething seconds, before tossing a slimy substance at her chest.

Shocked, Malajia's laughter came to an abrupt halt as she pulled the substance from her. "Is this seaweed?!" she shrieked, "Mark, did you just throw seaweed at me?"

"You shouldn't have been laughing," Mark confirmed, walking away.

"I can't wait to hit that club later," Malajia mused, opening a container of sour cream. "I'm ready to shake my ass somewhere."

"*What* ass?" Mark teased, grabbing a freshly made quesadilla from a large plate. "Lookin' like somebody kicked you in the ass with a work boot."

Exhausted from the sun, the group returned to the condo, showered, changed, and were in the process of eating lunch.

"First of all, every ass doesn't need to be as big as *Alex's*," Malajia groused, pointing to Alex's round behind, clearly defined through her tan yoga pants. "Mine may be small, but it's perfect."

"Perfectly non-existent," Mark returned, taking a bite. "Pancake ass."

Malajia stuck her middle finger up at him.

"Dude, can you at least wait until we set everything out?" Alex scoffed, smacking Mark's hand. "We spent all this time making these quesadillas, at least let us finish the presentation."

"*What* presentation?" Mark frowned. "Just open the damn salsa, and sour cream, put a spoon in it, and leave it alone. This ain't no damn restaurant."

"Whatever." Alex waved her hand at Mark dismissively. "Anyway, I'm glad we found an eighteen and over club to go to. I'm pretty excited."

Emily poured some freshly made lemonade into a glass. "Um, I'm not really comfortable with going to a club," she softly revealed. "Can we maybe go to a movie or something?"

Sidra, who was wiping off the counter top with a towel, let out a loud groan. *My God, not again.*

"You can take your sorry ass to a movie by your-damn-self," Chasity hissed. "Nobody's changing plans for you, Emily."

Jason grabbed some tortilla chips from the bag and put them on his plate. "Maybe we *should* find something else to do if she isn't comfortable with going," he advised. "We can't leave her behind; it wouldn't be right."

"Sure we can," Chasity said, pushing hair over her shoulder.

Alex shook her head at Chasity before turning to Emily. "You don't have to go to the club, Em."

"Emily why did you even come here with us?" Malajia exclaimed. "You went through this whole song and dance to be able to come on this trip, and for *what*? To sit in the house and do the same shit you do back home?"

Alex was fed up with them ganging up on Emily. "Look Malajia—"

"Shut up, 'Emily's-fuckin'-hover-cloud'," Chasity spat, staring daggers at Alex. "If the girl doesn't like what's being said, let her tell us herself."

Alex's mouth fell open. *So damn rude*, she fumed. She turned to Sidra for support and was astonished when Sidra closed her fingers together, signaling for Alex to keep her mouth shut. "Fine," Alex huffed, storming out of the kitchen.

Chasity smirked at Emily. "Now that your mouth piece is gone, you have something you wanna say?"

Emily stared back at Chasity, eyes nervous. She didn't know if Chasity was encouraging her to say something to defend herself, or if she was challenging her to say something so that she could jump across the counter island at her. Unsure, Emily simply shook her head.

"Well, it's settled, you're going," Malajia concluded, reaching for the plate of food. "And you're not wearing one of those curtains that you call dresses. I have an outfit for you."

Emily sighed. *Great, now I have to be uncomfortable and naked*, she thought, taking a sip of her juice.

"Come on, man!" Malajia shouted, slapping Mark's hand away from her quesadilla. "You've eaten damn near all of them already. I haven't had one yet."

"It's not my fault you're slow," Mark returned, reaching for her chicken and cheese filled triangle.

Malajia, trying to keep Mark from snatching her food, stuck her finger in the middle of her quesadilla. "I had my finger up my nose earlier," she announced, as he still grabbed hold of it.

"I scratched my ass earlier," Mark jeered.

"Eww," Malajia shrieked, releasing her food. She glowered at him as he put the mangled food on his plate. "Nasty bastard."

Unfazed by Malajia's comments, Mark did a silly dance and took a bite.

Chapter 25

The popular Miami club was packed. The DJ was spinning the hottest tracks, and music blared through the speakers. The group surveyed the hordes of people on the dancefloor.

"I'm making my way to those guys, over *there*," Malajia announced, pointing to a group of guys off in a corner. She began dancing in the direction, then grabbed Chasity's arm. "Come on bitch, *you* too."

"I don't wanna go over there. They're ugly," Chasity complained.

"Jason, keep an eye on them," Alex ordered, watching the girls disappear through the crowd.

"On it," Jason chuckled, following them.

Alex looked over at Emily, who was standing there with her arms folded. "You okay?"

Emily nodded as she forced a smile. The black shorts and red halter top that Malajia lent Emily wasn't her style. The black four inch sandals weren't comfortable, and the silver costume jewelry was too heavy. "I'm fine," she said finally.

"Feeling a bit naked?" Alex assumed.

"Just a little," Emily giggled. "But I like my hair." Clothing aside, Emily had to admit that the curly style that Malajia did on Emily's mid-length hair was certainly pleasing to her, and the subtle makeup did enhance her features.

"Well, for what it's worth, you look cute," Alex smiled.

"Yeeees, this is my song!" Malajia bellowed, dancing wildly with a random guy.

Chasity just shook her head as she watched Malajia with amusement. She then began dancing, grabbing a guy's attention. He walked up to Chasity and began dancing next to her. She tried to ignore him and move away, but he kept inching closer. The guy put his hand on her waist and before she could react, Jason appeared, stepping in between them.

"You cool, Chaz?" he asked Chasity, eyes glaring at the guy. Chasity smiled with satisfaction as the clearly intimidated guy walked away.

"Walk me to the bar to get a soda," Malajia said to Sidra after a half hour of dancing.

Sidra fanned herself as she walking alongside Malajia. "I hope you know I'm not buying you a drink," Sidra said.

Malajia stomped her foot on the floor. "Damn it, it's only three dollars and fifty damn cents. Stop being so cheap," she snapped.

Sidra raised an eyebrow at Malajia, before signaling for the bartender. Malajia smiled as she watched Sidra place her order. The bartender handed Sidra the glass of soda, and in return she paid him with five dollars, leaving him a tip. Sidra then grabbed the drink from the counter and walked off.

Malajia frowned. "Hey." Sidra stopped walking and faced Malajia. "So you really aren't gonna buy me a soda?"

Sidra took a sip of her ice filled drink. "I would've considered it if you hadn't raised your voice at me," she clarified, before walking off.

Malajia put her hands on her hips. "It's loud as shit in here. All you can do is raise your voice," she called after Sidra. She folded her arms in a huff when Sidra ignored her. Scanning the floor, she laid eyes on Mark, chatting up a young woman. A sly smile crept across her face as she made her way over.

"Yeah, I own like four cars and two houses down here," Mark crooned to the woman.

Seemingly intrigued, she smiled. "Oh really?"

"Yeah," he replied coolly. "I try to come down here like—"

"So you just gonna act like you didn't just sleep with me last night?" Malajia charged, slapping Mark on the arm.

Mark shot Malajia a confused look. "Huh?" was all that he could say.

"I guess you're also not gonna admit that you cried after lasting only two minutes," Malajia jeered, much to Mark's embarrassment. "Or that your dick looks like a short pencil."

"Malajia, you trippin'!" Mark wailed, eyes wide.

"You're sick," the young woman scoffed, throwing her drink in his face before walking away.

Mark held his arms out. "Yo, what the hell was that about, Malajia?"

Malajia busted out laughing as Mark wiped his face with the back of his hand. "You should be thanking me, the girl was ugly," she mocked, patting him on the arm and sauntering off.

"Blockin' ass," Mark fumed to himself.

Feet hurting and drenched in sweat, Malajia rested against the bar counter. She and the rest of the gang had been partying for hours. As the bartender sat a glass of juice in front of her, a man approached.

Malajia looked him up and down, taking in his body, face, outfit and shoes. *Nothin' but fine from head to toe*, she thought. When he smiled at her, Malajia felt a wave of heat flush over her.

"Hello beautiful," he gushed.

Hi yourself, you sexy black thing, you. "Hi," she smiled.

"You from around here?" He asked, taking a sip of the drink that he'd just purchased.

"No, just visiting," she answered, twirling some of her hair with her fingers. "I'm from Baltimore, but I go to college in Virginia."

"Really? I go to college here in Florida."

Malajia was grinning from ear to ear. She was so engrossed in conversation with her new interest that she didn't notice Mark walking up behind her.

Mark tapped her shoulder. "Mel." Malajia turned around, smile fading at the site of him.

"Not now, go away," she hissed, turning back around.

Mark held his cell phone to her face. "It's for you. It's important."

Malajia put her finger up at the man and spun around to face Mark. "What?" she snapped.

"It's your pharmacist on the phone," Mark yelled, a smile creeping across his face.

Malajia's eyes widened. *Oh no, Mark. No paybacks right now, please.*

"He said that your crotch itch medicine is ready for pick up!" Mark's loud voice carried, causing several nearby clubbers, including Malajia's interest to eye Malajia in disgust.

Malajia's mouth fell open as the guy backed away. "Don't listen to him, he's a liar." She sucked her teeth as the guy walked away. Furious, she delivered a stinging slap to Mark's arm. "That was uncalled for!"

"Yeah? So was lying about my dick," Mark returned. "Payback's a bitch ain't it?"

"Oh, whatever. You had no chance with that ugly girl anyway," Malajia argued.

"And now *you* have no chance with that corny looking dude *you* were talking to." Malajia glared at Mark's back as he danced away.

Night ruined, Malajia stormed over to where Chasity and Jason were dancing. "Can we get the others and go?" she sulked. "I'm over this scene."

Chasity looked at her. "Get away from me, I heard you have crotch itch," she joked.

Jason busted out laughing at the horrified look on Malajia's face.

"Damn, lies sure do spread fast don't they?" Malajia huffed, then eyed Mark off to the side dancing with a few girls. Catching her staring, he just waved to her in a taunting manner.

Yawns and stretches resonated through the car as Chasity pulled into the Torrence Hall parking lot, late Sunday evening.

"Aww, I miss Miami already," Malajia sulked, removing her seatbelt. She practically cried that morning as she and the rest of the group packed up for the long trip back to Paradise Valley University.

"Yeah well, we'll always have the memories," Sidra yawned, opening the car door.

Chasity turned the car off. "Bye y'all," she said to Malajia, Alex and Emily.

"Wait, you're not gonna give us a ride back to our dorm?" Malajia exclaimed.

Chasity shot her a confused look. "Why would I do that?" she hissed. "I just drove over seven hours straight."

"Chaz, that wasn't our fault," Alex slid in. "You're the one who said that you didn't want anyone else driving your car after the first few hours."

"Because Malajia almost ran us off a damn bridge!" Chasity exclaimed.

"Look, that's irrelevant," Malajia argued with a wave of her hand. "We have all these bags, so can you just drop us off?"

Chasity glared at the three smiling girls in the back seat of her car. Letting out a loud groan, she started the car.

Malajia began doing a happy dance in her seat, prompting Chasity to snap her head around.

"If you start dancing, I'll backhand the shit outta you," Chasity snapped.

"Sorry my sister," Malajia teased, earning a laugh from Alex.

"So silly," Alex mused.

Chasity pulled into the Wilson Hall parking lot a few minutes later and waited for the girls to get out of the car and remove their items.

"Wait, we're coming back over to your place," Alex announced as Chasity was getting ready to pull off.

Chasity let out a loud sigh "*Why?*" she barked. "We've been around each other all week, I'm *tired* of y'all."

"Lies, you love us," Malajia teased. "Now you might as well walk us inside."

Too tired to argue, Chasity stepped out of the car in a huff.

"I can't wait to see all the pictures we took," Malajia mused, walking down the hallway towards her room.

"I'll load them on my laptop when I go back to the room," Chasity promised dryly.

"The video's too?" Malajia asked, facing Chasity.

"Yeeeeessss," Chasity responded, exasperated.

Malajia narrowed her eyes. "Was that tone necessary?" she spat.

Alex giggled. "Malajia, leave the girl alone, you know she gets cranky when she's tired," she put in as Emily stuck her key in the door.

"Tired my ass," Malajia scoffed. "*Everything* makes her cranky."

"Including your big ass face," Chasity hissed.

"You know what—" Malajia began as Emily pushed the door open, laughing. "I'm sick of your smart ass mouth, you bi—" Malajia's insult was cut as her face, along with her friends' faces, held a shocked expression. "—tch," Malajia finished slowly.

"Mommy!" Emily exclaimed, coming face to face with the angered face of her mother.

"So, how was your project, Emily?" Ms. Harris spat, folding her arms.

Emily's eyes shifted. "Um I—"

"And before you start lying to me, I want to make you aware that I know *exactly* where you were this whole time!"

Emily flinched at the loudness of her mother's voice.

Chasity, Malajia, and Alex stood behind Emily, unable to think of what to say while Ms. Harris ranted at her horrified daughter.

Chasity and Alex exchanged glances and made gestures for each other to do or say something. Chasity sucked her teeth and waved her hand dismissively at Alex when she made a silly gesture. Both girls looked at Malajia, who was just standing there, staring at the back of Emily's head.

Chasity suddenly punched Malajia in the arm, hard.

"Ow!" Malajia howled, grabbing her arm and regarding Chasity in shock.

"I'm sorry, did that hurt?" Chasity quickly put out. "You need to go to the hospital, come on," she added, grabbing Malajia by the arm and pulling her out the door.

"I'll drive," Alex announced, hurrying out behind them, pulling the door closed.

Emily just stared at her mother. "Mommy I—"

"You lied to me!" Ms. Harris barked. "You told me that you were staying here for the week to work on your grade, but instead you were in Miami doing God knows what with those little...tramps!"

"Can you not talk about my friends that way?" Emily yelled back. Not intending to yell, she put her hand over her mouth.

Ms. Harris's eyes widened "How dare you raise your voice at me, young lady."

Emily rolled her eyes "Mom—"

"You see what hanging out with those girls is doing to you? You're defying me. How *dare* you take off like that! States away? Do you realize that something could've happened to you?"

"But nothing bad *happened*," Emily exclaimed, putting her hands on her head,

"It's obvious that you can't be trusted."

Emily sighed, trying to keep her composure. "You *can* trust me," she assured. "And I didn't want to lie to you, but you give me no freedom."

"Oh, quite the contrary. I think you have *too much* freedom," Ms. Harris contradicted.

Emily shook her head. *I don't! I have none, you hover over me even when you're not here,* screamed through Emily's head. She only wished that she had the courage to say the words out loud.

"I let you leave Jersey to come to school, and you start acting like you have no sense," she fumed. "I'll fix that."

Emily stood there confused.

"You're going to come home every weekend."

Emily's mouth fell open. "What?!" she hollered. "You can't do that to me! Mommy, I'm eighteen years old, I'm not a child."

"You *are* a child. You're *my* child, and you will do as I say and come home every weekend, and next semester I'm going to make sure that you get your own room."

Emily put her hands over her face and cried hysterically as her mother continued to speak.

"I saw some campus apartments that are being renovated, and I put your name on the list for next semester."

"Mommy, please don't do this," Emily sniffled. "You're controlling my life."

Ms. Harris walked over and placed her hand on Emily's tear streaked cheek. "I *gave* you life, so I can do what I *want* with it," she hissed.

Emily glared at her mother as the woman made her way towards the door.

"I'll be here to get you next Friday," she threw over her shoulder before shutting the door, leaving Emily to dissolve into tears.

Chapter 26

"That's it, I've had it with these classes," Malajia complained to Alex, clutching her books to her chest. "I just found out that I have a freakin' ten page paper to write on the Historic preservation of some buildings, or some bullshit."

Alex let out a little laugh. "Or some bullshit, huh?" she teased.

"Yes," Malajia scoffed. "Who the hell cares about some old ass buildings anyway?"

Alex simply shook her head. She hated to admit it, but Malajia touched on something. She too was over classes, and was looking forward to another break.

"Well, May will be here in a few days. It won't be much longer until we're finished for the summer," she advised.

"Well, it needs to hurry up," Malajia groused. Both girls nearly reached their destination of the cafeteria, when Malajia smiled brightly at a familiar face.

"Hey Praz, baby," she cooed.

Praz stopped and gave her a hug. "How've you been, beautiful?"

Malajia rolled her eyes. "Irked with these classes," she jeered.

"Same here," he chuckled, adjusting the book bag on his shoulder. "Hey, did either of you hear about what happened last night?"

"No, what happened?" Malajia asked, intrigued.

"Clive got attacked and robbed," he revealed.

Malajia and Alex's mouth dropped. "What?" Malajia exclaimed.

"You mean Clive from Contemporary Writing class? The quiet one?" Alex asked.

"Yup."

"The one who walks like he's about to take off running all the time?" Malajia added. Alex shook her head at Malajia's description.

"That's the one," Praz confirmed. "It happened a little after midnight. He was on his way back from the computer lab, and he was attacked by a bunch of guys. It's a shame man, he's a nice guy."

"What the hell?" Alex was shocked; she'd never imagine that robberies would happen on their campus. "Is he okay? Campus security wasn't around?"

"Alex, you know those flashlight cops stop patrolling the campus after like ten," Malajia bit out. "Like the trouble makers don't stay out past that time or something."

"He's okay, just got some bumps and bruises," Praz replied. "He said he went to the police and everything. I think he's gonna go home for a few days. He's pretty shaken up."

"I can imagine," Alex sympathized.

"I gotta get to class, you ladies be careful," Praz urged before walking off.

"That's terrible," Alex commiserated, Malajia nodded. "I hope they catch those thugs."

"You know what? Now that Praz said that, the girl who lives across the hall from us told me yesterday that she was coming back from her boyfriend's dorm the other night, and she saw a bunch of guys huddled by that gate behind the corny dorm—Daniels Hall," Malajia revealed. "It's probably no connection but…"

"We should still be careful," Alex concluded.

Sidra cradled her phone between her ear and her shoulder as she grabbed a pair of pajamas from her dresser, several days later.

"Mama these attacks going on around here are freaking me out," Sidra said, sitting on her bed. "I swear, it's been one on campus every other night."

"Sidra, I want you to be careful," Mrs. Howard urged. "I really think that you should come home until they catch these people."

"Mama, I'm not going to do that," Sidra replied, removing the clip from her hair, allowing it to fall past her shoulders. "I'll be careful. I already try not to go out after a certain time anyway, and these attacks seem to be taking place after midnight."

A sigh came through the phone. "You just make sure you check in with me constantly until this is over okay?"

"I promise," Sidra assured.

"You tell your friends to stay safe too."

Sidra frowned slightly. She'd been on the phone with her mother so long that she completely lost track of time. Glancing at the clock on her dresser, she noticed the time. *Midnight! And Chasity hasn't gotten back from the library yet.*

"Mama, I have to call you back," Sidra announced. Once she ended the call with her mother, Sidra went to dial her roommate's cell number, but a commotion from the hallway distracted her.

She jumped up from her bed, snatched the door open, and stuck her head out. One of her neighbors was crying hysterically and being consoled by other residents, including the RA.

"Drea what happened?" Sidra asked the resident advisor, who was trying to help keep the crying girl calm.

"She just got robbed," Drea informed, stroking the girls hair.

Sidra's eyes widened. "Are you serious?" she exclaimed. "Another one?"

"Everybody has to be careful when going out after midnight, since this seems to be when these robberies are taking place," a resident advisor in Wilson Hall announced to the group of girls piled in the front lobby.

As the number of assaults and thefts escalated, the president of the school ordered all dorms to call an emergency meeting.

One resident sucked her teeth. "I don't know why everybody has to be down here to hear this. Not everyone is out after midnight," she scoffed, pulling her throw blanket over her shoulders. "*I* for one am *always* in before midnight."

Malajia shot the girl a side glance; she couldn't stand her. Having bumped heads with her on several occasions over Malajia's long shower times, she couldn't resist the urge to make a smart comment.

"You're right Mya," Malajia agreed. "You *are* always in before midnight...In somebody's damn *bed*."

"You're one to talk, *Stank*ajia!"

Malajia rolled her eyes. "First of all, booo," she jeered of Mya's altering of her name. "Second, people just *think* I'm a ho. You actually *are* one."

"Yeah, you wish," Mya hissed.

"Everybody sees your fast ass sneaking back in the dorm after two in the morning," Malajia ranted. "That's why you be real hype about people taking long showers. You just wanna hurry up and wash those crabs off you."

Alex put her arm out, blocking Malajia from taking a step towards the girl. "Chill out, Mel," she urged.

"Alex, you better talk to your girl before she gets slapped," Mya warned, pointing to Malajia.

"That won't be necessary," Alex assured, evenly. This argument was pointless; she was more concerned about the robberies.

"You mad cause you nasty," Malajia taunted.

"Ladies!" The resident advisor barked over the noise. "I let you release some steam, now it's time to get serious."

While the RA finished the rest of her announcement, Malajia felt her phone vibrate in the pocket of her jeans. Sneaking off to a corner, she put the phone to her ear. "Yeah Sid, what's up?"

"Mel, where are you?" Sidra asked.

Malajia frowned at the urgency in Sidra's voice. "In the dorm with Alex and Em; we're having a meeting about the robbery that just happened." she informed. "What's wrong? You sound funny."

"Is Chasity there with you?"

"No, she's not," Malajia frowned. "I know her butt better not still be in that library with all this crap going on out there."

"I tried calling, but she's not answering her phone," Sidra ground out. "The girl who was just got robbed lives across the hall from me. I'm freaking out."

"Tell me about it," Malajia agreed, running her hand through her hair.

Chasity quickened her step along the path from the library towards her dorm. She'd lost track of time in the library and was in a hurry to get back. Digging into her purse for her room key, she pulled out her phone and frowned. *Why do I have all these damn messages from Sidra, Malajia, and Jason?*

Letting out a sigh, Chasity listened to the first message. "What the hell?" she bit out to herself as she listened to Malajia's loud, threatening message. "That girl is certifiably crazy."

Noticing a familiar figure storming towards her, she moved the phone away from her ear.

"Chasity," Jason barked, voice stern and deep.

"What," she answered calmly. Chasity pushed some of her hair behind her ears as Jason came face to face with her.

"What are you doing out here by yourself?" Jason asked, not hiding his frustration "Somebody else just got robbed."

Chasity frowned slightly. "I didn't know that. I was in the library," she replied.

"What's up with your phone?" he asked, tone sharp. "I've been calling you."

Chasity refrained from snapping at Jason for his harsh tone towards her; she understood that he was just concerned. "I had it on silent," she slowly replied, putting her hands up. "You wanna see?"

Jason's face relaxed from its frown. "I didn't mean to snap on you," he said. "It's just that Sidra called me and told me that you were out and not answering your phone...I was worried and I came out here to look for you."

"I get it," Chasity assured him. "I'm good."

Jason nodded, gently grabbing her book bag from her. "Come on, I'll walk you to your dorm," he said, slinging the heavy bag on his shoulder.

Reaching the dorm within minutes, Chasity opened the door and a fluffy blue pillow flew towards her. She ducked, and the pillow hit Jason's broad chest instead.

"Damn, Sid," Jason chuckled, retrieving the pillow from the floor.

"Sorry sweetie, I was aiming for the stupid chick next to you," Sidra spat, pointing at Chasity. "Have you lost your mind? Why were you out there this late with everything that's going on?"

"Soooo, you think trying to sneak me with a pillow is a mature response to me not answering your phone calls?" Chasity returned, folding her arms.

Sidra too folded her arms. "Mature, maybe not. Warranted? Absolutely," she countered. "Be more careful, damn it. You're not invincible you know."

"Yes, I know that," Chasity ground out.

Jason chuckled at their antics. "I'm gonna head back."

"You be careful too, Jase," Sidra ordered. "Or the pillow will be *meant* for you next time."

Jason put his hands up in surrender. "Yes Ma'am," he joked, walking out the door.

Malajia, Chasity, and Alex walked into Torrence Hall Friday evening, and were greeted by a lobby full of dorm residents, RA's, security guards, and several Paradise Valley police officers.

"What's going on?" Chasity asked Sidra, who was standing near the staircase.

"The local police are here to give us all updates on the robberies," Sidra revealed. Even though the university doubled security and students took precautions by traveling in groups, especially after midnight, the robberies still happened. The staff and police were at their wits end.

Malajia sucked her teeth. "What they *need* to do is update us when they find these bastards," she bit out, glancing at her watch. "We have to get going if we're gonna make this movie, it's almost ten thirty."

Alex frowned at her. "I think that this is more important than some movie."

Malajia waved her hand at Alex. "Please," she scoffed.

"Where's Emily?" Sidra asked.

"Home," Malajia replied, voice filled with amusement. "Hover mother picked her up after her last class."

"All right ladies, may I have your attention?" The police officer's loud voice radiated off the walls, grabbing the room's attention. "I know that everyone is aware of these after-midnight robberies that have been taking place on campus lately…Some of these robberies have involved brutal attacks. Unfortunately, we have no suspects at this time."

Malajia once again glanced at her watch, sighing loudly "Come oooon officer won't-shut-up," she complained.

Chasity snickered, earning both her and Malajia a glare from Alex.

"Even though we have tried to provide more security here, we can't be everywhere at once," the officer continued. "And so we have made the decision to place a curfew on campus until these thugs are apprehended."

Complaints were heard around the room. "Curfew?" someone exclaimed

"Yes. Everyone has to be back in their dorms by midnight, every night," the officer confirmed, much to the dismay of all of the residents. "Anyone found outside after this time will immediately be apprehended and questioned."

"Are you freakin' kidding me?" Chasity barked.

"Curfew?! I'm not freakin' twelve. I'm nineteen, you can't give me a damn curfew," Malajia protested loudly. "My *mother* don't even give me a damn curfew. I'm not following no damn curfew."

"Malajia, calm down," Alex urged, looking at Malajia.

"I'm *not* following it Alex, he can't give me no curfew," Malajia fumed. "He can curfew my *ass, that's* what he can do."

Alex just shook her head. *Malajia is so damn dramatic.*

"Do you really think that keeping us on lock down after twelve is going to do anything?" Sidra asked, calmly. "I mean, you haven't caught them yet. Do you really think that this is going to work?"

"Sidra, why are you even wasting your time talking to them?" a girl spat.

Sidra frowned. "You might want to check that tone, sweetheart," she bit back.

"My tone doesn't need to be checked, *honey*," the girl returned, tone nasty. "They're trying to treat us like kids on lockdown, and you're over there talking all calm."

"Bitch, shut your ugly ass up," Chasity snapped, before Sidra had a chance to respond.

Sidra couldn't help but chuckle. *Gotta love her*, she thought of her abrasive roommate.

"You stay running your mouth, when your teeth look like you've been chewing on concrete all damn day," Chasity hissed.

"Teeth lookin' like you've been sharpening pencils with em'," Malajia chimed in.

"Teeth looking like you've been cutting grass with them," Chasity jeered.

Alex put her hand over her face to keep from laughing out loud.

"Lookin' like you start fires with those teeth," Malajia laughed.

"Looking like somebody punched you in the mouth with a brick," Chasity added.

"Stop, stooooooppp!" Sidra screamed with laughter as the embarrassed girl stormed up the steps.

"You both are going straight to hell for talking about that girl's teeth like that," Alex chortled.

Malajia just shrugged as Chasity folded her arms. "She know her teeth are mangled, and steady talking that bullshit," Chasity ground out.

"All right ladies, enough of the bickering," the officer interrupted, putting his hands up. "The curfew will take place immediately. Your RA's will be doing a room check."

"Oh come on!" Malajia hollered.

"Room checks?" Chasity complained. "Y'all are insane, you can't *do* that."

"Ladies, I'm sorry, but we would rather have you all hate us than to have you get hurt," he replied.

"This is some straight bullshit," Chasity spat to the girls as the crowd dispersed.

"And they just *had* to do this shit on a damn Friday," Malajia complained.

"Come on ladies, they're only trying to keep us safe," Alex pointed out. "This shouldn't last too long."

"Well, so much for the movie," Sidra groused. "I'm going to eat a bunch of chocolate and watch a DVD. You want to join me, roomie?"

"No," Chasity spat.

"You act like you have a choice," Sidra laughed. "Where else do you have to be?"

"All right Mel, let's get going," Alex sighed, giving Malajia's shoulder a soft poke.

"I don't *wanna* go in the room; it's boring in there," Malajia whined, stomping her foot on the floor.

"Get over it," Alex shot back, nudging Malajia toward the exit.

"I wonder how the guys are taking the news," Sidra wondered aloud to Chasity as they walked up the steps.

"Come on, with this childish shit!" Mark shouted at the top of his lungs.

"Mark, did you just curse at the officer?" the RA frowned.

Mark's eyes shifted nervously "No," he lied.

The residents of Daniels Hall, having just received the news about the curfew, were seething. "Gentlemen this is our only option right now," the officer informed.

"Your only option is to lock us down because *you* can't find who is responsible for these attacks?" Jason barked. "You're punishing us because you can't do your job."

"Get em' Jase," Mark instigated.

"Guys, arguing with the police isn't going to change anything. We have to honor this, President Bennett said so," the RA said.

Mark sucked his teeth. "What's up with these damn room checks though?" he asked, exasperated. "Y'all corny with that."

"Get over it Mark," the RA bit out.

As the crowd started to disperse, Mark snatched his baseball cap off his head and slammed it to the floor. "I can't believe this shit, man," he complained. "It's Friday, and I gotta be stuck in my room with my wack ass roommate. I was supposed to be going over some chick's room later for a night cap."

Jason shot Mark a side glance. "Man, cap *these* with your lyin' ass," he snapped, walking out.

Josh and David started laughing. "A 'night cap', please," Josh teased.

Mark looked over at David, who was doubled over with laughter. "Dave, what the hell are *you* laughin' at?" he asked. "You can't get a girl to save your life."

David stopped laughing and narrowed his eyes at him.

"Aren't you still a virgin anyway?" Mark mocked. "Oh my bad, maybe not, if you count the times you were fuckin' your text books and your glasses."

David and Josh stared at Mark for a few seconds. "That was corny!" Josh howled, voice full of laughter.

David folded his arms. "Do you have any idea how much sense that *didn't* make?" he asked. "You sound like a complete and utter fool sometimes."

Mark just stood there looking stupid.

Chapter 27

"This don't make no damn sense," Malajia groaned, leaning back in her seat and taking a sip of her soda. "I feel like I'm back home with this curfew shit. There's supposed to be a reggae party this weekend, and I can't even go."

Chasity rubbed her temples with her fingers. "Malajia, please give my nerves a break and stop talking for *one* second," she snapped.

Malajia rolled her eyes at Chasity's sharp tone. Having suffered through several days of the campus wide curfew, Malajia was on edge, and the cafeteria food wasn't helping to change her mood.

"Mel, you have to admit that the curfew *does* keep us safe," Alex put in, taking a bite of her tuna hoagie.

Malajia sucked her teeth. "First off, you hype as shit eatin' all that tuna," she ground out, pointing at Alex's sandwich. "Second, this curfew isn't keeping no-damn-body safe. They've detained ten students so far."

"Well, if they would've stayed inside like they were supposed to, then they wouldn't have been caught," Sidra pointed out.

"This whole thing is scary," Emily put in, adding sugar to her iced tea.

"Scary for *who*?" Malajia spat out, raising an arched eyebrow. "You don't go out past eight, and you go home on the weekends, so this doesn't affect you."

"Malajia, don't be sour," Alex hissed. "It's not Emily's fault that you're bored."

"And there goes the big ass mouth piece again," Chasity mumbled, earning a glare from Alex.

Emily sighed; she wondered why she bothered to say anything sometimes. "Well, I'm sorry that your nights are ruined because of all of this," she said.

"I don't need your pity," Malajia spat.

Mark reached over and grabbed a few orange slices off of Sidra's plate. "I usually don't like anything that Malajia's simple ass says, but I agree with her," he said.

Malajia narrowed her eyes at Mark. *Always gotta be a jackass.*

"Hell, I have a date tonight," Mark revealed. "I'm not tryna be rushed. I might get laid." Mark's prediction earned skeptical stares from the girls.

"Yeah, okay," Malajia laughed. "No girl in her right mind will give up her goodies to the bum ass, freeloading, slacking, corny, likes of *you*."

"Spoken like someone who can't get laid to save her life," Mark bit back.

Malajia sucked her teeth as Sidra shook her head.

"Face it, this curfew hasn't helped any," Mark continued, going back to his original thought. "The police still haven't caught the bastards."

"Because everybody has been inside for the most part, so there's nobody to rob," Jason put in, eyes focused on his text book. He looked at his watch. "Chaz, it's almost six, time for your tutoring session," he announced.

Chasity rolled her eyes. She'd almost regretted asking him to tutor her for a big test that she had coming up for Calculus 2, "Fine," she huffed, grabbing her book bag.

"How are the sessions going anyway?" Sidra asked. "Jason, is she as difficult as she was last semester?"

"Oh absolutely," Jason chuckled, directing his attention to Chasity. "But she knows it doesn't bother me. Isn't that right, beautiful?"

"Let's just get this over with Jason," Chasity hissed, rising from her seat.

"Just for that attitude, today I'm going to make you find the tangent lines to the parametric equations for twenty minutes." Chasity threw her head back and let out a loud groan, inciting a laugh from Jason as they headed out of the cafeteria.

"Shoot, I forgot to ask Chaz if she can take me to Mega-Mart later," Sidra realized, grabbing her purse. "I'm out of instant coffee...and chocolate."

"You act like she won't be back later," Alex giggled.

"Yeah, but by that time she'll be all flustered and irritated from her session, so she's more inclined to say 'no'," Sidra joked, standing from the booth. "If I get a 'yes', do you ladies need me to pick up anything?"

"If you get a 'yes', we'll just ride with you," Alex replied. Sidra shrugged and headed out.

Malajia nearly choked on her soda. "Wait, did Jase say it was almost six?" she asked, eyes wide.

Mark stared at her as if she was crazy. "Yeah."

"Shit, Mark, we gotta go to Sociology." Malajia quickly gathered her belongings.

Mark waved his hand at her. "Man, fuck that class," he bit out, folding his arms.

Malajia hopped out of the booth. "That's fine, you repeat that class again if you want to, I'd be damned if *I* do."

Mark rolled his eyes as he watched Malajia dash for the exit.

"Mark, if you're gonna go to class, you better get to running—you know that Mr. Bradley will lock you out for being late," Alex advised.

"Damn it," Mark huffed, grabbing his book bag and taking off after Malajia.

"I can't believe it's ten minutes to midnight!" Sidra exclaimed, jerking her purse strap on her shoulder.

"This is Alex's fault," Malajia complained.

"*Mine*?" Alex looked at Malajia in shock. "*You* were the one who had to go up and down every damn aisle in Mega-Mart."

Sidra was able to get a 'yes' from Chasity after all, and both girls, along with Alex and Malajia, took a much needed trip to Mega-Mart after picking Alex up from the Pizza Shack. Losing track of time, the girls just pulled onto campus.

"We were late in the first place because we had to pick *your* broke ass up from that dusty ass Pizza Shack," Malajia shot back.

Alex sucked her teeth. "I had to pick up my check."

"But you didn't have to wipe off those tables," Malajia bit back.

"Placing the blame isn't helping," Sidra pointed out, unbuckling her seat belt as Chasity pulled into the first empty parking space that she found.

"Chasity, why are you parking at the apartments?" Malajia bellowed, craning her neck out of the window. "Do you realize how far this is away from our dorms?"

"Bitch, I don't have time to drive around and find a closer spot," Chasity snapped, opening her door.

"But, I have stiletto sandals! I can't run in these," Malajia whined.

"You're not the only one wearing high heels," Sidra scoffed, pointing to her black pumps. "So shut your mouth and get to running, before we get caught."

Out of the car, the four girls took off running towards their dorm.

"Ow!" Malajia howled, limping. "A twig just flew in my damn shoe."

Chasity laughed as Malajia's pulled the sharp twig out of her shoe. Irritated and embarrassed, Malajia tossed the twig at Chasity's back. Chasity stopped dead in her tracks, spun around, and tried to grab for Malajia. Alex grabbed Chasity's arm and nudged her back on her path.

"Kill her later, we gotta keep running," Alex urged.

"What time is it?" Sidra panted.

"Three minutes to twelve," Alex answered, hand over her chest.

A familiar figure appeared from around a corner and darted past them at top speed. Sidra frowned at the boxer shorts, white socks, and t-shirt that the tall, dark-skinned guy had on.

"Mark! What are you doing out here in your underwear?" Sidra shouted after him.

"No time to explain!" Mark hollered, not looking back.

The girls split off, running towards their dorms. Chasity and Sidra ran up the steps to Torrence Hall.

"Get the key, get the key," Sidra panicked as Chasity frantically fished through her handbag in search of her keys.

"I'm trying to find it," Chasity assured. "I have too much shit in this bag."

"Hurry up, Chasity."

"Where's *yours*, Sidra?" Chasity snapped, glaring at Sidra who simply scratched her head.

"Never mind that, just open the door."

As Chasity pulled the key from her bag, the girls noticed a police car approaching from afar.

"Shit," Chasity panicked, jamming the key in the door.

"Oh my God, come on. I don't wanna go back to jail," Sidra whined as the lights began flashing.

Chasity pushed the door open. They ran inside and raced up the steps to their room. Sidra and Chasity both collapsed on the floor once the door was locked behind them.

"I can't do this," Sidra panted, throwing her arm over her face. "My chest hurts."

Chasity stood from the floor just as a knock was heard at the door.

"Who could *that* be?" Sidra whispered, standing up. Chasity shrugged, looking at Sidra, who silently gestured for her to open the door. Chasity shook her head.

"*You* open it," Chasity quietly hissed.

Sidra frantically shook her head as the knock grew louder. Rolling her eyes at her roommate, who clutched a pillow to her chest, Chasity opened the door.

"Glad to see you two made it," Drea chuckled, closing the belt on her plush lavender robe.

Chasity simply stared at her resident advisor, not saying a word. *It would be her nosey ass*, she thought.

Recognizing the voice, Sidra walked over to the door. "Hey girl, what's up?" she smiled.

Drea folded her arms. "You two were lucky this time, you almost got caught."

"I don't know what you're talking about," Chasity hissed.

"Yeah, we've been in here the whole time," Sidra added, leaning on the door.

Drea looked back and forth between the two girls. "Um hmm," she ground out, pulling something out of her robe pocket. "Sidra, you should be more careful when you're running—you dropped your earring."

Sidra's eyes widened as she grabbed her ear. She recognized the blue crystal drop earring. *Crap, it must have fallen out of my ear mid-run.*

Sidra simply gave a nervous laugh as she retrieved the earring from Drea.

Chasity rolled her eyes as she shut the door.

Malajia and Alex darted through the front door of Wilson Hall. Hearing a snap, Malajia fell to the floor.

Alex spun around in mid-run to the staircase. "Mel, what the hell?" she whispered, not hiding the urgency.

"The heel just broke on my shoe," Malajia whined, holding up her broken heel. "This was my favorite pair of shoes."

"That's what you get for buying cheap shoes just because they're 'trendy'," Alex chided, grabbing Malajia's arm and dragging her limp body towards the stairs. "Now, come on."

Hearing a noise, Malajia jumped to her feet and both girls ran on tip toes, up the steps and down the hallway.

"I hope that Em is awake," Alex hoped, digging into her large brown satchel. "I can't find my keys."

"What else is new?" Malajia spat, turning the doorknob, which, much to their surprise and relief, was unlocked.

Emily bolted up in bed as Malajia came through the door, snatching off her shoes with Alex following close behind.

"Where *were* you guys?" Emily rubbed her eyes. "I tried to wait up for you."

"We were late getting to Mega-Mart and got held up," Alex informed, removing her lightweight jacket.

"Ask her whose fault it was, Emily," Malajia barked, pointing her broken shoe in Alex's direction.

"I'm not going to go back and forth with you on this again, Malajia" Alex shot back, flopping down on her bed. "Anyway Em," she added, turning her attention to Emily. "We just had to hide for like five minutes while a patrol car drove up and down the street…Now ask whose fault *that* was."

Malajia sucked her teeth at Alex's glare. "Chasity's," Malajia bit out, rubbing her foot. "I told her I can't run in these shoes. She should've parked closer."

Alex shook her head. "You can never take responsibility for your part in *anything,* can you?"

Malajia shrugged. "Nope."

"My ankle hurts," Malajia complained, lifting her leg up to examine it as she rested her back against the bench.

"All you do is complain," Alex laughed. "It's too nice of a day for you to be so miserable." The weather definitely felt like a typical spring day. Sun shining, breeze light, Alex relished taking it all in while sitting out with her friends in the campus commons area.

"Shut up, Alex," Malajia hissed, rubbing her right ankle. "*You* didn't bust your ass last night."

"Not my fault or anybody else's that your heel broke," Alex returned, pulling her hair back into a ponytail.

"And only *you* would bust your ass as soon as you get *in* the damn dorm," Chasity teased. Having heard the story from Alex earlier that morning, she couldn't wait to take a dig at Malajia for it.

Unable to think of a snappy comment, Malajia just rolled her eyes.

"I heard you girls almost got caught out last night," Jason said, taking a sip of his canned soda.

Sidra looked at him. "Who told you that?" she asked. "I mean we *did*. We were coming back from the store, but who told you?"

Without saying a word, Jason pointed to Mark, who was busy concentrating on the chips in his small foil pack.

Sidra leaned over in Mark's direction and cleared her throat. "And so did *he*," she announced.

"What could you have possibly been doing that would have you out after midnight?" Josh teased.

"Mind your business, pizza boy," Mark sneered, putting a chip into his mouth.

"No, I think we'd *all* like to know what you were doing out at nearly midnight, in your underwear, t-shirt, and socks," Sidra mocked, putting her hand up.

Mark noticed the prying eyes of his friends. "Whatchu mean, jelly bean?" he joked.

"Don't call nobody jelly bean, that's wack," Malajia jeered, shaking her hand at him.

"What were you doing?" Sidra pressed.

"Why you all up in my business?" Mark barked. "I didn't ask *y'all* where you were coming back from last night."

Alex looked at him with confusion. "But you didn't *have* to ask us, because we just told you."

"I'm not y'all," Mark grumbled.

Sidra narrowed her eyes at him. She knew that Mark's avoidance could only mean one thing—wherever he was, or whatever happened, must have been embarrassing. "Whose room were you in?"

Mark put his hand up. "Sidra, chill."

"Everybody stare at him," Sidra commanded. Mark sucked his teeth as all eyes fixed on him. He felt like eight sets of lasers were burning a hole into him.

"Look, it was just some girl," Mark revealed. "I was in her room getting…*serviced* and I looked at the time and just rolled out and left my shit there."

"Eww," Sidra scoffed at the thought of her friend receiving fellatio.

"What girl?" Josh asked, curious.

"You don't know her," Mark assured.

"Boy this campus is small and loud, we know everybody," Malajia ground out, getting close to Mark's face.

Mark rubbed the back of his neck. "It was um...Marilyn."

Sidra's eyes widened. "Hold on, from Torrence Hall?" she exclaimed. "Why would she be in Shippens Hall?"

"Her best friend lives over in that dorm," Mark clarified, "She was gone for the week, so Marilyn slept in there…and she invited me over." Mark lowered his head and shook it, as Chasity busted out laughing.

"You mean the girl whose teeth look like she carves concrete sculptures with em'?" Chasity laughed.

Malajia laughed. "Wait, is that the girl we were bussin' on, Chaz?" she asked. "The one who got smart with Sidra?"

"Yup, that's the one," Sidra nodded.

"Aye, her teeth don't look that bad…just that one snaggle one," Mark argued.

"His shlong got teeth marks on it and shit," Malajia teased, much to Mark's embarrassment.

"She was carving hieroglyphics into his man and shit," Chasity jeered, earning a playful backhand from Alex who was trying to control her laughter.

Jason winced and laughed at the same time. "Damn bro," he teased. "Were you that desperate?"

Mark rolled his eyes at Jason and glanced over at David, who was practically falling out of his seat. "You laughing kinda hard over there, glasses man," he bit out. "At least I got some, and didn't have to use my hand like *you* do."

"Trust me, I speak for all us guys when I say that *nobody* wants what you got last night," David shot back.

"She carved 'Marilyn was here' in his dick and shit," Chasity teased.

"Oh my God, Chasity!" Malajia screamed with laughter. Malajia could honestly say to herself that Chasity was the one girl in the group who could keep her laughing.

Mark was seething at the sound of his friends' laughter. Even innocent Emily, although she tried to hide it, joined in the laughing. "You know what, fuck y'all," Mark bit out, rising from his seat and hurrying off.

"Aww, where're you going, dick nibbles?" Malajia called after him.

Josh grabbed his stomach and doubled over in laughter. "Yoooo," was all that he could get out.

Sidra put her hand over her face. *These people are so damn vulgar.*

Chapter 28

Alex tapped her mouse vigorously before placing her head in her hands. "God, I wish I could afford a laptop," she mumbled. She'd been in the computer lab, located in the Science building across campus, typing two papers, for the past four hours. "I hate sitting in this damn lab all night."

"*You*?" Malajia complained, pushing her notebook across the table. "Try having a laptop and it being broke."

"Malajia, I already told you that if you kept looking up penises on the thing, eventually a virus was gonna invade it," Alex tiredly said.

Mark laughed, eyes not leaving his computer.

Malajia shot Mark a glare. "Shut up," she hissed at both him and Alex, while retrieving her notebook. "I'm mad as shit I gotta type this twenty page paper."

Alex sighed as she looked over at Jason, who was staring intensely at his computer screen. "How's your program coming?" she asked, noticing the drained look on his face.

"Its fine," he answered evenly as his fingers moved along the keyboard. He'd been in the lab way before Alex, Mark, and Malajia entered the room. Having met with his programming professor hours earlier, he'd opted to stay in the building and work in the empty lab as opposed to going all the way back to his room to work on his laptop. However, once Mark and Malajia started running their mouths, he regretted his decision.

"Don't you and Chaz have the same class?" Alex asked, sticking her flash drive into the computer tower.

Jason leaned back in his seat and rubbed his eyes. *Damn this bright screen.* "Yeah, we do," he answered. "But you already know she finished writing this program the same day it was assigned."

"My girl, the computer genius," Malajia gushed, shutting down her computer.

"Why are you shutting down? You barely typed any of your paper," Alex chided, removing her drive.

Malajia pointed to the now black computer screen. "Fuck that paper," she spat. "I'm over it."

"She about to fail and shit," Mark laughed.

Malajia sucked her teeth at him as she delivered a light tap to the back of his head. "What are you doing in here, anyway?" she asked, annoyed. "You've been surfing the damn web all night long."

"I'm minding my damn business," Mark barked.

Realizing that he wasn't going to get any more work done, Jason saved his progress and shut the system down. He'd ask Chasity to check it later.

Alex stood up and stretched. "I'm starving," she announced, glancing at the large black and white clock on the wall. "Is that time right?" she frowned.

Jason, Mark, and Malajia simultaneously glanced up.

"Yeah," Jason answered. It took a few seconds for them register what the time actually said. "Shit, its eleven-fifty!" Jason exclaimed, jumping up and gathering his belongings along with the others.

Jason darted for the door and opened it, finding the halls dark. The others ran up behind him and poked their heads out the door. Seeing a flicker of a flashlight at the end of the hallway, Jason signaled for them to get back inside. When they didn't immediately move, Jason glared at them. "Get back inside," he loudly whispered.

"I can't believe this is happening again," Alex said, running her hands through her hair as Jason quietly pulled the door closed. "How do we keep losing track of time?"

"How are we gonna get out of here with that damn flashlight cop walking around out there?" Mark asked.

Jason scanned the room with his eyes. Spotting a window on the other side of the room, his eyes lit up. "I see a way out," he announced, pointing.

"Oh no, I'm *not* climbing out a window," Malajia protested, putting her hand up. "I have on a damn dress."

"Look it's either *that* or you get caught, it's up to you," Jason shot back, voice stern. He was in no mood for Malajia's complaining.

"Come on Malajia, at least we're on the first floor," Alex added.

Malajia folded her arms. "I don't care *what* y'all say. I'm not climbing out the window."

Mark waved his hand at her. "Man, forget her ass, I'm outta here."

As Jason and Mark took off for the window, Alex grabbed Malajia's arm and gave her a hard yank. "Come on girl, stop playing games," she scolded.

Jason quickly but carefully opened the plate glass window. Seeing a screen, he carefully tried to open it. "Shit, it's stuck," he complained, giving it another jerk.

"We're gonna get arrested," Malajia panicked.

"No we're not, just calm down," Alex promised.

"Jase, let's kick this thing out," Mark suggested, realizing that the screen wasn't going to budge.

Mark and Jason began giving the screen a hard kick. They paused when they heard footsteps.

"That's the guard," Malajia panicked. "We're going down, we're going down."

Alex put her hands on Malajia's shoulder. "Pull yourself together," she commanded.

Jason gave the screen one last kick and it went falling to the ground. "Malajia, cut the bullshit," he barked. "Let's go."

Alex was the first to climb out the window with Malajia following. Mark took his time climbing out. Jason glanced at the door and heard the doorknob jiggle. *Crap!*

Jason looked back at the window, and seeing Mark halfway out, gave him a push sending him falling the rest of the way.

"Ow!" Mark yelped. Just as the door opened Jason dove out the window. The guard walked in, looked around the room and seeing the open window, walked over and flashed the light outside on the lawn. The four teens practically held their breaths as they laid on the ground as close to the wall as possible. Sighs of relief resonated through them once the window shut.

"That was close," Alex declared, voice low.

"Why did you push me?" Mark spat at Jason.

"Cause you were taking too damn long," Jason shot back.

"I was trying not to rip my jeans."

Seeing police lights nearby, Alex snapped her fingers. "Hey, shut up." She crawled away from the window. "We have to get out of here and fast."

After making their way from the Science building, they carefully ran to the next building, hiding behind walls while searching for other squad cars.

"I can't keep hiding like this," Malajia whispered as another car passed.

"Coast is clear, come on," Jason urged.

Jogging along the deserted path, they nearly passed Torrence Hall when they saw another car. "Hide, hide," Mark commanded, pointing to a cluster of bushes along the path. They scurried and dove behind the bushes, just in time for the car to pass.

"I landed on some damn branches," Malajia complained.

"So did *I*," Jason groaned, lifting his shirt to examine the blood covered scratches on his ribs.

Alex looked at the others. "Listen, there's no way that we're gonna make it to our own dorms right now," she announced. "Our only option is to get Chaz and Sidra to let us in *their* room," she said.

"And how are we gonna get them to do *that*?" Malajia asked, voice dripping with sarcasm. "It's not like we can just walk up and ring a doorbell."

"Yes, I'm aware of that smart ass," Alex bit back. "We'll have to go around back."

Malajia's eyes widened. "Hell no, I'm *not* climbing that damn tree."

"Do you have a better idea?" Alex quizzed.

"She never *does*," Mark chimed in, peeking over a bush.

"You okay, Jason?" Alex asked, noticing the pained look on his face as he held his side.

"I'll live," he assured. "Let's move."

"Chaz can you turn the light off, please?" Sidra asked, settling down in her bed.

Chasity flicked the switch to the overhead light before lying down in her own bed.

Hearing a light tapping sound, Sidra bolted up. "Did you hear that?" she asked Chasity.

"No," Chasity replied, pulling the covers up over her head. Hearing the noise herself, she snatched the covers off. "*Now* I did."

Sidra jumped out of bed as the tapping became louder. "I think it's coming from the window," Sidra concluded. "Go see what it is."

Chasity looked at her. "No, *you* check it," she shot back. "I'm tired of checking every-damn-thing."

"But...you're so fearless," Sidra smiled.

Chasity folded her arms. "Not working."

Sidra rolled her eyes and let out a huff. "Fine." She slowly walked over to the window. "It's probably a branch or something." Kneeling on the loveseat, she pulled back the curtain and opened the blinds. Shocked to see a weird face staring at her, Sidra let out a scream.

Chasity jumped out of bed and ran over to the window. Looking at the face, she frowned, then turned to Sidra who was still panicking.

"Sidra," Chasity said calmly. When Sidra continued to let out screams, Chasity grabbed both of her shoulders and shook her. "Sidra, Sidra!" Sidra stopped screaming and stared at her, wide eyed.

"There's somebody—"

"It's Mark," Chasity announced, tone even.

Sidra looked at her with confusion. "Huh?"

"It's Mark," Chasity repeated, guiding Sidra's face towards the window with her hand. "Look."

Sidra focused. Realizing that Chasity was right, her expression went from frightened to angry. Sidra pulled the window open to find Mark still staring at her with the same crazy facial expression. "What are you doing?" she snapped. "Are you out of your damn mind?"

"Um, can you let us in? It's a little uncomfortable out here," Mark replied, face now normal.

"*Us*?" Chasity frowned.

"What are you doing here?" Sidra asked, reaching for his arm to help him inside. Her mouth fell open when she saw the others climb in after him.

"What the hell?" Chasity asked, seeing them collapse on the floor. "Are y'all crazy?"

"I'm never climbing that mutant tree ever again," Malajia promised, dusting herself off.

Sidra put her hands up. "Excuse me, you still haven't answered my question," she pointed out.

Alex leaned back against the chair as she fanned herself. "Long story short, we lost track of time in the computer lab and have to hide out," Alex informed. "There's like ten patrol cars out there."

"In other words, we might as well get comfortable," Mark said, sitting on Sidra's bed and removing his sneakers.

"Aren't you guys worried about the room checks?" Sidra asked, running her hands over her blue satin scarf.

"Girl please, our lazy RA stopped doing room checks after the first night," Malajia chortled.

"Lucky you," Sidra said. "Ours is taking this room check thing a little too damn far."

"Cause Drea has no life," Malajia replied, removing her sandals.

Chasity glanced at Jason, "Did you finish your program?"

"Almost," he answered.

Noticing the pained look on his face and his labored breath, Chasity frowned in concern. "You okay?"

Jason winced as he felt the soreness of his side. "I have a few scratches," he said, lifting his blood stained shirt.

Chasity made a face of disgust at the site of the scratches. "Come on," she said, grabbing his arm and pulling him towards the bathroom. "I should have some stuff to clean that up."

"Sid, pass me a throw pillow," Mark commanded, as the bathroom door shut.

"Sure, cause you're gonna need it on that hard floor," Sidra replied, folding her arms. "Oh what? You thought that I was sharing my bed? You must be crazy," she added, noticing the surprised look on Mark's face.

A knock at the door halted any response that Mark was about to give.

"It's after midnight, who is that?" Alex whispered, as everyone froze in place.

"Sidra, Chasity. I heard a scream, open the door," the female voice urged from the other side.

"Shit, it's Drea," Sidra declared, recognizing the voice. "You have to hide, cause her nosey butt is going to come in here."

As soon as the words left Sidra's mouth, Alex, Malajia and Mark scurried around the room looking for a place to hide. Mark tried to hide under Sidra's bed but was greeted by large plastic storage bins.

"Damn sis, how much shit do you *have?*" Mark whispered, jumping up from the floor.

"Girls open up," Drea insisted, knocking again. "I have to check on you."

Sidra walked over to the door. "Just a minute," she called, signaling for her friends to hurry up and hide.

Alex ran for Chasity's closet and ended up colliding with Malajia who was also running for the door. Malajia backhanded Alex on the arm as both girls squeezed into the closet. Mark darted for Sidra's closet, but seeing a large trunk blocking the door, he sucked his teeth and ran for Chasity's closet.

"Come on!" Malajia barked as Mark crammed his long body into the closet, squishing Alex and Malajia in the process.

"Shut up and shut the damn door," Mark ordered. Alex pulled the door closed.

"Sidra!" Drea hollered, through the door.

Sidra snatched open the door. "Hello Drea, what brings you here at this hour?" she smiled.

"Don't play cute with me, Sidra," Drea sneered, entering the bedroom. "I heard a scream come from in here."

Sidra scratched the back of her neck. "A scream?...*I* didn't hear a scream," she lied.

"Oh really?" Drea regarded Sidra skeptically.

Sidra's mouth dropped open. "Are you implying that I'm hiding something?" she asked, sounding offended. "I am insulted and appalled. You must leave, now." She pointed to the door in dramatic fashion.

Drea smiled. "Nice try, where's Chasity?"

Sidra's eyes shifted nervously.

Chasity, having heard her name from inside the bathroom, slightly opened the door. Her eyes widened when she saw Sidra talking to Drea, her back facing the bathroom. Holding an alcohol soaked rag to Jason's wounds, Chasity, catching Sidra's attention, gestured for her to get rid of Drea. Sidra made a slight gesture with her eyes and her arms, letting Chasity know that she was trying.

Drea turned around; causing Chasity to pull her head back inside the bathroom. "Shit, it's that fuckin' RA," she bit out to Jason, still holding the rag on his cuts.

Jason was making faces as he felt the alcohol sting him. "Um, Babe—Baby this stuff is peeling my skin off," he complained, pointing to the rag.

Chasity quickly removed the rag. "Oh, sorry."

"Chasity, come out here please," Drea called.

"Yes, come out here please," Sidra followed up.

"I'll be right there," Chasity assured, teeth clenched. "Just be quiet," she whispered to Jason.

"Why would I say anything?" he whispered back.

Waving her hand at him dismissively, Chasity opened the door and stuck her head out. "Sidra, come here for a second," she commanded.

"Chasity enough of the games, it's late, just come out," Drea insisted.

Chasity felt her temper shorten. "Don't tell me what to do, Drea," she warned.

"Okay, okay let's not get hasty Chaz; she's only doing her job," Sidra cut in, knowing how quickly things can escalate. Sidra headed for the bathroom. "What is it?" she whispered, coming face to face with her roommate.

"You have to distract her," Chasity said, voice low.

"That's what I've *been* doing."

"I have to get Jason out of here, cause you know that she's gonna try to make up some excuse to use the bathroom."

"Okay, okay I'll try," Sidra assured. "I'm bad at this you know."

"Yes, I know," Chasity teased as a reluctant Sidra walked away from the door.

Sidra let out a sigh and was getting ready to say something, when she heard a loud thump from the closet, followed by a high-pitched shriek.

Sidra looked around nervously. "Ow!" she shrieked, grabbing her stomach. "My cramps!"

"Are you okay?" Drea asked.

"I'll live," Sidra said. They heard another thump.

"Sidra what was that?"

"That?" Sidra asked, failing to hide the panic in her voice. "Oh um, it's probably our neighbors. They're always loud and I wish that they would SHUT UP!" she hollered towards the closet.

Hearing a muffled female voice say "sorry" from the closet, Sidra closed her eyes and grabbed the bridge of her nose with two fingers. *Of course, Malajia would be the one to do that,* she fumed to herself.

As Drea proceeded towards the closet, Chasity opened the bathroom door and gave a signal to Sidra. Sidra looked over at Drea, who was standing in front of the closet with her ear to the door. Sidra, not sure of what to do, put her hands on her head. *Think Sidra, think damn it!*

Suddenly she walked over to Chasity's night stand and knocked her leg against it. "Shit!" she exclaimed, grabbing her leg.

"Oh my gosh, are you okay?" Drea asked, rushing to Sidra's side. In pain, Sidra looked up at Chasity who was staring at her with a confused look.

What the hell, Sidra? Chasity couldn't understand why Sidra actually hit her leg, when she could have just made a loud outburst to get Drea's attention.

While Drea was tending to Sidra; Chasity pushed the door all the way open and signaled for Jason to come out. Jason quickly ran and dove under Chasity's bed as Chasity hurried to Sidra's side. "Wow that looks bad, let me get a first aid kit," Chasity quickly blurted out, before running back for the bathroom.

"I'll go with you," Sidra said, limping alongside her.

"No, enough with the games," Drea snapped, grabbing both girls by the arm, accidentally scratching Chasity in the process.

"Bitch, you scratched me!" Chasity snapped.

Drea turned her back to the girls, ignoring Chasity.

Sidra quickly grabbed Chasity's arms as she went to grab for Drea's neck.

"I don't appreciate you two playing games," Drea ground out.

Chasity snatched away from Sidra. "You know what, you're taking this shit *way* to seriously," she snapped, pointing at Drea. "You are a resident advisor, not a *parent,* not a *security guard,* not the fuckin' *police.*"

"Okay," Sidra mumbled in agreement.

"You don't have the right to go searching in people's rooms, I don't give a shit *what* anybody else says," Chasity added.

"Look, I'm just doing my job, Chasity," Drea argued. "I have to make sure everybody in this dorm abides by the rules. I'm in charge, and you need to realize that. It's called respect."

Chasity glared at her "Respect for who? *You?*" she hissed. "Don't get full of yourself Drea. Nobody respects you. Hell half of us don't even like your ass for real…including *me.*"

Drea's round face fell. It was apparent by the look and silence that Chasity had hurt her feelings. "You ladies have a good night," she sulked, before walking out of the room, shutting the door behind her.

"Wow Chaz," was all that Sidra could say.

"Were you not thinking the exact same thing?" Chasity returned.

"Maybe," Sidra admitted, sitting on the bed. "All right guys, you can come out now," she called to the closet.

The closet door opened and Mark, Malajia and Alex came falling out as Jason emerged from under Chasity's bed.

"What was all that noise in there?" Sidra bit out.

Alex stretched. "It was Malajia and Mark playing around," she revealed.

"Mark was pinching me," Malajia exclaimed.

"Your ass was in my face," Mark countered.

"Can y'all leave now?" Chasity asked, tired. "I'm over this entire ordeal."

Malajia stood from the floor. "Oh Chasity, I found a cute pair of shoes in your closet that would go great with an outfit that I have," she announced, holding up an expensive pair of silver high-heeled sandals.

Chasity shot Malajia a death stare as she slowly folded her arms. Unfazed, Malajia simply smiled.

Chapter 29

Malajia's high heels clicked along the brick path towards the cafeteria. She'd been running for nearly five minutes and didn't realize how much her feet hurt until she busted through the cafeteria door and began walking to her usual booth, seeing Alex and Sidra sitting.

"Why are you out of breath?" Alex asked, looking up from her grilled chicken salad.

Malajia put her hand on her chest and signaled with her finger to give her a minute. Malajia flopped down in the seat. "I ran all the way from class," she panted, picking up Sidra's cup of iced tea and taking a sip.

"Why?" Alex asked, confused.

"I have some good news," Malajia smiled, now breathing normally. "The curfew is lifted." When she didn't get the reaction she hoped for from the girls, she slammed her hand on the table. "Did you hear me? We're free. They caught the assailants last night."

"I know, I heard earlier," Sidra sullenly replied. "They got caught trying to rob an undercover."

Malajia's eyes shifted from Alex to Sidra, taking in the sour look on both of their faces. "What the hell is wrong with you two?" she asked. "You don't think this is good news? No more ducking and dodging patrol cars or missing out on parties...Come on; we had that curfew for like three weeks."

"Malajia, we hear you and we get it," Alex huffed. "It *is* good news, but that is the farthest thing from my mind right now."

Malajia raised her eyebrow. Alex's tone was much too harsh for her liking. "Um...You wanna tell me what has you and Princess Prissy so bitchy today?" she sneered.

Alex and Sidra glanced at each other, then turned back to Malajia. "We got called before the Dean today," Alex informed.

Malajia frowned. "For what?" she asked, grabbing a french fry off of Sidra's plate.

"For the fight that we had with Jackie and her friends," Sidra added.

Malajia dropped a fry back on the plate. "What?" she exclaimed.

Alex nodded. "Yup, we got letters sent to our room this morning, telling us to go to the office," she revealed. "They heard about the fight at the store and wanted to talk to us about it."

"Before we even had a chance to explain, they told us that the president of the university wants to meet with all of us to get to the bottom of the whole situation," Sidra added.

"Are you serious?" Malajia fumed. "They need to haul Jackie and those ratchet friends of hers in front of the damn president."

"Apparently, they already spoke to Jackie and those rats," Sidra fussed. "The bitch complained that we started the whole thing."

Malajia's mouth fell open. "Oh really?" she ground out. "And how did she twist the whole 'jumping' situation? Stupid, lying bitch."

Alex shrugged. "I have no idea, but all I know is that we have to come back here sometime during the summer and stand before President Bennett, and once she has all of the information, she'll decide what she wants to do with us," she concluded.

"And what does *that* mean?" Malajia asked.

"It means…that we could get kicked out of school for this," Alex answered.

"Oh no, the hell we're *not*," Malajia protested. "There's no way in hell Jackie can spin this. Not with us standing in her damn face." She folded her arms. "You know, I was wondering why I haven't seen none of their asses sliding around campus lately."

"Oh, they've been avoiding us ever since the fight," Sidra confirmed, wiping her hands with a napkin.

Appetite gone, Alex tossed her fork down on her plate of half eaten salad. "Now I have to spend the rest of the semester worried."

"Why not just have this damn meeting *now*? Why wait until the summer?" Malajia fussed. "Ruining my summer and shit."

"Summer?" Sidra groused, leaning forward. "Forget the summer. Our *lives* could be ruined if we get kicked out of school."

"That's not happening." Malajia was confident that their school president would see through all of Jackie's lies. "Does Chasity know about this?" she asked.

Alex put her hands on her head. "Crap, I don't know," she said, grabbing her book bag. "Come on. Let's go find out."

The three girls left the cafeteria with haste, and had arrived to Torrence Hall within record time. Sidra opened the door to find Chasity sitting at her desk, typing on her laptop.

"Sis, you okay?" Alex charged, sitting her bag down on the floor.

"Uh huh," Chasity mumbled, not turning around.

Malajia and Sidra exchanged glances. "Um…did you get a letter telling you to go in front of the Dean today?" Sidra asked.

"Uh huh," Chasity repeated, same even tone.

"So did you *go*?" Malajia pressed, annoyed with the nonchalant responses.

Chasity spun around in her seat, and seeing the enraged look on her face, the girls were sure that Chasity wasn't feeling as nonchalant as her voice led on.

"I guess you feel exactly how *we* do," Alex concluded, sitting on the loveseat. "You wanna talk it out?"

"What do you want me to say, Alex?" Chasity drew her words out slowly.

Alex shrugged. "Something other than 'uh huh'," she returned. "We're all angry about this, but bottling your emotions won't help."

Chasity rose from her seat. "Don't start this shit with me today, Alex," she hissed. "Let me keep it in for now because if I don't…" Chasity paused as she felt her temper rising. Chasity had been trying to contain her temper ever since she saw the letter under her door when she returned from class earlier that morning. She recalled fighting the urge to lunge across the desk at the Dean when he accused Chasity of being an angry troublemaker. Talking to her aunt didn't make her any calmer; Trisha in so many words told Chasity to control her temper, stay calm, and that she would handle it. "It's taking everything in me not to tear this room, the Dean's office, and Jackie's *face* apart right now…So I'm begging you, don't ask me about how I'm feeling right now."

Alex nodded slowly as she put her hands up in surrender. "I get it," she promised. "But I will just say this."

The girls let out loud sighs. "Here she goes," Malajia mumbled, sitting on Sidra's bed.

Alex ignored the reactions. "We're all in this together."

Malajia had a thought. "Do we need to bring our parents?" she exclaimed. "Cause if we do, I'm just gonna leave school on my own."

Alex shook her head. "They'll probably want someone there…I mean we're adults, but I'm sure we should still have them come down," she suggested, running her hands through her hair. "Might as well let the cat out the bag."

"No, that cat can sit its ass right on in that bag," Malajia refused. "I can't deal with the reaction that I'll get from my parents if they find out. I'm already the bad seed in their eyes."

"No you're not," Sidra contradicted.

"Trust me, I *am*," Malajia bit out.

Chasity let out a sigh. "Trisha will be here," she revealed, voice low.

"Really?" Malajia asked, voice full of hope. It was when Chasity nodded that Malajia let out a sigh of relief. "Thank God."

"Your aunt is such a life saver," Alex added, grateful.

"She said she'll make sure we're treated fairly," Chasity added, rubbing the back of her neck. "She said that she donates too much money to this school for them to think they're just gonna kick us out."

Malajia clasped her hands together. "I so love her," she gushed. "And I love you too for being related to her."

Chasity narrowed her eyes at Malajia and shook her head, too mentally drained to fire off a snappy retort.

Alex, there's no point in stressing yourself, everything will work out fine. Those words swirled around in Alex's head for the past two days. She kept trying to convince herself and the other girls that everything would be okay, but she still wasn't sure if she believed it.

Shaking her head in an effort to remove the worrisome thoughts, Alex stopped walking. "Hey guys, I have an idea," she blurted out, grabbing the groups attention as they walked out of the movie theater.

"Why are we stopping?" Mark asked, rubbing his stomach. "I'm starving and that popcorn was ass. Come on, let's go to that taco place."

"Mark, can you not associate food and the word 'ass' together please?" Sidra scoffed, putting her hand up.

"Okay, so I just had a thought," Alex proclaimed. "You know how much I love you guys—"

"Alex, don't start this sentimental mess," Chasity sneered.

Alex pointed to her. "Hush," she commanded. "Anyway, I think it will be fun if we all got to know each other on a deeper level."

"Such as?" Sidra asked, curious.

"Well…" Alex hesitated, unsure of how her suggestion would be taken. "I think we should spend the next few weekends visiting each other's families." Alex shut her eyes as the complaints resonated through the group.

"Are you out of your damn mind?" Malajia exclaimed, "*I* don't even wanna sit around my family for a weekend; you think that I want to bring *y'all* around them?"

"Look we already met and hung out with Chasity's aunt, and she was so much fun right?" Alex pointed out.

"Yes, I just love her," Malajia gushed. "I wish she was *my* aunt."

"No, you just love her money," Chasity hissed.

"Anyway," Alex began, ignoring Chasity's smart comment. "I think it'll be fun. We'll get to see how we all interact with our families."

"But why would we want to do that?" Chasity asked, confused. "You always come up with the dumbest shit for us to do."

"Chasity, are you cramping sweetie?" Alex ground out, earning a death stare from Chasity. "Because you're a little bit more snappy than usual…a little bit."

Chasity hesitated for a moment. "Maybe," she admitted, voice filled with disdain.

"Aww, you need a hug?" Mark offered, reaching his arm around Chasity's shoulder.

"Don't touch me," Chasity hissed, causing Mark to jerk his arm away.

Alex suppressed a giggle. "So, what do you guys say?"

"I say hell no," Malajia spat. "I'm not taking part in this happy-go-lucky nonsense."

Alex folded her arms and moved close to Malajia's face.

"What the hell are you all up in my damn face for?" Malajia barked.

"You're *going* to participate," Alex assured. "As a matter of fact, we're going to your house first."

"Y'all got me *all* the way chopped." Malajia stood firm. "There's no way that's happening."

Ten minutes later

"Yeah Mom, are y'all doing anything next weekend?" Malajia asked into her cell phone. "All right, well, I'm bringing my friends over to spend the weekend...all of them...yes the guys too, tell Dad to stop asking questions on the sidelines please?...yes I hear him...so throw the brats in the trash and make room."

Once her mother confirmed the plans, Malajia ended the call and shoved the phone back into her purse with a huff. "This is some straight bull."

"See, that wasn't so bad, now was it?" Alex teased.

"Fuck you, Alex," Malajia bit out. "That was low for you to threaten to show my parents the video you took of me while I was drunk."

"That's what you get for all the trash talk," Alex mocked, smiling.

Malajia just turned her lip up while she glared at Alex.

"This should be interesting," David mused. "Bringing eight people home with us."

"Seven," Chasity contradicted.

"No it's—"

"*Seven*….We all know that Emily's mom isn't gonna let her go anywhere but home," Chasity replied, gesturing to Emily who was standing there silent.

"Oh that's right. Sorry Emily," David said sympathetically.

"Tough luck Em," Mark added.

Emily looked away. *I don't need to be reminded*, she thought.

"Shit, don't feel sorry for *her*," Malajia fumed. "You should feel sorry for *me*. *I'm* the one who has to deal with my stupid family all weekend."

"Oh my God, nobody caaaares," Mark groaned. "Can we go eat, please?"

Emily grabbed her pink overnight bag from her bed and wrapped the strap across her shoulder. Hearing a light tap on the door, she sighed. "It's open," she called, knowing who was on the other side.

Her mother barged through the door. "Are you ready to go?"

Emily nodded, reaching for her room keys. Yet another Friday evening was upon her, meaning yet another unwanted trip home for the weekend. She almost cried when her friends walked out to go bowling not even an hour earlier. Emily hated herself for not being able to stand up to her mother, or anyone else.

As both women headed out the door, Emily stopped. "Mommy," she softly called, earning a look from her mother.

"What is it Emily? We have to get going," Ms. Harris urged. "I don't want to get stuck in traffic."

Emily fiddled with the string on her sweat jacket. *Just tell her.* "I don't want to continue going home every weekend," she blurted out. Emily looked at the floor to avoid her mother's piercing gaze. "I'm sorry, but I don't."

"You don't have a choice, Emily," she spat.

"But why do I have to keep doing this?" Emily returned. "I mean, I get that I lied and I'm sorry for that. But I think you're being a little um…extreme with this punishment…I learned my lesson. I won't lie again."

"Emily, we've already had this discussion."

"With all due respect, Mommy…*You* talked about it. I didn't get a chance to say anything."

Ms. Harris folded her arms across her chest as she stared her daughter down. "Emily the only reason why you're in college is to get an education," she said. "Everything else isn't important."

"But that's not true," Emily argued, voice rising slightly. "College isn't just about the books. At least that's what Daddy told me."

"You do not live with your father," Ms. Harris spat. "You live with *me* and I say that you won't be spending your weekends down here with these—these girls that have no respect for you, or anybody else."

"So this is about my friends?"

"Those so-called friends encouraged you to lie to me, I know it."

"No, they didn't," Emily corrected. "They said that I should've just asked you. But…I knew you would say no." Emily stomped her foot on the floor. "The lie was on *me*, not them."

Ms. Harris waved her hand dismissively. "I don't believe you," she insisted. "You've never done anything so sneaky, not since you started hanging around them."

Emily rolled her eyes as her mother continued her rant. *You have no idea what you're talking about*, she fumed silently.

"We're done with this discussion, do you hear me?" Ms. Harris declared, voice stern. When Emily didn't answer initially, she snapped her fingers. "Did you hear me, young lady?"

"Yes, I heard you," Emily answered, keeping the tone in her voice in check. She gritted her teeth as her mother stormed out of the room, signaling Emily to follow.

Chapter 30

"I don't know how I got talked into this mess," Malajia complained as Chasity pulled into the driveway of Malajia's home the following Friday evening.

"I blackmailed you," Alex reminded, voice filled with amusement.

Malajia rolled her eyes as the girls stepped out of the car. "I hate y'all for this."

"Hush up, whiny," Sidra teased, grabbing her overnight bag out of the trunk. "Your family isn't as bad as you're making them out to be."

"Oh, I'm gonna tell *all* your business this weekend," Mark promised Malajia, stepping out of his car.

"Do it if you dare," Malajia challenged. "I'll shave your damn hair off."

"You wanna start with my balls?" Mark jeered, flipping her off.

"Gross!" Sidra scoffed, stomping her foot on the concrete. "We don't want to be subjected to this kind of childish nonsense all weekend."

"We do this every day. You should be used to it by now," Mark laughed.

Malajia stomped up to the front door and opened it. She let out a groan when she saw toys all over the living room.

"Nice cleaning job, *Mom*!" Malajia yelled, stepping over the mess. Malajia's three younger sisters ran out of the dining room as the rest of the group stepped inside the disheveled house.

"Quit running!" Malajia screamed at the girls. "Mom, come get your children," she barked when the girls ignored her, running up the steps.

Mrs. Simmons hurried out of the dining room and hugged her daughter. She turned to the group and greeted everyone with a warm hug.

"Sidra," she exclaimed, hugging her the tightest. "My baby, I haven't seen you in years. Look how grown up and beautiful you look." Sidra gave a slight twirl.

Malajia sucked her teeth. "Oh please, Mom," she groused. "The only reason she looks so grown is because of those old ass clothes she has on."

Sidra frowned. She certainly didn't think that her pale blue skirt and matching short sleeved top looked old. "You could stand to dress a little more like me, and less like a street walker," Sidra sneered.

"That come back was wack," Malajia returned, adjusting the shingles on her long silver earrings.

"Okay, enough," Mrs. Simmons cut in. "Come on, I'll show you guys where you'll sleep."

"And where is that?' Malajia asked, face frowned.

Mrs. Simmons shot her a side glance. "*First* of all, fix your sour face. Nobody wants to be subjected to that all weekend."

Malajia rolled her eyes as she heard snickers resonate through the room.

"Now, I'm putting the girls in your room and the boys in Maria's room."

Malajia's eye widened. "Why can't the girls get Maria's room?" she whined. "I don't wanna sleep in the room with Geri."

"You share a room with Geri when you're home, what's the damn difference?" Mrs. Simmons barked. "Girl, I'm not for your attitude, hear?"

Malajia opened the door to her room and tossing her bag on the floor, let out a loud sigh. "Home, rotten home."

"Girl, will you quit complaining?" Alex laughed. "That's all you do."

"Just relax, and I'll let you know when dinner is ready," Mrs. Simmons said.

"I hope you ordered take out, cause nobody wants that goulash you make," Malajia complained.

Mrs. Simmons regarded her daughter sternly. "If you don't stop your damn whining Buttons, so help me, I will embarrass you in front of all your friends," she warned, before walking out of the room, slamming the door behind her.

Malajia stood there horrified at the fact that her mother just called her by her childhood nickname. Slowly turning to face the girls, who were desperately trying to conceal their laughter, she focused on Chasity who slowly raised her hand.

"What Chasity? What is it?" Malajia barked, hands on her hips.

"Who the hell is Buttons?" Chasity laughed.

"It was a childhood nickname, okay?"

Sidra put her hand on her chest, fighting the urge to laugh out loud. "Um…Why?"

Malajia rolled her eyes to the ceiling. "When I was little, my nose looked like a button that had been sewn to my face," she revealed. "Hence, the name 'Buttons'."

It was silence for a few minutes before the girls busted out laughing.

"It's not funny," Malajia wailed.

"I gotta see a picture. Please," Alex insisted.

"I burned them all," Malajia snapped. She focused her attention on Chasity, who was in tears. "Chasity, I don't know what the hell *you're* laughing at, because your nickname was Pebbles."

Chasity instantly stopped laughing. "Say *what* now?"

"Uh huh, Ms. Trisha told me that, during one of our many conversations about you," Malajia confessed. Chasity looked shocked. "She said when you were little, you used to take the little pebbles from your grandmom's vase and stick them in your diaper."

"She *told* you that?" Chasity seethed. She couldn't believe that her aunt would just spread her business like that. Especially business that she begged her never to reveal, and especially to Malajia—the big mouth of the group.

Malajia nodded. "And she said that you didn't get potty trained until you were four," she quickly blurted out. "Take that."

Furious, Chasity grabbed a pillow from Malajia's bed and threw it at Malajia, who ducked, sending it flying into the wall. "Missed, Pebbles," she taunted, dancing in place.

Chasity gritted her teeth as Sidra giggled. "Thank God, I don't have any childhood nicknames that I hate," she said.

"Maybe not, but you hate your middle name Ophelia," Malajia teased, still dancing.

Sidra stomped her foot on the floor. "Shut up, Malajia," she hissed. "There isn't even any music on."

Alex put her hands up. "I'm just gonna keep quiet, because y'all know how I feel about 'Alexandra'," she chortled.

Sitting down to eat over an hour later, Malajia grabbed a slice of pizza from one of the boxes that were on the large dining room table. "Mom, where's Maria?" she asked of her sister, sprinkling pepper over her pizza.

"Spending the weekend at Tanya's house," Mr. Simmons answered, opening a beer.

"Hey Mr. Simmons, how about you pass me one of those, will ya?" Mark smiled.

Mr. Simmons shot Mark a death stare. "Son, are you out of your mind?" he chided.

"A little bit," Mark joked, earning a backhand on his arm from Sidra.

"You actually think I'm going to give an under-aged college student beer? In my house?"

"Dad, ignore him," Malajia demanded. "I'm sure you remember how much of an idiot he can be…always."

Mark made a face at Malajia as he picked up his piece of fried chicken.

"So, how is your second semester coming along?" Mrs. Simmons asked, reaching for a bottle of soda.

"It's cool, I'm getting straight A's," Mark boasted, avoiding the gazes of his friends.

"Liar," Malajia sneezed, earning a few snickers.

Mark glared at her. "Can you please pass the salt, Buttons?"

Malajia's eyes and mouth widened. Embarrassed by the laughter, she pointed to Chasity.

"Malajia, don't bring it over here," Chasity warned, pointing back.

"Chasity's nickname is Pebbles cause she used to stick pebbles in her diaper," Malajia blurted out, much to Chasity's annoyance. "And she crapped on herself until she was four."

Chasity tossed her napkin down on the table. "Malajia smokes weed," she blurted out.

Malajia gasped, seeing her parents glare at her.

Her older sister Geri busted out laughing. "Ooooohhh," she teased.

"Chasity's an alcoholic," Malajia shot back.

"Malajia never wears clothes."

"I do so!" Malajia shot back.

"When?" Chasity countered.

Malajia slammed her hand on the table and shot Mark, who was bent over the table laughing, a glare. "Mark messes with a girl with rotten teeth!" Malajia exclaimed.

Mark nearly choked on his piece of chicken. "Malajia has crotch itch," he lied, pointing to her.

Malajia was seething. "Mark has scrolls etched in his man parts."

"How would *you* know that?" Mark shot back.

"Exactly." Mrs. Simmons folded her arms as she narrowed her eyes at her daughter.

Malajia looked at her parents, wide eyed. "Huh?"

"Alex trades dry pizzas for sex favors," Mark joked, pointing a chicken bone at her.

"Don't drag me into this mess," Alex hissed, putting her hand up.

"Alex has to put plastic at the bottom of her boot to cover the hole," Malajia jumped in.

Alex tossed her arms in the air. "I don't have a hole in my boots," she seethed. "But *Malajia* got drunk at a reggae party."

"Snitch!" Malajia wailed. She pointed to Jason, "Jason dances around his room in nothing but his sweaty jockstrap."

"Wait, what?" Jason asked confused.

"Again, how would *you* know that?" Mark questioned.

"Malajia flashes people in the subway," Alex put in.

Mark pointed to David. "David is a dork."

"Malajia chews flavored condoms like its gum," Chasity spat.

"What?" Malajia shrieked.

"Sidra's ponytail is fake," Mark lied.

"You wish," Sidra spat. "Mark strips for free food."

"I strip for *what*?!" Mark barked.

"Josh spies on Sidra while she's in the shower," Malajia added.

"David has sex with his glasses," Mark informed, earning laughter from the table. David looked at Mark and shook his head.

"All right, everybody chill out," Mrs. Simmons intervened, standing up from the table. Geri was doubled over with laughter, while Mr. Simmons concealed his laughter.

"It's all *Buttons* fault," Mark spat after a few seconds of silence.

"Bum," Malajia shot back.

"Pebbles," Jason teased.

"Jock strap," Chasity retorted.

"Nappy wig," Malajia said to Alex.

"Naked drunk," Alex returned.

"Glasses lover," Mark called David, laughing.

David slammed his hands on the table. "It wasn't funny the *first* time you said it, and it's not funny *now!*" he snapped.

Chasity glanced over at the time illuminating from the clock on the small white nightstand. *Two in the damn morning*, she thought, tossing and turning.

"I swear I should've stayed in a hotel," Chasity complained, sitting up from the floor.

"You and me both," Sidra groaned, positioning a pillow under her arm. "I don't do the sleep on the floor thing."

"Oh, shut up prissy and bitchy," Malajia sneered, sitting up in her bed.

"Says the one who's comfortable in a bed," Sidra shot back.

"You know what Mel, you could've given up your bed, they *are* your guests," Geri suggested.

"Please," Malajia barked. "I'm not sleeping on the floor in my own house. You give up *your* bed."

"They're not my company, stupid," Geri pointed out.

"She's right," Alex yawned.

Malajia shot Alex a glare, unsure if she could even see it through the moon lit room. "You always gotta add your two cents, shut up," Malajia barked. She kicked her legs wildly in the air. "I'm so bored," she complained.

"Well, we can't go anywhere. Everything is closed," Geri pointed out.

"You wasn't going anywhere with us *anyway*," Malajia mumbled.

"Oh heifer, I was *going*," Geri shot back.

Malajia rolled her eyes as she heard a light tap on the door. The door slowly opened and Mark, who was lying on the floor, stuck his head in.

"Boy, nobody said come in," Malajia spat.

"We can't sleep," Mark announced, ignoring Malajia's scolding. "Y'all wanna play a game?"

Sidra sat up. "What kind of a game?"

"Nobody wants to play 'let's grab an ass in the dark'," Malajia jeered.

"You have no ass to grab anyway," he shot back.

Malajia flipped him off in retaliation.

"Anyway." Mark rolled his eyes at her. "I think we should play hide and seek in the dark."

"Fine, but we need to be quiet," Malajia agreed.

"Cool," Mark smiled, pulling his head out of the room. "Guys," he called to the next room. "They're in...Sorry Josh, they said they didn't wanna play 'let's grab an ass in the dark'," he joked.

"I didn't even suggest that," Josh hissed.

The group crept out of the rooms. Once downstairs in the dark living room, they huddled together.

"It's dark as shit down here," Mark chortled. "Creepy ass house."

"You sound stupid," Malajia bit out. "The lights are off and the damn curtains are closed. It's *supposed* to be dark, fool."

"Seriously guys, we really have to be careful not to wake Mom and Dad," Geri whispered.

"Shit, screw *them*," Malajia scoffed. "We have to make sure we don't wake Melissa's loud ass," she pointed out of her two year old sister.

"Anybody who has the last name *Summers* is it," Mark announced, quickly.

David's eyes widened. "Come on, man," he barked.

"Sorry, those are the rules," Mark chuckled.

"*What* rules?" David snapped.

"Shhhh!" Sidra admonished, glancing at the stairwell.

"You're gonna wake people up, just count David," Mark commanded.

David sucked his teeth. "Fine," he agreed. "Base is the front door."

Everyone scrambled to find a hiding spot as David began counting. Geri and Malajia nearly came to blows over a spot in the corner behind a large faux tree. "Move," Malajia hissed.

"Get outta here, and stop following me," Geri shot back, giving Malajia a nudge. Realizing that she wasn't going to get into that spot, Malajia jumped over the loveseat and made a dash for the dining room.

Watching the scene unfold, Mark laughed while he slid in an opening between a book shelf and the wall.

"Ten," David announced, removing his hands from his eyes. He scanned the entire living room with his eyes, blinking in an effort to focus in the dark. He let out a loud sigh as he tiptoed in the kitchen. Jason, seizing an opportunity, hurried from his hiding spot in the dining room and ran for the base.

"Damn it," David fumed, watching Jason touch the door. As he ran into the dining room, Sidra jumped out of the small coat closet, and ran for the base. "Guys, come on, I can't see," David complained as Sidra and Jason celebrated with high fives.

"Clean those glasses," a deep, muffled voice jeered.

David slowly crept through the house in search of the voice. Chasity, seeing David walk pass, climbed out from underneath the coffee table and made it to base.

"Really Chasity? Under the coffee table?" David bit out.

"Did you find me?" Chasity boasted.

David saw movement from the kitchen. Once he took off running in that direction, Mark and Malajia jumped up from their hiding spots and started running neck and neck for the base.

"Move," Mark urged, nudging Malajia with his arm, causing her to slip and fall into the couch.

Geri nearly knocked the tree over as she busted out laughing.

"Damn it Mark," Malajia yelped, crawling to the base.

"Malajia, you're gonna wake up the baby," Geri laughed.

"Oh *fuck* the baby!" Malajia fumed. "I just got pushed into the damn chair by a jackass."

"You was up in my face lookin' all ugly and shit," Mark shot back, scratching his head.

Malajia checked her reply once she saw Josh and Alex run out of the dining room with David following close behind.

"Move moooove," Josh urged to the people standing by the base. Josh nearly made it, but he slipped on a satin throw pillow, falling to the floor. As laughter rang through the room, Josh reached his hand out and touched the base.

Alex was so busy laughing that she didn't realize that David had tagged her.

"Alex is it," David exclaimed, pointing to her.

"This should be easy," Malajia boasted, pulling her red satin robe on her shoulders. "Her wide ass can't run fast."

"Don't be jealous because I have junk in my trunk and you don't," Alex shot back, heading to the base.

Malajia sucked her teeth as Alex covered her eyes. "I *do* have an ass," Malajia mumbled.

As Alex began to count, she heard people scatter throughout the room. "Ten; ready or not, here I come," Alex announced, turning around.

She focused her eyesight and let out a loud sigh as she slowly walked over to a wall. Standing before her was Malajia, standing against the wall, holding a pose, staring off to the side, with a serious look on her face. Alex shook her head.

"I hope you don't think that you're invisible," Alex said, folding her arms. Malajia didn't budge, Alex stomped her foot on the floor "Malajia, you're in bright red against a white wall, are you serious? You could have at *least* made an effort."

When Malajia still didn't move, Alex slapped her arm. "You're it, stupid."

"Come on! They cheated," Malajia barked, snapping out of her pose. "Everywhere I went, somebody pushed me away."

"The point is to find your *own* damn spot," Chasity argued.

"Alex is right, you *could've* at least made an effort," Josh laughed.

"Standing there looking all stupid," Mark jeered.

Malajia stood there, seething at the teasing taking place at her expense.

"I know, right?" Geri agreed, looking at Mark. "Looking like a big ass cherry stain on the wall."

"Ha ha ha!" Malajia snapped. "You know what, fine. I don't give a shit *who* wakes up, I'm tagging every last one of y'all tonight," she promised, storming over to the wall. "Ten!" she shouted instantly.

"Come on Mel, you cheatin'," Mark complained as he and everyone else scattered.

"Naw, y'all got jokes, it's on," Malajia seethed, chasing. She chased Geri around the couch. Growing tired of running in circles, Malajia jumped over the chair, grabbed her sister, and pushed her into the door.

"Malajia, you're going overboard," Geri fumed, rubbing her arm.

Malajia took off after Josh, Sidra and David who were running around the dining room table. "Come on, get pass me!" she challenged.

"Why are you so mad?" Sidra laughed.

David tried to crawl under the dining room table, but Malajia, seeing him, kicked him in the shoulder.

"You salty, next," Malajia boasted as David crawled from under the table.

"You knocked my glasses off," David complained, holding the silver frames in his hand.

"You always worrying about those damn glasses," Mark complained from the living room.

Sidra gave Josh a push as they both tried to run out of the dining room. Malajia slapped Josh on the arm, then took off running after Sidra. Malajia pushed a small table over in an effort to get to her target quicker. Sidra let out a scream as Malajia grabbed her ponytail.

Sidra spun around. "Girl, what's wrong with you?" she hollered, slapping Malajia on the back.

"You mad. Who's next?" Malajia taunted, running back into the kitchen. Sidra rolled her eyes and stood in the corner next to an equally disgusted Geri.

Chasity was about to run out of the kitchen when Malajia ran in. "Where do you think *you're* going, Devil?" Malajia taunted.

"Malajia if you hit me or push me, I'm gonna fight you," Chasity warned, putting her hands up.

"I'm not scared of you," Malajia shot back, before making a dash for Chasity, but stopped when Chasity ran around the kitchen island. Malajia stayed to one side, trying to make sudden moves in both directions to try to get Chasity to run.

"Go ahead and run, I'll even give you a head start," Malajia promised.

Chasity looked at her as if she was crazy. "Do I *look* stupid to you?"

Malajia, annoyed that Chasity wouldn't budge picked up a piece of plastic fruit that was sitting in a large bowl on the island and threw it. Chasity ducked, sending the plastic decoration flying into a spice rack behind her, knocking the entire rack and its contents to the floor.

"What the fuck is wrong with you?" Chasity hollered.

"*Fuck* those spices!" Malajia took off running around the island, and Chasity darted out of the kitchen. As Malajia reached out to grab Chasity's shirt, she slipped on a pillow and went falling to the floor with a loud thud.

"Malajia! If you wake up Melissa, Mom and Dad are gonna kill us," Geri warned, angry.

"That's it, I quit," Chasity declared, seeing Malajia run after Jason.

Jason dodged Malajia and made a run for the door. "Screw you and your athletic ass," Malajia fumed.

"That's right, Jase," Sidra proudly exclaimed, giving Jason a high five.

"You thought I couldn't get away from you?" Jason laughed, wiping sweat from his brow with his black sleeveless t-shirt. "I play football sweetie, that's what I do."

"You're crazy, Mel!" Mark hollered as Malajia chased him around the dining room with a shoe in her hand.

The others dodged away from the door as they saw Mark and Malajia approaching at top speed. As Mark made his way to the door, Malajia tripped on yet another throw pillow, sending her flying into Mark, who went falling into a stand, knocking it over along with the large potted plant that sat on top of it. As Mark tried to steady himself, he stumbled back into the book shelf, knocking it over, along with the mirror that hung next to it.

The group froze, horrified looks stuck to their faces as they heard the cries of the youngest Simmons girl come from upstairs.

"Ooooooh," Geri said, pointing to Malajia and Mark, who were laid out on the floor.

"Why are there so many goddamn pillows on the floor?" Malajia hollered, tossing one across the room.

"What the hell is going on down there?!" Mr. Simmons boomed from upstairs.

"Shit, Dad," Geri exclaimed.

"I'm outta here," Josh declared, taking off running for the stairs along with most of the group, tripping over each other in the process. They hurried into their rooms just as Mr. and Mrs. Simmons snatched open their room door.

Mrs. Simmons hurried into Melissa's room. "What's going on? Who woke up my baby?" She was furious; it'd taken her hours to get the little girl to sleep.

Mr. Simmons ran downstairs and turned on the light to find the house a wreck and Mark and Malajia standing up against a wall posing with serious looks on their faces.

"Oh my God, Malajia is gonna get in so much trouble," Geri laughed from the room as Mr. Simmons began yelling at the top of his lungs.

"I knew it," Alex commented, pulling the covers up on her. "That's why as soon as she started that hype mess, I brought my ass right up these steps."

Ears were close to the door as Mr. Simmons continued his loud tirade. "You two are idiots! Y'all are too damn old to be acting so stupid! Malajia, you and this fool are gonna clean this damn house before you even *think* about going to sleep!"

"Dad it wasn't—"

"I don't care *who* else was involved!" He yelled, interrupting Malajia's excuse. "I saw *you two* standing here looking like dumbasses in a room full of mess! Now shut your damn mouth, and start cleaning."

"This is hilarious," Chasity laughed.

"He's gonna go on all night too, and so is Mom," Geri assured.

Mrs. Simmons snatched open Melissa's room door. "Malajia, you are such an idiot!" she bellowed, hurrying down the steps. "Look at my damn house!"

Sidra was in tears as the Simmons parents continued to holler. "I'm gonna throw this in her face like every day."

"Malajia, pull your head out of your ass and hurry up and clean!" Mr. Simmons barked. "Mark, get your goofy looking ass off the floor and pick up this glass."

"Can I have the broom?" Mark asked, voice low.

"Go get it out of the damn closet!" Mr. Simmons screamed.

Chasity heard her cell phone ring. "Hello?" she answered, between laughs.

"Yo he said 'get your goofy looking ass up'," Jason laughed into the phone.

"I know, this is the funniest shit ever," Chasity agreed, wiping a tear from her eye.

"There better not be a spot left down here when you're finished, do you hear me?" Mr. Simmons warned.

"Yes," Mark and Malajia answered in unison.

"What happened to my spice rack?!" Mrs. Simmons shouted.

Chapter 31

Emily could hear Malajia's loud voice come through the door as she stuck her key in, Sunday afternoon.

Forcing a smile, Emily pushed open the door. "Hey girls. When did you get back?"

"This morning," Sidra informed stretching out on Alex's bed. "You missed a hilarious weekend."

"Sidra, don't start your shit," Malajia warned, opening a pack of candy.

"Emily, Malajia and Mark got screamed so bad by her parents," Sidra revealed to Emily, ignoring Malajia. "What happened was—"

"Hey! We've had to listen to you laugh about it all damn weekend," Malajia loudly interrupted.

"And you will *continue* to hear it, because it was funny," Sidra shot back.

"Whatever." Malajia rolled her eyes. "Emily you didn't miss anything but a stupid game of hide and seek in the dark and karaoke…which was terrible."

"Yeah, none of y'all can sing worth a damn," Chasity chortled, running her hands through her hair.

"You probably can't, either," Alex teased. "You just didn't participate, so we don't know for sure." Alex giggled.

"And you never *will*," Chasity promised.

Emily slowly began to unpack her belongings amidst her friends talking. She didn't want to speak, for she knew that once she did, they would be able to hear the sadness and disappointment in her voice.

"I can't believe that this semester is almost over," Alex mused, changing the subject. She caught the sadness in Emily's eyes while they were reminiscing about their eventful weekend. "Just a few more weeks left."

"Thank God," Malajia sighed, climbing the ladder to her bed. "We'll finally be sophomores, and I won't be in this raggedy room or on this damn top bunk."

"Who knows Mel, you might still end up in this dorm," Sidra said.

"Yeah, whatever," Malajia scoffed. "I'm over Wilson Hall. They better be finished building those new dorms."

"What? Paradise Terrace and Court Terrace?" Alex asked.

"Those *are* the only two new dorms being built," Chasity spat, voice filled with sarcasm.

Alex shot her a glare. "I hope your next roommate is just as evil as *you* are," she jeered.

Chasity smirked. "If you can find someone who is, I'd love to meet her."

"No, *I'm* gonna be Chasity's roommate next year," Malajia promised, swinging her legs over the side of her bed.

"You can't pick your roommate," Alex pointed out.

"Yeah, okay," Malajia said, unconvinced.

"Malajia, if you end up being my roommate, I will kill you," Chasity warned.

Malajia waved a piece of candy in Chasity's direction. "No you won't. You'll love me," she smiled.

"That would be hilarious," Sidra giggled, then her smile faded. "Aww, we won't be roommates anymore, Chaz."

Chasity just shrugged nonchalantly, causing Sidra to toss a pillow at her.

"Girls…I think my mom is gonna try to get me into those apartments next year," Emily revealed, sitting on her bed.

"Why?" Alex frowned.

"Because she wants me in a room by myself," Emily answered. "You know that the apartments are all single rooms."

"She still has attitude about you being around us, huh?" Sidra fussed. "Emily, I hate to say this, but your mother has issues."

"You better check her ass, and soon. Or you'll be right in those wack apartments," Chasity added.

"Missing out on the fun and shit," Malajia put in.

Alex shook her head. "Em, your mother may be able to request a room for you in the apartments, but that won't guarantee that you'll end up there," she pointed out. "Have some faith sweetie."

Malajia jumped down from her bunk. "If Em's mom can request where she lives next semester, then that means I can request my new roommate." She darted for the door. "Chasity, I'm gonna put your name down," she quickly announced, running out of the room.

"Malajia, I swear to God," Chasity barked, taking off after her. "Stop playing with me!"

"God help who ends up being roommates with those two," Sidra giggled.

Emily just sat there, silent. *What am I going to do if I have to be by myself next year?* She let out a long sigh.

Alex walked into her Philadelphia row home two weeks later, smiling from ear to ear. "Ma!" she called, plunking her overnight bag on the floor.

"It's all small in here," Malajia teased, looking around the cozy living area. Her comment earned a backhand to the arm from Alex.

Alex was excited; it was her turn for her family to host the group for a weekend. Her home family and school family were important to her, and she welcomed the opportunity to merge the two.

"I'm just messing with you," Malajia laughed, rubbing her arm.

Mrs. Chisolm ran down the steps and greeted her daughter with a big hug. "My college baby!" she exclaimed.

"Where's everybody?" Alex asked, parting from the warm embrace.

"Your father is working a double, so we won't see him until tomorrow," her mother informed. "Your brother and sister are on their way home from your aunts' house."

Alex nodded. "Mom, these are the friends that I'm always talking to you about," she smiled, before making introductions.

"It's nice to finally meet you," Mrs. Chisolm smiled. "I swear I feel like I know you all already."

"Yeah, we know Alex runs her mouth like no other," Malajia teased.

"No, that would be *you*," Chasity sneered of Malajia.

Malajia's mouth fell open. "The nerve," she spat.

"Can't hold water," Sidra laughed.

A small laugh erupted from Mrs. Chisolm. "I made some lunch, so come on in the kitchen and have some."

"Ma, I'm gonna show them where they're going to sleep before we come in, okay?" Once her mother disappeared into the kitchen, Alex faced her friends. "All right, this isn't a big fancy house; there aren't a thousand rooms in here. So we're all sleeping in the basement."

"Come on," Malajia complained. "Is it even finished?"

Mark looked at Malajia with disgust. "Why do you always have to complain?" he asked, voice sounding as disgusted as his face looked. "Shut up."

Alex put her hand on her hip. "Yes, it's finished smart ass," she bit out. "Don't act bougie, cause we've seen *your* basement."

"It was bigger than this living room, I tell you *that* much," Malajia grumbled.

"There's one pull out bed down there," Alex informed, ignoring Malajia's smart comment. "And there's plenty of room on the floor."

"*I'm* not sleeping on the floor this time," Chasity declared.

"Y'all girls are not taking that bed, the guys are tired of sleeping on the floor," Mark contradicted.

"We'll figure it out later, let's go eat," Alex put in, leading the way to the kitchen.

Arriving in the kitchen, Mark laid eyes on the plate of homemade hamburgers, bowls of potato salad and pasta salad, and a pan of Bar B Q chicken. "Yeeeesss," he rejoiced, rubbing his hands together. "Good lookin' out. I'm starving."

"Ma, please monitor his greedy behind, because he'll eat *everything*," Alex warned, pointing to Mark.

Mrs. Chisolm laughed slightly. "Alex, leave him alone," she teased, heading out of the kitchen. "He can eat as much as he wants."

"You ain't said nothin' but a word," Mark said, grabbing a plate off of the kitchen table.

"Can you not take all the burgers, please?" Malajia hissed, watching him pile several on his plate.

"Mark, can you for *once* not eat everyone out of house and home?" Sidra chimed in, reaching for a plate.

Mark shot them glares as he took a bite of his burger. "She said we can eat, damn it!" he barked, a mouth full of food. "You're just mad cause you didn't get over here first!"

"You spit on me," Josh exclaimed, wiping a piece of chewed up burger off of his arm.

"Get away from me then," Mark shot back.

"I'm so tired right now," Sidra yawned as she helped Malajia pull the sofa bed out.

Alex shifted a stack of sheets and throw blankets in her arms as she walked down in the basement. "Here's some more blankets," she informed.

"I can't believe it's one in the damn morning," Malajia complained, grabbing a blanket from Alex.

"Well, who knew that playing Pictionary would take so long," Alex laughed. "Or be so draining."

"I was about to kick Mark in the face over that game," Malajia declared, flopping down on the bed.

"Yeah, that was quite stupid, even for *him*," Chasity added, wrapping a throw blanket around her shoulders.

"I mean, I drew a picture of a lion and he had the nerve to say…'uh a mouse-pig'."

"I know rig—" Alex paused when she heard the guys' voices at the top of the staircase. "Crap," she whispered. "Hurry up and get in the bed, before they try to take it."

The girls quickly jumped in the bed, pulling the covers up.

"Naw it ain't goin' down like that," Mark declared, running down the steps, followed by the rest of the guys.

"Too late," Sidra propped a pillow under her head.

"That's what *you* think," Jason bit out, snatching the covers back and squeezing his long body on the bed.

"What are you doing, stupid?" Chasity hissed, as Jason nudged her over.

"I'm not sleeping on that floor," Jason promised, trying to find a comfortable spot.

"There's no room!" Alex bellowed.

"And it's about to be *less* room," Mark chimed in, pushing his way on to the bed along with Josh and David.

"Oh my God, somebody's toe went in my eye," Malajia complained, frantically rubbing her eye.

"Come on, can y'all stop playing and get on the floor so we can get some sleep?" Sidra sighed, trying to pull the covers back up on her shoulders.

"Ahhh quite comfortable," Mark sighed, stretching out.

"That's cause you're laying on everybody," Alex complained, delivering a slap to Mark's leg.

"Look, this is how it's gonna be, so there's no use complaining," Mark replied, unfazed. The girls, too tired to protest any longer, simply sucked their teeth and laid down.

"Mark, how in the hell did you get a mouse-pig from a picture of a lion?" Malajia blurted out after several moments of silence.

"Malajia, it's late, can you do this tomorrow?" Alex groaned.

"Naw, cause I don't even know what a damn mouse-pig is," Malajia argued, sitting up in bed. "Where the hell did he get that from?"

"You can't draw, Malajia," Mark complained, voice tired.

"Mark! It was a *lion*, not a mouse, not a damn pig," Malajia hissed. "And *especially* not a combination of the two."

"Not my fault your drawing sucks ass," Mark jeered.

Malajia flopped her head back down on her pillow. "Idiot," she mumbled.

"Shut. Up. Malajia," Chasity hissed, drawing her words out slowly.

Alex grabbed the empty plates and cups from the coffee table and took them into the kitchen the following afternoon. "Sidra, I'm gonna need for you to stop using so many napkins," Alex chortled, seeing the pile of soiled napkins on Sidra's plate.

"You know I hate having food under my nails," Sidra returned from the living room.

"Well maybe if you'd eat your chicken wings like a *normal* person and stop picking the damn thing apart, maybe you wouldn't have all that mess under your nails," Malajia groused.

Alex giggled at the banter. Hearing a knock, she darted for the door, and snatched it open. Alex's eyes widened once she saw who was on the other side. "Stacey, Victoria!" she shrieked.

"I missed you," Stacey exclaimed, wrapping her arms around Alex.

"We ran over here as soon as your mom told us you were home," Victoria informed, stepping into the house. "It would've been nice if *you* would've told us."

Alex held a smile on her face as she ran her hand over the back of her neck. She hadn't seen her high school friends since winter break. Being so preoccupied with hosting her college friends, she'd forgotten to let Stacey and Victoria know that she was home for the weekend. And judging from the bite in Victoria's tone, she knew that that wasn't appreciated.

"Sorry about that. I have no excuse," Alex apologized. "But since you're here, come and meet my other friends."

"Nice to meet you guys," Stacey smiled, once the introductions were made.

"What's up," Victoria greeted, tone and facial expression opposite from Stacey's cheerful one.

Great, not only did Alex completely forget about us, now we have to be subjected to her new college friends, Victoria fumed internally.

Mark walked over to Stacey and grabbed her hand. "Enchanté Stacey," he cooed.

Malajia slapped her hand down on the arm of the chair, exasperated. "You don't even know what that *means*," she wailed.

"It means 'nice to meet you' in French, dick face," Mark shot back. Malajia, not having anything else to say, sat there with a stupid look on her face.

"He told *you*," Sidra laughed.

"Nobody asked you," Malajia hissed, embarrassed.

"Victoria and I have heard so much about you guys," Stacey said, sitting on the couch. "Her stories about y'all have me cracking up laughing."

"Girl, all we do is act a fool," Malajia said with a wave of her hand.

"Hmm, and here I thought that college was about *studying*, not acting a fool," Victoria sneered. "Silly me."

Chasity and Malajia shot her glances. "I was making a joke," Malajia replied, a phony smile plastered to her face.

"Oh. Well, I guess *I* was too," Victoria shot back with a smile just as phony.

Chasity narrowed her eyes at Victoria, *I don't like her already.*

"Alex, did you tell them about the time we went to the hotel for Thanksgiving?" Malajia asked.

"No, she didn't. But I'm pretty sure the story will be fun filled just like all the others," Victoria ground out. "Can we talk about something else?"

"Victoria, you seem pretty angry. Is something wrong?" Chasity asked, earning a snicker from Malajia. Malajia recognized Chasity's tone. She wasn't concerned about Victoria's well-being; she was being smart.

"Nope." Victoria's tone was dripping with disdain. "Just saying that we should talk about something other than all the fun *you guys* seem to have." Victoria scratched her arm. "*We* have some stories too, just saying."

"Funny," Chasity spat. "We haven't heard *any* of them."

"Boom," Malajia laughed.

Victoria gritted her teeth.

"Okay ladies, relax," Alex put in, turning on the radio. *Victoria, don't start this jealous stuff,* she thought.

Alex knew from the moment that Victoria laid eyes on her friends that her attitude would show. That was the real reason Alex didn't tell her that she was in town. She knew how territorial Victoria could be when it came to her friendship with her and Stacey.

Malajia leaned over to Chasity as the others began to dance to the loud music. "I think Alex's little friend feels some kind of way about us," she whispered.

"Um hmm," Chasity agreed.

Stacey leaned over to Victoria. "Vicki, what's your problem?' she whispered. "They seem like cool people."

"Whatever, Stacey," Victoria spat, voice low. "Why do we always have to hear about them from Alex? And why doesn't she talk about us to them? *We* knew her first."

Stacey shook her head. "You're trippin'. Alex is not our property, she can be friends with whoever she wants."

Victoria folded her arms. "Yeah well, all that's gonna change when we go to Paradise Valley University in the fall," she promised.

"We don't need to compete with her new friends," Stacey assured. "Alex won't leave us out when we get there."

"Oh, there won't be any competition. Alex is *our* friend." Victoria's tone was full of confidence. She couldn't wait for the fall semester of PVU to begin. She was going to get her friend back.

As Alex and the group continued dancing to the music blasting from the radio, Victoria didn't budge from her seat. Watching Stacey be so comfortable with the new group didn't help her mood. Even Alex's two younger siblings joined in on the dancing. Hearing a knock at the door, Victoria rose from her seat.

"Alex, I'll get the door for you," she announced. Not waiting for a response, Victoria walked to the door and opened it. She became startled as she came face to face with the person who was standing there. "Paul," she stammered, glancing behind her to see if anybody was looking. "What are you doing here?"

"I heard around the neighborhood that Alex was home for the weekend and I came to see her," Paul replied, voice sharp.

Victoria folded her arms. "I don't think she's interested in seeing you," she bit out. "So you need to leave."

Paul stuck his foot in the door, stopping Victoria from closing it in his face. "Alex!" Paul bellowed.

The music was so loud, Alex didn't hear him.

Victoria tried to move his foot "What are you trying to do?" she hissed.

"I need to talk to her," he insisted.

"Paul, you need to go. I mean it," Victoria snapped.

Malajia, in doing one of her dance moves, turned and noticed the commotion at the door. She stared at the guy arguing with Victoria, and frowned.

"Alex, who's that guy your friend is arguing with?" she asked, tapping Alex's arm.

Alex looked confused as she turned towards the door. "What the hell?" she said, storming over to the door. "Paul, what are you doing here?" she asked, voice not hiding her agitation.

She had not seen or spoken to her ex-boyfriend ever since she broke up with him last semester. Finding out that he cheated wasn't something that she could forgive or forget.

"I tried to get rid of him," Victoria quickly put in.

"It's cool. Give us a minute, will you?" Alex replied, eyes not leaving Paul's.

Paul briefly looked down at the concrete step as Victoria walked away. It was like Alex's angry gaze was burrowing through him.

"Hey, Alex…you look good," he stammered.

"What are you doing here?" she repeated, not interested in small talk.

"I need to talk to you," he said.

"What could you possibly have to say to me, after all this time?" she hissed, folding her arms.

"Something important," he assured her. "Something that you need to know." Paul glanced over and saw Victoria watching them like a hawk. "Can we talk outside?"

"No, we can't talk *anywhere*!" Alex snapped. "We're over. You cheated on me with Sherry. Or did you forget?"

Paul frowned in confusion. "Sherry? No listen—"

"I don't have time for this. I have company."

"Alex," he pleaded, gently grabbing her arm as she went to shut the door. He pulled a white envelope out of his jeans pocket. "Since you won't talk to me, please read this."

"What's this?" Alex sneered as he pushed the envelope at her.

"Just read it," he urged. "Please."

The urgency in Paul's face, made it hard for her to deny his request. She sucked her teeth and snatched the envelope from him. "Fine," she reluctantly agreed. "Just go."

Alex shook her head and shut the door once he left the porch. Alex looked at the envelope for several seconds before tossing it on a small table near the door. *I'll deal with this shit later.*

"What did he want?" Victoria asked, folding her arms across her chest.

Alex ran her hands through her hair. "Knowing him, nothing important," she bit out. "He gave me some letter and asked me to read it."

"Oh?" Victoria glanced at the envelope.

"Enough with him." Alex waved her hand dismissively "Come on, Vicki. Let's go party."

"Um, I'll be over in a second," Victoria promised, eyes still fixed on the envelope. Alex shrugged and walked off.

Victoria glanced over her shoulder to make sure Alex was out of sight. Scanning the room with her eyes, she made sure that no one was watching before she picked up the envelope and walked out of the door. Closing the door behind her, Victoria snatched it open and began reading the words handwritten on the paper. *That son of a bitch*, she fumed before storming off.

Chapter 32

"Did you receive your new room assignment in the mail yet?" Alex asked into the phone, holding up an envelope from the school. "I just got mine today, but I haven't opened it."

"What are you waiting for?" Sidra asked, tossing her gym bag on the floor near her closet. "I opened mine."

"I just got in from work at that crazy diner," Alex replied. "So? How do you feel about your new assignment?"

"I'm happy with my new roommate," Sidra vaguely revealed.

"Yeah? You wanna tell me who she is?" Alex chuckled. "I take it it's not Chasity again, because you said 'new'."

"No, it's not Chasity," Sidra confirmed, amusement filling her voice. "Although, I'm going to miss my devil roommate." Sidra smiled as she thought about how far she and Chasity had come as friends. "Who would've thought that we would be friends after the way we first met."

"Heck, who would have thought that we would *all* be friends," Alex clarified. "I'm going to miss Mel and Em as my roommates too. But I'm sure I'll like my new roomie."

"Oh, I have an inkling that you will," Sidra mused. "I'm happy about the dorm that I got in to. Paradise Terrace looks really nice. I can't wait for next semester to…"

Alex frowned when she heard Sidra's voice trail off. "What's wrong sweetie?"

"Alex…what if we don't get to come back next semester?"

"Sidra, please try to stay calm," Alex urged, hanging her apron on the back of her room door.

"How can I be calm, Alex?" Sidra hissed. "We have this damn meeting with President Bennett in a few weeks."

Alex sighed. She knew why Sidra was panicking; she was secretly doing the same thing. The upcoming meeting was the cause of Alex not being able to really enjoy her summer break. She had no idea whether she or her friends would even be allowed back at school in the fall.

"I know Sid," she temporized. "I get why you're nervous, but freaking out won't do us any good."

Sidra flopped down on her bed. "I guess you're right," she sighed. Sidra had been trying to keep her stress under control, even taking up jogging. But every time a topic regarding school was brought up, all of the thoughts would just come to a head. "I just want to get this over with so I can stop this sick feeling in the pit of my damn stomach."

"Have you talked to your parents about all of this?" Alex asked after a few seconds of silence.

"Absolutely not," Sidra scoffed. "I think this is one secret that I will take to my grave…Unless we get kicked out, then I guess I'll have no choice."

"We won't," Alex promised, snatching open her envelope. A smile crept across her face as she read her new room assignment. Her eyes fixed on the name of her new roommate. She was pleased. *God, please let us be able to return in the fall.*

"Besides, I see these letters as a good sign," Alex added, "I mean, why would they send these if they were going to kick us out?"

"Because they want to torture us," Sidra jeered. "Giving us false hope."

Alex rolled her eyes to the ceiling. She glanced at the clock sitting on her dresser; her eyes widened. "Oh crap! Sid, I gotta call you back."

"Everything okay?" Sidra asked, noticing the urgency in Alex's voice.

"I forgot to pick up dinner," Alex informed.

She darted out of the door once she ended her call with Sidra. As Alex quickened her pace down the block in route to the fast food place, she berated herself. *Why didn't you just bring something home from work?*

Turning the corner, her face frowned instantly as she spotted a familiar figure walking along the same path. *You've got to be kidding me*, Alex fumed as they were about to enter a corner store.

"Sherry," she spat, voice raised.

The tall young woman, hearing her name, turned around and locked eyes with Alex. "Alex?" she exclaimed, a bright smile on her smooth brown face. "Haven't seen you since graduation. How's college?"

Alex shot Sherry a confused look. "Are you seriously just gonna act all casual?" she hissed, much to Sherry's confusion. "Like nothing happened?"

"I'm not sure I know what you're talking about," Sherry declared, voice calm.

It took everything for Alex not to choke the former high school slut right then and there. She looked the slender, well-dressed girl up and down. She seemed to have ditched her cheap provocative attire for a more sophisticated and expensive look. But no matter how she changed on the outside, as far as Alex was concerned, she was still a slut.

"I usually don't use the word 'bitch', but I think it describes you perfectly."

Sherry folded her arms as she shot Alex a glare. "I know you didn't like me in high school, but it's been a year since we graduated," she hissed. "I would think that you would've let whatever grudge you had against me go by now."

"Don't you dare brush this shit off like it's some high school grudge," Alex fumed, pointing at her. "Paul and I were still together *after* we graduated."

"Paul?" Sherry raised her perfectly arched eyebrow. "You're snapping at me about Paul? Alex, I may have had a crush on him in school, but I guarantee that it stopped before we graduated," she assured. "He made it clear that he wasn't leaving you, and contrary to what you *think* you know about me, I don't sleep with other girls' men."

"Bullshit," Alex fumed. "You slept with him while I was away last semester. He cheated on me with *you*."

"What?" Sherry exclaimed. "That's impossible."

"How so?" Alex ground out. "This lie should be good."

Sherry took a deep breath. "I left Philly and moved to Baltimore a week after graduation," she informed. "I haven't seen anybody from high school since then, *let alone* Paul…As a matter of fact, I'm engaged now."

Alex was dumbfounded as she eyed the large princess cut diamond ring on Sherry's delicate, manicured hand.

"My man is rich and established," she boasted. "Why would I mess my relationship up for a boy who didn't even graduate on time?"

"Wait a minute." Alex put her hand up as she tried to gather her thoughts. "Somebody told me that they saw you with him last fall."

"And just *who* told you *that*?"

"That doesn't matter," Alex bit out. "Just know that I trust this person."

"Well, you better make sure that your trusted person was seeing straight, because they couldn't have seen *me*." Sherry shook her head as she saw the troubled look on Alex's face. "Take care of yourself, Alex," she said, and sauntered off.

Alex didn't say a word, she couldn't understand what had just happened. *But…Victoria told me that she saw them together,* she thought, running her hands through her hair.

"What the hell is going on?" she asked herself.

Emily put the top back on to the jars of peanut butter and jelly and placed them neatly back into the cupboard. She rolled her eyes at the sound of footsteps approaching from the living room. *Can I get one moment to myself?*

"Another day on summer break and another day of you stuck in the house...in my face," Jazmine spat, grabbing a bottle of soda out of the refrigerator.

Emily glared at the back of her older sister's head. *If you had a life or a job, you wouldn't have to see my face every day.*

Emily would give anything to not be in that kitchen with her sister. Ever since she'd come home for break a few weeks ago, she'd endured the constant teasing and put downs.

"I'll be leaving to go back to school in a few weeks, so you won't have to be bothered with me much longer," Emily assured, voice low.

Jazmine spun around. "Did you say something?" she taunted. "I can barely hear you over that whisper, Pasty face."

Emily felt her blood begin to boil as her sister continued on with her rant.

"I keep asking Mommy if you were adopted, cause why the hell would you be a completely different complexion than the rest of us?"

"I'm not adopted!" Emily snapped, slamming her hand on the counter. "And I've asked you to stop—" Emily's loud words were interrupted as Jazmine jumped at her, standing within a few inches of her face.

"What are you gonna do?" Jazmine taunted. A smile of satisfaction crept across her brown face when Emily simply turned away to avoid making eye contact. "Punk ass," she hissed, giving Emily a hard poke on her arm.

"What have I told you about picking on your sister?"

Ms. Harris's stern voice startled both girls. "Mommy, you know I'm just messing around," Jazmine lied, putted her arm around Emily's neck and rubbing the top of her head.

Emily jerked out of her sister's grasp as Ms. Harris pointed to the living room. "Jaz, go use your energy to search the classifieds," her mother bit out.

Jazmine rolled her eyes and stormed out of the kitchen.

Upon Jazmine's exit, Ms. Harris sat down at the kitchen table and stared at Emily's face. Her eyes glistened with tears that had not yet fallen. "You know your sister loves you. She's just picking with you."

Emily pushed her hair behind her ears as she slowly sat down at the kitchen table. "She bullies me," Emily clarified, wiping her eyes.

Ms. Harris waved her hand dismissively. "I'll deal with her later," she assured. "I have to run out to do some errands; do you want to come with?"

Emily shook her head.

"Okay, well, when I get back, we can watch a movie together. There should be some good ones coming on."

Emily wanted so badly to shake her head 'no' once more. Her mother made it a task every day to monopolize all of Emily's time. It was like she didn't want Emily to breathe without her. It was when her mother smiled a hopeful smile at her that she decided against it. "Sure."

Satisfied, Ms. Harris left the kitchen, leaving Emily to sigh loudly. Grabbing her peanut butter and jelly sandwich, she made her journey towards the staircase. Seeing the stack of envelops slide through the mail slot in the front door, Emily smiled.

"My room assignment should be here," she mused, rummaging through the pile. Her eyes fixed on the school heading, and she ripped the envelope open. "I hope I still get to room with one of the girls." Her smile was short lived as she began reading the words on the page. Tears filled her eyes again, this time spilling down to her cheeks. "I can't believe this," she fumed between sobs.

The warm sun and gentle breeze were a welcomed distraction from the thoughts in Chasity's head. Sitting on the front steps of her home, she relished the quiet.

The peace was short lived when she saw a familiar figure approach the end of her walkway.

"Ugh, fuck my life," she groaned, rolling her eyes.

"Hello to you too, beautiful," Jason chuckled, walking towards her.

"Oops, didn't mean to say that out loud," she jeered.

"Of course you did," he contradicted, knowing her all too well.

"What are you doing here, Jason?" Chasity hissed as he sat down next to her. "I just talked to you earlier."

"Yes, I know, and I didn't like the tone of your voice," he declared. "You sound like something is on your mind, and I came over to check on you." He smiled as Chasity just shook her head. "That's the beauty of living only ten minutes away from you."

Lucky me, she groused.

Jason recalled their conversation earlier that morning. She sounded different to him, not so much angry or sarcastic like she normally did, but to him she sounded defeated. Not satisfied with her answer of 'nothing" when he asked her what was wrong, he decided to go to her. He knew that she could only deflect for so long when he was in front of her.

"So? Are you okay?" he asked, concerned.

"Don't I look okay?"

"No, you don't," he answered honestly. "You know your face shows everything that you're feeling."

"Then there's your answer," she bit out, taking a sip of her iced tea.

Jason sighed. "Come on Chaz. If nothing else, I'm your friend," he said, voice caring. "Just talk to me."

Realizing that he wouldn't go away without an answer, and wanting to talk out what she was feeling to someone other than the girls, she sighed. "That meeting is coming up," she revealed.

Jason nodded slowly, now it made sense. She'd told him about the upcoming meeting a few days after she'd gotten home for summer break. "You're worried that you might get kicked out of school?"

"*That*," Chasity confirmed. "And I just...I wish that I wouldn't have let Jackie's trashy ass take me there, you know."

"I understand," Jason said. "But you can't beat yourself up for that. You did walk away the first time...after some persuading."

"I know...but still, this whole mess is my fault."

"It's *not* your fault," Jason assured, voice stern. "It's Jackie's, and I'm not gonna let you beat yourself up for this."

Chasity ran her hands through her hair as Jason continued to speak.

"She has had it out for you since first semester. Jackie is a trifflin' person. She provoked you and tried to put her hands on you, and you were right to fight back. I don't give a shit *what* President Bennett, or the Dean, or anybody *else* has to say about it."

Chasity looked at Jason. She saw the intensity in his face, and smiled slightly. She appreciated how he defended her, even though she didn't want to tell him that.

"So, no more beating yourself up," he ordered.

Chasity put her hands up in surrender. "Okay."

Satisfied, Jason stood and extended his hand. "Come on, let's go for a walk," he said. "We can go catch a movie."

Chasity was about to decline, when she saw the mailman approach. Taking the mail from him, she looked at the letter from her school. Opening it, she read its contents and groaned out loud. "You've got to be freakin' kidding me!" she wailed.

Curious, Jason peered over her shoulder. "What's that?"

Without saying a word, Chasity showed him the letter. Jason saw the roommate assignment on the paper, and snickered.

"That's funny?" Chasity barked, balling up the paper.

"No, not at all," Jason lied, before dissolving into laughter. "It isn't that bad, really." Seeing that Chasity was clearly not amused by her new roommate, he stopped laughing. "Looks like you need that walk."

Chasity stood up in a huff. "Maybe I *should* let them kick me out, so I won't have to deal with that idiot."

"Don't say that," Jason said, voice full of amusement as they walked down the walkway.

Malajia flipped through the channels on the flat screen television in her family's living room as she laid on the couch. "I'm so boooooored," she groaned aloud.

"Well, go find something to do."

Startled by her mother's voice, Malajia bolted up. "Were you spying on me?" she spat, turning the TV off

"Malajia, trust me when I say, I don't have the time or the energy to spy on you," Mrs. Simmons assured, flopping down on the loveseat across from her. "Are you ready to go back to school?"

Malajia rolled her eyes. "Ready for me to go already?"

Mrs. Simmons shot her a confused look. "What do you mean *already*? You've been back for two months. And yes, I *am* ready for you to go back. Your complaining irritates me."

Malajia wasn't shocked by her mother's bluntness, she was used to it. Her family never hesitated to let Malajia know how she irritated them. She only wished they would be that open with their feelings towards her when she didn't.

"Very funny, Mother," she jeered, hiding her true feelings. "Don't worry, I'm sick of y'all too. I can't wait to get back to my college life."

If I'm still allowed to go back. With the dreaded meeting only days away, Malajia's stress had been at an all-time high. Trying to remain calm, as well as trying to deflect any topic about school over the past few months, had taken its toll on her.

"Oh, I'm going to West Chester in a few days," Malajia revealed. "Chasity's aunt wants us girls to hang out with her." That was the half-truth.

"I'm fine with you going."

Malajia twirled some hair around her finger. "I wasn't asking your permission," she mumbled.

"What did you say?" Mrs. Simmons barked.

"Nothing," Malajia lied, feigning innocence. "You look so pretty today. Did you get your hair done? I see you got those gray hairs dyed."

Annoyed by her daughters' smart mouth, Mrs. Simmons picked up a throw pillow. "I don't have gray hair, smart behind," she fussed, tossing the pillow at her giggling daughter.

Malajia continued laughing as her mother disappeared from the living room. "No gray hair, my ass," she mumbled as her laughter subsided. Eyeing the mail on the coffee table, she flipped through it in search of a magazine. Her eyes fixed on a letter from her school.

"Shit," she panicked, ripping it open. "I know they didn't send a letter about this damn fight." As she read the letter, her face went from panicked to excited.

Mrs. Simmons hurried out of the kitchen at the sound of her daughter's high-pitched scream. "Malajia what happened?"

Malajia turned around, at the sound of urgency in her mother's voice. She frowned. "Mom, why do you have ketchup on your shirt?" she laughed.

Mrs. Simmons looked down at her soiled blouse and sucked her teeth. "I was putting some on my damn burger when I heard your dramatic butt scream, and I squirted it on myself."

Malajia was confused. "But, how——"

"What did you scream for?!"

Malajia held up her letter. "I got my new room assignment for the fall," she informed, much to her mother's confusion. She still couldn't understand why that would cause Malajia to scream.

"And?"

"*And*, I'm happy with my new roommate," she smiled.

Both hungry and irritated, Mrs. Simmons just walked back into the kitchen without saying a word, leaving Malajia to do a happy dance in her seat.

Chapter 33

"Time is moving so damn slow," Sidra complained to Alex, looking at her watch. "Eleven needs to come on, so we can get this over with."

Alex adjusted the collar on her brown blazer. Although Sidra felt time was slow, she felt the opposite. The last few days arrived quicker than she would have hoped. Now she was standing in the hallway of the main office building of Paradise Valley University, waiting to be called in front of the Dean and the President.

"My heart is in my stomach right now," Sidra groaned, holding her hand over her midsection.

"Yours and mine both," Alex agreed. "Not to mention that this suit is uncomfortable," she complained, tugging her blazer down over her matching wide-legged pants.

"I think it's a good look for you," Sidra teased.

Alex gave Sidra a playful nudge as Chasity and Malajia approached them. "About time you guys got out of that bathroom," she teased.

"My hair isn't acting right today," Chasity scowled, pushing her curled hair over her shoulder.

"And my damn stomach hurts," Malajia added. "I haven't eaten in like two days."

"It's just your nerves," Alex assured.

"Yeah, no shit," Malajia hissed, reaching for a piece of gum in her purse.

Sidra grabbed the gum from Malajia as she was about to put it in her mouth. "Gum isn't going to make your stomach feel any better," she said when Malajia went to protest. "Chasity, your hair looks perfect as usual." Sidra assured. She was proud of her friends for dressing professional for once. Malajia's red pencil skirt with matching jacket, and Chasity's black pant suit complemented them.

"Sidra, shut up. You're just happy to see us in these wack suits," Malajia jeered, tugging on her skirt. "How do you wear these things, Sidra? Where's the damn elastic? It's hot!"

Sidra shook her head, not wanting to engage in a verbal battle with Malajia over clothes. She was the most comfortable in her royal blue skirt and matching jacket, for dressing that way was an everyday thing for her.

"Where's your aunt?" Alex asked Chasity, who was staring off into space. "Chaz," she called, giving her a soft poke.

"Why are you touching me?" Chasity hissed, snapping out of her daze.

"Are you okay?" Alex asked.

"No, I'm not."

"Look, all of us are on edge right now—let's just focus," Sidra jumped in, putting her hands up.

"Yeah, I'll focus all right," Malajia mumbled. "Focus on taking this hot ass jacket off." Sidra grabbed Malajia's arm to keep her from yanking her blazer off.

Alex giggled at the byplay, until the sight of Jackie and her friends walking towards President Bennett's office caused her moment of delight to vanish.

Chasity locked eyes with Jackie as she was on her way into the office. Chasity's jaw clenched as Jackie smiled slyly at her. She could have run over and ripped her throat out right then and there.

"Ugly bitch," Malajia hissed as they disappeared into the office. "We should jump her ass after this is over."

"No, we *shouldn't*," Alex chastised. "Fighting is what got us into this mess in the first place."

Those words screamed in Chasity's head. The reason for her detachment was because she still felt that this was all her fault. No matter how many times Jason or any of the girls reassured her that it wasn't, she couldn't get those thoughts out of her mind.

"Okay ladies, it's time to go in," Trisha declared, approaching. "Just smile, answer all questions honestly, and no cursing, throwing things, or insults...*Chasity*."

Chasity rolled her eyes. Her aunt knew her all too well.

The nervousness that the girls already felt intensified once they walked into the large room. Instead of meeting in the President's office, they met in a conference room. A large table sat in the middle of the room, surrounded by cushy swivel chairs. The girls were instructed to take their seats on the opposite side of the table from where Jackie and her friends were seated.

Malajia leaned in close to her friends, "Jackie could've at *least* redone those fuzzy ass braids," she whispered.

"Shhh, Malajia behave," Trisha scolded.

Malajia folded her arms and sat back in her seat.

The Dean sat at one end of the table and President Bennett, once she entered the room, sat at the other end.

President Bennett smoothed her salt and pepper hair away from her dark face. Her eyes roamed over each young woman sitting at her table. "Do you all know why you're here today?" she asked, voice stern, matching her distinguished face.

"Cause Jackie got her ass beat and now she's mad," Chasity mumbled, earning a stern backhand on the arm from Trisha.

"We're here because those girls over there ambushed us," Jackie accused, pointing across the table.

"Make me break that finger off," Chasity threatened.

"Miss Parker, I suggest you curb that mouth of yours," President Bennett urged. "It's landed you in enough trouble."

Alex put a comforting hand on Chasity's arm as Chasity fought the urge to say another word.

"We may have ambushed those girls, but we only did that *after* they jumped Sidra," Alex informed. "I'm assuming that you didn't hear that part from them."

"I heard it," President Bennett confirmed. "I also heard that this all started because Miss Parker fought Miss Stevens. I have been led to believe that this is her fault," she stated, pointing to Chasity.

Chasity's leg bounced up and down in a nervous rhythm. Her fears were confirmed, causing her to feel both helpless and angry.

"Oh, hell no," Malajia blurted out, slamming her hand on the table.

"Miss Simmons, your mouth," Dean Watkins scolded.

"Fine. But I'm not gonna sit here and let those freaks of nature accuse my friend of starting this mess," Malajia argued.

"Jackie is delusional!" Sidra wailed. "She's had it out for Chasity ever since first semester."

"The girl can't seem to keep her name out of her mouth," Alex fumed, glaring daggers at the girls across the table as the opposing side feigned innocence.

Seeing Jackie stare at her, taunting her, made Chasity's temper rise at a rapid pace. "I should choke the shit out of you," she fumed.

"Yeah, *that'll* help your case," Jackie mocked.

"Girls, cool it," Trisha scolded. She signaled for them to lean in close. "She won't get away with what she's trying to do, but y'all need to stay calm."

"I can't," Chasity admitted.

"You *have* to," Trisha urged.

"I won't tolerate too much more of these outbursts," President Bennett said, folding her arms.

"They're sorry for that," Trisha assured.

Dean Watkins rose from his seat. "We're just going to get the rundown of the whole story from each of you girls," he declared. "This way we have all sides before we make our decision. Miss Stevens, please go first."

"Why does *she* get to go first?" Malajia whispered to her friends. "With her lying ass."

"Well, me and my friends went into the bathroom of the convenience store just off campus and—"

"Bitch can't even spell 'convenience'," Malajia jeered, voice low. Her outburst earned her a kick in the leg under the table from Alex. "Ow!" she shrieked, rubbing her leg.

Jackie rolled her eyes. "Anyway…all of a sudden those girls came running in the bathroom taunting us, before attacking us."

"And why do you think they did that?" he asked.

Jackie was confused. "I don't follow?"

Dean Watkins rubbed the back of his head. "I said that we needed a rundown of the *whole* story," he clarified. "That means even the parts where you *don't* come off as the victim."

Malajia slammed her hand on the table. "Boom!" she exclaimed.

"For the love of God Malajia, please stop with the outbursts," Alex snapped.

"Look, if you're referring to the incident with that girl Sidra, that only happened because she started with us first that night," Jackie lied, ignoring Malajia and Alex.

Sidra frowned in confusion. "I said it earlier and I'll say it again. You're delusional," she hissed.

"My girls saw that Sidra was trying to fight me, so they jumped in it because those are my girls," Jackie continued.

Sidra looked over at President Bennett. "Please tell me that you can tell that she's lying," she said. President Bennett simply put her hand up signaling Sidra to remain quiet.

"Malajia did anybody persuade you to participate in the plot to attack Jackie and her friends?" Dean Watkins asked.

Malajia frowned. "Persuade?" she scoffed. "No disrespect Dean, but nobody persuades Malajia Lakeshia Simmons to do *anything*," she assured.

"That's not what the basketball team says," one of Jackie's friend laughed.

Malajia, along with the other girls glared at her. "Oh, that's cute," Malajia jeered. "Maybe you should stop worrying about what you *hear* about me, and concern yourself with what's being said about *you*. Like the fact that your boyfriend is screwing your fat ass friend over there."

The girls' laughter quickly subsided as she stared at Malajia in shock. "Who?" she exclaimed. She looked as Malajia, along with Alex, Sidra and Chasity pointed to the girl sitting next to her. "Trina, seriously?!"

"She's lying," Trina argued.

"That's not what the basketball team says," Malajia mocked.

"This pointless mudslinging is only going to hold up this process," President Bennett spat. "This nonsense is what landed you all here in the first place."

"What landed us here is Chasity's damn anger issues," Jackie spat.

Chasity sat there, arms folded, leg bouncing, furious eyes fixed on Jackie. It was taking everything in her not to jump across that table.

"Miss Parker, do you think that you have an anger issue?" Dean Watkins asked.

"What, is that a trick question?" Malajia mumbled, confused.

Chasity, for fear of what would come tumbling out of her mouth if she dared to respond, said nothing.

"Miss Parker, are you going to answer that question?" President Bennett asked.

Chasity slowly shook her head.

President Bennett turned To Alex. "Miss Chisolm," she called, earning a wide eyed look from Alex.

"Ma'am?" Alex sputtered.

"Do you think that Miss Parker has an anger problem?" she asked, point blank.

Alex's eyes shifted as Chasity shot her a side glance and Malajia quickly shook her head 'no'.

Don't say it Alex, Malajia thought, hoping that her inner voice would be transferred to Alex somehow.

"With all due respect President Bennett, I don't understand what—"

"Just answer the question Miss Chisolm," Dean Watkins urged.

"Um, I—Uh." Alex hated being put in this position, she didn't want to hurt or incriminate her friend, but she couldn't lie.

"Just answer the question Alex," Chasity muttered, sensing Alex's inner struggle.

"Okay." Alex put her hand up. "Yes, I think that Chasity has an anger management problem," she admitted regretfully. "But she's *not* a trouble maker."

"That's it, they got us," Malajia threw her hands up in the air.

Chasity rolled her eyes.

"Miss Parker, can we get your recollection of what transpired?" President Bennett asked, studying the intense look on her face.

"You already heard what happened," Chasity answered evenly.

"I need *your* story."

"For what? You heard everything."

"Not from *you*," she insisted.

"What do you want from me?" Chasity spat, feeling herself getting ready to tear up. "It's already been established that I'm an angry bitch. What could you *possibly* want to hear from me that will change your minds?"

"Miss Parker, did you provoke Miss Stevens?" Dean Watkins asked.

Chasity's hands began to shake as she put them over her face momentarily. "No, I didn't."

"Is that so? You didn't start to taunt her before class the morning of the fight?" Dean Watkins asked.

Chasity frowned in confusion. "What?" she felt like she was losing her breath. "So, because I said something to her first *one* time, I'm the bad guy?" Malajia rubbed Chasity's shoulder in a comforting manner once she sensed that her friend was nearing a breakdown. "You want me to say that this is my fault? Fine! It's my fault! Just kick me out and be done with it."

Alex put her hand over her face as Chasity pushed herself back from the table and stormed out of the room with Malajia running after her, calling her name.

"What did I do?" Alex asked, voice muffled by her hands. Sidra patted Alex on the back as she sighed.

"Chaz, you have to calm down," Malajia urged, seeing Chasity pace back and forth along the marble tiled bathroom floor.

"Don't tell me to calm down, Malajia," Chasity snapped, pounding her fist on the wall.

"I get that you're pissed. Trust me, we *all* are," Malajia assured. "But you *have* to calm down. Don't let that bitch get the satisfaction of seeing you break."

"It's too late for that," Chasity said, still pacing.

Malajia stood in front of Chasity, bringing her pacing to a halt. Chasity shot Malajia a glare, yet Malajia refused to back down. Malajia just stared at Chasity and watched the tears began to fill her light eyes.

Not wanting Malajia to see her cry, Chasity tried to push her away, but Malajia grabbed her arm. "No, you don't get to do that," Malajia said. "You don't get to take this all on yourself. You don't get to feel alone in this."

"I can't deal with this," Chasity stammered, as the tears fell. "I can't—they're just attacking my character and it's no point in trying to defend myself." Chasity felt like she couldn't breathe. She was never one to handle the outpouring of her emotions well, which was why she always fought hard to keep them in. "Everybody already has their minds made up about me, what's the point? They want to blame me, just let them."

"We're not gonna let them do that. This is not your fault!"

"Malajia, just please leave me alone."

"No, I'm not," Malajia insisted, squeezing Chasity's hand. "I know how you feel."

"No you don't."

"No?" Malajia challenged. "I know what it's like to have people just make an assumption about you and hold on to that no matter what you say. According to every damn body, I'm the campus slut," she informed, raising her hand. "And I'm a virgin. So I get it. But knowing that my friends know the real me, makes it easier. And we *are* your real friends. We see you for who you really are."

Chasity allowed Malajia to pull her into an embrace as she tried to hold any further tears from falling.

"You know what, I've kept my mouth shut this long because I'm trying to let the girls hash this out, but you need to start telling *them* to watch their mouths just like you're telling *my* girls," Trisha fumed to both Dean Watkins and President Bennett. She'd resisted the urge to defend Chasity or even to go after her when she stormed out of the conference room; she was only there for moral support, not to fight her battle. But watching her niece get jumped on was making Trisha's temper rise.

If President Bennett responded, Trisha didn't hear it, because she was focused on Chasity and Malajia walking through the door. "You okay?" she asked as Chasity sat down next to her.

"I'm fine," Chasity replied, pushing her hair over her shoulder.

"Let's continue, shall we?" Dean Watson declared.

"Can I say something?" Chasity asked, holding her hand up. President Bennett gestured for her to go ahead and speak. "Look, maybe I *did* antagonize Jackie that morning—"

"Uh uh, President Bennett, she can't be using words that nobody knows the meaning to," Jackie ground out. "'Antagonizing', what does that mean? For all I know, she could be calling me out my name."

It was so silent, a pin could be heard dropping as all eyes fixed on Jackie, confused.

"Um...what?" Malajia asked, fighting the urged to burst out laughing.

"Just wow," Chasity sneered, rolling her eyes at Jackie's blatant stupidity. "Anyway, I did antagonize her, but that was only because Jackie has been doing that to *me* ever since our first semester," she revealed. "As a matter of fact, a few weeks before that, we almost fought, because she started her nonsense."

"Oh whatever, Chasity," Jackie barked.

"Miss Stevens," President Bennett warned.

"No, cause she wanna try to make an excuse for her part in this," Jackie argued. "Bottom line is that she can't handle conflict like a big girl." Jackie focused on Chasity. "What's wrong? You can't use your words? You gotta resort to throwing blows?"

"And what do you call what you did to *me*?" Sidra jumped in.

"*That* was called knocking your stuck-up ass down a peg," Trina hissed, causing Sidra to jump up from her seat.

"Bitch, I'll come across this table—"

"Sid, calm down," Alex urged, forcing Sidra back down in her seat. "Don't give them the reaction they want."

"And the only reason why you didn't fight me that day was because Jason held you back," Jackie fumed at Chasity.

Chasity smirked. "Jason," she said. "Yeah, he *did* hold me back. He has some strong arms too. They're just as strong as they look," she taunted, relishing the fury burning in Jackie's eyes. *Gotcha bitch.* "I'll admit it, I have a temper problem...I'm quick to fight and I *know* that. And for my part in getting my friends in trouble, I'm sorry," she directed to President Bennett. "But," Chasity said, turning back to Jackie. "I will never admit that I started this whole thing. *You* did, because of one simple thing...You're jealous."

Jackie slammed her hand on the table. "That's bull and you know it!" she yelled.

Chasity folded her arms, a smug look on her face. "It's okay, I understand why you are," she taunted. "I'm prettier than you, I have a better body than you, I have more money than you, I have better friends than you, and the one man that you can't get your trashy hands on...wants only me."

"Jason doesn't know what he wants."

"Sure he does, and it's me, sweetheart," Chasity boasted. "It's okay, you don't have to admit it, but just know that I will *always* be better than you in *every* way."

Jackie rose from her seat and tried to jump across the table, but was stopped by her friends.

"Miss Stevens, don't you dare!" Dean Watkins boomed, rising from his seat.

Chasity was unfazed. "What's wrong? You can't use your words?" she smiled.

Hearing her own words thrown back at her sent Jackie over the edge. She started screaming obscenities and tried to break out of her friends' grasps.

"She's saaaaaaltyyyyy," Malajia laughed as their nemeses were told to exit the room.

After taking a ten minute breather, President Bennett called all the girls back to the conference room. "Now, I asked you in the beginning if you ladies knew why you were here," she began, adjusting the pearls on her neck.

"Is it to kick us out of school?" Sidra asked, mentally drained.

"No, it's not," President Bennett answered much to the surprise and relief of the room.

"Really?" Malajia smiled.

President Bennett nodded. "I believe that your future is too bright for you to be removed from school due to one indiscretion. However, I wanted you girls to learn a valuable lesson from all of this." Her voice was stern. "Had it been anybody else sitting here in my place, this all could have turned out very differently." She turned to Chasity. "Miss Parker, your reputation precedes you," she stated. "But I know, even with all that mouth and attitude, that you are no trouble maker. I also know that Miss Howard did not start that fight with Jackie. I may not show my face that often, but I do hear about what goes on around my campus."

"So, you didn't buy Jackie's lies after all?" Alex asked, relieved.

"Absolutely not," she assured, fixing her stern gaze on Jackie. "Like Miss Parker, your reputation precedes *you too*, Miss Stevens." Jackie gulped. "You think I don't know the trouble that you cause on this campus? The gossiping, the taunting? You really think that you can go through life being this jealous, vindictive person?"

"But Pres—"

"But *nothing*," President Bennett spat, cutting Jackie's excuses short. "Jealously is a dangerous thing, and it's unnecessary. Everyone is unique and special in their own way, and you should never feel anger towards someone because you feel that they have what you don't. Stop it. If you continue to go down this path, not only will you eventually end up out of this school, but you will find that your life will be miserable. Stop worrying about what you don't have, and focus on what you do."

"Boom!" Malajia exclaimed, slamming her hand on the table.

"Miss Simmons," President Bennett warned.

"My bad," Malajia chortled, putting her hand up.

President Bennett scanned the room with her eyes. "Ladies, I want to see you all live up to the potential that I know you all have. So I am giving you this reprieve...Don't let it happen again."

"Yes Ma'am," the girls said as President Bennett and Dean Watkins exited the room.

"I don't ever wanna go through *that* again," Alex said, breathing a sigh of relief once they left the conference room. She turned to Chasity. "I'm sorry that I said that you have an anger problem."

"Why? You were telling the truth," Chasity replied. "I wasn't mad at you, Alex. I was mad at them...and myself. So don't worry about it."

"Now you girls can breathe," Trisha smiled. "I told you everything would be okay."

"Ms. Trisha, did you know that President Bennett wasn't actually going to kick us out?" Sidra asked.

Trisha shrugged. "I may have had an idea...Lucy is my sorority sister," she revealed.

"Who's Lucy?" Malajia chuckled.

"President Bennett," Trisha winked. "How about we celebrate? I'll get the car and take you girls out to eat."

"Thank God, I'm starving," Malajia beamed, snatching off her blazer. "I'm never wearing one of these again," she promised, slinging the garment over her shoulder.

"Your aunt is amazing, Chasity," Alex mused as she watched Trisha head down the hallway.

"Yeah, she's *some*thing all right," Chasity jeered.

"Chaz that was hilarious how you brought up Jason to make Jackie mad," Malajia laughed. "You just rubbed it all in her oily ass face."

Chasity shook her head.

"And don't think we didn't pick up on how dreamy your eyes got when you started talking about him too," Malajia teased. Chasity narrowed her eyes at her. "So are y'all gonna bang next semester or what?"

"Malajia!" Sidra exclaimed.

"I'm not banging *anybody*," Chasity ground out. "Drop it."

"Yeah, we'll see," Malajia chuckled.

"Okay Mel, stop teasing Chaz. She's had a hard day," Alex cut in, trying to hold her laugh in. "Hell, we *all* have. At least now we have next semester to look forward to."

Malajia clapped her hands together. "We'll be sophomores. I can't wait to school the freshman babies."

"School who?" Sidra sneered as they made their way down the hall towards the exit. "You're still fresh off the freshman bus yourself, chill out."

"Nothing you say can kill my mood right now," Malajia declared. "I'm worry free and can look forward to my new dorm *and* my new roommate."

Alex looked at Malajia. "Ooh, you got your assignment? Who's your roomie going to be?"

"I won't reveal it just yet."

"What is the secrecy for?" Sidra asked. "Do we know her?"

"All I'm going to say is that I'm very happy," Malajia said.

Annoyed by Malajia's vagueness, Alex turned to Chasity. "Chaz who's your new—"

"I don't wanna talk about it," Chasity spat out instantaneously.

Alex put her hands up in surrender. "Very well," she chuckled.

"We should call the guys and tell them that everything is good," Sidra suggested.

"Can we wait until after we eat?" Malajia asked. "I can't listen to Mark talk on an empty stomach...I need *some*thing in my stomach to throw up."

Chasity snickered at Malajia, but she would call Jason once she got in the car. He'd supported her so much that she wanted to fill him in as soon as possible.

As they pushed the front door open and headed down the stairs towards the brick path, Alex smiled brightly. "If this situation has done nothing else, at least it brought us closer together."

"Oh God," Chasity groaned as Sidra shook her head.

"What?" Alex laughed.

"You always gotta ruin shit with your mushy ass," Malajia teased.

"I own my mushiness, and I'm proud of it," Alex countered, giving Malajia a poke. The girls teasing didn't faze her. Alex was relieved, with that ugly situation with Jackie finally behind them, she was now able to look forward to the semester ahead of her. "Sophomore year, here we come."

CPSIA information can be obtained
at www.ICGtesting.com
Printed in the USA
LVHW080331220219
608422LV00009B/151/P